Night After Night

Janelle Denison

St. Martin's Paperbacks

To Carly Phillips, for holding my hand every step of the way with this book. Your friendship means the world to me and I can't imagine my life without you in it.

And to my husband, Don, because he's the reason I write romances and believe in happily ever after. I love you.

This is a work of fiction. All of the characters, organizations, and events portrayed in this novel are either products of the author's imagination or are used fictitiously.

NIGHT AFTER NIGHT

Copyright © 2011 by Janelle Denison.

All rights reserved.

For information address St. Martin's Press, 175 Fifth Avenue, New York, NY 10010.

ISBN: 978-0-312-37228-6

Printed in the United States of America

St. Martin's Paperbacks edition / October 2011

St. Martin's Paperbacks are published by St. Martin's Press, 175 Fifth Avenue, New York, NY 10010.

10 9 8 7 6 5 4 3 2 1

Chapter One

"Do you recognize the man in this photograph?"

Sean O'Brien glanced from his boss, Caleb Roux, to the picture he slid across the surface of his desk. Leaning forward in his seat, Sean reached for the snapshot, all too aware of Caleb's direct gaze watching him, waiting for some kind of reaction.

Sean found his boss's quiet intensity disconcerting, especially when it was directed at *him*. Something was up, and Sean could only wonder where this meeting would lead.

If there was one thing he'd learned about Caleb, it was everything he did had a distinct purpose. Especially when it came to doling out the cases exclusive clients hired him to investigate.

As the founder of The Reliance Group—a private organization he'd established to accommodate those who preferred a more untraditional approach to resolving personal, private matters—Caleb utilized each member on his team according to their experience and skills.

In Sean's case, his proficiency as an ex–con artist had come in handy on a few of Caleb's cases. Sean's prior life as a hustler wasn't something he was proud of, and he was grateful that Caleb had given him a chance to redeem himself. First, for offering Sean a job as a bartender at the Onyx Hotel & Casino when no one else would hire him, and second, for inviting him to be a part of The Reliance Group.

Realizing Caleb was waiting patiently for a reply, Sean finally glanced at the photograph in his hand, his stomach clenching at the familiar face staring back at him. Even though it had been twelve years since he'd seen this man, there was no forgetting the person who'd betrayed Sean's father.

Not that he had been innocent in his crimes. Hardly. But the man in the picture had been an equal accomplice and had ultimately sold Sean's old man down the river to save his own ass.

"Yes, I know him," Sean said, his tone bitter as he tossed the picture back onto Caleb's desk. "That's Elliott Cooke, the man who sent my father to jail." Sean suspected Caleb already knew that bit of information. He had a thick file on Sean and his past, and there was nothing Caleb didn't already know about him and his family situation.

"He goes by 'Grant Russo' now," Caleb told Sean.

Sean didn't give a damn what the bastard called himself. At the core, he was still a man who lacked morals and a conscience. "And this matters to me why?"

Sean's gruff attitude didn't faze Caleb at all; his gaze remained razor sharp and determined. "It matters because you're about to take on a case that's going to force you to face your past, and this man. Can you handle that?"

Sean's jaw clenched and resentment burned in his gut. He despised Elliott Cooke for a variety of reasons but mainly for ruining Sean's father's life.

Sean didn't know what Caleb's case involved but hoped it included serving up a large dose of overdue justice to Cooke so he could have the satisfaction of delivering the punishment himself. It was the least he could do to avenge his father and finally settle a long-overdue score between the two men.

Doing so would also provide Sean with the opportunity to ease some of his own guilt when it came to his father. In the twelve years that Casey O'Brien had been in prison, Sean had only visited his dad a handful of times, and that wasn't something he was proud of. Sean's own shame and embarrassment in failing his father's final request to stop the cycle of cons and build a better life for himself was something he desperately wanted to make amends for. Only then could he face his old man again.

"What do you need me to do?" Sean asked.

Caleb picked up his BlackBerry and tapped out a message on the small keyboard. "Before we go on, Valerie will be joining us so she can explain the case and what she knows."

Valerie Downing was also a member of The Reliance Group, though her main job was as casino host for the Onyx. She spent her days and evenings catering to the requests and whims of the high-profile gamblers, known as Whales, who frequented the establishment.

"How is Valerie involved?" Sean asked.

Text sent, Caleb set his phone back down before meeting Sean's gaze once again. "It was one of her Whales who heard about TRG and asked for our help. I have the case file and all the initial investigative reports right here for you to review, but Valerie can give you a better rundown of the facts and answer any questions you might have."

Within a few minutes, Valerie arrived. She knocked briskly on the closed door before entering Caleb's office. The casino host was young and beautiful, a brunette with soft brown eyes and a charismatic way about her that people were drawn to.

Wearing a black pantsuit with a beige silk blouse beneath the short-waisted jacket, she sat down in the chair beside Sean's. "Hey, O'Brien," she said by way of greeting.

"Val." Sean inclined his head. "I'm dying of curiosity here. Tell me what you know about Russo." The last Sean had heard, after evading prison time, the other man had sworn he was going to clean up his act and lead an exemplary life.

Yeah, right, like Sean believed that. *Once a con, always a con.* Once you played the game and reaped the rewards, it was like a rush and an addiction that coursed through your blood and made you crave more. And as Sean well knew from his own experience, living the high life of a scam artist was a habit that was difficult to break.

As a cocky teenager, Sean had been sucked into his dad's fast and loose lifestyle that kept a lot of cash in Sean's pocket and made him believe he was invincible and above the law. Until his last con as an adult had gone horribly wrong and the innocent woman he'd swindled had paid a hefty emotional and physical price for being such an easy, gullible mark.

While Sean's own stint in prison had given him a much-needed slap of reality and had scared him straight, he still harbored a load of guilt and regrets for what had happened to the woman. Spending months in a small concrete cell had given him a helluva lot of time to reflect and to make the decision to finally turn his life around for good.

But there were some things in his past he couldn't forget or forgive himself for. And that last con gone wrong, and the woman's life that had been irrevocably changed as a result of Sean's deliberate deception, was one of them.

Valerie tucked a long strand of brown wavy hair behind the shell of her ear, that intuitive gaze of hers meeting Sean's as she addressed his question about what she knew about

Grant Russo. "I never heard of the guy until one of my best clients came to see me about hiring The Reliance Group to find him. Conrad Davenport is a billionaire with his own investment company, and he's one of the Onyx's highest rollers. He doesn't think twice about spending an obscene amount of money on gambling in the casino. My job is to keep him happy, and right now, the man is fuming mad. Not at us, of course, but his anger at being conned is affecting his game play at the Onyx, which in turn affects our revenue, and so on."

The corner of Valerie's mouth quirked with a wry grin. "I'm sure you've heard the saying 'If a Whale isn't happy, then nobody's happy.' Trust me, it's true."

"I'm sure it is," Sean replied.

"Davenport's private company, Security Investment Group, is based out of Texas." Valerie went on to explain the specifics of the case. "About a year ago his company invested over fifty million dollars toward the development of a new casino and resort slated to be built on a huge parcel of land in the Las Vegas Valley. It appeared to be a legitimate investment opportunity. The land was owned by Russo, formal contracts were signed, and he provided all his investors with an impressive résumé of his past projects and a full-blown business plan for the development of The Meridian Resort."

Sean already had a strong feeling where this story was heading and how it would end. It was a familiar scenario and a repeat of the past and the other lives Elliott Cooke had shattered and destroyed through an organized Ponzi scheme.

Realizing just how quiet Caleb had been, Sean cast a quick glance at his boss and found him reclining back in his leather chair. He appeared relaxed, but Sean knew beneath that deceptively casual façade Caleb was processing every word Valerie spoke, as well as Sean's response.

"About three months ago they broke ground for the Meridian project and started grading. Shortly after that, construction came to an abrupt standstill, along with a bunch of excuses from Russo as to what was going on." Valerie crossed one leg over the other as she continued. "Davenport suspected foul play and called Russo on it, but Russo swore the investment was legitimate. When Davenport insisted on seeing current financial statements, Russo wasn't able to provide them and kept putting him off. Now, he can't even get ahold of the guy."

"Which is why he asked The Reliance Group to get involved," Caleb said, finally jumping into the conversation. "I put my best investigators on the case, but they couldn't find Russo, either. In fact, it's as though he's dropped off the face of the earth, and he's left a lot of personal and private investors very unhappy."

Sean wasn't surprised to hear that Russo had disappeared. An exemplary life, Sean's ass, he thought sarcastically. Obviously, Russo was back to doing what he did best—wooing the wealthy and gaining their trust, making grand promises of huge return profits on their investment, then padding his own pockets and supplementing his affluent lifestyle with their money.

Clearly, whatever latest scheme he'd been plotting had finally come crashing down around him. Most likely, he'd taken the investors' money and gotten out of Dodge and, unless he was caught, the investors were pretty much shit out of luck. Including Davenport.

"The Feds are about to get involved with a thorough investigation of the situation, and once that happens, all of Russo's assets will be frozen." Caleb absently tapped his pen on a file folder on his desk as he spoke. "All his money, including the investors', will be tied up in court for years. Chances are, nobody will ever see their money, and

Davenport is determined to recover his before this case breaks wide open."

"I still don't get how this case applies to me, and what, exactly, you need me to do," Sean said.

"You know the life and thought processes of a man like Russo," Caleb said, reminding Sean of everything he'd spent the past six years trying to forget. "Russo has a daughter, Zoe, and we believe she's our best connection to finding out where her father is. We need you to get close to her, gain her confidence, and uncover what she knows of Russo's whereabouts."

Sean shook his head, not liking the direction this conversation was taking. The last thing he wanted to do was dupe another woman, even if it was for the greater good of putting Russo's ass in jail where it belonged. "I doubt she's going to spill family secrets to a stranger."

"Not the first time you meet her, no," Valerie agreed, her eyes shimmering with amusement. "But after a few chance encounters I'm sure you could work it into the conversation somehow."

He rubbed his fingers across his forehead and groaned. "You've got to be kidding me." His own personal misgivings aside, he had no desire to babysit the daughter of the con man who'd sent Sean's father to prison.

"I'm quite serious," Valerie replied, and softened her words with a sweet smile. "And I know for a fact that you've got the personality and the gift of persuasion to pull this off. I don't think I've ever met a woman who has been able to resist your charm."

As he was unable to argue with Valerie's reasoning, a reluctant grin tipped the corner of Sean's mouth. True, he normally enjoyed seducing the opposite sex—and reveled in the fun while it lasted. He just hadn't anticipated having to flirt with a woman he'd never, ever, willingly choose to hook up with. But he knew that both Valerie and Caleb were counting on him to make this work, to retrieve the information they needed to find Russo for their client, and Sean couldn't bring himself to disappoint either one.

"So what do you want me to do, call her up and ask her out on a date?" Sean joked.

Valerie laughed. "Actually, you don't need to be so obvious. We've set up a legitimate way for the two of you to meet."

"Here's what we know about Zoe Russo," Caleb said as he opened a file folder on his desk and perused the first page of notes. "She's an up-and-coming designer, and she's currently looking for a place to open her first boutique here in Las Vegas."

"She designs the most amazing accessories," Valerie said, sounding as though she was a fan of Zoe's creations. "Scarves, purses, sunglasses, jewelry, those sorts of things. Everything is accentuated with sparkling crystals in some way, which is part of her brand and what makes her ZR Designs recognizable."

"Yeah, what she said," Caleb said, his tone wry. "I've been told that the Onyx is interested in adding her flagship store to the promenade of shops here, and you'll be standing in for the leasing agent to court her, so to speak, to sign a lease to open her boutique here. That will give the two of you plenty of face time, so be sure to use it to your advantage to establish a connection with her so you can find out what she knows about her father and his whereabouts."

Sean accepted the file that Caleb pushed across his desk toward him. Just like with every other job he'd taken on for The Reliance Group, Sean knew what the folder contained. Pictures of their mark. Personal information. Investigative reports. Everything he needed to familiarize himself with all the players in the game and get the job done.

He'd always enjoyed the excitement and thrill that came with taking on an assignment for TRG. He supposed it provided him with that adrenaline rush he'd always relished as a former con artist. But he'd never been handed a case with such a personal connection. One that dredged up his imperfect past yet offered him the opportunity to serve a bit of overdue justice to the man who'd screwed Sean's father.

And maybe, in the process, Sean would also be able to repair his own broken relationship with his dad and show his old man that he really *had* changed his life around.

It appeared that *complicated* had landed in Sean's lap in a big way. Now he just had to prove to Caleb that he'd chosen the right man for the job.

Sean had spent his entire adult life charming women. With a flirtatious wink or a slow smile he made them putty in his hands. Soft, warm, and willing. Sometimes he seduced them for fun. Other times, for pleasure.

Today, it was all about business.

Standing in front of a recently vacated storefront located in the promenade area of the Onyx Hotel & Casino, he watched as Zoe Russo approached their mutually agreed-upon meeting place for their two o'clock appointment. The grainy photograph in the case file Caleb had given Sean had completely missed the mark in capturing Zoe's true beauty. She was much prettier in person, with silky shoulder-length blond hair and side-swept bangs that framed her soft, feminine features.

His gaze quickly swept the length of her, summing up the entire enticing package in a single glance. She wore a pair of white jeans and a butter yellow one-shoulder-style summer blouse. The material draped loosely over her full breasts and was cinched around her waist by a gold chain belt studded with sparkling crystals, which matched the long, multi-strand crystal necklaces swaying in cadence with her purposeful walk. Every step she took in her designer heels was accompanied with an air of sensual sophistication that drew appreciative male stares as she continued toward the empty boutique where Sean waited for her.

Or maybe it was the woman walking beside Zoe who was attracting a good deal of the curious stares being sent their way—a tall, slender redhead with an abundance of spiral curls who was rocking a form-fitting teal minidress. He couldn't see the woman's face since she was wearing a huge pair of sunglasses, but there was something vaguely familiar about her that eluded him at the moment.

Probably because his main focus, and interest, was on Zoe. Not a good thing considering he'd been assigned to this case to discover what she knew about her father's shady dealings as a con man.

Hell, for all Sean knew, Zoe was just as crooked as her old man. Sean's own personal experience had taught him that the apple usually didn't fall far from the tree, and he was jaded enough to believe that scenario was possible with Zoe.

Regardless of her guilt or innocence, he had a job to do, and procuring Zoe Russo's trust was the first thing on his agenda. While the ability to coax secrets from a woman had always come quite easily to Sean and was an essential skill for any con man, he had to mentally push aside the twinge of guilt that reminded him of the potential of someone getting hurt.

Sean exhaled a deep breath and reminded himself that he wasn't using Zoe in a con—just as a vehicle to locate her father. No harm, no foul, as far as Sean was concerned.

The duo stopped a few feet in front of him, and that's when he noticed that the guy following the two women from a discreet distance halted as well. The big, muscular man crossed his arms over his wide chest, his expression intimidating as he kept a sharp eye on the people walking around the redhead and Zoe.

Zoe extended her hand and smiled, the friendly sentiment reaching her bright green-gold eyes. "Hi. I'm Zoe Russo. Are you Sean O'Brien?"

"That would be me," he said with a nod. "The retail leasing agent for the shops here at the Onyx." A temporary job title until he got what he wanted from Zoe; then it was back to the trenches of bartending.

Responding to her smile with one of his own, he shook her hand. Her skin was supple and warm against his palm, like soft silk, and he hated letting go.

She slowly pulled her arm back, and he didn't miss the hint of awareness in her gaze. "I hope you don't mind, but I brought my best friend along to take a look at the shop, too. She's familiar with how I intend to lay out the store with my merchandise, and her input is important to me."

"That's fine." He forced his attention to the beautiful woman by Zoe's side. "It's always good to have a second pair of eyes to make sure the square footage is what you have in mind for your counters and displays."

The woman finally slipped off the big sunglasses encrusted with crystals, revealing her entire face and surprising Sean with her identity. There was no mistaking who Zoe's *best friend* was—a pop-star sensation and GRAMMY Award winner who was currently taking the music industry by storm.

"I'm Jessica Morgan," she said unnecessarily.

"You certainly are," he replied, his tone wry as he shook her hand. Now he understood who the guy hovering behind them was—her bodyguard. "It's a pleasure to meet you."

Zoe looped her arm through her friend's and grinned enthusiastically. "Jessica is the face for my newest Zoe Russo collection out this fall. Am I lucky, or what?"

"Extremely." And he meant it. Considering Zoe was still an up-and-coming designer who was on the cusp of making a big name for herself, getting a star and a trend-setter such as Jessica Morgan to kick off her fall campaign was equivalent to striking gold.

Between Jessica's flashy sunglasses, her blinged-out purse, and the pair of crystal earrings she wore, it appeared that she was already taking her role as spokesperson for ZR Designs very seriously.

"Let's take a look at the store." Sean withdrew the key to the shop and sent Zoe one of his irresistible smiles. "Hopefully it's exactly what you need."

"I'll keep an open mind," she returned.

The promise in her soft, husky voice sent a jolt of un-expected desire through Sean. Not quite the reaction he'd anticipated having toward her. Bitterness and resentment because she was her father's daughter, yes. Fascination, hell no.

But he recognized the signs, the spark that went deeper than just professional interest. Under normal circumstances he wouldn't hesitate to pursue their attraction, but he wasn't there to cajole her into his bed, even if that thought did appeal to him. He had a job to do, information to unearth, and a scam artist to find.

Her father.

With Sean's mind back on his objective, he unlocked the door and pushed the sliding glass panels open for Zoe and her friend to enter the vacant boutique. Zoe walked past him, and the delectable scent of fresh, sweet peaches filled his senses.

Damn. He loved peaches, especially ripe, juicy ones,

and he couldn't help but wonder if she tasted as good as she smelled.

"I have to say I'm still a little surprised you contacted me about this store," Zoe said, glancing around the open space before meeting his gaze and tipping her head curiously. "How did you even know I was looking for a place?"

He shrugged, refusing to give away his source—Caleb, who had the uncanny ability to find out just about anything on anyone. Pushing his hands into the front pockets of his navy trousers, Sean tapped into old but not forgotten bullshitting skills and his ability to adapt to any situation with finesse and ease.

"A good retail leasing agent always has his ear to the ground when it comes to cultivating new talent for his clients."

Just as Sean had anticipated, she beamed at his well-placed compliment, but there were still questions in her gaze. "But you even knew I was seriously considering a boutique at Caesars Palace."

"Yes, for half the space and triple the price of what the Onyx is offering." Out of the corner of his eye, Sean noticed that Jessica was checking out the store, but she was still close enough to hear his and Zoe's conversation. "I also know that you're anxious to get a place before your fall campaign is unveiled, and our spots available, while Caesars Palace misses the mark by almost a month."

Zoe laughed and shook her head in disbelief. "How in the world do you know all that?"

"I never reveal my sources." He winked at her. "Just know that the Onyx would love to have your flagship store here in the hotel, and they're prepared to make you an offer you'll find hard to resist. This really is a prime spot," he went on, using the spiel the *real* leasing agent had instructed him to say. "It's located across from the nightclub

Taboo, which generates a good amount of foot traffic, and you'd be positioned between Coach and bebe. Those two stores, along with the club, are a perfect match for your targeted demographic of young, sophisticated women."

"You really *did* do your homework," she murmured, her eyes wide in amazement.

"It's my job to know as much about you and your business as possible."

"Well, *I'm* impressed," Jessica said as she came up beside Zoe. Jessica's tone was sly, and there was a devilish gleam in her eyes. "It's quite obvious that he wants you and he's willing to do whatever it takes to get you."

Zoe's cheeks turned pink in embarrassment at her friend's deliberate double entendre. "He wants my *business*," Zoe clarified, jabbing Jessica in the side with her elbow.

Sean laughed. "That, too," he teased, finding her bashful reaction a refreshing change from the bold and brazen behavior of the women he was used to dealing with as a bartender. "Why don't you take a look around and see what you think of the space, and then we'll talk specifics."

While Zoe and Jessica strolled around the empty boutique and made notes for possible layouts for the display, racks, and counters, Sean stood by the door and gave them time alone to discuss pros and cons and ideas without feeling pressured in any way. While he'd been assigned to get close to Zoe for a case, the Onyx truly wanted her business. She was a hot commodity, and it would be a huge coup for the hotel that opened her first boutique.

As for Sean, the sooner he discovered what she knew of her father's whereabouts, along with his involvement in stealing millions of dollars from unsuspecting investors, the sooner The Reliance Group could resolve the case they'd been hired to solve and give their client the justice he deserved.

Sean hated to think that Zoe might know about her father's shady dealings or, worse, be a part of his deception, but it was a possibility he couldn't discount. Which meant he had to tread carefully with her from this point on until he unraveled that particular concern.

His strategy with Zoe Russo had been planned out from the moment he first contacted her about the lease space at the Onyx. This first face-to-face with her provided him with the initial introduction he needed to establish a connection between them. The next step required a more personal involvement that would give him the opportunity to ask the necessary questions about her father in a casual, relaxed atmosphere that wouldn't raise her suspicions.

So far, Sean was right on track.

Twenty minutes later, Zoe made her way back to him, her eyes lit with excitement. "Well, I certainly like the place. It has a lot of potential for what I have in mind."

"That's exactly what I want to hear." He withdrew a lease contract from the leather portfolio he'd tucked under his arm and gave it to Zoe. "I took the liberty of drawing up an agreement based on the financial discussion we had on the phone."

She took the papers and gave them a quick glance. "As much as I love the store, I'd like to take a few days to think about the offer and have my attorney look over the contract."

"Absolutely," Sean said with an understanding nod. "It's a big decision."

She slid the agreement into her purse. "I'll definitely be in touch."

Knowing if Zoe walked away now he might not have another chance to get to that all-important next step with her, Sean spoke up. "One more thing before you go . . . would you like to have dinner with me sometime this week?"

"She'd love to," Jessica said before Zoe had the chance to reply.

Zoe shot her friend an *I'm going to strangle you* look that was tempered with affection. "Would you *stop*?"

Jessica shrugged, looking unapologetic. And very mischievous. "Hey, I'm just saying what your mind is thinking."

Sean rubbed a hand across his mouth to hide a grin, though he appreciated Jessica's support on his behalf.

"I don't know," Zoe said, the uncertainty in her voice contradicting the glimmer of desire in her gaze and the undeniable attraction between them. "I've got so much going on, with the fall collection coming out, getting a new Web site and store ready in time . . ."

Despite her busy schedule, he could see her indecision. Fortunately, he was a master at persuasion. "It's just dinner, Zoe, not a lifetime commitment," he said, injecting humor into his tone. "Leasing agents take clients out for meals all the time. You do eat, don't you?"

"Occasionally, and mostly on the go," she admitted sheepishly.

"Then it'll do you good to relax for a few hours and have a healthy meal."

Jessica nodded. "I have to second that."

"You would," Zoe replied, rolling her eyes at her meddling friend before glancing back at Sean with a genuine smile. "Okay. Sure. Dinner would be great."

"How about Wednesday evening?" he asked, wanting to get a firm promise from her. When she agreed, he added, "And no pressure to talk business, unless you want to. I'll make reservations and give you a call with the time and place."

"I look forward to it." She extended her hand in a too-formal, all-businesslike good-bye.

"Me, too." He enveloped her hand in his and deliberately stroked his thumb along her soft skin in a slow, sensual caress. He heard her slight intake of breath and knew he had her exactly where he wanted her.

Oh yeah. It was just a matter of time before she was putty in his hands. Soft, warm, and willing to spill all the secrets that would lead him straight to finding Grant Russo and sending him to jail.

Chapter Two

"So, what do you think?" Jessica asked.

Zoe settled into the back of the Town Car beside her friend, her mind already turning over all the creative possibilities of leasing the boutique at the Onyx. In comparison to the other places she'd looked at, the impressive square footage of the store was a designer's dream come true, and would allow for strategic and optimal placement of her accessories without overcrowding.

"The store is ideal," Zoe said as their driver pulled away from the hotel and gradually made his way toward the gridlock of Las Vegas Boulevard. "It's open and spacious, with plenty of room for me to grow and expand, which is essential. And the monthly rent is well within my budget. That's a big plus, since we'd like to make a profit at some point." *We* being her and Jessica, since Zoe's friend was her one and only silent investor.

"But, before I get too excited about the spot, I'll have to see what my lawyer has to say about the Onyx's contract and lease terms."

"Yes, I agree with everything you just said," Jessica replied with a patient smile. "But I was referring to the hunky *Mr. O'Brien,* not the boutique."

Zoe laughed and shook her head, not at all surprised by her friend's comment. "Of course you were."

Jessica turned in her seat toward Zoe, her green eyes bright and engaging. "So do tell, what do you think of *him*?"

The words *tempting, sexy,* and *heart-stoppingly seductive* immediately sprang to mind. Oh yeah, the man seemed to have the natural ability to make her feel weak in the knees. Between the slight dimples in his cheeks when he grinned, the deep timbre of his voice, and the hint of a bad-boy twinkle in his dark blue eyes, he was downright irresistible. He exuded male confidence, and she had a strong feeling Sean O'Brien was well aware of his effect on the opposite sex.

"He's quite . . ."

"Delicious?" Jessica supplied before Zoe could find the right word to describe the man.

"Charismatic," Zoe replied with a smile, though *delicious* definitely applied. "And I really didn't need you meddling the way you did."

"Yes, you did," her friend insisted. "You've been working so damn hard this past year, and I know for a fact that you haven't so much as gone out on a date with anyone. I just wanted to be sure you didn't pass up a prime opportunity, considering there was a mutual attraction going on between you two."

Zoe arched a brow. "Did it ever occur to you that my single status is by choice?"

"Who says you can't be single and enjoy a night out with a gorgeous and supremely hot guy?" Jessica countered as she twined an errant auburn curl around her index finger. "And maybe more, if you're lucky."

"I'm not looking to get lucky." Despite Sean's hotness factor, Zoe had never been a one-night-stand kind of girl, and she didn't do casual affairs, either. In this day and age of hooking up and friends with benefits, she sometimes felt like an anomaly in wanting to cultivate some kind of emotional attachment with a man before sleeping with him.

Straitlaced and old-fashioned, her ex-fiancé, Ian Croft, had called her, even after they'd been intimate and he'd put a ring on her finger with the intention of her becoming his wife. He'd always say the comments in a way that made her believe he was teasing, until she'd been slapped in the face with the evidence of the double life Ian had been living. One that included another woman and made a complete mockery of everything Zoe believed in when it came to a committed relationship: trust, honesty, and fidelity.

Because of Ian's betrayal, Zoe found herself questioning her judgment when it came to men and their sincerity. While she still believed in love and wanted it for herself, there was a wall around her heart and emotions that she knew would take a very special guy to break through. As a result, she vowed to be more careful before getting intimately involved with another man—definitely more aware and not so naïve.

But right now, she really didn't have the extra time to dedicate to any kind of relationship when her sole focus was opening her first boutique and building a name for herself as a designer. The first boutique of many, she hoped.

"By the way, when was the last time *you* went out on a date?" Zoe asked, turning the tables on her friend.

Deliberately avoiding Zoe's gaze, Jessica checked out her freshly manicured nails. "We're talking about *you* here, not *me*."

"Yeah, well, maybe you ought to take your own advice," Zoe said softly, but with heart and meaning behind her words.

"No time." Jessica waved a hand in the air between them, the simplicity of her reply belying the deeper issues that kept her from allowing any man to be anything more than a friend. "It's kind of hard to date anyone when I'm touring all the time. And right now, I have a new album out, music videos to shoot, and an insane schedule of interviews and guest appearances."

All excuses, even if they were legitimate. "Okay, okay," Zoe conceded, knowing when to back off of what was a touchy subject for her friend. "I get your point."

Jessica glanced out her tinted window, and Zoe sighed beneath her breath. She and Jessica had been best friends since high school, and Zoe was the only one who really knew just how deep Jessica's emotional and physical scars ran. Even though Zoe's parents had gone through a bitter divorce during her sophomore year, she'd never doubted that her mother and father loved her—even if her mother hadn't been overly demonstrative with her affection, verbally or physically.

In comparison, Jessica's childhood had been unstable and filled with volatile situations, and the awful things that had happened to her had shaped Jessica into the woman she was now when it came to men.

Guarded. Cautious. Cynical.

There was so much pain in Jessica's past, and she poured all her emotions into the songs she wrote and sang. Her soulful lyrics and the underlying theme in some of her songs told her life story—the good memories, the bad times, and the difficult choices she'd been forced to make. In that regard, she wore her heart on her sleeve, though she insisted in interviews that the words and verses in her songs were purely fictional.

If there was ever a woman who needed a white knight to sweep her off her feet and give her a happily ever after, it was Jessica Morgan.

"So, do you have anything fabulous to wear to dinner with Sean?"

Glad to see that things with Jessica were back to normal, Zoe played into her friend's not-so-subtle change of subject. "Itching for a little retail therapy, are you?"

Jessica flashed her one of those dazzling grins that made her appear as though she didn't have a care in the world. "What can I say? It's my cure-all for everything."

Unfortunately, tangible items didn't make up for the love and affection Jessica needed and deserved, but Zoe wisely kept that thought to herself. "Sure, I'm up for a bit of shopping. I just received the samples for my new Eye Candy collection, and they're stunning. I'd love to find a dress to show off the pieces."

"Let's do it," Jessica said, then told her driver to take them to The Forum Shops at Caesars Palace, where they were bound to find the perfect outfit to complement Zoe's new designs.

Fifteen minutes later, they were entering the upscale shopping mall. With it being a weekday afternoon, the place wasn't quite as busy, but Jessica's wild mane of hair and her rock-star quality were hard to conceal. It didn't take long for heads to start turning in their direction as people recognized the celebrity in their midst. Jessica's big, strapping bodyguard, Simon, walked close behind them, his intimidating presence and the firm show of his hand enough to keep fans from rushing up to her.

People stopped and stared, some pointed in excitement, and a few even shouted Jessica's name. She smiled and waved, completely at ease with the attention while Zoe watched it all with a sense of relief that she didn't have to deal with such an intrusive level of fame. The name of Zoe Russo was connected to her sought-out designs and accessories, not her face, which offered her a bit of anonymity unless she chose otherwise. Seeing what Jessica had to deal with on a daily basis made Zoe want to keep things that way.

As they walked through the forum of shops, a trail of people followed at a distance. When they stopped at Valentino, Carolina Herrera, and Roberto Cavalli to try on a few outfits, Simon remained by the front doors to keep any rabid fans from disturbing Jessica as she perused the latest fashions. Zoe felt like a zoo animal on display as the small group watched them through the shop windows, and for the most part she was able to ignore their stares—all but one, anyway.

Standing just off to the side of the crowd was an angry-looking man who seemed to be watching *her*. Wherever she went, his narrowed gaze seemed to follow, causing an unsettling sensation to shiver down her spine.

She pushed off her unease when Jessica selected a summery halter top and asked Zoe to accompany her into the dressing room to give her opinion. Welcoming the chance to duck out of sight for a while, she joined her friend, and ten minutes later they were leaving the store with Jessica's new purchase in hand.

As they stepped back outside, Zoe was grateful for Simon's protection as the bodyguard fell into place behind them and easily kept the throng of people from invading their personal space. Zoe glanced around for the man she'd seen earlier. Unable to find him, she exhaled a relieved breath and relaxed.

"I can't believe you haven't found anything yet," Jessica said as they passed other specialty shops. Then she grinned and pointed at a window display. "Check out that sexy off-the-shoulder dress at Michael Kors. It has your name all over it."

"Yeah, it does," Zoe agreed, attracted to the style and the gorgeous coral color certain to complement the rich jewel tones she'd incorporated into her Eye Candy accessories. "Let's go try it on."

Just as they reached the store, a trio of teenage girls

came running up to Jessica, reaching her before Simon could step in and stop their enthusiastic approach.

"Oh, my God, it's Jessica Morgan!" one of them squealed in excitement. "You're so awesome!"

"I just love your song 'Never Again,'" another gushed, her eyes wide with awe.

"Can I take a picture with you?" the third girl asked, and without waiting for a reply she wedged herself next to Jessica and handed one of her friends her cell phone. "My sister will never believe I met you unless I can prove it with a picture."

Jessica leaned close to the girl and smiled just as the cell phone flashed, drawing even more attention to the pop star. Zoe stepped away as other people crowded around, asking for an autograph or a picture, even as Simon did his best to keep the fans from overwhelming Jessica.

"It's okay," Jessica told her bodyguard as she accepted a pen from a woman and signed the napkin she pushed in front of her. Friendly and kind and always aware of the fact that her fans were the reason for her success, Jessica posed for snapshots, graciously accepted compliments on her music, and autographed scraps of paper and even a few T-shirts.

Certain that Jessica would be occupied for a while, Zoe headed into Michael Kors, knowing her friend would meet up with her as soon as she was done. Inside the store, Zoe approached a salesgirl and asked about the dress in the window, and a few minutes later she was in the changing room trying on the outfit in her size. As soon as the dress fell into place, Zoe turned in front of the mirror and smiled at her reflection. She loved the off-the-shoulder neckline, the way the straight skirt hugged her curves, and how the coral hue complemented her skin tone.

"What do you think?" the hovering salesgirl asked, her voice drifting from just outside Zoe's closed door.

"It's perfect. I'll take it." Once Zoe had the dress off, she cracked open the door and gave it to the girl to take up to the register, then slipped back into her blouse and pants.

As she left the changing room, she glanced back out the front windows. There was still a small crowd around Jessica, and Zoe could only shake her head at the insanity of it all. She made her purchase, and as she was heading back out of the store, a red gathered top caught her eye. Just as she lifted the blouse to take a closer look, someone grabbed her arm in a tight grip and spun her around.

Startled by the rough treatment, she gasped, her heart lurching in her chest as she came face-to-face with the man she'd seen earlier. Up close, with his angry features, dark, glittering eyes, and short-cropped brown hair, he looked more menacing. A definite threat that had her pulse racing in her veins, especially since they were mostly hidden next to a rack of clothes.

"Where is your father?" the man demanded, his fingers still biting into her skin.

She shook her head, confusion and fear mingling inside her as she tried to make sense of his question. "My . . . my father?"

"Grant Russo," the man said in a low, harsh tone. "Where the fuck is he?"

Wincing at the fury lacing the man's voice, she tried to pull her arm away, but his hold didn't budge. The dangerous glint in his gaze warned her not to scream or draw attention to them, and she swallowed hard, deciding she'd be smart to answer him. "He's out of town."

It was all she knew of her father's whereabouts, that he was in Chicago working on a business deal—information his own secretary had given Zoe when she'd placed a call to her father's office a few days ago to ask her dad out to dinner. It wasn't out of the ordinary for her father to be away on a trip, and she figured he'd give her a call when he returned, like he normally did.

The man gave her an impatient shake. *"Where?"*

"I don't think it's any of your business," she said, her own anger rising over this bizarre confrontation with a stranger.

He moved his face close to hers. "Yeah, well, I'm making it my business."

"Who *are* you?" She figured if she had some kind of name, she could at least press charges against this man for harassment and let her father know the guy was trouble.

"I'm someone who has a whole lot of money wrapped up in the Meridian project, and now that money has gone missing, along with your father," the man said bitterly.

There wasn't a person living in or around Las Vegas who hadn't heard of the upscale casino and resort her father's company was developing. It was a huge, billion-dollar project, and a job as big as that wasn't without disgruntled workers.

She tried her best to reason with him. "Look, I'm not involved in my father's company, or the Meridian project, so I really can't help you with whatever your problem is."

"Sure you can." He finally released her arm but remained in front of her, keeping Zoe trapped between racks of designer clothes and his formidable body. "How about you relay a message to your father for me. Tell him that he needs to get his ass back to Vegas, along with the money Bunny and I worked damn hard for. And unless he wants his daughter to start answering for his financial dealings, then it's in both of your best interests that he return and take care of business."

The man turned around and walked away, leaving her trembling deep inside and trying to make some kind of sense of what had just happened. She didn't even know the guy's name or exactly what he was referring to. But whatever his issue, she was certain her father would take care of the problem once he returned from his business trip. In the meantime, she'd make a call to her dad and give him a heads-up on what had happened.

"Zoe?" Done appeasing her fans, Jessica walked into the store, her concerned gaze shifting from Zoe to the man who strode past her and out of the shop, then back again. "Who was that guy?"

"I don't know," she said, dragging a shaking hand through her hair.

"Are you okay?" Frowning, Jessica slid a protective arm over Zoe's shoulders. "Did he hurt you? I'll send big, bad Simon after him if you want."

"No . . . no, I'm fine. Really." Well, not *really*, but she didn't want to cause a scene. "I have no idea how that guy knows who I am, but there's obviously some kind of mis-understanding between him and my father. As soon as I let my dad know what's going on, I'm sure he'll take care of the problem."

"Then by all means, give him a call *now*," her friend insisted.

Retrieving her BlackBerry from her purse, Zoe punched in her father's cell number. The call went directly to voice mail, and she left him a message.

"Hi, Dad," she said, deliberately sounding upbeat so she didn't worry her father. "I need to talk to you about something important, so call me as soon as you get this message. I love you."

She disconnected the call and smiled at Jessica, doing her best to put the recent incident behind her and enjoy the rest of her day with her best friend. "The good news is, the dress fits and looks amazing on, so I now have some-thing fabulous to wear Wednesday night."

"That *is* good news," Jessica said, amusement replacing

her concern as they strolled out of the store together. "What a day it's been. I sure could use a good, strong margarita. How about you?"

"Yeah. Maybe even two."

Jessica laughed and led the way back to Caesars Palace. "Sounds good to me."

"If you're trying to impress me, you've definitely succeeded." Settling into the plush red velvet chair Sean held out for her on their dinner date two days later, Zoe glanced over her shoulder and smiled at her gorgeous, sexy, and very charming date. "I'm in awe of your ability to secure not just *any* table at the highly celebrated, award-winning Alex Stratta restaurant at the Wynn hotel, but one at one of the private seating areas on the terrace. From what I've heard, most people need at least a two-week reservation for one of these exclusive tables."

"What can I say?" Unfastening the button on the front of his fitted charcoal gray blazer, Sean sat down in the seat next to hers, his playful grin showcasing those masculine dimples creasing his cheeks. "I called in a favor. It's nice to have connections, especially when I'm trying to impress a woman."

She raised a brow, certain this man had plenty of practice in dazzling the opposite sex and sweeping them off their feet with memorable romantic gestures. "You use this particular connection often?"

Unmistakable amusement shone in his eyes. "If you're talking about me bringing women to Alex Stratta for dinner, you're the first."

Her cheeks warmed at the thought, and she was grateful for the dim outdoor lighting that disguised the extra color suffusing her face. "Lucky me."

Unexpectedly, Sean reached out and skimmed the pad of his thumb along her jaw, then trailed his fingers along her bare neck in a sensual caress. "No, lucky *me*," he murmured huskily.

A delicious shiver coursed through Zoe. The feel of his long, strong fingers against her skin awakened her feminine senses, and her awareness of him as a man didn't stop there.

With his dark hair, striking blue eyes, and chiseled features, most likely a gift from his Irish heritage, he literally took her breath away. Add to the mix a pair of wide, strong shoulders and the promise of a hard, toned body beneath the fitted charcoal gray blazer he wore, and he'd attracted his fair share of appreciative female glances as he and Zoe had walked through the upscale restaurant.

It was truly a sin for a man to look so devastatingly handsome. To be so tempting and self-assured. Unfortunately, between his stunning good looks, flirtatious personality, and effortless ability to make her feel high with desire with just a look or touch, the man had "heartbreaker" written all over him.

He was exactly the kind of guy she avoided, the kind who'd rather play around than settle down. Having been down that route before, she recognized those bold, charismatic traits of his, and while she'd promised herself over a year and a half ago that she'd steer clear of potential playboys, for tonight Sean provided a nice, temporary distraction she was determined to enjoy.

She was certain that once she made a decision between the Onyx and Caesars Palace for her boutique, they'd go their separate ways. After all, he'd been the one to say to her that this was just a dinner, not a lifetime commitment, and that worked perfectly for her.

Tomorrow, and the things weighing heavily on her mind, would come soon enough. She'd left another voice-mail message for her father on his cell phone and even talked to his secretary, Sheila, who'd told Zoe she'd spoken briefly to Grant a few times, but that he was in the middle of intense contract negotiations and was incredibly busy.

While not hearing from her father wasn't unusual when he was on a business trip, Zoe was still feeling unsettled by what had happened at The Forum Shops two days ago. Hearing something, *anything,* from her father would go a long way in reassuring her that everything was okay.

Their waiter came up to their table and introduced himself, bringing Zoe's thoughts back to the present. After the waiter made a few recommendations, she made a quick decision on her meal; then Sean ordered his dinner and an expensive bottle of Cabernet Sauvignon. Their wine was delivered and poured, and once their server left and they were alone again Sean leaned toward her, the sandalwood scent of his cologne adding to the awareness already curling through her.

His dark gaze took in her features, then slowly drifted down along her exposed shoulders to the coral-hued dress she wore. "By the way, you look amazing tonight. Then again, I have a feeling you always look put-together."

She crossed her legs beneath the table and smiled at the compliment. "As someone who works in the fashion industry, I try to represent my name and designs in how I dress and look when I'm out in public. It's like being my own walking advertisement, if that make sense."

"It does." He picked up the long trio of tiered necklaces draped around her neck, the back of his hand lightly grazing the rise of her breast as he fingered the chain of glittering, colorful crystals. "Is this necklace part of one of your collections?"

"Yes." If he'd noticed the peak of her nipples against the fabric of her dress due to the brush of his hand, he was enough of a gentleman not to show it. "The bracelet and earrings, too."

"Very nice." Finally releasing the Eye Candy necklaces,

he reached for his glass of Cabernet, relaxed back in his chair, and took a drink. "Tell me about your business."

She picked up her wine, too, the vibrant stones wrapped around her wrist glittering from the lit candle in the middle of their table. "What would you like to know?"

"How did you get started in the fashion industry?" he asked, sounding genuinely interested.

She sipped her wine and sent him a smile. "You mean to tell me you don't know?" she asked, injecting a teasing note to her voice. "When we met on Monday, you seemed to know a lot about my company."

After setting his wineglass back on the table, he picked up her hand, his fingers clasping hers intimately. "I know a lot about your business, yes. *You,* not so much," he said as he stroked his thumb along the back of her hand. "And that's what interests me the most."

Oh yeah, the man was a pro at making a woman feel special, as though what she had to say really mattered to him. The inviting look in his blue eyes, his attentive nature, made resisting him impossible.

"Ever since I was a little girl, I've always loved dressing up. I can remember getting into my mother's clothes and jewelry and makeup and loving all the pretty, sparkly stuff. I thought I looked like a movie star, but looking back on the pictures my mother took of me, the truth is I really looked more like a drag queen wearing a glittering feather boa, bright red lipstick, and ridiculously gaudy costume jewelry."

He chuckled. "Well, if it makes you feel better, your tastes have improved over the years."

"Thank God," she said, and laughed, too. "In high school, I added designs and beaded stones to my belts and purses and other accessories and I made my own crystal jewelry. Even before I graduated, I knew I wanted to do something in fashion."

"Did you make your own clothes, too?"

Remembering her many disastrous attempts at sewing, she grimaced. "I tried, but I'm no seamstress. So, I decided to stick with what I was good at and doing what I loved the most. Designing accessories is my passion."

"I love a woman with passion." He winked at her.

The man was truly incorrigible. "I just bet you do."

His wicked grin said it all.

At that moment, their waiter arrived to deliver their first course—an escargot tart for Sean and a roasted-beet salad for her. Their server refilled their glasses of wine and left them alone again.

Zoe glanced at Sean just as he took a bite of his appetizer and tried not to cringe at the thought of him eating a snail, even if it was a French delicacy and was drenched in a rich butter sauce. She tried her salad, the taste of beets, goat cheese, pistachios, and balsamic dressing a delicious surprise.

"What did you do after high school?" he asked a few minutes later, jumping right back into their conversation.

She ate another bite of her salad, then swallowed a sip of wine before answering. "Since I already knew that I wanted a career in fashion, I decided to bypass a traditional university and went to the Fashion Institute of Design and Merchandising in Los Angeles. During that time, I shopped around my designs to trendy boutiques in Hollywood that I knew the rich and famous shopped at. Little by little I sold my merchandise, gained celebrity endorsements, and made a name for myself, until orders increased to the point that I couldn't do it by myself any longer and I had to hire a few people to help me out. *That's* when I knew I had a chance at making it as a successful designer."

Finished with his first course, he placed his small fork on his dish and reached for his Cabernet. "Now I'm the one who's impressed." He tipped his glass toward her in a silent toast before taking a drink.

"Thanks." She smiled, appreciating his comment. "My mother thought my interest in fashion design was just a carryover hobby from my teenage years and never really understood how important it was to me, or why I was so determined to make it on my own."

Her mother's philosophy in life, and what she hoped her daughter would emulate, was that a woman's chief goal should be to find and marry a rich man who would take care of her so she never had to worry about being financially stable. That was, after all, why Collette had married Grant Russo, and even after their divorce she'd gravitated toward wealthy men. Currently she was living with a billionaire oil baron in Texas and hoping for an engagement ring.

While Zoe loved her mother, her superficial views when it came to the opposite sex and marriage weren't something Zoe believed in, and she never would. She didn't want to rely on any man to support her, and when she did get married one day she wanted the union to be for pure, unadulterated love, along with mutual honesty and trust.

Their waiter came by and cleared their dishes. After promising that their main course would be out in a few minutes, he moved on to an inside table to take an order.

"Your mother must be very proud of you now," Sean said, his smile warm as he topped off her Cabernet.

"Now that I'm successful, she's come around. She likes the fact that her daughter is becoming 'famous,'" she replied, her tone deliberately droll. "According to her, that makes what I do acceptable."

"That has to be tough," he said, his tone soft and sympathetic.

"It is what it is." She shrugged, having learned a long

time ago what to expect, and not expect, from her mother. "I don't need her approval to feel good about myself and what I do."

"Good for you," he said, clearly respecting her confident attitude. "And your father? What does he think about your choice of career?"

"He's always been very encouraging, which makes up for my mother's lack of interest." His support had even extended to offering financial help in opening Zoe's boutique, which she'd flat-out refused, and he seemed to understand that this was something she needed to do on her own. From taking on Jessica as a silent investor to taking out a business loan for other expenses, Zoe was in complete control of her company's success. And it felt good, too.

Sean tipped his head curiously. "Are you two close?"

"My father and I? Sure." A fond smile eased up the corners of her mouth. "We've always had a good relationship. I'm an only child, and I'll admit that I'm a bit of a daddy's girl."

Sean studied her over the rim of his wineglass as he took a long drink, his blue gaze intense, as if he was trying to analyze her reply or maybe even *her*. She glanced away just as their waiter arrived with their dinners. After setting a fragrant plate of food in front of each of them, he made sure they were satisfied with everything before giving them privacy to enjoy their meal.

She enjoyed a few delicious bites of her sea bass, surrounded by a savory mushroom broth, while Sean cut into his pancetta-wrapped veal.

"So, about your dad—"

Tired of talking about herself, she immediately held her hand up to cut Sean off and softened the gesture with a smile. "You know, somehow we've spent the past hour talking all about me, and not so much about you. How is that?"

"Trust me, sweetheart," he said in a low, sexy drawl that was undoubtedly meant to distract her. "I'm not that interesting."

His reply was too practiced, too evasive. Like a man used to protecting his personal life but exceptionally good at unearthing other people's secrets. "I find that hard to believe."

"Then how about the truth?" His gaze met hers, the sapphire depths darkening with a compelling heat. "You fascinate me."

Oh, he is good, she thought, and glanced away to calm the butterflies fluttering in her stomach. What woman wouldn't want to be the sole focus of this gorgeous man's attention and interest? It was quite a change from other men Zoe had dated, the self-absorbed kind who liked the spotlight on them and spent the evening dominating the conversation.

Sean obviously wasn't one to put himself out there for a woman to analyze. His more reserved nature shouldn't bother her considering this was just a casual dinner date and most likely wouldn't turn into anything more, but it surprised Zoe to realize how much Sean fascinated her.

"Have you ever seen the Lake of Dreams show here at the Wynn?" Sean asked, indicating the hotel's entertainment about to begin just beyond the terrace where they were sitting—one of the perks of their private seating area. At the moment, the lagoon was still and tranquil, but the soft sound of music and the slow rushing sound of water indicated the start of the show.

If he was trying to shift the topic of conversation again, he was about to succeed, because she was anxious to watch the extravagant production. "I've seen it during the day, but never at night."

"Then you're in for a real treat. It's spectacular."

The lights out on the lake dimmed even more, and they watched the elaborate water presentation while finishing their dinner.

Just as the show ended and the lighting returned to normal, Zoe's cell phone rang. Done with her meal, she placed her fork on her dish for the waiter to take and retrieved her BlackBerry from her purse. The display indicated it was her mother, and since it was odd that she'd call during the evening in the middle of the week, Zoe didn't want to ignore the call.

"Excuse me for a minute," she said to Sean. "It's my mother."

Zoe connected the line and pressed her BlackBerry to her ear. "Hey, Mom."

"Do you know where your father is?"

Collette had never been one for pleasantries and small talk, not even to take an extra minute to ask how her daughter might be before getting down to the reason for her call. "As far as I know, he's out of town on business."

"Yes, that's what his secretary has been telling me," Collette said, her tone vibrating with annoyance. "I need to get ahold of him *now,* and Sheila isn't being very accommodating about making that happen."

That was Zoe's mother—expecting people to jump at her command. Zoe was grateful that Sean couldn't hear her mother's embarrassing rant. "All I know is that he's in Chicago. Is everything okay?"

"No, everything is *not* okay," Collette replied, and released an exasperated stream of breath. "He's late on his alimony payment!"

Zoe dropped her head, closed her eyes, and rubbed her fingers across her forehead. Good God, her mother could be such a selfish bitch sometimes. "And you called *me* for this?"

Collette made an affronted sound that Zoe clearly heard,

just as her mother no doubt intended. "I figured you've been in touch with your father."

"I haven't. Not lately. I've been incredibly busy trying to find a boutique to lease, and Dad is wrapped up in the Meridian project," she said, repeating what his secretary had told her. "Sheila has been in touch with Dad—"

"That doesn't do *me* any good, now does it?" Zoe's mother cut in impatiently.

Reluctantly, Zoe glanced back up and found Sean watching her. She gave him an apologetic look before trying to reason with her mother. "Mom, I'm sure you'll get your alimony check. It's probably in the mail."

"It'd better be, because I need it," she huffed. "If you hear from your father, let me know immediately."

"Okay, I will."

"Good-bye, dear." With that, her mother disconnected the call.

Zoe pressed the END button on her BlackBerry and sighed, feeling emotionally drained by the short but exhausting conversation. In hindsight, she should have let her mother's call go straight to voice mail, because Zoe was certain she'd effectively killed the light, romantic mood between her and Sean.

"I'm sorry about that," she said, and dropped her phone back into her purse. "I thought it might be something important, but it wasn't."

"Are you sure about that?" he murmured, his gaze both perceptive and kind. "You seem upset. Do you want to talk about it?"

"I appreciate you asking, but I'd rather not." He'd been a good listener so far, but her dysfunctional family drama wasn't something Zoe wanted to discuss on a date. Instead, she exhaled a deep, calming breath and summoned a smile in an attempt to lighten the atmosphere again. "Besides, there's nothing I can do about the situation right now, so I just want to enjoy the rest of the night with you."

"How about dessert then?" He leaned closer, his thigh pressing intimately against hers, sparking a heat in the pit of her belly, and lower. His voice dropped to a deep, husky pitch as he continued. "Something rich and decadent that'll give you a sugar rush and make you forget all about that phone call."

She bit her bottom lip. Never mind *dessert*. Sean O'Brien was more sinful than any pastry or candy she could think of, and she was certain he could make her forget her first name, among other things. He made her feel more desirable than she had in a long time, and she suddenly wanted to be alone with him. Just the two of them.

Feeling daring and spontaneous, she rested her chin in her hand and embraced the sensation. "I have a better idea," she said, her tone flirtatious as she lowered her gaze to his full, sensual mouth. "How about we go back to my place and have dessert?" She knew her question sounded like a shameless attempt to seduce him, but she really did have a chocolate cake sitting on the kitchen counter at home.

A slow, toe-curling smile started in his eyes and traveled quickly to his lips. "Now there's an invitation I'm not about to refuse."

Chapter Three

Sean followed Zoe into the foyer of her apartment at the Panorama Towers, a luxury high-rise known for its exclusive amenities and outstanding views of the Las Vegas skyline. She led the way into a spacious living room with a wide, wraparound couch, a glass-topped coffee table, and a mahogany entertainment center with a flat-screen TV. The contemporary décor was uncluttered and precise, yet warm and inviting.

Just like the woman who lived there.

"Nice place," he said, catching sight of the adjoining kitchen with stainless-steel appliances and beige granite countertops.

"Thanks. It's small, but functional. Only a thousand square feet and two bedrooms, but it's really all I need."

After setting her purse on a side table, she strolled through the living room in front of him, drawing his gaze to the provocative sway of her hips and a pair of long, slender legs that had his fingers itching to touch all that silky, bare skin.

"But it was the outside balcony and amazing view of the Strip at night that ultimately sold me on this place." She pushed open the sheer curtains covering a glass sliding door and floor-to-ceiling windows, revealing a spectacular sight of bright neon lights that stretched for miles.

She unlocked the sliding door and stepped outside, and he did the same, standing beside her at the concrete and wrought-iron railing securing the area. Even at twenty-one stories up, a balmy evening breeze reached them, lifting and playing with the few loose strands of her hair that had escaped the wide gold clip she'd used at the nape of her neck. Her smooth shoulders, completely exposed by the low, sexy neckline of her dress, gleamed like alabaster in the moonlight.

Pulling his gaze from her profile, he looked out over the city, so deceptively beautiful at night. "I bet this sight never gets old, does it?"

"Nope." She curled her fingers around the wrought iron and slanted him a sidelong glance filled with a beguiling amount of heat. "Especially on a night like this. Clear. Warm. *Sultry*."

The soft, throaty way she spoke the last word evoked images of steamy, erotic kisses and hot, lazy caresses in intimate places. Ever since she'd asked him back to her place, the attraction between them had become a slow tease of sexual awareness. The onslaught of arousal thrummed through his system, and she wasn't helping matters by looking at him like *he* was dessert.

God, she was messing with his head and making him want her more than was wise, considering how he felt about her cheating, lying father and Grant Russo's part in making sure that Sean's father spent years in prison for a crime *both* men had committed. And judging by the information Caleb had collected for their client on this case, it was clear that Russo was still in the business of scamming people.

Sean had agreed to accompany Zoe to her place to discover anything else he could about her father. Based on their exchange at dinner, it seemed like she had a somewhat close relationship with her dad, but after listening in on her conversation with her mother and watching Zoe's reactions, Sean was pretty much convinced that she wasn't aware of her father's shady dealings and genuinely believed he was on a business trip—in *Chicago,* she'd told her mother.

Sean planned to pass that bit of information on to Caleb as soon as he left Zoe's tonight so they could get a jump on that lead and see if that found Russo or if it was nothing more than a diversion.

Ultimately, Sean's main objective was to remain as close to her as possible in the hopes that she heard from her father. Zoe was his daughter, and contact with him had to happen *sometime.* And when it did, Sean wanted to be around to learn where the cowardly bastard was hiding out, so The Reliance Group could take him down.

Obviously, Sean couldn't be with Zoe 24/7 to monitor her actions and calls, but one of The Reliance Group's team members, an ex–computer hacker, had already put a tap on her cell phone, enabling them to track her incoming and outgoing calls, as well as text messages. They couldn't actually listen in on her conversations, but they were able to monitor her contacts and approximately where they originated. So far, there had been plenty of business calls but no interaction with her father.

"Let's head back inside," she said after a few quiet minutes, and Sean followed her into the living room. "Make yourself at home." She waved a hand in the general direction of the entertainment center. "There's a CD player in the wall unit. Why don't you put some music on and I'll be back in a few minutes."

As she started to walk away, he couldn't help but ask, "Where are you going?"

She stopped, tipped her head, and gave him one of those

slow, sweet smiles that made him feel sucker-punched. "To get out of this restrictive dress and change into something more comfortable," she said, as if that should have been obvious.

She disappeared into a nearby bedroom and shut the door behind her, leaving Sean alone to contemplate what, exactly, she'd meant by *comfortable*. All his fertile male imagination could conjure was something flimsy, with silk and lace and lots of bare flesh. He groaned and tried like hell to shove those images from his mind before they got him into trouble.

He was a man who was used to fast women and mindless sex when the opportunity arose—no names necessary. Admittedly, he was a player, and he never made excuses or apologized for his preference for casual one-night stands. Because of his less-than-favorable past as a con man, cultivating any kind of lasting relationship had never been on his agenda and most likely never would be.

Because, at the end of the day, what woman wanted a long-term commitment with a man who'd spent years scamming people, only to spend time in prison for his stupidity? With such a huge black mark on his résumé as potential husband and father material, he'd found it much easier to keep things with women simple and uncomplicated.

Fulfilling his physical needs had never been a problem for him . . . until now. Because the woman he wanted was someone he shouldn't touch. Not only did they reside in completely different worlds socially, but even more damning was the fact that he was dating her under false pretenses. He was using her for information, and if she ever discovered his deception she'd undoubtedly, and rightfully, hate his guts.

Knowing all that, however, didn't stop him from wanting her. Far more than was wise.

Feeling warm and knowing it had more to do with his

internal temperature than the outdoor weather, he removed his jacket and tossed it over the back of a chair, then discarded his tie as well. He unbuttoned the too-tight collar of his shirt as he made his way to the compact disc player, where he selected one of John Mayer's earlier CDs, then adjusted the volume so the music wasn't too loud.

Waiting for Zoe to return, Sean stood by the sliding glass door, hands in his trouser pockets, and gazed out at the brightly lit horizon until he finally heard her bedroom door open again.

Not certain what to expect, he turned around, initially relieved to find that there wasn't a bit of silk or lace on her anywhere that he could see. She wore a pair of pink drawstring sweatpants and a white camisole-type top with thin straps, and while there was nothing overtly revealing about what she'd changed into, the casual outfit showcased everything her dress had concealed—the tantalizing curve of her waist and hips and the full, rounded shape of her breasts. She had a stunning figure, the kind that had the ability to bring a man to his knees—for all the right reasons.

"Dessert is in the kitchen." Giving him a coy look, she crooked her finger at him to follow as she walked by.

The playful overture in her voice was unmistakable. *Dessert* took on a very suggestive meaning, and as he turned to follow her he nearly groaned when he caught sight of the word *JUICY* stamped across her perfect ass, which accurately described the way she smelled. Like a ripe, succulent peach he wanted to suck and savor before taking a big bite out of.

He shook his head. Hard. God, she was going to kill him with all her innuendo before the night was over. He was sure of it.

"I hope you like chocolate cake," she said, indicating the confection displayed beneath a glass dome on the counter.

He was both pleasantly surprised and a bit disappointed
to find she actually did have an edible dessert when he was
anticipating something more tempting. Like her. "You weren't
kidding."

She tipped her head to the side, her eyes dancing with
humor. During her quick change, she'd taken the clip out
of her hair, and now the soft strands fell over her shoulders, giving her a more youthful, girl-next-door appearance. "Did you think I invited you back here for a different
kind of dessert?"

He grinned, knowing better than to fall for that guile-
less look in her gaze. "I'll admit the thought crossed my
mind."

"I'm sorry to dash your hopes." Laughing, she lifted
the lid on the cake, filling the air with the delectable fragrance of rich cocoa. "My homemade chocolate cake is
Jessica's favorite. I made it for her, but there's so much
here I thought it would be a perfect dessert for us to have
here at my place."

She cut two generous slices and transferred them to
plates, added forks, then poured two tall glasses of milk.
They each carried their dessert to the living room and sat
down on the couch next to each other while John Mayer
crooned in the background. Sean took his first bite, and
for someone who wasn't a huge fan of sweets, he had to
admit that Zoe's cake was delicious. The moist cake and
chocolate buttercream frosting literally melted in his
mouth.

"Is Jessica staying here with you while she's in Vegas?" Sean asked, curious about Zoe's best friend.

"No." Zoe curled her legs beneath her on the couch and
turned so she was facing him. "She actually has a penthouse here in the towers, which is her home base in between touring and out-of-town obligations. She's like the
sister I never had, and I love having her living so close by."

Hearing the affection in Zoe's voice, he smiled. "How did the two of you become friends?"

She took a drink of milk before answering. "We met our freshman year in high school. Our personalities were so opposite in so many ways that we never really should have become friends. I was energetic and outgoing, and she was guarded and a loner. Whenever I saw her at school, her head was down, she never made eye contact with anyone, and she avoided any kind of conversation."

It was difficult for Sean to associate that insecure young girl Zoe spoke of with the confident pop star Jessica Morgan was today.

"It wasn't until we were paired up to work together on a monthlong project in our history class that I really got to know her." After taking a bite of her cake, Zoe licked the extra frosting off her fork, her expression thoughtful, as if she was thinking back and remembering. "She was very quiet and wary at first, but the more time we spent outside of school working on our project together, the more she opened up, and we just clicked. By the end of our freshman year, we were best friends and were inseparable. Unfortunately, her home life wasn't the greatest, which accounted for why she was so guarded and didn't let too many people get close to her."

"Yet here she is, a famous celebrity who sells out concert tours within hours of their release." He shook his head in amazement. "How did that happen?"

"I know. Crazy, isn't it?" Zoe tucked a silky strand of hair behind her ear before taking another bite of her cake. "She's definitely a different person these days. But back in high school, she dealt with the ugliness at home by writing songs and making music. Her choir teacher noticed what an amazing voice she had, then learned that she also played the guitar, and cultivated her talent. By the time Jessica graduated, she wanted to be a singer or songwriter."

"That's quite a long shot," he said, and drank the last of his milk.

"Yeah, she was a realist and knew how difficult getting into the music business would be. She'd originally planned on attending UNLV for a degree in business, so she'd always have that to fall back on, but things changed for her at home that summer."

Zoe grew quiet and reflective, the look in her gaze pained as she continued. "Something really bad happened, and she just couldn't stay at home any longer, so I insisted that she move into my small apartment with me in Los Angeles. When she arrived on my doorstep, all she had was the clothes on her back and her guitar and the fire of determination to make something of her life. When auditions opened up for a new vocal talent show called *Make Me a Star*, she tried out and made the top twelve, then went all the way to the final three. She didn't win the title, but being on the show was enough to get the attention of a few record labels."

The corner of his mouth tipped up in a grin. "And the rest, as they say, is history?"

"Yeah, pretty much." Nodding, Zoe set her half-eaten piece of cake on the coffee table in front of the couch. "At the age of twenty, she was recording her first album and touring, and it's only gotten crazier for her since."

"That's a great story."

"She's deserved every bit of her success." Zoe took his empty plate from him and placed it next to hers on the table. "So, what did you think of dessert?"

"It was pretty darn good," he replied honestly. Stretching his arm across the back of the sofa, he twined a strand of her hair around his finger, feeling just as ensnared by the woman herself. "Who would have thought you were so multitalented."

Husky, playful laughter escaped her lips. "Jessica insists my chocolate cake is better than sex. What do you think?"

The woman was such an adorable vixen. So delightfully daring and so damn irresistible. She was cavorting with the underlying fire that had been simmering between them all evening, and boldly traveling down a path rife with sensual possibilities. And damn if he didn't want to follow along and indulge in whatever she had in mind.

"It's hard to say what I think, since I haven't so much as kissed the cook."

The tip of her pink tongue skimmed along her bottom lip, dampening the pillowed flesh and filling Sean's head with too many erotic thoughts and images. "You want to see if my kiss is better than my chocolate cake?"

Her voice was breathless with anticipation, her eyes darkening with the same desire igniting a low, burning need inside of him. "It's the only way I can make an informed comparison," he murmured, using the gentle pull on the strands of her hair still wrapped around his finger to reel her in as he dipped his mouth closer to hers. "Your cake is probably the best I've had, but I have a feeling kissing you might be a whole lot more addictive."

She smiled, her lashes fluttering closed as his mouth brushed across hers, his teeth gently nibbling, tasting, teasing. Her cool palm touched his cheek, and her lips parted on a sigh, inviting him in, and he didn't hesitate to give her more. His tongue touched hers in a slow swirling caress that drew a purr of sound from her throat and made him harder than hell.

With effort, he pulled back, ending the kiss while he still had the ability to do so. She opened her eyes and looked up at him, the wanting in her gaze turning him inside out with a deeper, more insatiable hunger that threatened to consume him.

"Well?" She dragged her thumb along his moist bottom lip, and it took monumental effort on his part not to suck her finger into his mouth. "What do you think?"

Honestly, there was no comparison when it came to the flavor of her chocolate cake versus how rich and decadent she tasted. "I'm still not sure," he lied, hoping like hell she'd offer up another sampling.

She didn't disappoint him. Her fingers slid into his hair and around to the back of his neck, her expression filled with a seductive yearning. "Then by all means, let's try again until you're absolutely certain." She guided his head back down to hers.

At first touch, both their lips automatically opened and he rolled his tongue into her mouth. She took it and gave him her own, coaxing him deeper into the wild and willing kiss. What began as a fun, sexy dare quickly flared into heated lust, the kind that tightened his groin and threatened his control. In the back of his mind, he could hear John Mayer singing about her body being a wonderland, and Sean couldn't agree more.

Lush curves and silky skin awaited his touch, urging him to stroke his hands over all those alluring dips and swells that made her intrinsically a woman. Pushing her back onto the couch, he moved partially on top of her and slid a hard thigh between her legs, entwining their bodies intimately. Tunneling all ten fingers into her hair, he tipped her head slightly, fitted her mouth precisely to his, and took their kiss to a deeper, hotter level of pleasure.

Her soft moan of consent vibrated against his lips, and she shifted restlessly beneath him, seeking something more. He slid a hand along her thigh and over her hip, the clingy material of her sweatpants too much of a barrier when he ached to feel her naked flesh against his palm. Then his fondest wish was granted when his fingers grazed the soft, supple skin of her stomach, where her sweatpants ended and her camisole top began. He feathered his fingertips along that bared strip of skin, his pulse spiking dangerously high when she arched into him and wrapped a leg around his, so that his rock-hard erection had no choice but to nestle right up against her sex.

Sweet Jesus. She was so damn responsive. So incredibly sensual and passionate.

She rolled her hips against his, a slow, erotic undulation that made him growl deep in his throat and made him crazy with the need to shed their clothes and sink his cock to the hilt inside of her. Instead, he slipped his hand beneath the hem of her top and headed for the next best thing . . . the sweet, plump rise of her breast.

She wasn't wearing a bra, and when he closed his palm over her warm, pliant flesh and his fingers plucked at her stiff nipple, she shuddered beneath him and squeezed his thigh between her legs. He lifted his head to look down at her, taking in her flushed face, her pink, wet lips, and her heavy-lidded gaze staring up at him with undeniable wanting.

Unable to help himself, he went back in for another kiss, this one a long, slow, lazy exploration of lips and tongues, adding to the exquisite feel of her breast nestled so perfectly in his hand.

She unbuttoned his shirt, splayed her palms on his chest, and grazed her thumbs across his rigid nipples, coaxing a rough groan of pleasure from him. As one decadent kiss melted into another and each luxurious caress grew bolder than the last, he lost track of time, not that seconds or minutes mattered when he had such a gorgeous, vibrant woman pressed beneath him.

A while later her fingers slid into his hair and she tugged his head back, ending their kiss. They were both panting hard, their bodies taut with arousal, and he knew they were right on the verge of taking this make-out session one step further, to the point of no return unless one of them came to their senses.

"Oh, God," she said breathlessly, her expression soft and dreamy. "Why can't you kiss like a Saint Bernard and look like a troll?"

He chuckled. Not exactly what he was expecting to hear, but as the voice of reason in this runaway train of seduction, her humorous comment worked to bring them both back to reality. "I'm sorry."

"Me, too." She sighed, a languid smile easing up the corners of her well-kissed mouth. "It would make resisting you so much easier."

He dipped his head and nuzzled the fragrant curve of her neck. "Who says you have to?" he murmured into her ear, and gave her supple breast another gentle squeeze.

She shivered, twisted his hair tighter between her fingers, and tugged his head back again. "I do," she said, genuine regret in her tone as she pulled his hand from beneath her top. "The thing is, I'm not the type of girl who has sex with a guy unless it means something more than scratching an itch."

Her confession couldn't have shocked him more, and made him wonder just how experienced, or inexperienced, she actually was. "Are you . . ." How did he ask such a question?

"A virgin?" she finished for him, then laughed. "Lord, no. I love sex; I just don't do *casual* sex, even when I know it has the potential of being absolutely mind-blowing. Pathetic, but true."

"Ah-h, you're a good girl." Grinning, he propped his head in his hand and drew lazy swirls on her bare stomach with the tip of his finger, enjoying the way the muscles in her belly clenched in reaction. "Nothing pathetic about that. In fact, I find it incredibly sexy and refreshing."

Her morals said a lot about her character, and oddly

enough, her views on sex only made him respect her more. And it kept him from crossing lines he had no business stepping over. Hell, he never should have kissed her in the first place, but it was difficult to regret something that felt and tasted so good.

She looked relieved. "Then you're the first. In fact, I've been accused of being a tease, so I try not to let things get to the point of no return, if you know what I mean." Before he could reply, she rushed on to explain. "Don't get me wrong. I love kissing and touching and fondling, and all the other good stuff that goes with making out with a hot guy like you."

He lifted a brow. "The good stuff?" he asked, curious to hear her definition of that phrase.

Her shoulder lifted in a nonchalant shrug, though the delightful pink coloring rising on her cheeks told him she wasn't so indifferent to their candid discussion. "You know, *the good stuff*," she said, her blush deepening as her hands fluttered in the air between them. "Foreplay, an orgasm, but without actually having sex."

"Foreplay *is* the best part of sex." He winked at her, though he was completely serious. "So is the buildup of sexual tension over the course of a few dates."

She smiled. "Are you asking me out on another date?"

"I believe I am." She was still lying beside him on the couch, and he loved that she was so comfortable with him. "When can I see you again?" Being with her should have been all about the case and finding her father, but Sean knew deep in his gut his desire to be with her was too personal. Not a good thing, but his attraction to her was getting more difficult for him to fight.

"Soon, hopefully."

"Tomorrow?"

She laughed at his persistence. "I can't. I'll be tied up all day in marketing conference calls for my fall campaign and placing coordinating orders for the boutique with my manufacturer, and tomorrow night I already have a date."

The pit of his stomach twisted with an emotion that was foreign to him—jealousy. "You do?"

She nodded, an impish look in her eyes. "With Jessica."

Not a guy but her best friend. Thank God. The ten-pound weight sitting on his chest eased substantially. "Maybe I could crash your party," he teased.

"No boys allowed," she said, shaking her head. "We're ordering dinner in and watching a chick flick. It's something we do whenever she's in town."

"It was worth a shot." He grinned and ran the tip of his finger along the smooth slope of Zoe's nose. "How long are you going to make me wait to see you again?"

She thought for a moment. "Tell you what. How about I promise to be in touch over the next few days? Maybe we can get together this weekend . . . if you're lucky."

He chuckled, knowing she was deliberately playing him. "Yeah, you *are* a tease."

She certainly wasn't a simple mark or someone he could easily manipulate, and pushing the issue any more would only make him look too desperate and annoying. Her calls were already being monitored, but he'd have Caleb put surveillance on her until they were together again. Which Sean hoped wouldn't be long from now.

Moving off the couch, he stood up, then offered her his hand. "It's getting late and I should go."

After accepting his help up, she straightened her camisole, which did nothing to conceal the outlines of her nipples against the fabric. He grabbed his coat and tie, and she followed him to the door. For purely selfish reasons he didn't dare analyze, he stole another quick, heated kiss, something sweet to tide him over until he saw her again. Something that would leave her aching for more.

Too soon for his liking, he drew back and smiled. "Just

for the record, you're far more delicious than your chocolate cake."

She licked her bottom lip, as if tasting for herself. "That's
good to know."

Satisfied that he'd weakened her defenses and ignited the
slow burn of anticipation, he opened the door and looked
back at her one last time. "Don't make me wait long."

"So, did you get lucky last night?"

Jessica sauntered into Zoe's living room the following
evening, carrying a bag of Chinese takeout and a six-pack
of cheap strawberry daiquiri wine coolers, their favorite
girls'-night-in fare. She set their meal on the place mats
Zoe had laid out on the coffee table, then turned back
around, hands on her slim, jeans-clad hips and her expression direct and expectant.

"Well?" Jessica persisted, wanting details, as always.

Zoe settled on the couch, unable to stop the silly, giddy
grin lifting her lips. "I got lucky enough."

Jessica plopped down beside her and let out an exasperated breath. "First base? Second base? Come on, Zoe,
spill already. Let me live vicariously."

Zoe laughed, then told her best friend what she wanted
to know, because they pretty much shared everything. "We
kissed. *A lot.*"

And those seductive kisses had been so, so good. Just
remembering Sean's persuasive mouth on hers, his hard
thigh pressed between her legs, and his warm hand on her
breast made her heart pound like an infatuated school-
girl's all over again. He was the first man since her painful breakup with Ian to make her feel so desirable, and
she couldn't deny that Sean's attention, and their mutual
attraction, felt really nice.

"I'm jealous." Jessica exhaled a wistful sigh. "I can't
remember the last time I made out with a guy."

Zoe didn't bother to point out that Jessica's lack of a love life was by her own choice. Jessica Morgan the glamorous rock star had her pick of any guy she wanted. But Jessica the woman was wary when it came to men and what they expected of her because of her celebrity status. Did they really want *her* or the perks of her fame? She didn't trust easily, and even though she gave the impression of being a bit of a bad girl when she performed onstage, she had a soft, vulnerable heart she kept well protected.

Zoe's stomach growled, reminding her how busy she'd been all day long and that she hadn't eaten since breakfast. She unpacked their dinner and handed Jessica her take-out box of sweet-and-sour pork, along with chopsticks, then picked up her own entrée of chicken lo mein. Leaning back against the sofa cushions, she crossed her legs on the couch and dug into her meal.

"Are you going to see him again?" Jessica asked after they'd eaten a few bites.

Reaching for her wine cooler, Zoe took a drink of the strawberry-flavored beverage. "He asked, and I'd *like* to go out with him again, but honestly, right now just isn't the ideal time to jump into a relationship of any sort."

It was a thought Zoe had been wrestling with all night long and still didn't have a definite answer to. Physically and sexually, she and Sean meshed incredibly well, but Zoe wasn't sure she was ready to invest her emotions into any man when she needed all her focus on opening her boutique.

Jessica popped a piece of pork into her mouth and chewed. "There's never a *good* time."

"Yeah, like *you* would know," Zoe shot back, pointing her chopsticks in her friend's direction.

Jessica responded by sticking her tongue out at her.

Zoe shook her head and changed the subject, for both of their sakes. As they finished eating, they talked about

Jessica's upcoming tour and the different elements she wanted to incorporate into the show. They brainstormed ideas on props and backdrops, and an hour later they'd even come up with a few costume ideas for Jessica to discuss with her stylist and wardrobe coordinator.

Finished with her chicken lo mein, Zoe set her box on the table, wanting to share some exciting news with Jessica. Actually, there were two important things she needed to tell her, and Zoe retrieved the flat envelope she'd left within reach. "Before we start the movie, guess what I got in the mail today?"

"I have no idea," Jessica said, though her gaze flickered with interest. "Something good, I hope."

"Definitely good." Unable to contain her enthusiasm, Zoe pulled two glossy sheets of paper from the envelope and handed them to her friend. "It's the page proofs for the layout you did for *InStyle* magazine." A two-page spread featuring her Zoe Russo Fall Collection, starring Jessica Morgan as the woman wearing various jewelry, scarves, sunglasses, and other accessories for the upcoming season. "You look *amazing*. I couldn't ask for a better spokesperson for my collection."

"Are you kidding me? I genuinely love your stuff. Besides, you know I'd do anything for you, and if this helps to give ZR Designs the recognition it deserves, then I'm happy to be a part of it. Now you just need to get a boutique, because when this magazine hits the stands women are going to be clamoring for your accessories."

"Then it's a good thing I'll have one," Zoe said, getting to the second part of her news. "My lawyer called a few hours ago. The Onyx lease agreement is a go. I'll be turning in the signed contract and my first and last months' deposits for the place tomorrow afternoon. The boutique is mine."

"Oh, my God!" Jessica released a squeal of delight and

launched herself into Zoe's arms for a big, congratulatory hug. "I'm so thrilled for you!"

Zoe laughed, appreciating her friend's support more than ever. No one understood more than Jessica just how important all this was to Zoe. "Thanks."

Jessica pulled back and grabbed Zoe's hands. "Wow. Your flagship store. This is *huge*. How do you feel about all this?"

Zoe bit her bottom lip, trying to put a name to the various emotions she'd been experiencing since the call from her attorney. "Excited. Nervous. Scared," she admitted honestly.

"Yeah, like me and my first album, then my first concert singing live in front of thousands of people. I get it. You wouldn't be normal if you weren't a little scared." Jessica picked up her bottled wine cooler and raised it in a toast. "Here's to you, ZR Designs, and a prosperous, exciting future."

"I'll drink to that." Zoe clicked her bottle to Jessica's, then finished off the last of her strawberry daiquiri.

"There's only one thing left to do," Jessica announced enthusiastically.

Zoe tipped her head curiously. "And what's that?"

"See what Confucius has in store for us." Grabbing both of the fortune cookies that had come with their dinner, Jessica tossed one of them to Zoe and kept the other for herself. "He's usually a wise old man."

Sometimes they had a good laugh over the silly fortunes folded inside the cookies. Other times, the sayings were eerily accurate, applying to some aspect of their lives in a way that gave them goose bumps. They never took their fortunes seriously, but for some reason tonight Zoe was reluctant to read hers. Her life was going so well, personally and professionally, and she didn't want a stupid phrase to mess with her head or influence her thoughts.

"You go first," she said, giving herself a few extra minutes to get over her illogical worry. Geez, since when had she turned superstitious?

Without hesitation, Jessica cracked open her cookie and pulled out the white strip of paper tucked inside. "'Something you lost will soon turn up.'" She glanced at Zoe and grinned. "Maybe I'll finally find my favorite Cartier pen that I haven't seen since my trip to New York last month."

Most likely, Jessica's coveted pen was long gone, but Zoe wasn't about to dash her friend's hopes by saying so.

"Your turn." Jessica set her fortune on the coffee table, twisted the cap open on another wine cooler, and settled back against the corner of the couch.

Taking a deep breath, Zoe broke her cookie in half, retrieved her words of wisdom, and read them out loud: "'Sometimes the object of the journey is not the end, but the journey itself.'" She felt a ridiculous amount of relief that she hadn't been delivered a foreboding message but rather a harmless saying that could apply to anyone's life.

"Hm-m." Jessica made the thoughtful sound before taking a drink of her daiquiri. "I'm sure it has something to do with your new journey as a boutique owner, and how your business is on the verge of taking off."

Happy with Jessica's take on things, Zoe nodded and embraced her promising fortune and future. "I think you're absolutely right."

After all, what else could it mean?

Chapter Four

"Are you sure you don't want to consider a permanent job as a leasing agent?"

"No, thank you," Sean said, knowing he'd never trade in his bartending gig for boring, monotonous nine-to-five employment where he had to wear a suit on a daily basis.

As he unlocked the glass door to what would soon be Zoe Russo's boutique, he glanced at the woman who'd accompanied him to his Friday afternoon appointment. Janet Hayes, a sharp, business-savvy woman in her mid-fifties, was the leasing manager for the shops at the Onyx, and with Zoe turning in her contract today, along with deposits, it was Janet's signature that was needed on the agreement in order to seal the deal and make it legitimate.

Sean might have negotiated the deal for Janet, but *his* John Hancock on the final paperwork would be equivalent to fraud, since he didn't really work for the leasing company, and he was no longer in the business of scamming people.

Janet followed him into the empty shop and switched on the lights. "Well, I don't know what kind of magic you have up your sleeve, but this is one of the quickest, easiest negotiations we've ever seen."

Shrugging off her compliment, he pushed his hands into the front pockets of his pants and closed his fingers around the set of keys that would soon belong to Zoe. "It was just a matter of the right client at the right time. Zoe Russo needed a place, you offered her a great price and lease terms, and this boutique is exactly what she's looking for."

"Don't be so modest." Janet gave him a cougarish once-over that made him feel like a piece of raw meat she was looking to sink her teeth into. "I'm sure your good looks and charm helped to sway her. I know I'd be hard-pressed to say no to anything you offered."

Oh, hell. She started walking toward him, and he cast a quick glance outside the shop, grateful to see Zoe heading their way. The last thing he wanted to do was fend off Janet's advances. Again. The woman had made it more than clear that she was interested in him, but he certainly didn't reciprocate the feeling. Not even close.

"Here she comes," he announced.

Janet stopped and followed the direction of his gaze. "Which one is she? The blonde or the redhead?"

"Zoe is the blonde." The gorgeous, vibrant blonde who looked damn hot in a curve-hugging pair of black jeans, a fitted red button-front blouse that revealed just a hint of cleavage, and the kind of spiked high heels that conjured the erotic image of her naked, wearing nothing but those sexy shoes. "The redhead is her best friend, Jessica Morgan."

Janet's expression flickered with interest. "Ah-h, that explains the trail of people following her."

He laughed, watching as Jessica's bodyguard tried to keep the spectators at bay. "Yes, she does seem to draw a crowd wherever she goes." He glanced back at Zoe, and as soon as she saw him in the store waiting for her, her smile widened with pure pleasure.

He hadn't seen her since Wednesday night, but he knew

from his recent meeting with Caleb, less than an hour ago, that The Reliance Group still had her under surveillance. According to their phone log of her incoming and outgoing calls, there still had been no contact with her father, though it appeared she'd dialed his cell phone and left him messages. She'd also called her father's office a few times and spoken with her mother again, but Grant Russo still remained elusive.

When Zoe and Jessica reached the storefront, Jessica told her to go inside and she'd sign some autographs to diffuse the crowd around them and give Zoe the privacy she needed to complete the deal for the boutique.

As soon as Zoe walked into the shop, Janet welcomed her with a professional smile and a handshake and explained that since she was the manager, her being present when a lease agreement with a client was finalized was a routine business practice. Less than twenty minutes later, with the last of the paperwork completed, Zoe had herself a new boutique for her designs.

"Welcome to the Onyx family," Janet said, looking pleased that they'd managed to entice Zoe to sign with them, instead of their rival Caesars Palace. "We're so happy to have you as part of the chain of fine shops here in the hotel."

"Thank you. I'm very excited." Smiling happily, Zoe shook Janet's hand again, this time in a congratulatory manner.

Janet gathered up all the signed paperwork and tucked it into a file folder, along with her deposit payments. "My job here is done, so I'll let Sean finish up the last of the appointment. It was a pleasure meeting you."

"You, too," Zoe replied.

Sean waited until Janet left the store and he was alone with Zoe. He noticed that Jessica was no longer outside of the boutique; in fact, he couldn't see her or her bodyguard anywhere in sight. Which was fine with Sean, since he wanted extra minutes with Zoe to execute his next plan of action to spend time with her.

"Well, there's only one thing left to do," he said, reaching into his front pocket to present her with the best gift of the afternoon.

She tipped her head curiously. "What's that?"

He withdrew a silver key ring and dangled it in front of her. "Give you the keys to the store."

Her eyes lit up with excitement as he dropped the keys into the palm of her hand. "Oh, wow," she breathed, her voice awed. "This is a dream I've had for such a long time, and I can't believe it's really come true."

"It has, and now it's your reality," he said, enjoying the fact that he was there to share this special, life-changing moment with her. "Congratulations."

"Thanks." Her expression infused with pride, she looked around, taking in all the open space and empty shelves yet to be filled. "Now the work really begins. I have about a month to get this place organized with display units, stocked with merchandise, and opened for business." Hands on her hips, she looked back at him, delight dancing in her gaze. "I'm going to be *very* busy."

"Yes, you are." She didn't look at all overwhelmed by the enormity of what awaited her but, rather, determined to tackle the job ahead. "Now that our business has been wrapped up and we are no longer broker and client, I'd like to take you out tonight, as a *friend,* to celebrate the opening of your very first boutique."

She twirled her finger around the long crystal necklace around her neck, a sweet but mocking smile on her lips. "As a friend?"

It was hard to miss the playful note to her voice. Yeah, he knew it sounded ridiculous, considering the kisses they'd shared Wednesday night at her place had gone way beyond platonic friendship, but he didn't want to give her any reason to turn him down.

He grinned. "It's your decision if you want it to be more."

She crossed her arms over her chest, giving him a glimpse of her black lace bra peeking from the low, buttoned V in her blouse. "Okay, as a friend, or maybe more," she added with a cheeky smile, "I'd like to invite you to join me, Jessica, and a few other friends tonight. The three of us already made plans to spend the evening at Taboo," she said, indicating the Oynx's nightclub located just across the way. "The more the merrier, I say."

He jumped on the opportunity. "Count me in. In fact, I know the club's manager. If Jessica doesn't already have a room booked, I'll pull a few strings and make sure you all receive the VIP treatment, including a private balcony so everyone can just relax and have a good time without people bothering you."

"Thank you. I know Jessica will appreciate the offer." Zoe tilted her head to the side, regarding him with amusement. "You're very good at pulling strings, aren't you?"

"That's not the only thing I'm good at." He winked at her.

She blushed, obviously recalling how *good* their kisses had been. How *good* his hands had felt on her body. "Braggart," she teased.

He chuckled. "I'll send a limo to your place to pick everyone up at eight."

After signing over a dozen autographs, Jessica mustered another smile and posed for one last picture with a fan before giving her bodyguard *the look*—the one that told him she was feeling overwhelmed and desperately needed some breathing space. Simon, having been in her employment for the past four years, was exceptionally good at his job and knew exactly what to do to appease the last of the crowd while giving Jessica enough time to slip away unnoticed.

Confident Simon was watching where she went and would catch up to her as soon as she put some distance between herself and the avid fans, she crossed the promenade of shops and strolled casually past the Onyx's nightclub, Taboo.

The double doors were open a few inches, and she could hear one of her songs from her recent album playing inside. The lyrics to "Don't Turn Me Away" drifted out to where she was standing. Intrigued that someone was listening to one of her songs in the middle of the afternoon and before the club even officially opened for business, and seeing this as the perfect escape for a few minutes, she glanced back at Simon to let him know where she was disappearing to, then stepped into the nightclub.

She'd expected a darkened interior, but the main lights in the lounge area were on. The place was virtually empty, except for a few people doing what looked like cleanup and preparations for Friday night's crowd. A couple of the workers cast her a curious look, but to her surprise, none approached her.

Enjoying the moment of anonymity, she stood off to the side in the shadows, humming along to her own lyrics. No matter how many times she heard one of her songs on the radio or anywhere else, it was always an amazing, surreal experience, and this was no different. She never took her success for granted and knew she was so lucky to make a living writing and singing what was in her heart and soul. More than a career, it was therapy for her, a way to deal with the pain of the past and the heartbreak she still lived with on a daily basis.

Every lyric she penned, every verse she sang, told a story. She'd written "Don't Turn Me Away" a few years ago, but even now the message behind the words still rang true and had the ability to form a huge, emotional lump in her throat.

> *Let me inside where it's warm and safe,*
> *In your arms, your loving embrace.*
> *I know I was wrong, but the feelings are still so strong.*
> *Don't tell me no. Don't turn me away.*

"Excuse me, miss, but the club isn't open right now."

Startled by the deep, male voice coming from behind her, she spun around to apologize for intruding. "I'm so sorry. I heard the music playing and I just wanted . . ."

Her words trailed off and her heart slammed hard in her chest as she stared into a familiar pair of chocolate brown eyes. Dark, sensual eyes that invaded her dreams late at night and left her aching for his touch. Tender, trusting eyes she'd betrayed. The sweetest, most caring eyes she never, ever, believed she'd see again in person.

Noah Young. Her high school sweetheart. The only man she'd ever given her heart to, whom she had never forgotten. Never would. He was the one who got away or, rather, the one she'd run far and fast from rather than face the humiliation and shame of telling him the truth of what had happened to her.

Oh, God. The last time she'd seen him he'd been a tall, lanky, gorgeous eighteen-year-old who'd made her feel special and loved when her own mother had never missed an opportunity to tell Jessica how much she despised her daughter. Nine years later and he'd grown into a devastatingly sexy man who seemed larger than life, definitely more mature, and far more dangerous to her feminine senses, if the searing heat of awareness washing over her was any indication.

He looked good. Better than good. His facial features

were more refined, his brown hair a little longer than he'd worn it as the captain of the high school basketball team. His shoulders were wider now, his chest broader beneath the collared shirt he wore, and his dark jeans outlined strong thighs and long, lean legs.

She forced her gaze back up to his, feeling as though someone were sitting on her chest. "Noah . . ." Her voice cracked. Nothing had prepared her for seeing him again. She wasn't usually at a loss for words, but she had no idea what to say or do.

He stared at her with a combination of shock and disbelief, seemingly unable to comprehend the fact that she was standing in front of him after all these years.

"Jessie?" he asked, as if he needed her to confirm that it was, indeed, her.

She shook her head in denial, her mane of spiral curls swaying with the movement. "I . . . I'm sorry," she managed to say. For more than just being in the nightclub when it clearly wasn't open for business. The apology encompassed the wealth of guilt she'd lived with for the past nine years.

The urge to bolt, to run, overwhelmed her, and she backed away from him. "I've got to go." She whirled around and started for the entrance.

"Wait." He grabbed her arm, forcing her to stop.

She gasped, not because he'd hurt her in any way but because the heat of his touch threatened to unravel her. These days, she never lost control. Never let anyone or anything rattle her composure. Yet with just one touch Noah had stripped away all her defenses and left her reeling.

"What are you doing here?" he asked, his voice gruff as his hard gaze searched hers.

The animosity she detected in his tone was like a well-placed knife to her heart. "It was a mistake."

He finally released her arm and jammed his hands on

his hips, his narrowed gaze brimming with resentment. "Seeing me again is a *mistake*?"

"Yes . . . No. . . ." She was so nervous and unable to think straight, the words tumbled from her lips before she could censure them. She inhaled a deep breath and tried again, this time going for civil and polite. "How have you been?"

He laughed, the sound lacking any semblance of humor. "I haven't seen or heard from you in *nine years* and that's all you have to say? *'How have you been?'* Do you really even *care* how I am?"

Sarcasm spilled from him, but it was the hurt she saw in the depth of his eyes that cut her to the core. She'd done this to him. Made him bitter and angry toward her. He was a man who now hated her, with good reason.

"Of course I care." More than he'd ever know.

"Then you have a shitty way of showing it, Jessie."

To her horror, hot tears burned the backs of her eyes. What in the world could she say to that? How could she explain to him that what she'd done had been a matter of self-preservation? That leaving him had been her only option, because it would have happened eventually, when he discovered that she was no longer the girl he'd once known. That one terrible, awful incident had changed the course of her life and her future with Noah. By ending their relationship and cutting off all contact she'd managed to salvage a bit of her pride, even if it had been at the expense of breaking his heart and shattering the strong, intimate bond they'd once shared.

God, there were so many questions glimmering in his gaze. And the answers were just too painful for her to reveal—even if he did deserve an explanation.

"Jessica? Everything okay?"

Simon's concerned voice cut into her thoughts from somewhere behind her, and she watched as Noah shifted his gaze and scrutinized her burly bodyguard with something akin to contempt. She knew Noah was wondering who the guy was, and Jessica didn't bother to clarify Simon's presence.

"Yes, I'm fine," she said, loud enough for Simon to hear. Then, taking the coward's way out, she said to Noah, "I really do have to go. It was nice seeing you again."

She walked away, and this time he didn't stop her.

"Are you sure you still want to spend the evening at Taboo?" Zoe stepped out onto her apartment balcony, joining Jessica by the railing where her friend was drinking one of the leftover wine coolers from the other night and staring off into the distance—much too quiet and contemplative for Zoe's liking. "I completely understand if you'd rather not, and there's still time for me to call Sean and cancel the limousine he's sending for us."

"Don't worry about me." Jessica waved her hand in the air, causing the gold and crystal bracelets stacked on her wrist to make a soft tinkling sound. "I'm fine. Really."

Zoe's best friend was such a bad liar. Jessica wasn't fine. Outwardly she might look confident and spectacular in her sparkly, champagne-colored dress and Jimmy Choo heels, but internally she was an emotional wreck. Zoe could see the pain in Jessica's eyes, along with the guilt of what had transpired between her and Noah all those years ago.

When Jessica had returned from wherever she'd disappeared to when Zoe was signing her lease agreement, Zoe had known immediately that something was wrong. Jessica had looked shaken and pale, and as soon as they were sitting alone in the back of the Town Car, Zoe had insisted on knowing what had happened. That's when Jessica had spilled about running into Noah at Taboo. Come to find out he was the general manager of the nightclub.

"But I *am* worried." Leaning her arms on the railing, Zoe glanced at her friend's profile, hating that Jessica was hurting at all. "I don't want you feeling uncomfortable in any way. We don't have to go to Taboo."

"Yes, we do," Jessica said, turning a smile Zoe's way. "Because your hot man went through the trouble of making sure our group will be well taken care of and it would be rude to back out now. Tonight is all about *you,* and I'm not ruining your evening just because I ran into an old flame."

Not just any old flame, but the love of Jessica's life.

"I'm a big girl and I can handle this," Jessica went on, then finished the last of her strawberry daiquiri for a bit of liquid fortitude. "Besides, I doubt there's anything left to say between Noah and me. He wasn't thrilled to see me, so I'm pretty sure he'll ignore my presence tonight."

"Do you really want him to?"

"No . . . but yes." Jessica sighed, the sound tinged with anguish as she ran a hand through her curls and pulled them away from her face. "God, he looked so good. And he was so angry and bitter. After all these years, I hadn't expected that."

"You honestly thought he'd be happy to see you?"

She didn't even flinch at the brutally honest question Zoe asked. "Well, no, not exactly. But I didn't think he'd hate me so much."

Zoe had never agreed with how Jessica had handled things with Noah all those years ago, but she'd always been supportive of her best friend. And Zoe would continue to be so, no matter how Jessica decided to handle *this* situation.

"I doubt he hates you," Zoe said, trying to be reasonable.

Jessica's smile was sad. "You didn't see the way he looked at me. It was as if I'd devastated him."

Zoe wasn't sure what to say to that and considered the safest response. "It was a long time ago, Jess."

"You're right." Jessica pulled in a deep breath and visibly shook off her melancholy mood. "Isn't it about time for us to go? We've got some major celebrating to do tonight."

Jessica headed back into the living room to grab her purse, giving Zoe her cue to follow . . . and to leave their too-emotional conversation behind.

Chapter Five

By the time they arrived at Taboo, the place was already packed inside, with a line out the door. Sean met them at the nightclub's entrance and led the way up to the private skybox he'd secured for them for the night. Zoe, Sean, Jessica, and four of her band members had free rein of the VIP services, which included a buffet, an open bar, a sitting area, and a balcony that overlooked the lower dance floor and the live band currently rocking the joint.

"Here's your apple martini."

Shivering at the sound of Sean's deep, sexy voice, Zoe turned from where she was standing at the banister securing the lounge area and accepted the cocktail that he'd insisted on getting for her. She took a drink, tasting the tang of apple schnapps and the kind of premium vodka that went down smooth and easy. The sugar on the rim was just a bonus.

"Thank you," she said, licking a few sweet granules from her bottom lip. "It's perfect."

"Good." Settling in beside her, he leaned against the railing, his gaze taking in the chaos below. Tonight he was wearing a pair of black jeans and a dark purple pullover shirt that was unbuttoned at the throat, making him look more gorgeous than a man had a right to.

After a few moments, he glanced back at her, his blue eyes warm and inviting as they slid across her bare shoulders and took a second to appreciate the low-cut bodice of her dress and the soft swells of her breasts before making his way back up to her face. Knowing he'd been caught ogling her, he merely smiled unapologetically as he took a drink from his bottle of beer.

"Are you having a good time?" he asked.

"I am." Her only concern was Jessica, but she seemed to be okay.

Currently, she was talking with her drummer and laughing at something he said. All in all, she'd managed to put her own angst aside and appeared more relaxed. Zoe was sure the second cosmo her friend was gulping down was helping to give Jessica a false sense of complacency. Whatever worked to calm her was fine by Zoe.

Taking another sip of her apple martini, Zoe smiled at Sean. "I was just watching the crowd enjoy the music. It's crazy down there," she said, indicating the huge, spacious area jam-packed with party revelers. "It certainly isn't a place for someone who might be claustrophobic."

He laughed. "I don't know. It could be fun."

"You think?" She wasn't so sure.

"If you enjoy a little dirty dancing, then yeah, I'd call that fun."

His slow, shameless grin sent a rush of heated awareness through her veins. Feeling her skin warm with what was becoming an ever-present flush around him, she shifted her gaze back down to the throng of people and considered his comment.

Dirty dancing was an apt description for what was going on below. People were dancing to the music, the tight confines of the floor space forcing them to brush up intimately, and very suggestively, against their partners. There was a lot of rubbing, shimmying, and grinding going on between couples, and Zoe felt a bit like a voyeur watching it all.

After a while, Jessica joined Zoe and Sean at the railing to people-watch. The music was loud, and no one paid any attention to them in their private skybox. The band playing for the Friday night crowd had most everyone up and dancing, including Zoe and Jessica. With a bit of alcohol in their system, they were laughing and having a great time, letting loose and enjoying the evening until the band announced they'd be taking a short break.

Rippling sounds of disappointment filled the air, and as the band members headed off the stage a tall, dark-haired man wearing a navy suit stepped up to the microphone. Zoe did a double take, recognizing the guy as Noah Young. A grown-up, good-looking version of the teenager she remembered. Standing at the railing next to Jessica, Zoe cast a sidelong glance at her friend, noticing the frown that now replaced the smile she'd been wearing only minutes before.

"Hey, everyone," Noah said, greeting everyone in a loud, jovial voice. "I'm the general manager of Taboo, and I hope you all are having a great time tonight."

The crowd roared their approval.

"That's exactly what I want to hear," he said, and grinned. "Hopefully, it's going to get a lot more exciting. I've been told we have a celebrity in the house tonight," he went on just as a spotlight flashed up to the second floor of the club, illuminating Jessica and her halo of signature auburn curls. "Let's give it up for Jessica Morgan!"

The mass of people turned, looked up, and as soon as they spotted Jessica went wild, yelling and clapping enthusiastically. The sound was thunderous and deafening. With everyone's attention on Jessica, she smiled good-naturedly and waved, a performance in itself.

"Maybe you all could persuade Jessica to come on down and sing a few of her songs," Noah suggested, encouraging the crowd to increase their boisterous, relentless cheers.

It didn't escape Zoe's notice that Noah's gaze was locked on Jessica, and vice versa, in a silent battle of wills. He'd just issued her a direct challenge and was waiting to see how she handled the dare.

Zoe expected Jessica to be a little upset that she'd been put on the spot so blatantly, by someone who was clearly trying to goad her, but much to her surprise her friend was incredibly poised and a consummate professional in front of so many fans. Whatever animosity was simmering between Noah and her, Jessica wasn't about to show it with hundreds of people witnessing her every move.

Instead of politely declining the invitation, Jessica leaned over the railing and dazzled them all with a wide grin. "I'd love to give you guys a miniconcert! I'll be right down."

When Jessica turned back around and moved away from the banister, there was no missing the fire of determination blazing in her green gaze. It probably didn't hurt that she had a few drinks under her belt to help bolster her fortitude as well.

"He's such a jerk," she muttered, voicing her frustration to Zoe. "He knew I wouldn't say no to all these people and risk looking like a self-centered diva."

Unable to argue Jessica's point, Zoe instead grabbed her friend's hands and gave them an affectionate, and reassuring, squeeze. "Just treat this like any other concert. You've done this hundreds of times before and you're good at entertaining your fans."

Jessica released a low groan, revealing a moment of

vulnerability with Zoe. "It's unnerving to know that *he'll* be in the audience watching me."

"Then give him a show he'll never forget."

Her chin lifted and she pushed her shoulders back, standing tall and proud. "You're absolutely right. I'm going to do just that."

Two men, part of the club's security, came up to the skybox to escort Jessica and her band members down to the stage.

"Do Noah and Jessica know one another?" Sean asked as soon as the others were gone and the two of them were alone on the balcony.

"Yeah, you could say that." Noah and Jessica's story wasn't hers to tell, so Zoe kept the explanation simple. "They have a bit of a history."

"And chemistry, if I'm not mistaken."

So, Sean had noticed that, too. Interesting.

It took about fifteen minutes for Jessica to get up to the stage and for her band members to familiarize themselves with the previous group's instruments so they could play Jessica's songs for her.

She picked up the microphone and addressed everyone in the club. "How's everyone doing tonight?" she asked, ramping up the crowd again as they answered with resounding applause and zealous hoots and hollering. "Let's get this place rockin'!"

As if on cue, her guitarist started strumming his electric guitar and her drummer hit a heavy, driving beat that seemed to shake the floor beneath the soles of Zoe's shoes. Jessica started the set off with "I've Got It Bad," a recent number-one hit that showcased her sultry, husky voice, then followed that up by the more emotional "I'm Good Enough." When she started in on a rousing rendition of "Forget About It," the mob responded by jumping and screaming and pressing closer to the stage.

Zoe had been to a few of Jessica's concerts, but this performance was like none other she'd ever seen. Tonight, Jessica brought on the sex appeal, the heat, the energy that got people up on their feet and moving to the beat of the music. She strutted across the stage in her four-inch heels and sparkly, form-fitting dress and tossed her long hair like a sexy siren as she seduced the crowd with her voice and lyrics.

All for Noah's benefit, no doubt.

Suddenly Zoe wanted to be a part of the crowd's frenzy of excitement, instead of being alone with Sean up on the balcony, too removed from the fun and merriment happening below.

She turned to him. "Let's go downstairs."

After their conversation about how crowded it was on the lower level, her suggestion seemed to take him by surprise. "Are you sure?"

"Absolutely." She tossed Sean's own words back at him. "Could be fun." Especially if it meant dirty dancing with him.

As if he'd read her thoughts, a rakish grin spilled across his lips. "I'm game."

He grabbed her hand tight in his, and within a few minutes he'd managed to wend their way right into the middle of the melee, where they were shoulder to shoulder with the rest of the crowd and had a great view of Jessica up on the stage. With Sean standing behind her, Zoe rolled her hips in time to the pulsing beat of the music, bold and uninhibited, and all too aware of every time she brushed up against Sean.

It wasn't long before she felt his hands drift along her waist, tracing her curves and following the sway of her hips. Then his palm slid around and he splayed his fingers low on her abdomen, pulling her closer, until her bottom was tucked firmly against his groin.

There was no mistaking the erection nestled against her buttocks, made all the more erotic and forbidden because no one could see what was going on below their chests. Through the material of her dress she felt the pressure of his hand on her belly, felt the heat and slow caress of his fingers just a few inches away from that sweet spot between her legs.

She leaned into him and let her head fall back on his shoulder. Lifting her hand, she ran her palm along his jaw and into his soft hair and moaned when his lips touched her neck and skimmed up to the shell of her ear. She continued to dance, to shimmy her hips deliberately against his, and he picked up her seductive rhythm and moved his body in sync with hers.

Breathless and incredibly aroused, she turned in his embrace, and he locked an arm around her, crushing her breasts to his chest. Mixed in with the mass of other people, he pushed a knee between hers, firm and insistent, until she was riding his thigh and so turned on she almost no longer cared that they were in a public place. He could easily slide his hand beneath her dress, touch her, make her come, and no one would ever know.

She shivered at the thought while he stared down at her, his gaze dark and hot, and smoldering with need. No man had ever looked at her with such blatant lust, wanting her with a hunger that matched the one tightening deep inside her.

The next thing she knew Sean was pulling her through the packed nightclub, and she willingly followed, trusting him and whatever he had in mind. They exited Taboo, and with her hand securely in his, he strode purposefully through the casino and adjoining hotel lobby, then out a set of glass doors that led to the Onyx's pool area.

The immediate site was dimly lit, but as they passed the main pool and outdoor bar the pathway darkened, illuminated only by the soft glow of moonlight. The air outside was cool compared to the nightclub, but the evening breeze did nothing to douse the flame of desire still burning through her.

A manicured garden of foliage, flowers, and hedges gave way to another pool with rock formations and waterfalls that fed into various lagoons. "Where are we going?" she asked curiously.

"Somewhere dark and secluded where we can make out and not get caught."

Oh.

They reached the farthest pool, where it was completely unlit and deserted for the night. Private and isolated, just how he wanted it. They passed rows of cabanas, and he finally ducked into one of the tented structures furnished with a table and chairs and a few oversized, cushioned chaise lounges.

He settled onto one of the chaises, sitting upright and stretching out his long legs, then crooked a finger at her. "C'mere, Zoe," he said, his voice a mesmerizing blend of sex and sin.

As if she'd refuse the chance to make out with him again. The chair was wide, enabling her to climb onto his lap and straddle his waist with her knees. The hem of her dress stretched taut across her thighs, making it difficult to get as close to him as she wanted to.

He took care of the problem for her, boldly pushing the material of her dress higher, until the fabric bunched around her hips and he'd exposed her black lace panties. With a slow, wicked grin, he smoothed his hands around to her butt and dragged her forward, until her crotch came into contact with the hard ridge of his erection straining against the fly of his pants.

The wholly sexual contact made her moan. Aching to taste him, she framed his face in her hands and settled her lips against his. Slow, soft kisses gave way to a deeper hunger, a more aggressive need that had her moving restlessly against him. Her breasts swelled, her nipples tightened, and desire twisted and tensed between her legs.

One of his hands tangled in the hair at the nape of her neck, and he gently tugged her head back, his open mouth moving along her jaw before trailing damp, hot kisses down her throat. Her entire body shivered, and she whispered his name, a plea for more.

A lot more.

His lips skimmed back up the side of her neck to her ear, his breathing heavy. "I want to touch you," he said huskily, and she knew he was asking her permission to take things further than just kisses and fleeting caresses. "Let me make you feel good. Let me blow your mind, without sex."

For as much as every molecule in her body shouted *yes* to his generous offer, it didn't seem fair that he'd go without. In her experience, not many men would be so selfless. "That's very one-sided. What do you get out of it?"

"More than you can imagine," he murmured as he skimmed his flattened palm up her arm and slipped his long fingers beneath the thin strap holding up her little black dress.

She bit her bottom lip at the subtle tease of his fingers and the promise of pure, unadulterated satisfaction glittering in his blue eyes.

"Tell me," she said, needing to know why he was so willing to forfeit his own pleasure for hers.

"I get the enjoyment of feeling you respond to my touch," he said as he dragged the pad of one finger over the rise of her breast and watched her nipple peak against the low-cut top of her dress. "And I get the gratification of giving you an orgasm, and knowing that *I* was the one to make you come."

It was all about her, and she couldn't help but shake her head in disbelief. "Are you for real?"

He grinned, giving her a glimpse of the charming dimples creasing his cheeks. "I can show you how real, if you'll let me."

He was asking permission, and he wanted nothing in return. The fact that she was going to let him touch her intimately revealed just how much she trusted him. Because if she wasn't so attracted to Sean, if she didn't feel that there was something more between them, she'd never let things go so far.

Running her hands over his broad shoulders, she leaned in and touched her lips to his. "Show me," she said, and kissed him again.

His mouth opened beneath hers, his lips warm and inviting, his tongue just as persuasive as the fingers pulling down the straps of her dress, along with the flimsy cups of her bra. She gasped as he closed both hands over her breasts and used his thumbs to flick across her sensitive nipples. The tips peaked into hard points, and this time he groaned, broke their kiss, and dipped his head for a taste.

Pressing her breasts together, he licked her cleavage, then laved her nipples, the slow, deliberate stroke of his tongue so erotic she felt it all the way down to her core. She squirmed on his lap, opened her legs wider, and rocked shamelessly against the thick, hard length of him.

In response, he drove his hips against hers, increasing the pressure and friction, but it wasn't enough to give her what she ultimately desired.

She whimpered her frustration, and as if knowing exactly what her body clamored for, he dropped a hand to her thigh. The contact seared her skin and made her sex clench with the need to feel him touching her, stroking her . . . right *there,* she thought, and shuddered when his fingers slid beneath the lace edge of her panties and his thumb found her slick flesh.

Her head fell back, and she shifted just enough to give him the room he needed to slide first one finger, then two, deep inside her and begin a lazy thrusting motion. She tightened around him, and he gave an encouraging groan.

If that weren't enough to unravel her completely, he pulled a nipple into his mouth and sucked hard. From her breast to her belly, and lower, every sensation threatened to collide inside her.

It was too much . . . yet not enough.

Tunneling her fingers into his hair, she forced his mouth back to hers, her damp breasts puckering even more from the cool night air. She kissed him as deeply and greedily as the fingers penetrating her. He stroked her clitoris, mixing ecstasy with madness until she was tense and trembling and rushing headlong into a devastating climax.

When the tremors finally subsided, she collapsed against him, shuddering one last time as he removed his fingers from inside her.

Still trying to catch her breath, she buried her face against his neck, closed her eyes, and inhaled the warm, enticing scent lingering on his skin—a combination of sandalwood and aroused male.

While she recovered, he caressed one hand up and down her back while the other threaded through her hair. The moment was so tender and romantic. So caring, in a way that was dangerous to her heart and emotions.

"That was nice, and incredibly sexy," he whispered against her ear.

"Nice?" She lifted her head and gave him an incredulous look. "More like spectacular."

"Good to know." Smiling, he smoothed her hair from her face, then readjusted her bra and the top portion of her dress, making her presentable again. "Next time, we'll strive for phenomenal."

Next time. Already, he was counting on seeing her again, and while a few days ago she might have made excuses as to all the reasons why she didn't have the time to date anyone seriously, she knew it was futile to try to stonewall what was happening between them. Quicker than she ever could have believed, her feelings for Sean were developing into something more than those of just a business association or a casual relationship.

It had been a long while since she'd trusted a man, but maybe it was time to open herself up to the possibility again. To have a little faith in her feelings and her judgment of Sean as a person. As an honorable, worthwhile man who wouldn't lie to her, or betray her as her ex-fiancé, Ian Croft, had done.

Despite all the reasons for her not to dive headlong into a relationship, she was already falling hard and fast for Sean. To the point that she was too far gone to turn back now. And she honestly didn't want to. So, instead, she decided to embrace the warm glow of infatuation spreading through her and see where it led.

"What are you smiling about?" Sean asked.

She sighed contentedly, though she wasn't quite ready to share her newfound feelings with him just yet. "After what we just did, you have to ask?"

He chuckled. "You have a point."

As much as she hated to end their idyllic time together, she knew they needed to head back to the nightclub before they were missed. "You ready to go?"

"No." He skimmed his thumb along her jaw in a gentle caress. "I'd rather stay right here with you and not share you with anyone."

Feigned or not, the slight possessive note to his voice

made her smile. "You know all the right things to say to make a girl feel special, don't you?"

"Not any girl. Just *you*." In the moonlight, his gaze shone with sincerity.

Oh, wow. Her heart skipped a beat, making her feel like a teenager all over again, experiencing her first crush. Except as a grown woman, she didn't have to deny her attraction or suppress her desires, and she wasn't about to do either with Sean.

"As much as I'd like to grant your wish to stay out here indefinitely, at some point Jessica is going to wonder, and worry, about where I am."

"Fair enough," he said, and nodded.

He helped her off his lap, and she pulled down the hem of her dress as he stood, too. Before she realized what he intended, he kissed her again, soft and sweet—romance and charm in its purest form. His firm, sensual lips molded so perfectly against hers, like he was made just for her enjoyment.

He'd already given her body an incredible orgasm, one that should have kept her satisfied for a good long time, yet with just the touch of his lips, the silky glide of his tongue against hers, and the clench of his fingers around her waist, the sizzle of arousal ignited all over again.

With effort, she pulled back, before she gave in to the urge to push him back onto the chaise and have her way with him. And vice versa.

She stared into his darkened blue eyes and gave him a chastising look. "Stop trying to distract me."

He laughed, the sound low and husky and without a hint of contrition. "It was worth a shot."

Chapter Six

She was magnificent. As a performer, Jessica Morgan captivated and enthralled her audience. As a woman, she was strikingly beautiful, naturally sensual, and literally took his breath away in every sense of the word.

Standing off to the side of the stage and deliberately shrouding himself in the shadows so Jessica couldn't see him, Noah watched in reluctant fascination as she belted out an upbeat tune that had the crowd dancing and singing along. He should have felt a twinge of guilt for calling her out tonight, but he didn't regret issuing her the dare, not when it enabled him to see her so comfortable in her element as a pop star.

Much as it pained him to admit it, he respected her fortitude for calling his bluff and treating the clubgoers to an impromptu concert.

And treating him to a side of her he'd never seen before.

He'd always known she was talented. Back in high school, it had been her angelic vocals and the soulful lyrics she wrote that had initially caught his attention. He could still remember that day in vivid detail, when he'd been walking through the school's empty hallways after basketball practice and heard the strum of a guitar and a soft, female voice singing a poignant melody that had stopped him in his tracks. Curious to put a face to the amazing voice, he'd peeked into the choir room, surprised to find Jessica Morgan, the shy, pretty girl he'd been attracted to from afar.

He'd known her name and spent too much time in the classes they shared together staring at her curly auburn hair, gazing at her graceful features, and every once in a while, when he was really lucky, catching a rare glimpse of her stunning green eyes. While he'd been completely infatuated with her, it hadn't taken him long to realize that she was a loner, and the only times he saw her laugh or smile were with her good friend, Zoe Russo. Jessica never met his gaze, and whenever he saw her in the hallway she walked with her head down, always reserved and guarded.

In the choir room, she was completely alone, lost in her music and unaware of his presence. He stood quietly in the back of the room, his heart beating crazily in his chest as he listened to her sing, waiting patiently for her to finish so he could talk to her without anyone else around. He knew he was risking a rejection, but he also knew he'd always regret not taking advantage of this opportunity if he walked away now.

After the last note of her song drifted away and the room went quiet, he finally spoke.

"You have a beautiful voice," he said, startling her.

She jerked around, and as she realized that she was no longer by herself a mortified look came over her face, followed quickly by a wariness that would have sent most guys scurrying back out the door. Not him. He'd walked toward her, complimenting her on her song, trying to put her at ease while attempting to ask her easy, casual questions that would start a conversation between them.

She'd stonewalled him with one-word answers and

still he wasn't discouraged. He invited her to join him and a group of his friends to a party on Friday night, and she'd politely but flatly refused. Then she stood up, told him that it was late and she had to get home, and he let her go . . . even though he wanted to ask her to stay.

As captain of the basketball team, he could have had any girl in high school, and there were many who made it very clear that they were more than willing to put out for a star athlete like him. He hadn't even been tempted. Unfortunately, the only girl he was interested in didn't want to have anything to do with him.

Undeterred, he set out to change Jessica's mind and spent the next month courting her. He gave her silly, flirtatious notes. He put handpicked flowers into the slats of her locker to surprise her. He walked her to every single one of her classes and carried her books, despite her insistence that she could carry them herself.

He joined her and Zoe at their lunch table and discovered that Jessica loved peanut butter and strawberry jelly sandwiches. He did everything he could think of to make her feel special and valued when it started becoming painfully clear to him that her home life was less than ideal and her time in the choir room after school was a form of escape for her.

In time, his efforts paid off. Slowly, eventually, she started to smile at him. Laughed at his stupid jokes. Glanced at him with pleasure and longing, instead of distrust. Let him listen to her sing without being embarrassed. And, most important, she started sharing things about herself that gave him better insight as to why she was so guarded.

Weeks later, in the choir room, he kissed her, and ridiculous as it sounded, he saw fireworks and his future with her. Their slow, evolving friendship turned into something more intimate, and he discovered that falling in love with Jessica Morgan was the best feeling in the entire world.

He learned that he was the first guy she'd ever kissed.

Her first boyfriend.

Her first lover.

He wanted to be her last.

They remained together, practically inseparable, for a year and a half. She spent most of that time with his family, staying away from her mother, and her emotional abuse, as much as she possibly could. She and Noah talked about getting married someday, after college, and having a big family. They had huge dreams, and he wanted to make every one of them come true for her. For them.

Then came high school graduation, and two months later, in August, he departed for Allegheny College, where he'd been granted a full-ride basketball scholarship. In Pennsylvania, all the way across the country from her, while she remained in Vegas, where she planned to attend The University of Nevada, Las Vegas.

It never happened. Within a few weeks of him being gone, something changed. Jessica changed. During phone calls home she was cool and distant, and whenever he pressed her to tell him what was wrong, they'd argue and fight and she'd shut him out. Then, out of the blue and without a reason why, she broke up with him.

He thought it was a matter of giving her time and space to deal with whatever was bothering her, but a few days after that she just . . . left. Gone, without an explanation. Disappearing on him and everyone else without telling anyone what she was doing, where she was going, or why.

Even after he'd discovered that she'd gone to Los Angeles and was living with Zoe, Jessica had thwarted every attempt he made to contact her. The blow had been devastating, leaving him confused, angry, and unable to make any sense of what had happened between them.

A year later, he was watching her on the hit TV show *Make Me a Star* and wasn't surprised when she made the final three. Throughout the years he'd followed her career, bought every one of her CDs, and watched her enjoy huge success as a pop star, but he was never able to get over the way things ended between them. Unresolved issues. Unanswered questions. And a whole lot of bitterness on his part that had affected every relationship he'd tried to have with a woman since her.

Most of all, Noah never stopped wondering if walking away from what they had together had been worth it to her. He saw this as his opportunity to finally find out. To confront Jessica and finally get the answers that she owed him so he could get on with his life, like he should have years ago.

He glanced from the unruly crowd to the dynamic woman up onstage with the glorious mane of auburn hair. Despite everything, this confident woman—so opposite of the quiet, introverted girl he'd once known—intrigued him. The soft, smooth voice he'd once known was now more refined, definitely sultry, and raspy enough to appeal to the men in the room.

As her head-turning body did.

Full, firm breasts, shapely hips, and long, slender legs made for one helluva bewitching package. When she was a teenager, her figure had been slim and lithe, everywhere. Now, she possessed the kind of *Penthouse* curves that men fantasized about and lusted over, and the way she dressed only accentuated her sex appeal.

They were changes he as a man couldn't help but notice and appreciate.

She finished up her set of songs and thanked the crowd for their enthusiastic response before heading backstage, where Noah had instructed security to escort her to the luxurious green room reserved for celebrities. It was a fully stocked private lounge, a place for entertainers to cool down and relax after a performance.

All he wanted was a few minutes alone with her before she returned to the upper level with her band members and friends. Heading to the green room, he gave a nod to the security guy guarding the door, then stepped inside the lounge.

Jessica was standing across the room, tipping her head back as she dabbed the perspiration from her face and throat with a plush hand towel, giving him a handful of seconds to admire the wild tumble of her hair and the sensual arch of her neck before she turned to look at him.

Her complexion was flushed from the show, her green eyes bright with the exhilaration of performing, which quickly dimmed with caution as she met his gaze. Not that he could blame her for being leery, considering how their first encounter earlier that afternoon had ended.

She set the towel on a nearby table, then ran her fingers through her hair, pushing the damp strands away from her face before crossing her arms over her chest. "You sure know how to put a girl on the spot."

"You do this for a living," he said with a casual shrug, refusing to feel bad or apologize for provoking her. "I didn't think it was a big deal."

The corner of her lush mouth twitched with what he swore was a hint of humor. "Then you won't mind when you receive the bill for my private concert here at Taboo."

He didn't know whether she was joking or not, but he was willing to pay the price for her up close and personal performance. "Whatever the cost, it was worth it."

"So, you enjoyed the show?" She sounded surprised and pleased.

"Very much." Why lie? She had an incredible voice and used it to her advantage. She also had a dozen GRAMMYs and other industry awards to validate her amazing talent.

Not that he'd ever openly admit to following her career so closely.

"Would you like a drink?" He indicated the wet bar behind her.

"Sure," she said with a nod. "Water would be great."

Walking around her, he fetched a chilled bottle of water from the refrigerator, twisted off the cap, and handed the bottle to her. "Here you go."

"Thank you." She took a long drink, then licked the excess moisture off her bottom lip with her tongue.

"Quite a nice career and life you've made for yourself," he said, the first twinge of resentment creeping into his voice. "Was it worth it?"

Obviously hearing the accusation underlying his words, she stiffened, her entire posture shifting into defense mode. "Was it worth what?" she asked tentatively.

"Giving up *us*," he clarified, not bothering to sugarcoat his feelings. "You and me and the future we'd planned on having together."

A hurt look passed across her features, and she took another drink of her water before setting the bottle on a table. "It wasn't like that, Noah," she said softly, her voice sounding raw and pained.

"Could have fooled me," he said, steeling himself against the bit of vulnerability he saw in her gaze. "I leave for college, and a few weeks later you take off for Los Angeles without a word. And when I finally find you, you ignore my letters, my calls, and any attempt I make to contact you . . . all for *this*," he said, waving his hand around the lavish comforts of the green room and all the perks that went with her pop star status. "I can't believe I was so wrong about you."

She flinched at the bitterness seeping into his tone; then her chin lifted obstinately and she glared at him. "Go to hell, Noah."

His jaw clenched tight. "Baby, you already sent me there."

It was the truth. The past nine years had been torturous when it came to memories of her, of them. Nine years spent wondering what the hell had happened between them that made her cut him out of her life so completely.

So many emotions raged through him, and with her standing there looking so proud and defensive and gorgeous he couldn't stop from doing something shocking to shake her calm, too-controlled composure. He advanced determinedly toward her, and her eyes widened as she realized his intent. Automatically, she took a step back as he continued to close the distance between them, again and again, until she came up against a wall and had nowhere left to escape.

Finally reaching her, he shoved his hand into the wild mass of curls falling around her shoulders, then slid his fingers around the nape of her neck so she couldn't turn her head away. Before she could take another breath, before she could utter a word, his mouth was on hers, harsh and hot and unrelenting. She gasped in shock, her lips parting to his demanding tongue, and he took the kiss deeper, delving in with total domination.

She made a sound in the back of her throat and lifted her hands between them, splaying them against his chest. The heels of her palms dug into muscle, initially trying to push him away; then slowly, gradually, her fingers fisted in his shirt and she didn't fight his sensual assault. Instead, she kissed him back, and that's when everything shifted and changed between them.

Softened.

Became more about pleasure than punishment.

Her mouth yielded beneath his, the tension in her stiff body evaporated, and all the anger he'd harbored toward her melted away. Her lips molded perfectly to his, so sweet and achingly familiar. As was her slow, gradual surrender and the surge of desire that settled low in his belly.

This was why he couldn't move on. Why no other woman—and there had been quite a few—had managed to erase Jessica from his memory. The undeniable heat of passion was still there between them, as if they'd never spent a day apart. As if she were still his and had never stopped loving him.

Which she didn't.

Too soon for his liking, she shook her head, dislodging his lips from hers and ending their kiss. They were both breathing hard, and he pressed his cheek against hers, unwilling to let her go just yet.

"Noah, don't," she rasped, her voice thick with regrets. "Please, *don't*."

Her words, her demand, snapped him out of his fantasy world and brought him right back to the present with a jolt. Disgusted with himself, he pushed away from her and jammed his hands on his hips. "Don't what, Jess? Don't want you? Seems like that's out of my control, despite every reason I have to hate you."

She visibly recoiled from the sting of his words, and all those emotional walls he'd just torn down with a kiss, she shored right back up again.

Which pissed him off even more. "I'm not like you. I can't just shut off my feelings and forget everything we shared like it never happened."

"Dammit," she said, her voice rough with frustration and her eyes suddenly shimmering with moisture. "You have no right to do this to me."

"Don't I?" he countered, shoving his hands deep into his pants pockets when a part of him wanted to kiss her again. "You're the one who walked away without so much as a good-bye. The least you can do is tell me why you left. Give me at least that much respect." He wanted, *needed,* that closure to a past he couldn't forget.

She swallowed hard and her hand flitted to her stomach, pressing against her sparkly dress. "I left because I had to. I left because I had no choice."

"There's always a choice," he refuted, "and the one you made, for whatever reason you made it, was damn selfish."

"I know," she whispered, and glanced away while brushing a tear from her cheek with her fingers. "And I'm more sorry than you'll ever know."

It wasn't the cavalier, uncaring answer he'd been expecting and the animosity inside of him slowly ebbed away. "Dammit, Jess, what happened?"

She shook her head, her remorse nearly palpable. As was the sadness in her gaze. "It's been nine years, Noah. Just let it go. *Please*."

He wished that were possible, but he just couldn't do as she asked. "I've tried to let it go, let *you* go, but I can't," he said, revealing much more than he'd intended. "I spent the past nine years wondering what I did wrong. What I might have said to make you end things so abruptly. And I just can't figure it out."

She stepped away from him, back into the middle of the room where it was open and safe and there was no chance of him touching her again. "It wasn't you, Noah."

He followed her with his gaze but let her have the space she seemed to need. "Was it someone else?" he asked, his gut clenching as it always did when he considered that scenario.

"No, there's no one else," she said with a shake of her head.

Whether intentional or not, her reply encompassed past and present tense, letting him know that it hadn't been a guy to break them up and currently there was no man in her life, either. Why that relieved Noah he wasn't about to analyze.

Right now, at this moment, Noah knew that she wasn't going to open up and give him the answers he needed. She was back to being guarded, and pushing her any more tonight would do no good. But that didn't mean he was willing to let her walk right back out of his life a second time, without giving him the closure he deserved.

"Can I see you again?" he asked, knowing it was a long shot that she'd agree. Especially after everything that had just transpired in this room with her tonight.

She gave him a small smile. "I really don't think that would be a good idea."

Her reply didn't surprise him. Instead of pushing her and risking her completely shutting him out, he decided to give her the space she seemed to need before he contacted her again.

And the next time he did, he'd do so in a way that she wouldn't be able to refuse him.

Chapter Seven

Sean couldn't do it anymore. He was in way over his head with Zoe, beyond anything he'd ever thought possible. After Wednesday evening at her place and again tonight out in the cabana, he'd crossed professional lines—and, he feared, emotional ones, too.

Getting close to Zoe should have been about nothing more than doing a job for The Reliance Group, but the guilt of deceiving her was starting to weigh heavily on his mind, and that was something that had *never* been an issue for him in his prior life.

He'd never allowed his conscience to get the best of him. He'd always managed to keep his eye on the prize and his feelings out of the equation. Outwardly he might have been charming, amicable, and everyone's best friend, but deep inside he'd been cool, indifferent, and focused, just as his father had taught him.

Nothing had ever interfered with that drive and determination that pushed him toward getting what he ultimately wanted. Even if it meant lying, cheating, and deceiving his target to achieve his goal. It was all a part of how the game was played. And with each con, remaining emotionally detached had become easier to do . . . until the day he'd seen physical proof of what one of the hoaxes he'd been a part of had cost another person.

Sean had only been the "seal-the-deal" guy on the con, the middleman to an old friend who'd set up a wealthy and bored housewife as their mark. The other guy had romanced the woman to gain her interest in making a quick turnaround profit on a bogus investment, and Sean had only stepped in to back up his friend on the deal and collect the cash.

It was only after Sean and his friend had been arrested for fraud in connection with that last scam that Sean had discovered the extent of the damage he'd caused. When he was on trial, he and the jury had been presented with a photograph of the woman he'd exploited. In the picture, her face was swollen and bruised, courtesy of a massive beating by her prick of a husband when he'd discovered she'd lost their savings after being stupid enough to fall for Sean's scheme.

Sean hadn't been the one to physically hurt the woman, but he felt just as responsible. He'd been overwhelmed with shame, and he'd known then that something had to change.

That *he* had to change.

When he'd been sentenced for his part in the con, he'd taken the punishment as his due, though the time he served in prison had probably been more lenient than he'd deserved considering all the past scams he'd gotten away with.

When Caleb had hired him as a bartender for the Onyx, even knowing his history, Sean accepted the chance to start fresh, to put the past behind him and create a new, respectable life for himself—even though he still harbored a ton of guilt for what he'd done.

And now he didn't want to add Zoe to his long list of regrets.

Working for Caleb, Sean had never found himself in a quandary quite like this, where his relationship with a mark started presenting a direct conflict of interest with the job he was hired to do.

As he walked back into the hotel lobby from the pool area with Zoe on his arm, the turmoil inside of him burned like acid in his stomach. He needed to talk to Caleb and be up-front and honest with the man about what was happening between him and Zoe. Despite still needing to find her father, Sean refused to continue to lead her on emotionally while keeping her in the dark about his true intentions.

"You know what?" Zoe asked, the excitement in her voice pulling him from his troubled thoughts. "I'm feeling lucky tonight. How about you?"

He managed to chuckle as they strolled through the casino area, which was packed with Friday night gamblers. "I'm with you, aren't I? A guy doesn't get any luckier than that."

"You're such a sweet talker," she said, smiling up at him, her complexion still glowing from their outdoor tryst and the orgasm he'd given her. "I haven't played roulette in forever, and it's calling to me. Can you spot me a twenty?"

"Sure." He followed her to the game, pulled a twenty-dollar bill from his wallet, and gave it to her, welcoming the new distraction.

She found an open spot at the crowded table and without hesitation placed her entire bet on black. The dealer turned the roulette wheel, then spun the small white ball in the opposite direction. The ball eventually dropped into the pocket for black twenty-four. When the dealer paid out Zoe's winnings, she gave Sean his twenty back, then let the one still on the table ride for another spin.

She won again, and again, and kept letting the money go another round. For the next half hour Sean watched in fascination as she switched her bet from red to black depending on whichever urge struck her, doubling her bet each time, and the ball seemed to play to her whims.

She kept her attention on the numbers that hit, calculated the odds to the best of her ability, and went with her gut instinct. It served her well, and before long she drew a crowd of spectators around the table to cheer on her success. Some people even placed their bets in accordance to hers and reaped a few wins of their own.

Eventually, she rolled the initial $20 into $320. Instead of taking the money and walking away, in true gambling spirit she took a deep breath and pushed all her chips onto the number black seventeen. Everyone else at the table followed her lead, stacking their bets around hers.

"Are you sure you want to do that?" Sean asked from where he stood beside her.

"Yes, I'm sure." She met his gaze, her expression bright and exuberant from her recent wins. She grabbed his hand, threading their fingers together. "I have a strong feeling about this one. But win or lose, this is my last bet. I promise."

The dealer spun the wheel, added the white ball, and Sean found himself holding his breath as the ball bounced from number to number . . . and finally stopped on black seventeen. Zoe gasped in shock, and the crowd around the table let out whoops and cheers that had everyone in the gaming area looking their way to see what all the commotion was about.

"You won!" Sean said, laughing in disbelief. His mental calculations came up with a payout of over eleven thousand dollars.

"Oh, my God!" She launched herself into his arms and hugged him tight. Caught up in the excitement of the moment, she kissed him in front of everyone, a quick but passionate kiss that openly displayed her feelings for him and garnered cheers from the small crowd around them.

She finally pulled back and beamed up at him. "You must be my good-luck charm!"

He chuckled, still amazed at the amount she'd managed to win . . . until he caught sight of a very angry-looking man standing just off to the side watching Sean interact with Zoe. Instantly recognizing the guy as Conrad Davenport, Sean realized just how bad this too-intimate situation might look to the other man who'd paid The Reliance Group to track and find Zoe's father. Conrad looked pissed, and Sean's main concern was that the other man might say or do something to unwittingly compromise Sean's investigation.

Sean transferred his gaze back to Zoe and produced one of his charming, easygoing smiles that belied the sudden apprehension swirling in his stomach.

"I see a business associate of mine I'd like to say hello to," he said, keeping his tone casual. "Why don't you collect your winnings and cash out your chips and I'll meet up with you in a few minutes?"

"Sure." Still basking in the high of her recent win, and oblivious to Sean's inner unease, she turned back to the roulette table and gathered up her impressive payout.

With Zoe otherwise preoccupied, Sean headed toward Conrad, who wore a dark, furious scowl and was holding a highball glass of amber liquid. As Sean neared, he immediately recognized the signs that indicated the other man was intoxicated. Between the bloodshot, bleary eyes and his being unsteady on his feet, it was apparent that the drink in Conrad's hand wasn't his first. Not a good sign.

"Davenport," Sean said, acknowledging the other man, whom he'd met the day Caleb had briefed him on the Russo case. At that meeting, Conrad had been provided with the initial investigative reports on Russo, which included a picture of his daughter, Zoe, so witnessing the cozy, more-than-friends kiss between Sean and Zoe had no doubt enraged Davenport.

"You being here right now isn't a good idea," Sean said calmly, and patted the other man on the back. "Maybe you should go and relax with a good cigar in the players' lounge."

Conrad ignored Sean's suggestion, contempt blazing in his eyes. "What the hell are you doing with that *woman*?" he demanded, his voice too loud and belligerent.

Obviously, what Sean was *doing* with Zoe was complicated on many levels, and it didn't help that Conrad thought the worst as well. "Now isn't the time or place to have this discussion."

"Bullshit," Conrad replied, his words a bit slurred as he waved his glass of liquor in the air, sloshing the liquid over the rim. "It's been nearly a week since you started on this case. Where the hell is that son of a bitch and the money he owes me?" the other man roared in frustration.

Sean inwardly winced—at the man's harsh words and the strong fumes of alcohol on his breath. Davenport might be a smart businessman when sober, but he was incredibly stupid and obnoxious when drunk.

"Look, why don't I get ahold of Caleb, and he'll explain things to you?" Sean took hold of Davenport's arm and attempted to guide him toward the security offices before he started attracting too much attention in the casino. People were already looking their way.

Conrad shook Sean off and glared, clearly not done with his drunken tirade. "Grant Russo is off somewhere spending the millions of dollars I invested in his fucking project, and I paid The Reliance Group to find the lying, cheating bastard. Why aren't you working on *that*, instead of fooling around with his daughter?"

"Sean, what is he talking about?"

Both Sean's and Conrad's heads swiveled to the left to

find Zoe standing there, her expression confused and wary.

Oh, shit. Sean's entire body flashed hot, then cold, as a sinking sensation settled in his chest. *How much had she overheard?* Sean wondered. Too much, he was certain.

Sean thought fast on his feet and shook his head. "The man's had a bit too much to drink," he said, but knew that didn't explain what Davenport had said or his accusations.

Before Zoe could say anything else, Sean caught sight of Kane Briggs, another TRG member who also worked undercover security in the casino, followed by Valerie, making their way toward them. Relief poured through Sean. Upstairs surveillance must have witnessed the confrontation and contacted Valerie and Kane to diffuse the situation.

As soon as they arrived on the scene they pulled Davenport away from the gaming area, leaving Sean alone with Zoe. Undoubtedly, he needed to talk to her, but first he needed a few minutes with Valerie without Zoe listening in on the conversation.

He grabbed her hand and gave it a light squeeze that did nothing to dispel the skeptical look in her eyes. "Give me a sec to talk to the casino host and I'll be right back."

Zoe was the one who pulled her hand from his and crossed her arms over her chest, physically withdrawing from him. "I'll be here. I think you and I have a few things to discuss."

Yes, they did. Sean nodded, then strode over to where Kane stood guard beside an irate Davenport while Valerie tried to placate the man and soothe his temper.

As soon as Valerie saw Sean coming, she said something to Kane, who led Davenport away. Before Sean could say a word or blow the fuse that was simmering below the surface, she held up a hand so she could speak first.

"I'm so sorry. I can't believe he did that," Valerie said with a shake of her head. As he was one of the casino's wealthiest Whales, Valerie had known Davenport for a few years and had established a strong business relationship with the man, as was her job as a casino host. She knew him better than anyone else in the casino did.

"Earlier this evening he lost over three hundred thousand dollars at the craps table," she went on to explain. "He's been in a bad mood all day, and losing all that money pretty much topped him off. He's also been on edge with this whole Grant Russo case. Add to that a half-dozen shots of straight-up whiskey, then seeing you kiss Zoe, and he just lost it."

"Getting shit-faced does not justify what he just did," Sean said, trying to keep his own temper in check. "He blew my cover, Val, and outed me right in front of Zoe. There is absolutely no question in my mind that she's thinking about every single fucking word he said and putting two and two together." It was only a matter of time before the jig was up—and much sooner than Sean had anticipated.

"Are you going to take her up to Caleb's?" Valerie asked.

"No. Not yet." Sean knew he was breaking protocol by not immediately involving Caleb in this situation, but Sean had already breached a few of TRG's rules by getting personally involved with Zoe, so what did it matter now? "Telling her the truth is something I need to do myself." He owed Zoe that much, even though he knew she'd most likely hate his guts before this night was over.

The thought caused a huge lump of dread to settle in his stomach.

"I'm really sorry this happened," Valerie said softly, her gaze searching his in a way that made him uneasy because it felt like she was looking right into his soul. "You like her, don't you?"

Despite Valerie's perceptive comment, Sean wasn't about to admit anything to his co-worker. "She's a nice girl and doesn't deserve to be hurt by her father's bullshit."

Valerie paused for a moment, then asked, "Are you absolutely certain that she's not involved in, or aware of, her father's business dealings?"

"I'd bet my life on it," Sean stated without a shred of doubt. "How about you?"

She crossed her arms over her chest and shrugged. "I don't know her like you do."

He almost smiled at Valerie's nonchalant attitude. "Don't try to con a con man, Val. What does your women's *intuition* tell you about Zoe?" he asked, knowing that Valerie's insightful observations about people went much deeper than just female insight.

"Honestly, my *intuition* tells me that if you gambled your life on her being uninvolved, it would be a safe bet," Valerie said, confirming what Sean already knew in his gut. "You go and do what you have to do with Zoe, and I'll take care of Davenport."

They went their separate ways, and Sean met up with Zoe right where he'd left her.

"Care to explain what all that was about?" she asked without preamble. While her voice was calm, her question was direct and to the point. "And *please*, do not lie to me."

That last plea felt like a kick to Sean's midsection. In any other circumstance, he might have done what he did best and smooth-talked his way out of this mess, but he knew it was time to come clean and put the truth out on the table. No more lies or deceiving her, even if it meant shattering the trust he'd worked so hard to build between them.

"We need to talk," he said, an understatement if there ever was one. "And I'd rather not have the conversation out here in the open. There's a private room close by. Will you come with me?" After what she'd just witnessed, he wasn't about to assume she'd go anywhere with him.

She considered his request for a few seconds before replying. "Okay," she finally said, leading him to believe that her desire for answers must have outweighed any reservation she had about being alone with him.

He started toward the far end of the casino, and she fell into step beside him. Her stiff and guarded body language screamed, *Don't touch me!,* and as much as he wanted to slip his hand into hers, or even rest his palm at the base of her spine as they walked side by side, he didn't dare.

Reaching the bank of elevators, he escorted her into the next empty lift, then withdrew his employee key card from his wallet and swiped it through a reader. He punched the button labeled G1, which took them down to a restricted floor for casino employees. Without a word, she followed him down another short hallway and into the first empty conference room he came to. He turned on the lights and shut the door behind them.

She immediately put distance between them, crossing the room to the other side of the large conference table dominating the area. She might have been quiet this entire time, but her actions now spoke volumes. Outwardly she appeared cool and reserved, and instead of jumping to conclusions and venting her outrage over what she might have overhead between him and Davenport, she was obviously going to try to give Sean the benefit of the doubt in hopes that there was a logical explanation for the other man's tirade.

God, Sean absolutely *hated* that he was going to disappoint her and crush any hope she harbored that Davenport's accusations had all been a huge misunderstanding.

She lifted her chin, seemingly shoring up her strength

for what was about to come. "What did that man mean when he said he'd paid some group that you're obviously a part of to find my father?"

It didn't escape Sean's notice that she'd avoided Davenport's other claim, the one where he'd accused Sean of fooling around with Grant Russo's daughter while on the job. Which was fine with Sean, since what had transpired between himself and Zoe had nothing to do with the case and everything to do with him falling for the sweet, open, sensual woman she was. And allowing himself to cross those lines between business and pleasure had been a *huge* mistake on his part.

He exhaled a deep breath, unsure where to start. He decided to open the discussion with Davenport and go from there.

"Conrad Davenport, the man who caused the scene in the casino, is a highly respected businessman from Texas who invested millions of dollars into the development of The Meridian Resort here in Las Vegas."

A small frown creased her brows as she made the connection. "That's my father's current project."

"Yes, it is." Sean slowly strolled closer to her and was gratified when she didn't step away, even though her emotional barriers remained firmly in place. "Did you know that construction on the Meridian project has been at a standstill for almost a month now?"

A casual shrug lifted her shoulders, as if that bit of information wasn't anything new. "My father mentioned he was having some permit problems with the building and safety departments, and that could easily hold up construction until whatever issues exist are resolved."

It was a plausible explanation, but Sean knew better. "That's obviously what your father wants everyone, especially his investors and the press, to believe."

"Are you saying it's a lie?" Her voice rose incredulously, and her eyes flashed with anger. "That's ridiculous! Why else would construction be halted on such a major project?"

He loathed being the one to shatter her illusions, but he had no choice. "Because there isn't enough money to pay contractors and complete the job because your father has been skimming the coffers for his own personal gain."

She jerked back as if Sean had slapped her. "You're *wrong*! My father would *never* do such a thing."

"Zoe," he asked gently, "do you know where your father is right now?"

She crossed her arms over her chest. "He's on a business trip. He takes them all the time," she added defensively, trying to justify his reasons for being gone.

"A business trip to where?" Sean persisted.

"Chicago, as far as I know." Agitated with his line of questioning, she threw her hands up in the air. "Why does it matter where he is, anyway?"

"Because we've attempted to track him to Chicago, without any luck at all, and there are a lot of unhappy people who have big money involved in the Meridian project who are trying to locate him."

Her eyes widened ever so slightly as a flash of realization passed across her features, an *oh my God* moment that Sean instantly latched onto.

"Do you know something, Zoe?" he asked, keeping his tone even and calm, in the hope that she'd open up and tell him what was going on in that mind of hers.

She shook her head and wouldn't look him in the eye. "No. Just what I've told you."

Which wasn't much. Watching her reaction, he'd wager a guess she was hiding something from him. Something important she didn't want him to know. And now that she no longer had any reason to trust him, she wasn't about to share anything that would incriminate her father.

"So, tell me something, Sean," she said, her composure back in place as she finally lifted her gaze to his. "What is your part in all this?"

He scrubbed a hand along his jaw, taking a few moments to choose his words carefully before replying. This was the part of their conversation he wished they could skip altogether, because he knew his answers were going to hurt Zoe. Badly.

But lying wasn't an option. Not with her.

"Conrad Davenport hired The Reliance Group, the company I work for, to find your father," Sean said, keeping his explanation as straightforward as possible. "After trying to track Russo and having every lead come to a dead end, I was put on the case to help find your father in a more direct way."

"Through *me*," she said, her voice flat and emotionless.

Her tone might have been apathetic, but her gaze was filled with the pain of complete and utter betrayal. Sean's stomach cramped at the thought that he was the cause of her misery. "Yes, through you."

A bitter laugh escaped her and she swept him with a look of contempt. "Are you even who you say you are?"

He buried his fists into the front pockets of his pants. "My name *is* Sean O'Brien, and I work for the Onyx and The Reliance Group."

She stared at him in disbelief. "You're not even a leasing agent, are you?"

"No, it was a cover, but the leasing agreement you signed for the boutique is legal and binding. The store is yours." He wanted to make sure she knew the contract was the real deal.

"Under false pretenses," she said heatedly.

He couldn't argue her point, and if she decided to break the lease under that claim no one would be able to refute her allegation. Sean hoped it wouldn't become an issue.

"So you lied," she said, the words more a statement of fact than any kind of question he needed to answer or confirm. "About *everything*."

God, the disdainful way she looked at him was killing Sean and made him feel lower than a snake—which was nothing less than he deserved. She believed he'd used her, and he had as a source to find her father, but in no way had Sean faked his attraction to her, as she seemingly thought.

"Not everything was a lie, Zoe." And he was tempted to prove it with a hot, deep kiss that would leave no hesitation in her mind as to how much he wanted her. Not as a lead to her father but as a woman Sean strongly desired.

"Everything that mattered *was* a lie, and I was nothing more than a means to an end for you." She shook her head in disgust and turned away from him. "God, when will I ever learn?" she muttered beneath her breath.

He had no idea what she was talking about. Sean only knew that right now, with her emotions at an all-time high and the sting of deception fresh in her mind, there was no convincing her of his sincerity—that while the parameters of the case dictated he get close to her to find out what she knew about her father's disappearance, what transpired between her and Sean had been, and was, very real.

She glanced back at him again and dragged her fingers through her hair, pulling the strands away from her now-pale face. "How long were you going to string me along before you told me any of this?"

There was no sugarcoating his answer. "Long enough to find your father."

She cut him with a look, and more of that scorn flashed in her eyes. "Well, I have to give you credit. You're good at what you do, Sean. Very convincing, too."

God, could he feel any more like shit than he already did? Apparently so.

"I just have one last thing to say to you," she said, her

voice strong and unwavering. "I know my father a helluva lot better than you or anyone else does, and whatever is going on, I know there's a reasonable explanation. He's a good man, and not the criminal you're making him out to be."

Of course Zoe would defend her father. What daughter wanted to believe her parent was corrupt? Sean could have easily marched her up to Caleb's office and let her read the case file they had on Grant Russo, along with her father's shady past as a con man. What she discovered would indisputably shake the very foundation of who she believed her father was and leave her devastated.

And that was ultimately the reason why Sean didn't force the issue. He'd already given her so much to think about and process, and he couldn't bring himself to compound her anguish with the unvarnished truth of her father's fraudulent past—which tied to all the evidence pointing to Russo's current scam.

"Let me take you home," Sean said, knowing there was nothing left to say.

"No, I think you've done enough," she said, the double meaning in her words slicing him to the core. "I'll find my own way home."

Clearly, she wasn't going anywhere alone with him, so he escorted her back up to the casino, where she insisted on heading back to the nightclub on her own. He watched her go, and as soon as she walked into Taboo, Sean reluctantly headed up to Caleb's office, where he was no doubt waiting to talk to his employee after what had happened with Davenport.

Chapter Eight

"Men are dogs."

Zoe gave a weary laugh as she sat down next to Jessica on her living room couch. Lifting her cup of steaming coffee, she clicked it to her friend's mug, wholeheartedly agreeing with her sentiment. "I'll drink to that, girlfriend."

They each took a sip of their morning cup of coffee, both of them needing the jolt of caffeine after a night spent tossing and turning more than sleeping—all because of *men*.

"Life is so much simpler without them," Jessica grumbled.

"Isn't that the truth," Zoe concurred, and sighed.

Last night, after Zoe and Sean had parted ways, she'd found Jessica back in the private skybox at Taboo, looking just as upset as Zoe felt after her troubling conversation with Sean. Neither one of the women had been in the mood to stay at the nightclub any longer, and instead of waiting for a private car to arrive to pick them up, they'd taken a cab back to their apartment building.

With each of them needing an understanding friend to vent her evening's frustrations to, Zoe suggested that Jessica hang at her place for the night, which she had. After changing into pajamas and scrubbing the makeup from their faces, they'd gorged on Ben & Jerry's Chocolate Fudge Brownie ice cream while ranting about the men who'd done them wrong.

Zoe curled her legs beneath her and made herself more comfortable at the opposite end of the sofa. "I swear, my luck with men sucks," she said, and took another long drink of her coffee. "I really thought I had a good feel for Sean, that he was sincere and genuine in his interest in *me*." Her stomach swirled with self-disgust at just how mistaken she'd been. "God, I feel like such a fool for falling for him and for believing everything he said to me."

"You couldn't have known he was playing you," Jessica offered softly.

"I *should have* known," Zoe argued. "Did I learn nothing with Ian and his charming ways and all the excuses and explanations he had for everything? I must have the word *gullible* stamped on my forehead."

"No, you don't. I promise," Jessica assured her with a smile. "You just have a big heart and you like to see the best in people."

With a groan, Zoe dropped her head back against the couch and thought about the *other* man she'd trusted who'd ended up completely shattering her romantic illusions.

Zoe had met Ian Croft at a cocktail party when she'd been living in Los Angeles and had been instantly attracted to him and his charismatic personality. Gossip had it that he was a player, but he'd swept her off her feet, romanced her, and single-mindedly pursued her until she couldn't resist him any longer. For two years they'd dated, and she'd honestly believed that he was *the one* when he'd asked her to marry him and put an engagement ring on her finger.

Stupid her.

As a hotshot corporate attorney he'd traveled often to New York, and she'd never questioned his trips, believing they were all business-related . . . until one day she'd come across a very intimate text on his cell phone from another woman. A woman, Zoe later learned, he'd been seeing on a regular basis during his trips to Manhattan. The only consolation to that discovery, if any, was learning that his New York mistress had no clue about Zoe, either.

Looking back, Zoe knew there had been other signs of his infidelity—some she'd overlooked or passed off as inconsequential, and others she'd questioned. But Ian had been a master at manipulating the truth and giving her answers that were believable and made sense . . . and also made her feel bad for thinking he would ever have an affair behind her back.

Sean might not have cheated on her with another woman, but he'd deceived her about his intentions and used her for his own purpose. And for her, the betrayal was just as painful.

As was the fact that she'd let him kiss her, touch her, and do intimate things she never would have allowed if she'd known.

Stupid, stupid her.

"What are you going to do about the boutique?" Jessica asked.

Zoe turned her head so she was looking back at her friend. It was a good question, and one Zoe had thought about while staring at the ceiling in the middle of the night, unable to sleep. "I'm keeping it. I'll need to check with my lawyer to make sure everything is still legitimate, but I want the store." She already had a conference call set up with her merchandiser on Monday, displays were on order, and everything was falling into place for her to open the boutique within the next month.

Jessica finished her coffee and stood with a sigh. "As

fun as man-bashing has been, I need to get back to my place. I'm supposed to have lunch with my manager today to discuss the radio interview I have scheduled for Monday at K-one-oh-three."

Joining Jessica in the kitchen, Zoe rinsed out their coffee cups and put them into the dishwasher. "What are you going to do about Noah?" she asked as she dried her hands on a terry towel.

Jessica shrugged. "Absolutely nothing. By this time next month I'll be back on tour and he'll forget all about me."

Zoe didn't believe that for a second, but instead of disagreeing, she merely nodded and walked Jessica to the door, where they gave each other a big, warm hug that encompassed friendship and deep affection. Once Jessica was gone, Zoe headed into her bedroom, stripped off her pajamas, piled her hair on top of her head, and stepped under the spray of a steamy, hot shower.

Between hearing about Jessica's crazy confrontation with Noah and thinking her own upsetting thoughts over Sean and the accusations that had been made toward her father, Zoe was wiped out and exhausted. Mentally and physically drained. Closing her eyes, she dropped her head forward and let the water massage her tense shoulders and the steam gathering in the shower clear her head so she could sort out what to do next.

She needed to try to call her father again, and if she got his voice mail this time she had to stress to him that it was an emergency and he needed to call her back immediately. Her father had never not returned her calls, even while he was away on a business trip, and not being able to get in touch with him concerned her more with each day that passed without talking to him. She needed to hear his voice. Needed to be reassured that whatever was going on with the man who'd confronted Sean about her in the casino last night was a huge misunderstanding.

She lathered up with her peaches-and-cream body wash, rinsed off, and got out of the shower praying that this call to her father would yield some kind of answer and prove Sean wrong. It was a Saturday; therefore her father wouldn't be stuck in a meeting and, she hoped, would take her call.

With a fresh application of makeup on and her hair pulled back into a chic ponytail, Zoe dressed for the day in jeans, a tangerine-colored blouse, and white strappy sandals, then headed into the living room to retrieve her BlackBerry. With a deep breath, she hit her father's number and pressed the phone to her ear. The call connected once again to voice mail, but instead of Grant Russo's deep tone instructing her to leave a message, an automated voice informed Zoe that her father's voice-mail box was full—which put a whole different, and worrisome, spin on the situation.

Biting her lower lip, she severed the call, her mind whirling with doubts and a wealth of concern. It was one thing for her father not to return her calls because he was busy with work and another for him not to pick up his voice-mail messages at all.

And that meant one of three things. Either he'd accidentally left his cell phone behind and the voice-mail messages had piled up; something bad had happened to him; or he was deliberately avoiding contact with anyone.

Zoe didn't care for the niggling bit of apprehension settling over her. Something wasn't right, and the overwhelming unease she was starting to feel was something she couldn't ignore.

As she paced her living room, she thought about the things that man in the casino had said about her father, and also the insinuations Sean made about her father's business dealings. There were certain things she could no longer completely discount—foremost in her mind was her inability to reach her father and how he'd seemingly cut himself off from everyone. And how could she forget the man who'd accosted her in Michael Kors while she'd been shopping with Jessica and the comment he'd made about him and someone named Bunny having a lot of money wrapped up in the Meridian project and how that money had gone missing, along with her father?

Oh, God. Zoe pressed a hand to her churning stomach. She honestly didn't know what to think anymore. Zoe only knew that she desperately needed answers. And somehow, someway, she had to find her father to get them and, she hoped, prove his innocence.

Obviously, she couldn't do it on her own. Despite the way things had ended between her and Sean, Zoe needed him. Sean and the company he worked for were most likely going to continue their search for her father, and she'd be better off being a part of the case rather than an uninformed bystander.

Besides, Sean had just spent the past week using *her* for information, so she had no qualms about turning the tables and doing the same with him.

Decision made, there was only one thing left for her to do. She lifted her phone and dialed Sean's number.

Sean stood by the large black onyx lion statue that separated the lobby of the Onyx Hotel from the casino, where he'd told Zoe he'd meet her that afternoon.

Her phone call that morning had been an unexpected surprise, as was her request to see him again. And while he'd like to believe she'd forgiven him for his deception, her curt *"we need to talk"* told him this appointment was all about business.

He'd spent all last night telling himself it was for the best that things were over between them—better now than when they were even more emotionally involved. Anything beyond a brief fling wouldn't have worked out, and she didn't do no-strings-attached affairs like he did. Besides those obvious reasons, there was his own past as a con man that would undoubtedly be a deal-breaker for her, not to mention how her father's past was directly linked to Sean's father's stint in prison.

All that ugliness would have eventually been brought to light, and the end result between her and Sean would have been the same. Keeping everything business-related going forward from here would save her a ton of heartache in the future.

The lecture was a solid, logical one—until he saw Zoe walking toward him and his chest tightened with desire and something else no other woman had ever made him feel. Instant awareness, pure pleasure, and a surge of excitement just at the thought of being near her.

He watched her approach him, a proud tilt to her chin and a determined gleam in her eyes. She was dressed casually with her hair in a sleek ponytail and minimal makeup, but there was still an air of sophistication in every step she took.

Despite the lines of fatigue around her eyes—most likely courtesy of a restless, sleepless night spent thinking about everything that had happened with Davenport— she still managed to look so damned beautiful and sexy.

She stopped a few feet away from him. "Thanks for agreeing to meet with me," she said, her tone and demeanor so cool and detached she could have been talking to a stranger.

"No problem," he replied, keeping his own voice neutral as well. "Before we discuss anything, I'd like you to meet my boss, Caleb, since he's directly involved in this case." Along with a few other Reliance Group members who'd been recruited to help track her father.

"Okay," she agreed with a nod.

"Then come with me." Gently Sean grabbed her elbow to lead her away, and was relieved when she allowed him that simple touch and followed without an issue. He guided her through the casino, up to the security offices, and into a conference room where everyone was already seated and waiting for the two of them to arrive.

Upon seeing there were a few extra people in the room, she stiffened and glanced at Sean warily. Not wanting her to feel uncomfortable in any way, he immediately sought to put her at ease and launched into introductions. He started with Caleb, then went on to Valerie, whom Zoe had briefly met last night during the altercation with Davenport.

Then there was Lucas Barnes, The Reliance Group's security analysis technician, which was a fancy name for computer geek. He was TRG's go-to guy for anything involving hacking, file manipulation, and computer fraud—both perpetrating and preventing it, depending on the situation. He was the one responsible for hacking into Zoe's cell phone to trace her calls. Not that any of them were about to share that bit of information with her. For as long as they were searching for her father, the tap on her phone would remain intact.

Zoe sat down across from the trio, who'd all been very warm and polite with their hellos, and Sean took the seat next to hers. She looked them all in the eye, and if she felt intimidated by being outnumbered, she didn't show it.

"I'll get right to the point," she said, and folded her hands together on the table in front of her. "I'm well aware of the unwarranted claims being made against my father, about him being involved in some kind of scam. And now I also know that your company has been hired by some uncouth businessman to find my father because he's being accused of stealing funds that were invested toward developing the Meridian project."

Caleb jotted notes on the pad of paper he'd brought with him to the meeting. "Yes, all that's true," he confirmed with a nod.

She exhaled a deep breath. "I want to help find my father."

Beside Caleb, Valerie looked a bit surprised by Zoe's announcement. "What made you come to that decision?" Val asked the one question the rest of the group was thinking.

"For starters, I know you're going to continue looking for my father with or without my help, and I'd like to be involved as much as possible." She cut a quick glance at Sean before looking back at Caleb. "After all, you did assign Sean to find out what I know about my father's whereabouts, right?"

"Yes," Caleb replied unflinchingly. He wasn't a man who couched the truth, no matter how painful his answer might be.

"Well, now I'm openly offering my services. I'll share whatever I know or find out about my father, as long as you keep me in the loop on your end, as well."

Caleb thought about her proposition for a moment before agreeing. "Okay."

Whether or not Caleb intended to keep his end of the bargain remained to be seen. Sean already knew plenty of things they were still keeping from her.

"Bottom line, I want to find my father to clear his name." She continued laying out her terms, her voice direct and confident. "No matter what he's being accused of doing, he has the right to defend himself. It's as simple as that."

So, she was playing the *my father is innocent until proven guilty* card, which was understandable. It was Zoe's way of protecting her father, even if Grant Russo didn't deserve her blind faith.

It would be so easy to put an end to any hopes she had of her father's innocence by handing over the investigative reports Caleb had on Russo that outlined the man's corrupt past in vivid detail. But those in-depth reports would also reveal Sean's ties to Zoe's father, and both Sean and Caleb had decided beforehand that opening that can of worms would do more harm than good. They'd also determined that doling out information on her father, or the case, would be done on a need-to-know basis.

And right now, they both agreed that Zoe didn't *need to know*.

"I'm also very worried about my father," she said, her tone much softer now.

Caleb stopped writing on his notepad to look back up at Zoe, his interest obviously piqued by her comment. "Why's that?"

For the first time that afternoon, Sean saw a crack in Zoe's tough composure, her professional demeanor giving way to a more vulnerable side.

"For the past week, I've tried getting in touch with my father," she said, sharing her own information with the group, as promised. "According to his secretary, Sheila, he's away on a business trip, which is nothing out of the ordinary. But what isn't normal is that he never returned any of my calls or the messages I left for him. And this morning, when I called his cell phone again, the voice-mail box was full, which tells me he hasn't picked up any of his messages recently."

Caleb absently tapped his pen on the tablet of paper. "And why do you think that is?"

"There's the chance that he forgot his cell phone when he left on his trip, but if that were the case, he would have gotten a new one right away. His cell phone is his lifeline when it comes to his business."

Her explanation was logical and made perfect sense,

yet the frown marring her delicate brows told them just how troubled she was.

"He'd never let his voice-mail messages pile up like that," she went on. "Nor would he ignore my calls for an entire week. Also, last night Sean told me that you were unable to trace my father to Chicago, where he's supposed to be, and that's something else that concerns me. I'm afraid that something *bad* has happened to him."

Sean met Lucas's gaze and knew what the computer guru was thinking. People who were on the lam didn't take traceable electronics and other identifiable items with them. They used disposable cell phones and didn't send e-mails since the originating IP address was easy to locate. They spent cash instead of swiping credit cards and used an alias.

Most likely, Grant Russo was operating under those basic principles, because Caleb's top investigators had tried all those other traditional methods of tracking Russo, only to come up empty-handed.

At this moment, Zoe was in a state of denial about her father's guilt, and they had to do everything possible to ensure her cooperation in this case—and not alienate her, or devastate her, by showing her proof of her father's history as a con man. What she was proposing in terms of forging an alliance with them was something they didn't want to compromise in any way.

"Your father hasn't made it easy for us to find him, so it would be great to have your help," Caleb said diplomatically. "Would you happen to have a key to your father's house or his office?"

A look of confusion passed over her features. "I only have a key to his house. Whatever you might need from his office I can try and get from Sheila on Monday."

"We'll start with your father's house." Caleb made another note on his pad, then met Zoe's gaze again. "I'd like you and Sean to head over there this afternoon if you're free, to see if either of you can find anything that might give us an idea of where he might have gone."

"Sure, we can do that," Zoe said, obviously unnerved by Caleb's directness.

Sitting to the left of Caleb, Lucas spoke up. "While you're there, if you find any kind of computer, I need you to bring me back the hard drive."

"Lucas is a data-recovery specialist," Sean explained for Zoe's benefit. "What's on your father's hard drive could be very helpful in terms of providing us with information on where he might be."

"Okay then, let's go see what we can find." Zoe pushed away from the table and stood, her body language resolute.

Sean stood, too, and nodded at Caleb. "I'll be in touch." He hoped with some kind of information that would accelerate this case and give them a jump on Russo's location.

As Sean followed Zoe out of the conference room, he couldn't help but wonder how she felt about the two of them being paired up again. Obviously, she was still miffed at him and she was trying like hell to be cool and indifferent as far as he was concerned.

Sean was smart enough to realize that if he didn't do something to diffuse the tension between them, they might end up at cross-purposes on this case, and that was the last thing he wanted. But after deceiving her once, he'd be a fool to expect her to immediately trust him again just because he wanted her to. Her respect was something he had to earn from scratch, and he didn't doubt it would not be quick or easy.

That her forgiveness made a difference to him caused his chest to constrict with the knowledge of how much he'd come to care for her—and how much her opinion of him mattered. God, he was in way over his head when it came to her, and there wasn't a damn thing he could do about the emotions she stirred in him that would undoubtedly cause her more pain than anything else.

His own personal feelings aside, there was one thing he could do that might help him earn a place back in her good graces. For once, he didn't want to rely on his boyish charm, a bouquet of flowers accompanied with an endearing smile, or any of those other flirtatious tricks he'd normally use on a woman to soothe her bruised ego.

No, with Zoe, he was going to have to step up to the plate and do something more meaningful.

Chapter Nine

Sitting next to Sean in the close confines of his sporty black Camaro Coupe was agonizing for Zoe. Despite every valid reason she had to remain pissed off at him, her reaction to Sean as a totally hot and sexy man was chipping away at her resolve, bit by bit. Every breath she took was filled with the arousing scent of him, and with his arm resting on the console between them, if she so much as relaxed, her body brushed against his and the sensation and heat within her intensified.

God, even watching him shift gears with those long, strong fingers of his that had touched her so intimately and feeling the growl of the car's engine reverberating through her entire body made her feel antsy.

Squirming restlessly in her seat and annoyed with herself for allowing him to affect her so profoundly, she glanced out the passenger window as they drove past various casinos lining the Las Vegas Strip. In the afternoon sunshine, the hotels lacked the glitz and glamour that they had at night, and during the day the town didn't look quite as dazzling and exciting.

Since she and Sean had left the security offices at the Onyx, the only conversation they had engaged in had been out of necessity. He'd asked for her father's address, and she'd given it to Sean to punch into his GPS system. Other than the mechanical female voice occasionally instructing him where to turn, the inside of the car had been uncomfortably quiet.

Finally, Sean spoke, his deep voice cutting through the silence and adding to the awareness swirling through Zoe.

"Zoe . . . can we talk?"

No. His tone was so gentle and caring that she was certain any kind of interaction with him would be dangerous to the emotions she was desperately trying to keep *out* of this new business relationship of theirs.

Releasing a deep sigh, along with a good amount of tension gathering in her neck and shoulders, she glanced at Sean. He'd stopped at a red light, and he was watching her intently, his eyes a dark, sensual shade of blue that made her pulse kick up a notch.

Steeling herself against his irresistible charisma, she shrugged as if it didn't matter what they did. "Sure. We can talk."

The car started forward again, and he made a left-hand turn onto a street leading to the outskirts of Vegas.

"I owe you an apology."

She closed her eyes and turned her head away. *Damn him.* She didn't want Sean to be a nice guy. Didn't want to soften toward him when he should stay at the very top of her shit list, right where he belonged.

But here he was, *apologizing,* which was something she never expected him to do. She would have thought he'd chalk up the fact that he'd deceived her to just doing his job and had done so without an ounce of regret or remorse. At least, that was *her* experience when it came to men and their egos.

Either that or she really did have *gullible* stamped across her forehead.

"I really am sorry for everything that happened last night, Zoe. And for misleading you."

Her eyes shot back open when she felt his hand on her knee, his touch like a shock of heat to her entire system.

"The last thing I meant to do was hurt you." Sincerity laced his voice, along with hope, too—that she'd accept his peace offering.

She completely melted. Zoe wasn't the kind of person who held grudges, and she knew it was going to be impossible to stay mad at Sean. So, why even try?

Fine—she could forgive him so they could start fresh and work together toward a common goal without issues or animosity standing between them, but she wasn't about to let her guard down with him again. As the saying went, "once burned, twice shy," and this time around Zoe knew what to expect.

"Okay," she said, and very deliberately she removed the heavy weight of his hand from her thigh, letting him know with that single action where things stood between them.

"Okay . . . what?" he asked cautiously, and cast her a quick, sidelong glance.

"Okay, I accept your apology." She folded her hands in her lap, still feeling the burn of where his fingers had been on her thigh. "And thank you."

He frowned in confusion. "For?"

"For being man enough to admit you were wrong."

His brows rose in surprise, and the corner of his mouth twitched with humor. "Is that what I just did?"

She wanted to smile, too, but didn't dare. "You absolutely did."

"Okay, then." Male amusement deepened his voice. "You're very welcome."

With those words, a truce was born. Zoe was relieved, because it was too hard to maintain her anger toward him and she honestly didn't want to. There needed to be as much open communication between them as possible in order for this new alliance to work.

The car stopped at the guard shack in front of the gated community of Siena, where her father lived, and Sean rolled down the driver's side window as a uniformed man approached the vehicle. The older man bent low to look at Sean, then saw her sitting in the passenger seat and grinned.

"Hi, Martin," she said, knowing the guard by name since he'd been working the same day shift since her father moved into the area over six years ago.

"Hey, Zoe," Martin greeted her in that jovial way of his. "Good to see you. Your father must be on a business trip, because I haven't seen him in over a week now."

"He is," she verified. Martin knew everyone who lived in the community, and their extended family, and he took his job as a security guard very seriously. There was no way he would have let Sean past the gates without her with him. "My father asked me to take care of a few things for him at the house while he's gone."

"Sure thing." Martin tipped his hat at them. "You two have a good day."

Sean put the window back up while the big metal gates slid open, allowing them entry into the wealthy neighborhood. Secluded beyond a six-foot-high masonry perimeter was an exclusive community with a health-and-fitness facility and a wellness center, along with a clubhouse and a pristine golf course landscaped with a lake, elegant gardens, and waterfalls.

"It must take a helluva lot of money to live in a place like this," Sean said as he drove into the residential area and followed the GPS to her father's street.

Zoe wasn't sure what kind of point Sean was trying to make with his comment, nor did she understand the slight hint of resentment she detected in his tone. "My father is a developer and he *makes* a lot of money," she pointed out, even though Sean and the organization he worked for had to be well aware of Grant Russo's net worth.

"He knows how to spend it lavishly, too," Sean muttered as he parked the Camaro in her father's driveway, then cut the engine. "Let's do this and get it done."

Sean got out of the car, and she sighed in annoyance. After retrieving the key to her father's house, Zoe tucked her purse beneath the passenger seat so she didn't have to carry it with her, then met up with Sean at the paved walkway leading to the front of the house. Whatever his problem was with her father's wealth, Zoe decided to take the high road and not call Sean on it. Besides, it was his issue to deal with, not hers.

She unlocked the main door, then stepped inside and quickly disengaged the alarm. Sean walked in behind her, his gaze sweeping the area, taking in the open Mediterranean architecture, the imported Italian flooring, and the rich décor embellishing the sprawling one-story house.

His jaw clenched ever so slightly as he glanced back at her. "Let's start in your father's bedroom and go from there," Sean suggested.

She nodded in agreement. "It's this way."

Setting her key ring on a table near the door, she led the way down a wide hallway and into the spacious master bedroom. Everything was neat and tidy, including the comforter on the bed, which was smooth and undisturbed. The adjoining bathroom was also spotless, most likely due to her father's housekeeper, who came by once a week to clean the house.

Sean started with the nightstand drawers and worked his way around the room from there while Zoe glanced through the bathroom drawers and medicine cabinet but couldn't tell what toiletries were missing, if any. The clothes in her father's walk-in closet were hung up in a neat and orderly manner. There was nothing to indicate he'd packed in a rush, nor could she find anything out of the ordinary to give her cause for concern.

Back in the bedroom, she watched as Sean continued searching through her father's dresser drawers, then looked behind all the artwork hanging on the wall, his movements efficient and methodical. It felt wrong and invasive rummaging through her father's personal things, but she knew it was necessary to find him and prove his innocence.

From there, she and Sean moved on, going from room to room and doing a thorough check of each, including the kitchen, and came up empty-handed. Zoe was both relieved that they didn't find anything incriminating against her father yet disappointed there wasn't anything tangible to confirm his business trip to Chicago.

But she and Sean still had one last place to search—her father's spacious home office. If there was any information to be found, that would most likely be the spot where he'd keep his business-related paperwork.

As soon as she and Sean walked into the room the scent of leather, mingled with the rich, woodsy fragrance of her father's cologne, wrapped around her like a warm, familiar embrace. The kind that reminded her of being a little girl and sneaking into her father's office while he was working, and how he'd stop whatever he was doing to give her his attention and a piece of the candy he kept in one of his desk drawers just for her. It was a comforting childhood recollection she didn't want tainted by something unpleasant, like the possibility that her father was capable of the things Sean had accused him of last night.

"Zoe?" Sean asked from beside her. "You okay?"

Realizing she'd gotten lost in her thoughts, she shook her head of the past and met Sean's gaze. "I'm fine," she said evenly, certain he wasn't interested in hearing about those warm, fuzzy memories about her father. Not when Sean believed the worst about Grant Russo.

"Why don't you check the bookshelves and I'll go through the file cabinets and desk?" he suggested, obviously giving her the easier task.

Not that she minded, considering how just stepping into her father's office had triggered her emotions. "Sure."

Sean headed toward the desk and she veered to the right, where a wet bar and built-in bookcase lined the wall. She wasn't sure what, exactly, she was looking for that might be stored in a bookcase, but she went ahead and scanned the hardback novels and expensive-looking trinkets sitting on the shelves. There was also a collection of bronze sculptures that had undoubtedly cost a small fortune, along with the Waterford crystal decanters of alcohol and glasses monogrammed with his initials that were situated above the wet bar.

Her father had always enjoyed the finer things in life—from the artwork he bought to the cars he drove and even the beautiful women he was attracted to, Collette Russo included. Zoe's mother might not have come from money, but she sure knew how to spend it and even now, after the divorce, *depended* on it.

"Damn it," Sean muttered from behind Zoe.

Curious to know what had set Sean off, Zoe turned around and found him tugging the handle on a drawer, which didn't budge. "What's wrong?"

Frowning, he checked the next drawer down and again met with resistance. "All the filing cabinets are locked."

Zoe wasn't surprised. Most filing cabinets held personal, private, and business-related items, and if her father was out of town for an unspecified amount of time, why wouldn't he secure confidential paperwork until he returned? Still, Sean was clearly annoyed that he didn't have access to the files.

"You mean to tell me you don't know how to pick the lock open?" she asked, the teasing note in her voice overriding what should have been sarcasm.

"Sure I do," he said, flashing her a sexy dimpled grin. "Except I left my lock-picking kit at home."

She didn't know if he was serious or not but was more inclined to believe a man like Sean knew his way around something as simple as a lock. "You could always do like MacGyver and try using a paper clip to toggle it open."

Sean smirked at her attempt at humor. "You're very funny."

"You strike me as an innovative type of guy," she said with a shrug. "Seriously, I think you'll find whatever you need on the computer's hard drive." At least she hoped he did. She didn't relish the thought of Sean, or anyone else for that matter, rifling through her father's personal bills and business transactions, and unless speculation turned into guilt, she was going to do her best to dissuade anyone from that particular invasion of privacy. It was bad enough that they were pillaging information from his computer, but even *she* was hoping Lucas would find *something* that would explain where her father was.

"You're probably right," Sean said as he stepped back to the large desk and set his sights on the computer sitting on the surface. "But it would have been interesting to see if there was anything worthwhile in the filing cabinets."

Worthwhile, meaning evidence of her father cheating people out of millions of dollars. The thought made her stomach churn.

Exhaling a deep breath, she returned her attention back to the bookcase. She glanced at the last section of shelves, and the first thing that caught her attention was the handcrafted humidor she'd given to her father for Christmas a few years ago to store his favorite cigars. Absently she ran her fingers over the smooth lacquer finish and her father's initials, carved into the mahogany wood, ridiculously happy to see that he actually used the box and had it on display.

Below that, on a separate shelf, was a framed picture of her and her father—a photograph she easily recognized as the one Jessica had taken of the two of them the day she'd graduated from the Fashion Institute of Design & Merchandising in Los Angeles, magna cum laude. Her father had driven the four hours from Las Vegas to attend her ceremony and awards reception and to hand her the keys to a brand-new Lexus as a graduation gift.

Smiling, she picked up the snapshot, remembering that exciting day oh so well. Her father had been so proud of her accomplishment, the pride and joy shining in his eyes evidence of just how much he supported her dreams, no matter what they entailed. Unlike her cool, detached mother, who felt her daughter's aspirations were frivolous and unnecessary, her warm, loving father had always believed in her abilities, and she had him to thank for encouraging her and building her confidence from a very early age.

"When was that picture with your father taken?" Sean asked from behind her.

His conversational tone prompted her to answer, "The day I graduated from the Fashion Institute." She set the frame back on the shelf and glanced at Sean as he quickly and easily removed the side panel of her father's desktop computer, as if he'd done the same thing a dozen times before.

He cast her a quick, curious look before reaching inside the open computer and tinkering with something she couldn't see. "How come your mother isn't in the picture?"

Zoe crossed her arms loosely over her chest, content for the moment to watch Sean as he worked. "Because she wasn't there," Zoe said, her tone matter-of-fact.

His hands stilled, and he glanced up at her, his expression incredulous. "She didn't attend your college graduation? Was she sick or something?"

"Or something." At the time, Zoe had been hurt that her mother hadn't made the effort to be there but ultimately not surprised with the reason why she hadn't attended such a monumental event in her only child's life. "She was in Italy with some guy she was dating at the time, and to her, that was far more important."

"Wow."

Sean sounded as stunned as he looked, but Zoe had had years to get used to her mother's selfish choices and skewed expectations. "I wasn't exactly a priority to my mother, unless it was for something that benefited her," Zoe explained as she strolled to the desk and propped her hip on the corner. "Even when I was growing up, she missed a lot of milestones, but my father always tried to be there for me, no matter how busy he was."

"Ah-h, you were a daddy's girl," Sean drawled.

His comment triggered her defenses. Sure, her father had doted on her and lavished her with affection and even bought her nice things, but he'd never spoiled her to the extreme and she'd always been grateful for the nice things she'd had. She knew her father just wanted her to have every advantage to succeed in life, and while she'd appreciated his support throughout the years, she'd been so relieved when he'd understood her need to make it all on her own with ZR Designs and her first boutique.

Most *daddy's girls* would have taken the substantial amount of money he'd offered to fund her business venture, knowing he never expected her to pay the money back, but she'd turned down the cash because she wanted, and needed, to be independent and self-sufficient. For herself and because unlike her mother, Zoe didn't ever want to rely on a man to support her financially.

"He was a good father," Zoe said of her dad. Despite whatever faults he might possess, she wanted Sean to know that Grant Russo had been a decent and caring parent, a father who'd loved her unconditionally.

Sean concentrated on pulling a small, square metal box out of a slot inside the computer and disconnected the attached cables. "I never said he wasn't."

Maybe not directly, but there was no doubt in her mind that Sean questioned her father's integrity. "Considering what you *think* you know about my father based on investigative reports you've read, he was *always* there for me."

Sean lifted his head and met her gaze, the barest hint of emotion flickering in his blue eyes. "Then you were very lucky."

His comment led her to believe that his childhood had been less than ideal and made her curious to know more. "What about your parents? Where do they live? Here in Vegas?"

"My mother died when I was twelve," he said, his tone taking on a curt edge. "And my father has been out of the picture for years."

Sean's answer was cut-and-dried and didn't welcome further prodding about what, exactly, had happened to each of his parents, and Zoe didn't push further to find out. "Any brothers or sisters?"

Shaking his head, he set the hard drive aside and snapped the side panel back in place. "Nope. I'm an only child."

"Well, what do you know," she said, deliberately injecting a light, humorous note into her voice in an attempt to lighten the mood in the office. "We actually have something in common."

The atmosphere between them definitely shifted and changed, and the slow, sensual smile curving the corners of Sean's lips made her heart race just a bit faster. "Sweetheart, we have a whole lot more than that in common, and you know it."

Like their mutual attraction and her sexual awareness of him that she couldn't suppress, no matter how hard she tried. But feeling that hot rush of need for Sean and acting on those desires were two different things, and she was determined not to cross that line with him again.

Sean picked up the slim metal box he'd left on the desk. "I've got the hard drive, so we're ready to go."

Grateful for the change in subject, Zoe nodded and led the way back to the front door. She set the alarm, locked up the house, and followed Sean back to his car. Once she was in the vehicle, she reached beneath her seat for her purse just as a beep chirped from her cell phone, indicating she had a voice-mail message. Praying her father had finally called, she dug her BlackBerry out of her handbag and punched in the code to listen to the message.

Her hopes plummeted the moment she heard her mother's voice. Zoe listened to what Collette had to say, then with a resigned sigh erased the message, since it was nothing she needed to save.

"Was that message anything important?" Sean asked as he pulled onto the main road just outside of her father's gated community.

Obviously, he, too, was hoping that Zoe's father had finally gotten in touch with her. "No," she said, and even though she was certain Sean wouldn't demand to know who'd called, she told him anyway. "It was my mother calling to tell me that she still hasn't received her alimony check from my father, and that she's leaving tonight for a weeklong trip to New York. So, when I *do* hear from my dad, she wants to make sure I tell him that she needs her money." It really was unbelievable just how superficial she was.

"Is he usually late on his payments?"

"No, as far as I know, he's normally very prompt." Zoe dropped her cell phone back into her purse, trying not to think of all the reasons why he'd be late on his alimony payment, which included the possibility that he *was* on the run. "By the way, I'm going to stop by my father's office on Monday afternoon and talk to Sheila face-to-face and see what kind of information I can get out of her about where my father is, like a hotel name or a copy of his itinerary, and find out how she's been contacting him. She takes care of all that stuff, and being his daughter, I have a right to know where my father is."

"Good idea." Sean turned onto Las Vegas Boulevard and headed toward the Oynx. "If your father's secretary doesn't have anything to hide, I'm sure she'll cooperate."

And if Sheila didn't give Zoe what she asked for . . . well, she'd deal with that issue when and if she met with resistance.

A few minutes later she and Sean arrived back at the Onyx Hotel, and he drove Zoe to where she'd parked her car earlier, before her meeting with Caleb and The Reliance Group. Sean came to a stop behind her Lexus and pushed the switch to unlock the passenger door.

"I guess we'll be in touch if either of us has any news?" she asked.

He nodded as he casually draped his wrist over the steering wheel. "It might take Lucas a few days to decode what's on your father's hard drive, but if anything comes up, I'll let you know."

"Okay." With nothing left to say, she slid out of the Camaro and shut the door, feeling Sean's eyes on her backside as she walked to her car. Like a gentleman, he waited until she was securely inside her vehicle before taking off, leaving her wishing they had a legitimate excuse to spend more time together that didn't include investigating her father's whereabouts.

She exhaled a heavy sigh and turned on the car's engine, knowing that going their separate ways was the smartest thing to do. She had a ton of work to get done over the next few days for ZR Designs, including spending all day Sunday reviewing and modifying orders and conducting the half-dozen interviews she'd set up for Monday morning to find a manager for the boutique.

She really didn't have time for anything non–business related, and she most certainly didn't have the extra time to spend with a sexy, charming man who would leave her with nothing more than a broken heart.

Chapter Ten

"This is Benny Davis and you're listening to KJOY, Las Vegas's classic hit radio," the popular DJ sitting across from Jessica announced into the airwaves. "This afternoon we have a special treat for you. The beautiful and talented Jessica Morgan is in the house, and she'll be letting us know what to expect from her in the near future."

Jessica smiled at the friendly DJ—a young, twentysomething male sporting a faux 'hawk, guy-liner, and a collection of colorful tattoos covering the length of both of his arms—and leaned toward her microphone. "Thanks for the welcome, Benny, and for playing my songs on the radio. I really do appreciate it."

Her label expected her, as a recording artist, to do interviews and appearances to promote her albums and upcoming tours, which Jessica didn't mind doing. But today was mostly about raising money, and awareness, for Wishes Are Forever, the foundation she'd established a few years ago. The organization was directly linked to The Children's Hospital of Nevada and granted wishes to the young children who had a long-term stay at the facility. Whenever Jessica was in town, she spent time visiting the sick kids and enjoyed getting personally involved in making their wishes come true.

"We're happy to have you here. After all, you are one of Las Vegas's own who made it big," Benny said, referring to her stint on the hit show *Make Me a Star* and how her career had skyrocketed after her time on the show. "Before we get to the good stuff, we need to go to commercial, so stay tuned to KJOY to find out all the latest on Jessica Morgan, and to hear about how you can win an evening in her company and VIP backstage passes to her concert next month here in Vegas."

Benny pressed a button on the panel in front of him, disconnecting their microphones until the reel of commercials ended. During the quick three-minute intermission, they discussed the details of the auction Jessica had planned and how Benny would handle the calls and bids. Once the interview part of her visit was over, she was putting herself up on the auction block for a date night with one lucky winner, with all of the proceeds benefiting Wishes Are Forever.

"We're back on air with Jessica Morgan," Benny said, once the radio station fulfilled their advertising obligations. "Why don't you tell us about your new album and your upcoming tour?"

Jessica worked the PR angle, telling the radio station's listeners what to expect on her album—more of the soulful lyrics her fans had come to expect from her, along with a bit more edge to some of her songs. Her latest tour, It's All for You, was kicking off at Las Vegas's Mandalay Bay, and that concert was already a sold-out event, which made the VIP backstage passes all the more valuable.

"You sure are one busy woman," Benny commented. "What do you do on your downtime?"

"Downtime? What's that?" She laughed, and so did the

DJ. "Seriously, when I do have free time, I like to hang with my friends, write new songs, read books. You know, normal, everyday things. When I'm not on tour, I'm quite boring."

"I find that hard to believe," Benny said, obviously opting to believe the gossip rags that touted her as a party girl, which was the furthest thing from the truth about her lifestyle.

"It's true," she insisted, hating that one part of being a celebrity—the scrutiny and speculation of everything she said and did and how it was twisted into sensationalized fodder for the masses to believe whatever they wanted, and it was usually the worst. "I'll go out with friends occasionally, but I'm just as happy staying at home for the evening."

A sly grin eased up the corners of the DJ's lips, and she knew exactly what direction this conversation had just veered into, even before he spoke. "I know the male population is dying to know, are you dating anyone right now?"

This was the part of interviews she hated—the focus on her private life. But the personal questions came with the territory and she handled it politely when she really wanted to just tell him it wasn't any of his, or anyone else's, business.

"No, no one seriously," she said lightly. Or even casually, for that matter. Over the years she'd gone out with a few guys, but she hadn't been intimately involved with anyone since Noah in high school. She blamed it on her busy schedule, but she knew her hectic career was more of an excuse to mask a deeper issue—one that kept her from developing a meaningful relationship with any man out of fear of being rejected when he discovered the physical and emotional scars she carried that would most likely be a deal-breaker for him.

"Did you hear that, guys? The gorgeous, sexy Jessica

Morgan is single and available!" Benny said enthusiastically, a ploy to generate excitement for the upcoming auction. "We've got the auction up next, so guys, here's your chance to win a date with Jessica, and ladies, if you want to party with a rock star for an evening, pick up the phone and open your wallet for a good cause, the Wishes Are Forever foundation. All it takes is a winning bid and she's yours for the night, so be generous."

With that said, Benny pressed a button on the console in front of him and played a song from her recent album. By the time "Don't Turn Me Away" ended, the auction was ready to begin. Benny opened the phone lines to KJOY's listeners, and the switchboard lit up with callers willing to place a bid for the opportunity to spend a few hours in Jessica's company. All she had to do was sit back, relax, and wait to find out who the winning bidder turned out to be.

The opening offer of one hundred dollars came from a young girl who wanted Jessica to perform for her sixteenth birthday but was quickly eclipsed by a higher bid. The hundred-dollar bids quickly jumped into the thousands and kept rising from there. A group of girlfriends had pooled their money in hopes of winning a cocktail party with Jessica as the guest of honor, but they were no match for the many men calling in, who were very competitive and cutthroat in their attempts to become the highest bidder.

The whole process, and the amount of money someone was willing to pay to spend time with her, made Jessica's head spin—in a very good way.

Eventually, the calls began to dwindle as the bidding climbed to sixty-five hundred dollars, until a male caller made an offer of seven thousand dollars and no one else called to top him.

"Very nice, dude," Benny drawled, obviously impressed

with the man's generous bid. "Six thousand dollars going once . . . going twice . . . going—"

Benny abruptly stopped his countdown as a phone line lit up, flashing like a bright beacon. "Hold on, folks. Looks like this auction is not done yet." Grinning at Jessica, he connected the call. "What's your bid?"

"Ten thousand dollars."

Jessica sucked in a shocked breath—at the staggering amount and because the deep, masculine voice that had made the offer was an all-too-familiar one. The hot, sexy, and very determined Noah Young.

She certainly hadn't seen *that* coming.

Benny looked just as surprised. "Now *that's* an impressive bid."

"You got that right, man," the caller before Noah said, his tone both disappointed and annoyed. "I'm tapped out and can't compete with ten grand. You win."

"So, let's make this official, then," Benny said, relishing his role as auctioneer. "Ten thousand dollars going once . . . going twice . . . going three times . . ." He dragged the last part out, but when no one else rang in, the DJ made a loud clapping sound with his hands in lieu of pounding a gavel to signal the end of the auction. "Caller, you just won an evening in Jessica's company, along with VIP passes to her upcoming concert. What's your name?"

"Noah," he said, confirming what Jessica already knew. But that didn't stop her heart from racing ten miles a minute at the knowledge that he'd placed a hefty bid for a date with her.

"Well, Noah, that's quite a chunk of change you just plunked down. You must want this date with Jessica really badly."

"Who wouldn't?" Noah drawled, his deep, masculine voice resonating through Jessica like a slow, seductive caress. "Besides, the money is going to a great cause, so it's a win-win situation."

Jessica knew that listeners were probably expecting her to say something to the winner, to at least congratulate him, but her tongue felt tied. No matter how she tried, she couldn't wrap her mind around *why* he would spend that kind of money on her—or even for her foundation. If it was all about doing a good deed, he could have just written a check directly to Wishes Are Forever and not torture her in the process. Because she couldn't imagine he actually wanted to spend time with her on a date, unless it was to dredge up the painful past again, and she so wasn't going there with him.

Not now. Not ever. Despite the regrets she still lived with, her life had irrevocably changed all those years ago and there was no repairing the damage done.

Jessica cleared her throat and forced herself to speak. "Thanks for the generous donation, Noah."

"My pleasure." Again, his husky tone rippled along Jessica's nerve endings, making her body come alive as if his voice alone had the power to awaken all those desires she'd squashed after leaving him nine years ago. "I'm looking forward to our time together."

Unaware that Jessica actually *knew* Noah, Benny focused on the business aspect of the auction: "We'll get our PR person, Jackie, on the phone to make arrangements for your payment, and to get your personal information to pass on to Jessica so the two of you can set up a time and place for your date."

"Sounds great," Noah said.

The DJ switched Noah over to Jackie to handle the transaction while Benny wrapped up the interview portion of Jessica's visit. Even though her mind was distracted by everything that had just transpired, she managed to answer the final questions, quickly mentioned her album and up-coming tour one more time, then stopped by Jackie's cubi-cle to collect Noah's contact information.

Jessica's bodyguard, Simon, was waiting for her out in the reception area, and as soon as he saw her he stood and fell into step a few feet behind her as they left the radio station, then made their way out of the building to the Town Car waiting to take her back home.

Except parked at the curb, right behind her chauf-feured vehicle, was a sporty black BMW with none other than Noah leaning casually against the passenger door, his arms folded over his broad chest and his jean-clad legs crossed at the ankles. A warm summer breeze ruffled his thick hair, and sunglasses shaded his eyes and kept most of his expression concealed.

She came to a sudden stop, unable to believe he'd been waiting right outside the radio station the entire time the auction had been going on. The man was bold and cocky and too damn persistent.

Simon halted beside her and narrowed his gaze at Noah. "Is there a problem?" Simon asked her in a low, gruff tone, ready and willing to take care of said *problem* with one word from her.

"No, it's okay," she assured her bodyguard, whose tense forearms immediately relaxed. "I'll be fine. I know him, and he's not a threat."

Except, of course, to her emotions.

In that regard, Noah Young caused all kind of havoc—with his dominating presence, his too-confident attitude, and mostly his delicious, addicting kisses. Like the ones he'd planted on her Friday night after her impromptu con-cert at Taboo. Those kisses had started a slow burn inside of her that had made her feel restless ever since.

She glanced at Simon. "Give me a few minutes to talk to him."

Simon gave her a nod and headed toward the Town Car, and Jessica started in Noah's direction, annoyed by the fact that the dark pair of shades he wore blocked his eyes. But despite those sunglasses, she could still *feel* his gaze on her, most likely taking a slow, leisurely perusal over her dark purple gauze blouse, down her skinny black jeans, to her lace-up ankle boots—and all the way back up again. Maybe it was a good thing she couldn't see his eyes and what, exactly, he was looking at.

Jessica stopped a few feet away from him and kept her expression neutral. "Was all that really necessary?" she asked. She wanted to sound irritated but didn't quite pull it off.

To his credit, he didn't pretend to not know what she was referring to. "Yes, it was very necessary," he said, his voice smooth as silk. "I didn't think you'd go out with me willingly, and I figured this was something you couldn't back out of."

Jerk. A clever jerk, she admitted begrudgingly, but a jerk nonetheless. "Why would you want to go out with me at all?" It wasn't as though the last time they'd been together had been all romance and roses. In fact, there had been a ton of animosity between them, and she couldn't imagine spending hours with Noah steeped with anger and resentment.

Now that sounded like a fun time together. *Not.*

"Why, Noah?" she persisted.

Shrugging, he finally slipped off his sunglasses, his gaze a direct and piercing shade of brown. "Because you and I have unfinished business to resolve."

She stiffened, her defenses rising. "No, we don't," she said adamantly. The past was the past, and she wanted it to stay there. For her, that term was nonnegotiable.

He thought for a long moment, as if trying to come up with some kind of compromise. "Okay, what if I promise to be on my best behavior and we both make an effort to enjoy the date?"

God, with the history between them, was that even possible? Could they put the past aside and just go forward as friends? Honestly, it wasn't as though she had a choice. The man had just spent an exorbitant amount of money for a date with her—how would it look if word got out that she'd backed out on a legitimate auction? Her publicist could no doubt handle the damage control, but Jessica had never reneged on a deal before and she wasn't about to start now with Noah—no matter how bad of an idea this was.

"Fine." She absently adjusted the strap of her purse over her shoulder, telling herself she could handle a few hours with Noah, especially since they'd both agreed to play nice. Once her obligation was fulfilled, they could go their separate ways. Thank God she was leaving in a few weeks to begin her concert tour, which would assure there would be plenty of distance between herself and Noah.

"What are you doing here, at the radio station?" she asked. She knew he'd handled the donation payment over the phone, so it wasn't as though he needed to show up in person.

His smile encompassed a wealth of male arrogance, which only made him look hotter. Sexier. "I knew I was going to win the auction, so I wanted to be here when you left so we could discuss the details of our date."

She bit her bottom lip to keep from grinning, because she didn't want him to think she was amused by his gigantic ego, which she was. "You are so full of yourself. What if someone kept outbidding you?"

"Not possible."

With those two words he told her that he'd been prepared to drop far more cash for a date with her, if necessary. As for the details of their date ... "Well, your ten-grand donation bought yourself an evening in my company, so we need to decide on a day and time that works with your schedule."

"How about right now?"

Was he serious? "It's two in the afternoon on a Monday."

He arched a dark brow. "I'd like to think that ten thousand dollars would buy me a few extra hours of your time."

Oh, he was good. Or bad, as the case might be. "So, you want the afternoon *and* evening?"

"Sounds fair to me." He pushed away from his BMW, straightening to his full height so that she had to tip her head back to look at his face. "Unless you have other plans today?"

"No plans. But don't you have a nightclub to run?"

He shook his head, causing soft strands of his hair to brush across his forehead, giving him a boyish look when he was anything but. "Taboo is closed on Monday and Tuesday nights."

How convenient was that? She hadn't anticipated going out with Noah so soon and would have appreciated the extra time to mentally and emotionally prepare herself to spend so many hours with him. "I'm not exactly dressed for a date," she said, the excuse sounding lame even to her own ears.

To her surprise, he reached out and grabbed her hand, the heat of his touch making her stomach do the kind of somersaults she hadn't felt since their first face-to-face encounter in high school. "You're dressed perfectly for what I have in mind for the first part of our date."

"First part?" she asked curiously.

"Yep, it's a two-part date." His thumb caressed the back of her hand, and the gold in his brown eyes all but mesmerized her. "And you're perfectly dressed for the second part, too."

She released a soft sigh. When things were like this between them, friendly and civilized, the lack of hostility made it so easy for her to do anything he asked. As long as he kept his promise to leave their history where it belonged—in the past—and she was trusting him to do just that.

Deciding to make the best of the situation, she gave Noah a genuine smile. "Okay, I'm all yours." As soon as the words left her mouth, she realized how brazen her reply sounded.

And, of course, being a guy, Noah immediately jumped on the chance to acknowledge the double entendre. "I like the way that sounds."

His deep, wicked chuckle made her shiver and her cheeks grow warm.

He tugged her closer and lowered his head to speak into her ear. "One more request. Can we ditch your bodyguard?" Noah asked hopefully, nodding his head toward where Simon was waiting patiently for her by the Town Car. "I promise to keep you safe and protected the entire time you're with me." He gave the hand he was still holding a gentle squeeze.

Oddly enough, she believed him and trusted him. There was a time when he'd been her knight in shining armor, her defender against the unpleasant memories shadowing her youth, and her sanctuary when her own mother had treated her only daughter like she wished Jessica had never been born. Unfortunately, he hadn't been around to save her from what happened on the worst day of her life.

She didn't blame him for that, but those events had

forever changed the course of her future . . . one in which Noah Young no longer had a place.

"Yeah, we can ditch Simon," she told Noah.

And for tonight she, too, was going to put the past aside and enjoy her time with the only man she'd ever loved.

Chapter Eleven

By four o'clock Monday afternoon, Zoe was ready to call it a day—at least at the office. She still had plenty of work to do relating to the boutique and getting her flagship store ready to open within the next month, but most of the remaining tasks she could handle from home on her computer or by phone. Between her and Brittany—Zoe's trusted assistant who'd been with ZR Designs for the past year—they'd accomplished everything on Zoe's to-do list for that day and more.

They'd placed orders for inventory, found a commercial builder to install the shelves and racks and cases she wanted in the boutique, and even interviewed three potential managers for the store earlier that day. Since there was something else Zoe needed to handle outside of the office, Brittany was staying behind to call references on the applications to see which candidate received the best recommendation from past employers. Then came background checks, drug tests, and Zoe hoped by the end of the week she would be able to hire one of the women as a boutique manager and could put her to work as well.

"Thanks for taking care of the dirty work, Britt," Zoe

said, as she gathered up her purse and laptop case, to her assistant handling the rest of the application process. "If you need me for anything, just give me a call. Otherwise, I'll see you bright and early tomorrow morning."

"Okay, boss." Ever the efficient, multi-tasking assistant, Brittany didn't even glance up from whatever she was typing into her computer as Zoe passed by the petite blonde's desk. "Have a good evening."

"You, too. And don't stay too late," Zoe said over her shoulder, knowing that Brittany had a bad habit of getting so engrossed in what she was doing that she worked well past quitting time. It was a quality Zoe appreciated but didn't want to take advantage of. "Tomorrow's another long day."

Abruptly Brittany stopped typing and glanced up at Zoe, her gaze soft with understanding. "Hey, good luck at your father's office."

"Thanks." Brittany was one of the few people Zoe had told about her attempts to contact her father and how worried she'd been because he hadn't been in touch, but she'd kept the darker accusations against her dad to herself. Until she had any kind of solid evidence to prove The Reliance Group's claim against her father, she wasn't about to add fuel to the rumors.

Twenty minutes later she stopped her car in front of her father's office, immediately noting the lack of vehicles parked in the lot. Counting her Lexus, there were three cars total, which she found odd. Her father's development company employed over a dozen people, from site and project managers to estimators, an accounting and payroll department, and a few secretaries to handle overflow work for the Meridian project.

As she'd witnessed in the past, usually in the late afternoon the office was a hub of activity, but today the place looked and felt like a ghost town. Unease twisted through her as she entered the building, and things only got worse from there.

The phone lines at the front desk were ringing persistently, but the receptionist was nowhere to be seen. In fact, as Zoe walked past the reception area to where workstations and smaller offices were located, she found the place abandoned.

Including Sheila's cubicle and Zoe's father's office.

Then she heard voices coming from a corner office and headed in that direction, hoping to find a familiar face who could tell her what the heck was going on, because she didn't like the sense of foreboding settling over her like a dark, brewing storm.

She reached the far office and recognized both men inside—Jeremy, one of the site managers for the Meridian project, and an older gentleman, George, her father's controller, who'd been with the company for the past five years. They were arguing about a check that had bounced to one of their sub-contractors—and it was just what Zoe *didn't* want to hear.

She knocked on the wooden door, startling both men out of their heated conversation. "Hi, guys," she said when both pairs of eyes turned to her. "Where is everyone? This place is practically deserted."

The two men exchanged a not-so-discreet look that only added to Zoe's suspicion that something was very, very wrong. When neither of them spoke, she directed her gaze to the man she knew best. "George, what's going on around here?" She couldn't keep the wariness from her voice or prevent the nausea that was beginning a slow roll through her stomach.

Jeremy shook his head, looking both frustrated and angry. "I have somewhere else I need to be, so I'll let George be the bearer of bad news."

Jeremy brushed past her and out the door, leaving Zoe alone with the older man, who appeared worn-out and weary. George ran his fingers through his receding hair, then sank down into the leather chair behind his desk while Zoe waited not so patiently for him to speak.

"Things aren't going too well around here," he finally admitted as he tugged on the knot of his navy blue tie as if to loosen the fabric so he could breathe easier. "Quite honestly, we're having a bit of a cash flow problem, and I'm having a helluva hard time trying to locate your father."

Confusion, and something more oppressive, enveloped her. "He's supposed to be on a business trip in Chicago."

"That's what I thought, too," George said. "Do you know where in Chicago he's staying?"

"No." It wasn't a good sign that one of her father's trusted employees was hoping that *she* had some insight to her father's whereabouts. "Wouldn't Sheila have that information?"

The older man laughed, but the sound lacked any real humor. "Yeah, that's her job as your father's secretary. She sets up your father's business trips and keeps his itinerary. All last week she gave me the runaround about getting ahold of your father, along with a bunch of bogus excuses, until I finally confronted her on Friday evening and demanded she give me the information. Which she did right before she left for the day, except the hotel whose name and number she gave me doesn't have anyone under the name of Grant Russo registered."

Zoe walked farther into the office, each step feeling as though her shoes were weighed down with lead. "What did you say to Sheila when she came in today?"

George's mouth twisted grimly. "She didn't come in today. No call, no show. No answer on her house phone or her cell phone."

Nope. Not good at all. "Where's the rest of the office staff?"

He met her gaze, his expression turning harsh. "They haven't gotten a paycheck in two weeks, so most of them have walked out until they get paid or they've just flat-out quit."

Oh, God. Feeling as though the rug was being pulled out right from under her feet, Zoe sat down in one of the chairs in front of George's desk. "That's not all, is it?" She instinctively knew there was more and it wasn't going to be pleasant.

The man shook his head. "Not only are checks bouncing, but big money is missing from accounts that normally hold money in reserve. The Meridian project has shut down, without a legitimate reason that I can find, and we've been inundated with calls from angry sub-contractors who did work but haven't been paid and now I can't locate your father to get answers. All I know is that whatever is going on, it's bad, and I have a feeling it's going to get worse."

She thought about the man who'd confronted her a week ago and how bitter and angry he'd been because he hadn't been paid. There was also that Davenport man who'd made a scene at the casino Friday night. That was two people out of a dozen or more who were probably furious with her father, and the company, for withholding their money. What if someone had gone so far as to hurt her father, or worse, in their attempt to exact retribution?

She forcibly swallowed the huge lump of dread that had gathered in her throat. "Do you think something bad happened to my father?"

"I don't know," George said, his features suddenly softening with an emotion that looked like empathy. "But I have to be honest with you about something, Zoe, because you have the right to know. I've been doing my damnedest to figure out what went wrong with the finances, and all signs are pointing to your father having embezzled millions of dollars from the investment accounts. I've found discrepancies in financial records and bank statements, and possible evidence of wire fraud, and it just doesn't look good that nobody seems to be able to locate your dad."

An instant denial sprang to her lips to defend her father, but she could no longer ignore the very real possibility that her father *was* guilty of fraud and had gone rogue. She didn't want to believe it, but it was as though everything she'd been denying for the past week was slowly unraveling and becoming her worst nightmare.

"I'm sorry, Zoe," George said, his tone compassionate. "If your father doesn't show up, and soon, there is no doubt in my mind that the Feds are going to get involved and things are going to get very, very messy."

She could only imagine. Her conversation with Sean last Friday night played through her mind, along with the undisputable fact that The Reliance Group had been hired by a respected businessman who'd invested millions of dollars into the Meridian project, and how that same man was trying to find her father to reclaim his loan because the project had been shut down without legitimate cause— except the lack of money to pay people.

Everything Sean had tried to tell her was now being backed by someone from the inside, a man who had access to records and accounts and *the facts*. As much as it pained her to do so, she had no choice but to face the truth, because there was no ignoring the cold, hard, irrefutable evidence piling up against her father.

And what was up with Sheila giving George false information and disappearing, too? Was there any chance Sheila was intimately involved with Zoe's father and was protecting him and the millions of dollars that were missing from the company?

Zoe had a difficult time believing that the two of them were lovers. Sure, Zoe's father had always talked very highly of Sheila as a competent, efficient secretary, yet Zoe had never seen her dad treat Sheila with anything other than courtesy, respect, and professionalism. Not only that, but Sheila wasn't even close to the type of woman Grant was attracted to and dated. In every way, Sheila was the antithesis of the young, blond, silicone-enhanced arm candy Zoe's father preferred.

Which made the thought of Grant Russo running off with Sheila all the more confusing to Zoe.

Her temples throbbed with the beginnings of a headache. She felt as though she were trying to put together a giant, convoluted jigsaw puzzle and was missing crucial, key pieces. She needed some kind of solid, concrete answer, something tangible to confirm, or affirm, her doubts and uncertainties about her father's relationship with Sheila.

An idea came to Zoe, one that might prove helpful if she was able to get George to cooperate. "I need to ask a favor. With Sheila now being gone, too, I'd like to take the hard drive from her computer."

George frowned, looking confused. "What for?"

"I know someone who can analyze the information on hard drives, and since Sheila is my father's main secretary who plans all his trips and itineraries, I'm hoping he might recover something that could indicate where my father is." And Sheila's whereabouts, too.

Zoe figured if Lucas wasn't able to find anything incriminating or helpful on her father's home computer hard drive, Sheila's might prove to be more useful. It was worth a shot, anyway.

George hesitated for a moment, then released a heavy sigh and finally relented. "Fine. Take it."

They walked to Sheila's office, and Zoe waited while George retrieved the hard drive out of the secretary's computer. He handed to Zoe the component, which she'd pass on to Sean tomorrow.

Still feeling numb from everything she'd just learned, Zoe left the building as though she was operating on autopilot. She got into her car and just sat there, staring blankly through the windshield, her mind spinning with daunting thoughts and an awful, sinking sensation taking up residence in the pit of her stomach.

None of this made sense to Zoe. The Grant Russo she'd known all her life was honest and generous and kind. An ethical, hardworking businessman who treated his employees fairly and had built a reputable development company. He wasn't some kind of scheming, cheating con man who would, without conscience, bilk innocent people out of paychecks and investments due to them.

Her eyes burned with tears she valiantly tried to blink back as she navigated her way home. She *needed* to find her father and wanted desperately to believe he'd be able to explain away all the claims against him and everything would return to normal. She clung to that bit of hope, because it was all she had left.

God, she felt so lost and alone and confused. She knew she'd made a promise to keep Sean informed of any new revelations concerning her father, but she couldn't find the strength to admit that Sean might be right and that some of the things he and Caleb had alluded to were proving to be true.

She picked up her cell phone to call Jessica and tell her what had happened but remembered that Jessica was on a date with Noah. Zoe didn't want to interrupt her best friend to vent about her own personal family drama—or give Jessica an excuse to cut her evening with Noah short to comfort her. Those two had things to work out between them and needed whatever time they could get together before Jessica left on tour.

Briefly Zoe thought about contacting her mother, but if Zoe relayed what she'd just learned from George, she knew without a doubt that Collette Russo would freak out. Instead of offering her daughter a sympathetic shoulder or ear, her mother would give Zoe nothing but grief over the fact that *she* wasn't getting her alimony. And that was the last thing Zoe wanted to hear from her self-centered parent.

Resolved to spend the evening alone to try to process everything she'd discovered that afternoon, Zoe continued toward her place. When she reached the Panorama Towers, she punched her code into the gate-control box, then gave a friendly wave to the familiar guard at the security shack as the electronic iron gate opened for her.

As she drove forward, she heard the loud, high-pitched sound of a motorcycle and glanced in her rearview mirror just in time to see a red and black low-profile bike zoom through the small opening seconds before the gate slid shut.

The motorcycle followed her into the parking garage and all the way up to the third level. She parked her vehicle in her designated spot while noticing that the motorcycle had stopped closer to the stairwell. Putting the other person out of her mind, she gathered her purse and laptop case and got out of her car, then headed toward the bank of elevators.

That's when she realized that the man who'd been on the motorcycle was now striding purposefully toward *her*. He was still wearing his helmet, and the tinted face shield kept his identity concealed from her view and kicked her unease up a few notches. She glanced around, but there wasn't anyone else in the parking structure, and she slowed her steps as he continued his determined approach.

She was beginning to feel stalked and trapped, since there was no getting to the elevators unless she walked around the guy, and something was screaming inside of her to run in the opposite direction. A rush of adrenaline spilled through her veins, bringing on a surge of panic she heeded.

Trusting her instincts, she turned and ran back toward her car, using her remote to unlock the driver's side door. Too frightened to look back, she quickly slid behind the wheel, slammed the door shut, and locked herself inside— just as the motorcycle man reached her vehicle.

Standing by her window, he withdrew a long, lethal-looking knife from the sheath strapped to his leather belt and held it up for her to see. The steel glinted menacingly, and the sharp, pointed tip of the blade made her breath catch in her lungs.

Finally, the man flipped open the visor part of his helmet, giving her a glimpse of dark, angry eyes glittering with contempt. The same ones she remembered as belonging to the guy who'd approached her a week ago at Caesars Palace. He was back, and this time he obviously had some kind of vengeance in mind.

He narrowed his gaze and kept that threatening, deadly-looking knife within her view. "Where the fuck is your father?" The man's voice was deep and loud enough for her to hear through the rolled-up window.

She swallowed the lump of fear lodged in her throat and forced herself to answer. "I . . . I don't know!"

"Well, you'd better find out, and fast. That bitch and your father double-crossed me!" he snarled bitterly. "I put my ass on the line to get all that money, and now Bunny and that bastard screwed me over! I want what's *mine*."

His words made no sense to Zoe. The first time this man had confronted her she'd thought he was a disgruntled investor—now he was yelling about being betrayed,

and that was something altogether different. And who
was this Bunny person he kept referring to?

"What are you talking about?" Zoe asked, her voice
quivering with confusion.

"Your father will know exactly what I mean." The man's
thin lips twisted with a chilling malevolence. "Here's another message for you to give to him, to let him know just
how serious I am about getting paid for all my hard work."

He proceeded to walk around her car and brutally slashed
every one of her tires. She had no idea what the man intended to do next, and the scenarios flashing through her
mind filled her with an irrepressible terror. He was big and
strong enough to break her window with one blow from the
butt of his knife, and she would be helpless to stop him.

Shaking off the paralyzing fear gathering within her,
she scrambled for her phone, her hands trembling as she
dialed the one person she instinctively knew she could
count on, no matter what.

As soon as he answered, she spoke the words she'd
never believed she'd ever say to him.

"Oh, God, Sean . . . I need you."

Sean, I need you.

Even through a raspy voice tinged with tears, Sean immediately recognized Zoe's voice and the panic in her
words. He'd been sitting next to Lucas Barnes in one of the
security offices, the two of them discussing some of the information the computer technician had unearthed on the
hard drive Sean and Zoe had retrieved from Grant Russo's
home computer.

But now Sean's attention was completely focused on
the phone call from Zoe and how she was babbling inco-
herently about a guy on a motorcycle who had a knife and
had slashed her tires.

What the hell? Frowning in concern, Sean stood up and

paced away from Lucas's desk, trying to make sense of what she was saying. "Sweetheart, slow down," Sean said evenly, even though Zoe was anything but calm. *First things first,* he thought, and asked, "Where are you?"

"I'm . . . I'm sitting . . . in my car," she said, her voice shaking so badly she sounded as though she were freezing to death, which was impossible in the ninety-degree summer weather.

He needed details. *"Where?"*

"The . . . the parking garage," she said, her voice dropping to a frantic whisper. "At my place. I'm . . . I'm too afraid to get out of the car." A sob broke over the line. "He's gone now, but he said he's going to slash my neck the next time if my father doesn't pay him what he's owed."

The blood went ice-cold in Sean's veins at the thought of her being in danger of any kind. The threat against her was enough to send him over the edge. "Who, Zoe?"

"I don't know." There was still a slight quiver to her voice. "It's some guy who's been following me."

She made it sound as though this wasn't the first time this guy, whoever he was, had approached her. And that wasn't good. Not at all.

"I need you," she said again, her words a panicked plea he'd never expected to hear from her lips. Not after the way he'd betrayed her. *"Please."*

"I'm on my way," he promised. There would be plenty of time later to find out what, exactly, had happened to her—when he knew for certain she was safe and with *him.* And then he wasn't going to let her out of his sight. "Just hang on a sec while I let Lucas know what's going on. Do *not* hang up the phone," Sean ordered.

"Okay."

Knowing his expression was as grim as he felt inside, Sean glanced at Lucas. "Tell Caleb that something important came up with Zoe and I'll get in touch with him later."

Lucas nodded in understanding and waved a hand for Sean to go. "Will do."

Within minutes Sean was in his car racing through the streets of Vegas toward Zoe's place. He kept her on the phone the entire time, doing his best to keep her calm by letting her know how close he was and making sure she knew he'd never let anyone, or anything, hurt her.

It was a huge promise he had no right making, considering *he* posed the biggest threat. Because there was no question in his mind that when she discovered how Sean's father was linked to hers and how the two of them had been involved in a Ponzi scheme together years ago she was going to be devastated. And she'd probably hate Sean, too, for wanting revenge against her father, the man who'd sent Sean's dad to prison.

Add to all that the fact that Sean used to be a con man just like her old man and had more than a few black marks on his record and she'd start to wonder who the monster in all this really was.

"Give me your access code," Sean said as he reached the security gate, so he didn't have to deal with the guard at the shack and take precious time to explain the situation.

Zoe gave Sean the number, he punched it in, and the gates slid slowly open—which made him wonder how the mysterious motorcycle man had made it past security without being stopped or questioned.

Sean intended to find out.

He drove up to the third level of the parking structure and came to a stop directly behind Zoe's car, then got out of the vehicle. As soon as she saw him in her rearview mirror, she flung open her door and plastered herself against him. She wound her arms around his neck and clung to him for dear life.

Knowing she needed the comfort and reassurance of

feeling safe, he wrapped her in his warm embrace, savoring the rare moment of tenderness and trust between them.

Having her in his arms felt so damned good. Better than good, actually. Except for the trembling part. Her entire body was shaking with the residual remnants of fear, and he tenderly caressed his hands up and down her back until she relaxed and softened against him.

"You're okay," he whispered in her ear, trying like hell not to think about the crush of her full breasts against his chest and how badly he wanted to kiss her and ease her pain with something more pleasurable.

After a short while, she pulled back, her red-rimmed eyes filled with genuine appreciation. "Thank you for coming."

"No thanks necessary." Reluctantly, he let her go, before he gave in to the urge to taste her soft lips, or more. "Let me get your things out of your car. I'm taking you back to my place for the night."

She didn't argue, which said a lot about just how frightened she was. He tossed her purse and laptop case into the backseat of his Camaro, then buckled her into the passenger seat before sliding behind the wheel and heading to his small, modest house in the suburbs.

Now all he had to do was keep his hands to himself for the night and off of her and they'd be just fine.

He had a feeling it was going to be easier said than done.

Chapter Twelve

"How's Zoe doing?" Caleb asked.

"She's okay, all things considered." Cell phone pressed to his ear, Sean walked out of his living room and into the adjoining kitchen so he could talk to Caleb privately.

Currently, Zoe was curled up on the far end of Sean's sofa, legs tucked beneath her, watching the ten o'clock news—though he doubted she was really paying attention to the show. Not only had she had an exhausting day emotionally and mentally, but they had just spent the past few hours talking about what she'd learned of her father's deteriorating business, his secretary's mysterious disappearance, and even the attack against Zoe in the parking garage earlier that evening.

"Zoe told me that today isn't the first time she's been approached by the man who slashed her tires," Sean said as he leaned against one of the counters in the kitchen that gave him a view into the living room so he could keep an eye on Zoe. "About a week ago the same guy accosted her while she was shopping with her friend, demanding to know where her father was and letting her know that Russo owed him money. It's clear that this guy is getting bolder and more hostile with his confrontations and now he knows where she lives."

"And we're taking that threat very seriously," Caleb said, his tone adamant. "Looks like you'll be on security detail with Zoe until either the guy is caught or things with her father finally get resolved."

In other words, Sean was now Zoe's personal bodyguard. "That's not a problem." He'd rather have her close by and know that she was safe than constantly worry about her welfare when they were apart.

"I didn't think it would be."

Sean wasn't certain whether Caleb was alluding to something more personal between him and Zoe or if it was just Sean's own imagination making more of his words, but he certainly wasn't going to ask. "Look, I need you to contact security at Panorama Towers and find out what kind of video footage they have on the guy on the motorcycle and the attack against Zoe. Hopefully one of the security cameras got his license on tape and we can trace that information through DMV to find out who the bike is registered to."

"I'll get Nathan on that first thing tomorrow morning," Caleb said, giving the assignment to another Reliance Group member who'd been a vice cop and had connections in all the right places.

Sean switched his cell phone to his other ear and continued on, relaying what Zoe had told him about her time at her father's office and what she'd learned about the failing business. It was information The Reliance Group was already privy to thanks to their private investigators, but it let Caleb know that Zoe was beginning to realize just how serious her father's disappearance was. She no longer believed Grant Russo was on a business trip, and with George confirming that there was big money missing from the company accounts, there was no denying her father was looking guiltier by the day. And now it appeared that Grant's secretary might be involved somehow, too.

"By the way, Zoe managed to retrieve the hard drive from her father's secretary's computer," Sean said, still surprised that Zoe had been thinking straight enough to do so. "I'll bring it in tomorrow morning for Lucas to analyze."

"Perfect. Lucas has pulled a few things from Russo's hard drive that we intend to follow up on, but overall the history cache was pretty clean, which is to be expected from a man with Russo's past experience. He's smart enough not to leave a trail of evidence on his personal computer, but maybe his secretary wasn't as careful."

While Caleb talked, Sean's gaze traveled back to Zoe. Since he hadn't taken the time to get anything from her apartment when he'd picked her up, she was currently wearing one of his T-shirts and a pair of his drawstring shorts, which she'd changed into after taking a long, hot shower after their discussion. Her hair had dried into soft waves and her face was devoid of makeup, making her look so much younger than her true age and twice as vulnerable.

After everything that had happened to her today, he knew she was feeling less than balanced and questioning everything she thought she knew about her father. And the growing knowledge of what Grant Russo was capable of was tearing her apart inside.

Unfortunately, it was going to get a whole lot worse for her, because now that she was coming to terms with the reality of what her father was being accused of, there was a lot more she needed to know. Like the fact that this wasn't the first time Grant Russo had scammed millions of dollars from unsuspecting investors.

Since there was no longer a valid reason to put off the

inevitable, Sean released a deep breath and let Caleb in on his thoughts. "I think it's time to give Zoe the file on her father's past."

On the other end of the line, Caleb was silent for a long moment, as if contemplating the consequences of those actions. "Are you ready for that?" he asked quietly.

Closing his eyes, Sean pinched the bridge of his nose with his fingers, his stomach in knots. No, he wasn't prepared for Zoe to discover just how closely their pasts were intertwined and how Grant Russo was responsible for making sure Sean's father enjoyed a nice, long sentence in prison for a crime both men had committed together. How, without guilt or remorse, *Elliott Cooke* had turned his back on his business partner to save his own ass.

And then there was Sean's hatred and resentment toward Grant Russo that would always stand between him and Zoe.

God, what a freakin' mess.

Sean clenched his jaw. He was far from ready for Zoe to learn the truth, but it was necessary, and honestly, it was a secret he no longer wanted to keep from her.

"Considering how fast everything is escalating, she's going to find out about her father's past eventually," Sean said. "I think she'll be better off knowing the facts so she has time to digest the truth before the real shit hits the fan."

"Okay." Caleb's tone was even and without judgment. "It's ultimately your call."

Sean appreciated Caleb's support but knew if he thought it wasn't the right time to show Zoe the files, he would have said so.

"I'll see you tomorrow," Sean said, and disconnected the line.

Setting his cell phone on the counter, he released a deep breath and walked back into the living room. Zoe glanced from the TV to him, her normally bright green-gold eyes filled with a sadness that made his heart ache for her and the betrayal he was certain she was feeling.

"Why didn't you tell me about the first time this guy attacked you?" Sean asked, sitting next to her on the couch. "If I'd known you were being harassed, I *never* would have left you alone." As it was, he felt sickened that she'd endured such brutality without anyone around to protect her.

"The first time it happened, I didn't know that you were investigating my father," she pointed out, though there was no trace of bitterness in her voice, which Sean was grateful for. "And I thought it was a one-time thing and he was a disgruntled investor. But now, thinking back on both attacks, there were things he said that first time, then again tonight, that were . . . *off*."

Sean frowned. "Off how?"

She drew her knees up and wrapped her arms around her legs, her gaze troubled. "The first time, at Caesars Palace, he made a comment about telling my dad to get back to Vegas, along with the money he and Bunny worked so hard for. Then, tonight, he said something about how 'that bitch' and my father double-crossed him, and how he put his ass on the line to get all the money and now Bunny and my father have screwed him over."

Sean processed what Zoe had just told him, finding it both interesting and intriguing, as it put a whole different spin on things. "Do you know someone named Bunny who knows your father?" Sean asked.

Zoe shook her head, her expression as weary as the day had been long. "No, and I don't mean to be stereotypical, but I have to admit that the name does sound like someone my father would date. He likes younger women with more fluff than substance, and 'Bunny' certainly fits the image."

Sean cracked a smile at Zoe's wry tone. "Well, it sounds

like this guy who attacked you is definitely connected to your father and the missing money somehow, along with whoever this Bunny person is."

Most likely the duo had been Grant's partners in crime—and it sounded as though he'd double-crossed at least one of them. No big surprise there, considering how easily the guy had betrayed Sean's father. Deceiving people was what Russo did best.

"I'll make sure to pass that information on to Caleb tomorrow, and Lucas as well, since he's reviewing the hard drives," Sean said, and stood. "But for now, it's after eleven and you've had a long day. How about we put you to bed?" He extended his hand to help her up.

"Sure." Her tone emotionless, she placed her fingers in his palm and stood, then followed him to the guest bedroom.

He pulled back the comforter on the bed, and when she was settled on the mattress he covered her with the sheet and blanket. "I'm right down the hall if you need me for anything."

He turned to go, but her soft voice stopped him before he reached the door.

"Sean?"

He glanced back at her, steeling himself against her somber expression when he'd much rather see her smiling or laughing. "Yeah?" he asked, his tone huskier than he'd intended.

"Thank you," she whispered. "For everything."

Her words were like a knife in the chest, because while she might be filled with gratitude tonight, she wasn't going to be thanking him tomorrow, when her world as she knew it came crashing down around her a second time and he was the reason why.

"No problem." After turning off her light, he locked up the house for the night before retiring to his own room.

He stripped down to his boxer briefs, got into bed, and managed to doze off—until the creak of the wooden floor, along with the soft sound of footsteps, jarred him awake. He blinked his eyes open and found Zoe standing beside his bed, a shaft of moonlight silhouetting her body and shimmering off her blond hair like a halo.

Immediately he sat up, concerned that something was wrong. "Are you okay?"

"Not really." She shifted on her bare feet and bit her bottom lip anxiously. "After everything that happened today, I . . . I don't want to be alone tonight. Can I stay in here with you?"

"Of course you can." Even knowing that letting her sleep beside him was probably going to keep him awake and most likely aroused all night long, he couldn't bring himself to refuse her. Tossing back the covers, he patted the mattress next to him. "C'mere."

She crawled into his bed and lay on her side facing him, her gaze searching his in the shadows. "Sean . . . ," she whispered longingly, "will you hold me?"

The muscles in his abdomen tightened at her request. Was she trying to test every ounce of willpower he possessed? Didn't she realize that he had very little self-control when it came to her? Apparently not, since she took it upon herself to close the distance between them before he could reply. She snuggled up to his side and rested her head on his chest, trusting him when he'd given her very little reason to.

Oh, hell. Wrapping his arm around her slender waist, he pulled Zoe closer to him—right where she belonged. Her body relaxed against his, and she sighed, her warm breath fanning across his bare chest.

Succumbing to temptation, he threaded his fingers through her silky hair, offering her the physical kind of affection and comfort she seemed to need tonight. He skimmed his hand along her arm in a tender caress, loving the feel of her soft skin beneath his palm, and whispered caring, soothing words that lulled her to sleep.

He gave her the warmth of his embrace, the safety of knowing she wasn't alone, and a brief escape from the harsh reality she'd faced today. But the one thing he couldn't give her was the reassurance that everything was going to be okay. No, that would be a lie, and he wasn't about to give Zoe any more false illusions.

With a happy smile on her face, Jessica rested her head against the passenger seat in Noah's BMW, feeling more exhilarated than she had in a very long time. And wiped out, too, since they'd just spent the past four hours at the Adventuredome at Circus Circus, where they had played carnival games, eaten junk food, and she had screamed her head off as they rode the Canyon Blaster roller coaster and other thrill rides meant for adrenaline junkies.

Of course, Noah chuckled the entire time, enjoying the fact that she'd clung to him on the wilder rides while her stomach bottomed out and her throat grew hoarse from all her high-pitched shrieks.

Just like old times.

Back when they were teenagers and dating, her time with Noah had always been fun and carefree and filled with laughter, the exact opposite of the anger and hostility she'd been subjected to at home. Then and now, he made her feel special, and she realized that being with a man, without pressure or expectations, was something she'd missed having in her life.

As promised, there had been no talk of their past or why she'd left him, which made the time with Noah that afternoon even more enjoyable. It also made her glad that he'd won the auction, instead of a stranger, because she'd been able to just be herself, and the outing had given her a sense of normalcy.

Releasing a sigh of contentment, she glanced over at Noah, admiring his strong, masculine profile and the easy smile on his lips. His dark hair was mussed from the rides, but the tousled look only made him sexier. "If you were trying to wear me out, I think you succeeded."

"Yes, that was all part of my nefarious plan, so I can have my wicked way with you later." He waggled his brows at her.

She laughed at his teasing remark. That's how relaxed she'd become with him over the last few hours. He was no longer her adversary but had established himself as someone she could fall for all over again.

Noah might have been on his best behavior when it came to not discussing their past relationship, but that hadn't stopped him from flirting shamelessly with her. He hadn't missed an opportunity to touch her as they stood in line for the attractions, or put his arm around her when they sat next to each other on the rides.

When he'd won her a prize at one of the midway games, she'd been so excited she'd given him a hug, and it hadn't escaped her notice that he'd held her longer than necessary or that his hands had *accidentally* brushed over the curve of her bottom before letting her go.

The incident, along with the heat of desire darkening his eyes, had brought on a rush of awareness she hadn't been able to shake since. And she was beginning to wonder if she even wanted to. Dangerous thoughts, considering they had no future together.

Determined not to allow any negative energy to ruin her time with Noah, she glanced down at the cute stuffed pink orangutan with the words *Be Mine* stitched on its soft belly sitting on her lap. "By the way, thanks again for

my orangutan," she said, fingering one of the fuzzy ears.
"I love it."

"It was my pleasure." He took his eyes off the road for
a second to grin at her. "It wouldn't be right if I took you
to a circus and didn't win you a stuffed animal."

"Well, it's not as though it was *that* difficult," she
drawled, giving him a hard time. "You were a basketball
star in high school and college, and you chose the Hoop
Shot game. Of course you're going to make every shot and
win the best stuffed animals."

He placed a hand on his chest and feigned a wounded
look. "Man, you're killing my fragile ego."

Amused laughter escaped her. "From what I can see,
there's plenty more where that came from." The man had
male arrogance to spare.

He didn't argue. Instead, he turned his gaze back to the
road. "Are you hungry?"

"Yeah," she said, just as her stomach gave a growl of
agreement. "After those nachos, popcorn, and cotton candy,
I'm hungry for *real* food."

"How does Italian sound?" Noah asked as he turned
off of the main Strip and headed toward the outskirts of
Las Vegas.

"Sounds fantastic. Where are we going for dinner?" she
asked curiously.

"My place," he said, his tone casual.

His reply surprised her. She would have thought he'd
try to impress her by taking her to a fancy, high-dollar
restaurant. But a quiet dinner, without having to worry
about people watching her or fans approaching her for a
photo opportunity or autograph, was more her style. But
then again, there was the flip side of being completely
alone with Noah at his house and just how tempting that
had the potential to be.

"Are you going to cook dinner for me?" she asked. Now *that* would definitely impress her.

He cast her a lazy grin. "I'd love to say yes, but I had my mother make up a dish of her baked ziti with mini-meatballs and it's waiting for us in the refrigerator to heat up for dinner."

"Oh, my God. That sounds *amazing*." Her mouth nearly salivated at the mention of the savory home-cooked meal. "I love your mother's baked ziti and meatballs."

"I know," he said, and winked at Jessica.

She shook her head, shocked that he'd remembered something so simple. Not to mention the forethought that had gone into arranging their date and dinner. "Everything today was so well planned, including my favorite dinner. How did you manage that?"

He shrugged as if it were no big deal. "When I heard the radio station promoting the auction for a date with you, I set everything up ahead of time."

There was that self-confidence again, and she had to admit he wore it well. "You were *that* certain you'd win," she said, her comment more of a statement than a question.

"I was," he said, his tone unapologetic.

She hugged the soft orangutan to her chest, feeling oddly special that Noah had gone to such great lengths to make her happy today. "Well, if I haven't already said it, thank you for the generous donation. It'll go a long way in making a lot of kids at the hospital very happy."

He made another turn into a middle-class residential area and slowed his vehicle when he saw kids playing on one of the sidewalks. A little boy waved at Noah as he drove by, and he gave a friendly wave back. "I know you founded Wishes Are Forever, but do you spend time at the hospital with the kids?"

"When I have the time. Usually in between touring, like now," she told him, wondering how much he knew of her foundation, and her career, too. "The foundation keeps me informed of the various wishes, which I have to approve, and I also like to be involved with the setup of the wishes as much as possible. The kids deserve a bit of happiness in their sick lives."

"Well, it's a noble cause." He pulled into a driveway and cut the engine. "Here we are."

She glanced out the passenger window at his two-story house, taking in the well-maintained appearance and beautifully landscaped front yard, which told her he took a lot of pride in where he lived. The neighborhood was far from ostentatious, but there was a warmth and charm about the area that she really liked. It was the kind of place a couple could raise a family and be a part of a community—which was something that Jessica had always secretly wanted for herself.

She followed him up the walkway and into the house, finding the inside just as cozy and inviting. Decorated in shades of beige and hunter green throughout, with oak trim and leather furnishings, the place had a definite masculine vibe. He led her into the spacious kitchen, where he gave her the task of making a salad while he prepared the garlic cheese bread to go with the pasta dish.

While she pulled the lettuce and other veggies out of the refrigerator, he put the ziti into the oven to heat, then poured each of them a glass of red Zinfandel.

"Thank you," she said, and took a sip of her wine before asking, "So, does your mother know who she made this ziti for?"

Noah came up beside Jessica where she was standing at the granite island chopping lettuce and set a loaf of bread, grated cheese, and a garlic butter spread on the counter. "Of course I told her. I've never asked her to specifically make it for me before. She was curious *why,* and I wasn't going to lie."

Jessica winced and took another gulp of Zinfandel before focusing on cutting up the tomatoes. "I'll bet she hates me, just like you do."

He stopped spreading the garlic butter on a slice of bread. "She doesn't hate you . . . and neither do I, Jessica," he said softly.

She tossed the tomato slices into the glass salad bowl and started in on a cucumber. "You had an odd way of showing it the other night," she said, forcing a wry note into her voice. She didn't even know why she made the comment, because it really shouldn't have mattered how he'd treated her a few nights ago at Taboo.

But it *did* matter, and she hated that it made any difference at all.

Sighing, he placed the bread on a baking sheet, added the shredded cheese, and turned to face her, his expression sincere. "Look, I know I acted like a jerk at the nightclub, but seeing you again after so many years, with so much left unsaid between us, it brought up *old* anger." He reached out and ran the back of his fingers along her cheek, the touch so gentle and caring. "There's still a level of hurt there, because I have no idea what I did wrong, but I loved you too much at one time to ever hate you."

He *had* changed his behavior toward her, and she swallowed the emotional lump that had jammed in her throat. She glanced away before she did something incredibly stupid . . . like throw herself into his arms and beg his forgiveness.

Picking up her glass, she took another drink of her wine, realizing that she'd already consumed the entire amount he'd poured. Then she pasted on a bright smile. "Well, at least you've moved on, right?" She nearly groaned as the idiotic words slipped out of her mouth. Why would she ask such a thing when she really didn't want to know the answer?

He moved around her to put the bread in the oven to toast, then returned to her side with the bottle of Zinfandel and refilled her glass. "If you're asking about having relationships with women, sure, I've had a few over the years, but nothing lasting," he said as he began setting the small dining table with plates and silverware.

She tossed the salad with Italian dressing and placed it on the table before returning to the kitchen, where he was checking the pasta dish. "What, you just haven't found the right woman?" God, could she get any more clichéd?

"No, I found her." He turned to face her, his eyes a startling shade of brown. "Once, a long time ago. I thought I was going to get married, have a big family with her, grow old with her."

The emotion that swelled within her was almost suffocating in its intensity, because she'd wanted those things, too, until a cruel twist of fate had changed everything.

She looked away and decided the best thing to do was not respond to his comment. After such a wonderful day with each other, the last thing she wanted was a discussion about the past to ruin what was left of the evening and their time together.

He didn't push the issue, either, which she appreciated. The timer on the oven buzzed, announcing that the ziti and cheese bread was done, and they put the rest of the food on the table and sat down to eat.

She wasn't as hungry as she'd been an hour ago, but she scooped up a nice amount of the baked ziti onto her plate, along with some salad and bread. And once she started eating and Noah steered the conversation toward his family and bringing her up-to-date on his parents and siblings, her appetite, and cheerful disposition, returned.

Until he unwittingly brought up another touchy subject she had no wish to broach.

"How's your mother these days?" he asked, his tone conversational as he finished off a piece of garlic cheese bread.

Jessica set her fork down on her plate and wiped her mouth with her napkin. Judging by the genuine interest in his gaze, he obviously had no idea just how unpleasant this particular topic still was for her—that the years that had passed had done absolutely nothing to mend the volatile mother–daughter relationship that had started way before her father's fatal heart attack.

"Honestly, I have no idea how my mother is," Jessica replied, and took a drink of her Zinfandel.

Noah tipped his head, a slight frown creasing his brows. "You don't talk to her?"

"No." And it was no big loss to Jessica. Not after the horrible accusations her mother had made against her right before she'd kicked Jessica out of the house that summer she'd graduated. The day her mother's much younger boyfriend had ruthlessly raped her and Cheryl Morgan had walked in on them just as he'd finished.

Of course, Cheryl chose to believe that Jessica had seduced her boyfriend in an attempt to take yet another thing away from her mother, and the asshole who'd assaulted her insisted that's exactly what had happened.

That day had changed Jessica's life forever, in so many ways. She'd lost the innocence she'd only ever shared with Noah. She'd been cast out of the only home she'd ever known. And, most devastating, she'd been stripped of the ability to ever have a family of her own. The family she'd dreamed of having with Noah.

Realizing that Noah was studying her too intently, Jessica glanced at her wineglass, watching as her fingers absently stroked the crystal stem as she gathered her composure.

Finally, she spoke. "The last time I saw my mother was three years ago, when she came to one of my concerts, made her way backstage afterward, and asked for money because she'd blown through every cent my father had left her, including the money she'd received from his half-a-million-dollar life-insurance policy."

"Nice," Noah drawled sarcastically. "I guess some things never change."

When Jessica and Noah had been dating, he'd been the one person other than Zoe whom she'd confided in about just how difficult things had been between herself and her mother, so he knew all about Cheryl's erratic and unstable personality. "I'd expect nothing less from her," Jessica said, unable to keep the note of disgust from her voice. "And she didn't take it too well when I told her that she'd never see a dime from me, then had security escort her out of the building, along with the message that if she ever approached me again I'd have a restraining order put out against her."

"I don't blame you."

Jessica appreciated Noah's comment and his understanding. Ever since the moment she had been conceived, it had been her mother's intent to use her as a pawn to coerce marriage to the wealthy man Cheryl had deliberately captivated and charmed. As a stripper in one of Vegas's upscale gentlemen's clubs, she had seen the older-by-twenty-years Liam Morgan as her meal ticket, but what she'd never anticipated was the strong, unbreakable bond between daughter and father. Jessica had been a daddy's girl, the light of her father's life, and her mother's jealousy over their close relationship had made her bitter and vindictive toward Jessica.

The marriage between Cheryl and Liam was far from a love match, and while Jessica's father took care of Cheryl and bought her whatever she wanted, it was never enough. She'd had affairs that her husband had turned a blind eye to, because he refused to divorce Cheryl, fearing she'd demand full custody of Jessica out of spite and that he'd rarely, if ever, see her and not wanting to take that risk. Liam had put Jessica's welfare above his own happiness and always made sure she felt loved and secure, and she'd been devastated when he'd died.

Her mother couldn't have been happier. Within days, every trace of her husband had been erased from the house and Cheryl's current boyfriend had moved in. From there, it had been a revolving door of men in Cheryl's life, booze and partying, and lavish spending sprees on herself. And those times when Jessica made the mistake of crossing paths with her mother, Cheryl always made sure that Jessica knew how much she despised her.

Yeah, her mother had been a real piece of work. Still was, apparently. Except now Jessica no longer had to put up with Cheryl's crap.

"Damn," Noah said, cutting into Jessica's less-than-pleasant thoughts. "I really am a mood killer tonight, aren't I?" he asked, seemingly realizing that he'd dredged up bad childhood memories.

She laughed and decided to make light of things. "Yeah, a little bit. How about I help you clean up?" she asked, indicating the meal they were done eating. That was as good a distraction as any.

"Now there's an offer I won't refuse." Standing, he started stacking their plates and utensils.

She helped him clear the table, and while she rinsed dishes and placed them in the dishwasher, he put away all the leftover food. They worked together companionably, sharing in the domestic chore, and it made Jessica wonder what married life with Noah would have been like. She had a feeling that being his wife would have been amazing, and it was difficult to ignore the pang of regret that squeezed her chest.

"Would you like me to take you home, or would you

like to stay a while longer?" Noah asked once they finished cleaning the kitchen.

There was nothing sexual in his offer, just a friendly overture to Jessica to spend more time with him . . . if she wanted to. And if she was ready to leave, she knew he'd respect her decision and drive her back to her apartment.

Her choice was an easy one to make. "It's been a really nice day, and evening, and I'm not ready for it to end just yet." She spoke honestly, from the heart. It just felt good and right being with Noah, in some ways as though they'd never been apart.

His smile was filled with relief, and boyish charm, too. "Good. Me, either."

Chapter Thirteen

Jessica watched as Noah picked up both of their wine-glasses, which he must have refilled while she'd been doing the dishes.

"It's a gorgeous night out; let's go sit outside for a while," he suggested.

She followed him out a sliding glass door to a patio, and he continued on to the concrete pool in the backyard. He'd left the outdoor lights off, but she didn't mind because the clear sky was filled with bright stars and a nearly full moon, which was plenty of illumination for her, even if it did make for a more romantic, intimate setting.

He led her to the two padded chaise lounges, and she sat down on one of them and he took the one next to her, then set their glasses of wine on the table between them. A cool summer breeze ruffled through her hair and rustled the tall palm trees in his landscaped yard, the sound relaxing and soothing.

As the years had passed, Jessica had always wondered what kind of life Noah was living, and now she knew. "Looks like you've done well for yourself."

He shrugged. "I've done okay."

She reclined back on the lounge chair and smiled at him. "I never would have thought you'd become the manager of a hot nightclub like Taboo." She'd always envisioned him in a more traditional type of career.

"It wasn't intentional," he said, swirling the red wine in his glass before taking a sip. "I got a business degree because I wanted to keep my options open as far as what type of job I wanted to do. But when I came back to Las Vegas after graduating college, there wasn't anything that really inspired me, career-wise. I'm not really a corporate kind of guy. So, while I figured out what I was going to do with the rest of my life, I got a job at Taboo as waitstaff, and from there I gradually worked my way up to shift supervisor, then assistant manager, and now here I am, *the* manager."

He sounded content and happy, and ultimately that's what mattered. "And you like what you do?"

"Sure. It's crazy at times, and stressful, too, but what job isn't?"

"True," she agreed, and reached for her Zinfandel.

"What about you?" he asked, his tone curious. "What's your life as a singer and songwriter like?"

She stretched her legs out on the chair, feeling relaxed and mellow from the wine. "Busy. Hectic. Stressful." She laughed, because it sounded just like *his* job.

"You enjoy it?"

"I do. Singing is like a release for me, a way to express myself. It's very therapeutic," she said, revealing more than she probably should.

His gaze met and held hers, his dark eyes shining with flecks of gold. "The songs you write seem very personal."

"A lot of them are," she said softly, truthfully.

"Like 'Don't Turn Me Away'?" he asked of the song she'd written one night when she'd been thinking of him, missing him.

She bit her bottom lip, and even knowing just how revealing her answer would be, she refused to lie. "Yes."

His expression softened as he stared at her. "'Let me inside where it's warm and safe,'" he said, reciting the words to the song as if he'd written them himself. "'In your arms, your loving embrace. I know I was wrong, but the feelings are still so strong. Don't tell me no. Don't turn me away.'"

A lump of emotion gathered in her throat, and she forced herself to speak around it. "Wow, you've got a great memory."

"The words in your songs are very real and honest," he said, letting her know that he listened very carefully to the songs she wrote and had probably followed her career just as closely. "I wouldn't turn you away, Jessica," he whispered in the shadowed darkness, his voice a low, husky rasp of sound. *"Ever."*

Oh, God, she wished she could believe him. With everything she was, she ached to trust in his promise that he'd always be there for her, no matter what. But she wasn't the girl he'd once known and loved, and when he learned the truth of what had happened to her and that she could never give him the family she knew he wanted, her biggest fear was that he *would* turn her away.

He sat up on his chair, his hands clasped between his spread knees, and for a moment she thought he was going to call it a night, which she really didn't want, despite the personal turn to their conversation. But instead, she watched as a slow, devastatingly sexy grin curved his lips.

"It's a warm night and that water looks very inviting," he said, nodding toward the pool, an irresistible gleam in his eyes. "What do you say we go for a midnight swim?"

Her stomach did a free-fall jump, and she fought the temptation of indulging in something so intimate with him. "It's kind of hard to swim in jeans and boots," she said, her excuse sounding lame even to her own ears.

"I was thinking of swimming in the buff." He stood up, towering beside her chaise lounge as he toed off his shoes. "Or at least stripped down to our underwear."

She gulped, feeling a light-headedness that had nothing to do with the wine she'd consumed and everything to do with where this late-night swim with him might lead. "Are you serious?" It was a stupid question, because Noah always meant what he said.

"Absolutely." And to prove his point, he stripped his shirt over his head, giving Jessica her first physical glimpse of the man he'd become.

Oh, wow. As a teenager, Noah had always had an athletically honed body, but because of his height he'd always been lanky. Not so now. He'd filled out to perfection. His chest was nicely defined, his hips narrow and lean, and when he reached down to pull off his socks she watched in fascination his abdominal muscles rippling as he executed the move.

A long-forgotten desire coiled through her, as did the urge to reach out and touch him, to feel the warmth of his taut skin beneath the tips of her fingers.

He lowered his hands to the waistband of his low-slung jeans and slowly unzipped them, unerringly drawing her gaze to the crisp, dark hair circling his navel, then arrowing down his flat, hard belly and gradually disappearing into his navy boxer briefs.

He pushed his pants off and stepped out of them, and her mouth went completely and utterly dry. He wasn't naked, thank God, but he might as well have been, because the material of his underwear molded to everything that made him masculine.

Unexpectedly he leaned over her, bracing his hands

against the chaise on either side of her head, his face only inches away from hers. "Come on, sweetheart," he cajoled in a deep, mesmerizing voice meant to seduce. "I remember a time when you liked to be a little reckless and daring. And judging from your performance the other night at Taboo, I think you still have a bit of a wild streak in you."

"That was just an act." And with him there had never been any pretenses. He'd been the one to make her feel reckless and daring, a willing partner to whatever he asked. And even now, she was finding it so damn hard to fight his allure.

"Well, it was a really *hot* act, and I really enjoyed it," he told her, grinning wickedly. "Come join me for a swim, Jessie." He dropped one of his hands to the button on her jeans and expertly flicked it open, then started pulling the tab of her zipper down.

She gasped, both shocked and aroused that he'd be so bold. "Noah, stop," she said, and gently pushed his hand away, because the thought of him undressing her was more than her body could handle.

He straightened, but the sinfully determined light in his eyes told her he wasn't done trying to persuade her. "Chicken?"

"Hardly." Oh, she was such a liar. Her biggest fear was that if she got into that water with him things would turn steamy.

"Then prove it," he said, issuing a direct challenge she no longer wanted to resist. "Join me in the pool and we'll play a game of Marco Polo."

With that last invitation, Noah walked away and dove into the pool, leaving the final decision up to her.

She remembered another time when they'd played Marco Polo at night in his parents' pool and how the game had been all about building sexual awareness between them and, ultimately, her seduction.

Jessica knew that if she agreed, this time would be no different.

Noah surfaced at the deep end of the pool, then started a slow swim back to the shallow end. "Well, what's it going to be?"

She was dying to join him, to shed her inhibitions and be wild with someone she trusted. There was no justifiable reason why she couldn't just enjoy whatever Noah had to offer. They were both consenting adults, and the attraction was still as strong as, if not stronger than, before. And the best part was, she was leaving on tour in a few weeks, so that would eliminate any awkward good-byes between them—they'd just go their separate ways and chalk up their time together to a summer fling.

It was all she could give him, anyway.

She glanced around, noticing that the fence surrounding his backyard was so high she couldn't see the neighboring yard and the pool was dark, too, which helped to reassure her that they wouldn't be putting on a show for his neighbors.

She released a deep breath to shake off any lasting doubts. "I'm coming in," she said, and stood up from the lounge chair to start undressing.

Except Noah was watching her, making her feel way too self-conscious.

Heat seared her cheeks and slowly spiraled down her body. "Be a gentleman and turn around," she said, unable to bring herself to be as brazen as he'd been in shedding his clothes.

"I'm no gentleman," he warned her, grinning like a rogue. "Besides, I let you watch me."

She shook her head, trying not to laugh, because that

would just encourage him. "Sorry, but I'm not putting on a striptease show for you."

"Awww, you're no fun," he grumbled good-naturedly, then turned to face the opposite side of the pool.

She kicked off her shoes, then quickly pulled off her top and jeans and ditched her bra, too, leaving her clad in just her pink lace panties. Before she changed her mind or Noah got impatient and glanced back at her, she dove into the pool. The cool water felt like a sensual caress as it rippled across her bare skin, stroked like fingers along her full breasts, and swirled between her thighs. She reveled in the provocative sensations until her lungs forced her to come up for air, and she surfaced as far away from Noah as she could.

Still in the shallow end, with moonlight reflecting off his broad, wet chest, he started walking toward her, a purposeful light flickering in his gaze before he closed his eyes. "You have ten seconds to hide before I come and get you."

The sight of him stalking her with the intention of catching her caused a frisson of excitement to zip through Jessica's veins. She ducked beneath the water but didn't move far from her current position or head into the shallow area like he'd expect. Nearly a minute later she emerged as quietly as possible just as he called out, "Marco."

"Polo," she replied, and when he turned toward the sound of her voice she disappeared into the water again. Opening her eyes underwater, she watched his murky shadow canvas the area, searching for her, moving closer.

A rush of adrenaline gave her an extra burst of energy, and she kicked off the side of the pool and swam away before he could find her. She surfaced in waist-deep water, and she immediately scanned the dark pool, looking for a silhouette and finding none. The anticipation of not knowing where Noah was made her heart race, and she nearly jumped when he came up for air behind her, less than a few feet away.

"Marco," he said, and waited for her reply.

Nerves jittered in her stomach. She knew it was unfair not to say anything, but knowing just how close he was, she couldn't bring herself to answer and get caught, because she knew that once he had her in his grasp the fun and games would be over.

"Marco?" he called again, this time a little louder.

She shivered as a cool breeze tickled her wet skin, even as she remained super still and quiet while waiting for an opportunity to escape.

"I know you can't still be under the water, so you must be really close by," he guessed, his voice deeper, huskier, than before. "Marco."

Polo, she thought, and bit her bottom lip to keep from saying the word.

"You're not answering me," he murmured much too patiently. "And that's cheating, sweetheart."

Beneath the surface of the pool, she felt the water shift and undulate around her legs and gently lap around her waist, telltale signs that he was slowly moving toward her. She remained silent, praying he'd somehow miss her, and couldn't suppress a groan when his body brushed up against hers from behind.

He placed his hands on her hips, his long fingers spanning across her bare belly. "Marco," he whispered in her ear.

She shuddered, the tips of her breasts puckering, her thighs trembling. Even though he'd found her, she still didn't move or try to evade him. He'd caught her fair and square. Besides, there really was no place to escape to, and she no longer wanted to avoid what she wanted so badly. *Him.* Even if it was just for one night or a few weeks. She'd take whatever she could get and enjoy every minute of it.

She turned her head to the side, welcoming the feel of

his lips grazing her cheek, his warm breath on her skin. "Now who's cheating?"

"You gave me no choice. I had to open my eyes to make sure you were okay and not drowning, because you weren't answering." He pulled her closer, so that his chest aligned with her spine and she could feel his solid erection pressing against the curve of her bottom. "I'm thinking there should be some kind of penalty for that."

Oh yes, she thought, and hoped it was a very sexy punishment. "What did you have in mind?"

"For starters, a long, deep French kiss." He turned her around so she was facing him, his gaze burning hot as he stared at her mouth and his hands drifted up over the indentation of her waist until his thumbs brushed the undersides of her bare breasts. "Do you think you can handle that?"

She was ready to handle anything he dished out. "Yeah, I think I can," she whispered, and tilted her head up, meeting him halfway.

Pleased with her acquiescence, he smiled and covered her mouth with his, and her lips automatically parted for him, welcoming the slow, delicious slide of his tongue. While the kiss at the nightclub had been fueled by anger and aggression, this one tasted of unadulterated passion and literally took her breath away. His arm curled around her back, and he hauled her against his body, crushing her breasts against his rock-hard torso.

Her blood started to simmer, making her feel more alive, more turned on, than she had in a very long time. Since *him,* to be exact, and she'd almost forgotten what real, true desire felt like. She'd only known this kind of hunger with Noah, and now, as adults, it was so much hotter and stronger. And far more intense.

A relentless surge of arousal thrummed through her, and not wanting the wonderful sensation to end, she framed his face in her hands and kissed him wholeheartedly. Beneath the water, she wrapped her legs tight around his waist so the hard ridge of his erection pressed against her aching sex, fervently wishing that they'd both stripped off their underwear so she could feel his thick length stroking along her soft, wet folds. Or better yet, thrusting deep inside her body.

Groaning at her enthusiastic response, he twisted the long strands of her wet hair around his fist and pulled her head back. His lips left hers, and he kissed his way across her jaw to her neck. Another longer, firmer tug on her hair had her back arching and her breasts rising, firm and pale and glistening damply in the moonlight.

"Beautiful," he murmured in awe, just before he dipped his head to taste her.

She felt his breath on her skin, a warm, steamy rush of air just before he swept his tongue around a taut, sensitive nipple. She shuddered and moaned in frustration and need. Her hand palmed the back of his neck to pull him closer, urging him to take more.

He wasn't to be rushed. He teased her mercilessly, laving the aching peak with his tongue, using his teeth to heighten the pleasure/pain, and when he *finally* opened his mouth over her breast and sucked she went wild.

She started to pant, and of their own accord her hips bucked against his in an attempt to seek some kind of relief for the building pressure gathering between her thighs. Shamelessly she rubbed against him, and he pressed back, grinding into her, knowing exactly what her body needed, and it didn't take long for her to go up in flames.

His mouth came back to hers as she climaxed, absorbing her soft cries while his hands stroked her back. When the last of her orgasm faded, she buried her face against Noah's neck and sagged full-weight against him, grateful that the water, and the hands now beneath her thighs, helped to keep her body afloat.

"I want you, Jessie," he whispered in her ear.

There was no mistaking the raw emotion in Noah's voice or the echoing response resonating in her soul. She lifted her head to look into his dark eyes. "I want you, too."

Relief etched his features. "God, I was hoping you'd feel that way."

Sliding a hand between them, she stroked his thick shaft through his briefs, relishing the deep, guttural groan that escaped him.

"Condoms are in the bedroom," he said, his voice now sounding like gravel.

It was on the tip of her tongue to tell him that they didn't need one, but she caught herself. That statement would raise questions she wasn't prepared to answer. So, instead, she smiled at him and unlocked her legs from around his waist. "Then what are we waiting for?"

They got out of the pool, and Noah helped her to dry off with one of the towels folded on a nearby table, then wiped himself down, too. He scooped up their clothes, grabbed her hand, and she followed him back into the house, a bit modest about walking around in her panties and nothing else. He led the way up a darkened staircase, and when they reached the spacious master bedroom and he reached to turn on the lamp on the nightstand next to the bed, she caught his wrist.

"Leave it off," she said, her tone soft and more insecure than she'd intended, because in the light there were things she couldn't hide. Things she didn't want him to see. Like the scar from her emergency hysterectomy.

"No way," he said, and switched on the lamp, illuminating the bedroom.

He retrieved a condom from the bedside drawer and tossed it onto the mattress. Quickly he stripped off his wet briefs, giving her only a handful of seconds to admire his impressive erection before he stepped up to her and slipped his fingers into the waistband of her lace undies. He skimmed them over her hips and down her thighs, until they dropped to the floor at her feet.

Her hand automatically moved to cover the scar on her abdomen, but he caught both of her wrists and gently held them away. "I want to see you, Jessie," he said huskily, obviously thinking she meant to cover other aspects of her body. "All of you. In the light."

He pressed her down onto the mattress so she was lying on the soft comforter, then pushed her thighs apart for him to kneel in between, leaving her utterly exposed to his slow, thorough perusal. His heated gaze traveled from her face down to her breasts and continued leisurely over her belly, past the thin line of her scar, and came to a stop when he reached the apex of her thighs.

Placing his hands on her knees, he caressed his palms up the inside of her legs, spreading them wider as he moved closer to her feminine core. His breathing deepened as his fingers touched her wet heat, glided through her slick folds, and stroked her clitoris with his thumb until her hips were moving in tandem with his slow, exquisite, torturous exploration.

"I want to see you," he said again, watching with heavy-lidded eyes as he slid a finger deep, deep inside of her and she arched shamelessly against his hand, whimpering her need for him. "Just . . . like . . . this. You're so gorgeous. Every single inch of you."

Her body wept for him, and another climax gathered strength within her. She fought the fluttering sensation between her legs, because this time she didn't want to go over that crest alone, without him, and told him so. "As good as this feels, I want to come with *you* inside me."

His eyes blazed with heat and hunger. "It's hard to turn down that kind of invitation."

"Then don't."

While she watched, he rolled on the condom; then he moved over her, his mouth curved in one of those adorable, boyish grins she'd thought she'd never see again. But the memories of her youth didn't last long, not when Noah, the man, filled her to the hilt in one smooth, hard thrust.

She gasped, and he groaned, deep and low, as her inner muscles clamped tight around him. She had little time to adjust to the size of him, to let her body reacquaint itself with the heat and fullness of having a man inside her again before Noah increased his pace, the quick, unrestrained pump of his hips leaving her no choice but to slide her arms around his shoulders and hang on for the pleasurable ride.

"You feel so damn good," he growled, his voice infused with raw hunger as the molten friction between them burned brighter with every stroke of his body inside of hers. "So tight and hot and . . . *Jesus,* I'm going to come."

So was she.

He tossed his head back and arched high and hard, and she watched him lose control, lose himself in her, a man reduced to pure emotion and desire. It was that thought that ultimately sent her over the edge right along with him.

When they'd both caught their breaths, Noah pressed his lips to hers in a soft, sweet, romantic kiss before lifting his head and staring deep into her eyes.

"I missed you," he said, the words so honest that Jessica was compelled to be just as truthful.

"I missed you, too." Every single day they'd been apart.

The feeling of contentment spreading through her was something Jessica had spent the past nine years searching for . . . but had never been able to grasp. And as much as she reveled in the peaceful sensation filling her, she knew it wouldn't last forever.

But for now, for tonight, her world was perfect once again.

Chapter Fourteen

Drifting somewhere between slumber and a dream-like state, Zoe decided it was a lovely place to be, and she didn't want to wake up anytime soon. Not when she was curled up to Sean's warm, muscular body, the musky, male scent of his skin teasing her senses and eliciting a slow burn of desire down low, between her thighs.

Sighing and embracing the luxurious sensations, she snuggled even closer, pressing her face against his neck and sliding her calf between his, wishing they were both completely naked. Her hand, which had been resting on his flat stomach, began to move in a curious exploration, up over the pecs defining his chest, skimming across the nipples that were as stiff as her own, and down the ridges lining his abdomen.

His muscles grew taut and his breathing deepened, but if he was conscious he didn't make any move to stop her.

She was glad, because he felt good. Really good. Touching him and letting the arousal and anticipation simmer and build was such a nice, pleasant distraction from the reality of what she knew she had to face once she awoke.

Slowly, blindly, she followed the sexy trail of hair dusting his belly as it spiraled downward, and when she reached the waistband of his briefs she slipped her hand beneath the elastic barrier. The moment the tips of her fingers grazed the taut crown of his engorged shaft and her thumb caught the slick moisture beading on the plump head, her lazy quest came to an abrupt end.

With a deep, animalistic growl, he circled his fingers around her wrist and jerked her hand from his shorts. Quicker than she could gasp, he had her flat on her back, her hand pinned next to her head. He loomed over her, his masculine features etched with lust, the dark stubble on his jaw adding to the edgy, bad-boy attitude. The blatant heat in his eyes pierced straight to her soul, the depths of his gaze an intense shade of midnight blue.

A shameless excitement rushed through her veins, and his stare dropped to the pulse beating wildly at the base of her throat, then lower, to the unbound breasts and hard nipples outlined in the soft fabric of the T-shirt he'd given her to wear. A muscle in his cheek ticced and he dragged his gaze back up to hers, blasting her with a look so carnal she felt branded.

Last night he'd held her without sexual intent, comforted her with platonic caresses, and played her knight in shining armor with chivalry and respect. He'd proved to be a man she could depend on and trust, which was becoming a rarity in her life, and his kindness had been exactly what she'd needed at the time.

There was no trace of that subdued gentleness this morning, and the aggression and barely leashed need tightening his body was exactly what she wanted from him now.

"Don't . . ." His gruff voice trailed off and he shook his dark head, looking agonized and conflicted. "Just *don't.*"

Her heart was beating erratically in her chest, and while she heard the warning lacing his voice she didn't heed it. "Don't what?" she whispered in a challenge.

His jaw clenched. "Don't touch me like that."

She smiled, which he didn't seem to appreciate. After everything that had happened to her yesterday, she wanted to replace all the pain, fear, and even the awful truth with something she could believe in and trust. And that something, that *someone,* was Sean.

With her free hand, she glided it up the slope of his back, letting her fingers dig into firm muscles, and felt him shudder beneath her palm. "What if I want to touch you like that? And more?"

The fingers still trapping her other arm on the mattress flexed, but he didn't let go. "You don't know what you want right now," he snapped irritably. "You're still half-asleep."

Not anymore, she wasn't. She was wide awake and knew exactly what she craved. "You don't want me?" It was a stupid question, but it was the only way to get him to respond the way she knew he would.

He didn't disappoint. Swearing beneath his breath, he ruthlessly shoved his solid erection against her hip, so there was no mistaking his desire for her. "Does it *feel* like I don't want you?" he asked, his eyes shining with frustration. "I'm so fucking hard right now, have been all night long; that's how bad I want you."

He was being so noble, and it was the very last thing she wanted from him. "Then take me," she said, and lifted her head, touching her lips to his in a soft, teasing kiss.

Another curse fell from his lips, and she felt something in him snap loose—like his too-gallant restraint. Letting go of her hand, he slid his palm around to the nape of her neck, his fingers delving into her hair, then fisting in the strands as he kissed her back, much harder and deeper than what she'd just offered. His tongue swept into her mouth, seeking, searching, *demanding,* and she responded just as avidly.

As his mouth ravaged hers, he shifted closer, and she

twisted her legs around his, trying to adjust their bodies so the length of his rigid shaft was grinding against her sex, but all he allowed was the press of his muscled thigh between hers.

It wasn't enough. She wanted her clothing off and full body contact—skin on skin. Her entire being shook with need, and she clutched at his shoulders, arching desperately into him. Her hips undulated frantically against his, aiming for a deeper, hotter connection he didn't seem inclined to give.

He broke their kiss, and she whimpered in frustration, which was quickly replaced by a soft sigh of relief when his hands reached between them and tugged her shirt up and off. Tossing the wad of material to the floor, he didn't waste any precious time in dipping his head and pulling a nipple between his damp lips. He groaned against her breast as he sucked hard on the taut bud, then bit gently.

She inhaled a quick, shocked breath, then purred with pleasure when he soothed the sting with his soft, velvety tongue before switching to her other breast and giving it the same delightful treatment. The swirl of his tongue laving her nipple and the deep suctioning heat of his mouth had her moving restlessly beneath him.

She fisted her hands in the covers to keep from thrashing. "Sean, *please*."

"Shhh. I'll give you what you need," he promised as he scattered hot, damp kisses down her torso, then flicked his tongue into her navel.

She gasped, feeling that wicked stroke even lower, between her thighs. Impatiently he tugged the front ties loose on her drawstring shorts, and she lifted her hips so he could pull them, and her panties, down her legs. The clothing joined her shirt on the floor, leaving her completely naked for the first time in front of him, while he still wore his briefs.

So not fair, but she figured he'd get around to removing them eventually.

"Spread your legs for me, sweetheart," he murmured huskily.

She complied, and he let his appreciative gaze slowly trail over her body—across the straining peaks of her breasts, the softness of her belly, then finally where she was wet and swollen with need for him.

His eyes darkened, stealing the breath from her lungs, but not as much as his next calculated move did. Moving lower on the mattress, he settled between her thighs, his broad shoulders forcing her legs even farther apart. He glanced up over her prone body, capturing her gaze with his, the unbridled hunger gleaming in his eyes making his intentions very clear.

Oh, God, *he was going to go down on her.*

Then every thought flew from her mind as he did just that—with enthusiasm and passion. She moaned, her hips jerking involuntarily at the first wet, rough rasp of his tongue against her. Then she shuddered when he added longer strokes and a firm fluttering of his tongue on her clitoris. He gave a murmur of approval and added his talented hand into the mix to explore her intimate folds, rubbing her slick flesh, and slipped one finger, then two, inside of her.

Between his wicked mouth and skillful, thrusting fingers mimicking the act of sex, she turned liquid with desire. The tension coiling within her escalated, higher and tighter, making her restless with the need for *more.* His fingers slid from her channel, but before she could issue a form of protest his tongue was there, pushing deep inside of her in a greedy, openmouthed French kiss.

It was like nothing she'd ever felt or experienced before. Her initial gasp of shock gave way to a low, sultry moan and total body ecstasy. She threaded her fingers through his soft, silky hair as what promised to be a rapturous climax rose inside of her. She fought the sensations, wanting to savor every last second, but Sean was so avid, so determined, and she didn't stand a chance against his seduction tactics.

Closing her eyes, she tossed her head back on the pillow and cried out as a wave of sexual bliss crashed over her and she came in a hot rush of intense pleasure. He rode out the orgasm and kept kissing her intimately, deeply, until the tremors wracking her body finally subsided.

She expected him to move over her and take his very generous foreplay to its logical conclusion, but instead, with an agonized groan, he pressed his cheek against her stomach, as if he was trying to regain his composure. His breathing was so harsh, his body undeniably aroused and strung tight, and she didn't understand what he was waiting for.

Gently she dragged the tips of her fingers through his hair, wondering what had gone wrong when everything had felt so right only moments ago. "Sean?"

"Don't." Jerking away from her touch, he stood up at the side of the bed, his gaze both anguished and angry as he yanked the covers up over her naked body. He muttered a curse word that singed her ears, then turned and stalked off to the adjoining bathroom, closing the door a little harder than necessary.

Stunned and confused, Zoe tossed the covers right back off and sat up on the edge of the mattress. She stared at the bathroom door and frowned.

What the *hell* was that all about? She honestly didn't have a clue. For some reason, he was resisting her when that was the last thing she wanted, and she had no idea why he'd ended things so abruptly. Especially after what he'd just done to her. It didn't get more intimate between two people than *that*.

She was a grown woman, capable of making her own choices, and her decision to have sex with Sean hadn't been made lightly. He was the one person who'd been there for her, the person who'd made her feel safe and secure when her life as she'd once known it was falling apart before her eyes.

After the attack in her parking garage, she'd wanted that comfort, that closeness with him, and while he'd given her an amazing orgasm and her body was physically satiated, deep inside she felt empty, as though something vital was still missing—an emotional connection she knew Sean was capable of giving her, even if he had his doubts.

If he thought he was doing her a favor by walking away, he was wrong. And Zoe intended to prove it to him.

Physically aching and emotionally rattled, Sean stepped beneath the spray of hot, steaming water, his entire body screaming with the need for sexual relief. He'd never been one for cold showers; they were more torturous than helpful to the cause, and he'd learned long ago that it was just easier to take care of business and get it out of his system.

Yeah, like he'd *ever* be able to get Zoe out of his system.

Shit. After he had watched Zoe come apart for him, after he had felt her every response to his intimate kisses, after he had tasted the depths of her passion, everything about her was indelibly etched into his memory. And when she'd cried out with the force of her climax he swore he'd never heard anything so sweet, so sexy, so cock-swelling erotic that he'd nearly orgasmed right along with her.

The recollection caused his stiff dick to throb painfully, and with a scowl he dipped his head beneath the showerhead, drenching himself completely in the heated cascade of water.

As much as he'd been tempted to bury himself deep inside Zoe, to take what she was offering and slake the lust that had been riding him hard all night long, Sean ultimately couldn't do it. He knew that sex *meant* something to her, and what scared the crap out of him was the realization that it was beginning to mean something to him, too, when he'd never allowed any woman to be anything more to him than a good time in the sack.

He honestly, truly cared about Zoe, and he knew developing any further feelings for her could lead nowhere. Their lives were too different, their pasts too intertwined and complicated. He despised her father for what he'd done to Sean's dad, and once Zoe knew the depths of her father's deception, along with Grant Russo's connection to Sean's dad, she'd never accept a man like Sean in her life—a man who'd also once been a con artist and used people's weaknesses for monetary gain.

While he'd turned over a new leaf when Caleb had given him a second chance to clean up his act when he'd gotten out of prison years ago, Sean would never be able to erase his past or forget the less than honorable things that he'd done. And no woman—especially a sophisticated, successful woman like Zoe—wanted the stigma of being with an ex–con man.

For the first time ever, Sean experienced a twinge of pain at having to let a woman go because of the stupid, senseless choices he'd made in his past. And it royally sucked—which was why this was a great example of why he didn't do relationships or long-term commitment. And a woman like Zoe would eventually want both.

He inhaled a deep breath of steam, not surprised to see that even his oppressive thoughts had done nothing to deflate his straining erection. No, there was only one way to take care of that particular problem, and if he was going to be spending most of his time around Zoe, then he desperately needed the release now.

Reaching for the liquid soap, he lathered his palms until they were slippery and took his cock in hand. All he needed was a few minutes, fast and furious, and he'd be able to get on with his day without being half-aroused around Zoe.

Closing his eyes, he began stroking his shaft in his fist and went with the first fantasy that tumbled into his mind—where he finished what he'd started with Zoe in his bed less than ten minutes ago. He imagined crawling over her soft, curvy body and groaned when he thought about how wet and tight she'd be when he sank into her and how she'd wrap her slender legs around his waist and encourage his heavy, driving, pounding thrusts. . . .

Oh yeah . . . he was so close, so damn close . . .

The soft click of the shower's glass door opening, then closing, yanked him back from the orgasm gathering force. He clenched his jaw in frustration, knowing Zoe was standing behind him. Despite being caught in the act, he didn't turn around, and he refused to release his nearly bursting, aching cock from his tight grip. Nor was he about to apologize for jerking off, either, because it was her own fault for coming into the bathroom unannounced and catching an eyeful.

"What are you doing in here?" he asked gruffly as the shower spray battered his chest and water sluiced down to his groin. He knew she was probably getting wet, too, but didn't care about that, either. He just wanted her gone.

He tensed when he felt her hand on his back and bit back a groan as she oh, so slowly slid her fingers down the slope of his spine in a wet, sensual caress. "Why did you leave me?"

He didn't have to ask what she meant. Even though he'd given her a shattering orgasm, he knew he'd left her wanting. He never should have touched her in the first place, but she obviously didn't know the meaning of *don't*, and he'd been weak and unable to resist her. "I left you because it was the right thing to do."

"Says who?" she asked softly while the tip of one finger traced the crease in his buttocks, all the way down to the crux of his thighs.

Jesus. With his legs braced apart, her fingers dipped lower, brushing over the lightly furred skin of his taut balls. In his palm, his cock surged. Reflexively his fingers squeezed, and his heart thundered in his chest as he desperately held on to his sanity.

"Says me," he rasped. "Trust me, you'll thank me later." When she discovered everything about him. Things that would shock and disappoint her.

She closed the distance between them, aligning the front of her body against his back. Her bare chest seared his skin, as did the pointed tips of her breasts. Against his ass, he could feel the soft, feminine tuft of hair that covered her mound, and it was all he could do not to turn around and take her up against the tiled shower wall.

Her flattened palms slid around his torso and over his abs, adding to the lust brewing within him. One hand glided up to his chest, where her fingers plucked at his nipple, while the other skimmed down his belly to his groin. She nudged his hand out of the way and replaced it with her own snug grasp around his shaft.

"I'd rather thank you *now,* by reciprocating the pleasure you gave me," she said.

A deep, primitive groan rumbled in his chest. "Zoe . . ."

"Shhh. I'll give you what you need," she persisted, repeating the words he'd said to her earlier, just before he'd seduced her with his mouth. "Just put your hands on the wall and let me take care of you."

He knew he ought to object and stop her, but his control was hanging by a thin thread and he was quickly learning that he had absolutely no willpower when it came to her. And when she dragged the pad of her thumb over the crown of his cock, teasing him with the promise of ecstasy, he decided that he'd rather come in her hand than his own.

He splayed his palms on the wet tiles and let her have her way with him. Whatever kind of sensual madness she wanted to inflict, he was game. And it was a good thing, too, since she seemed to want to take her time and make him suffer. Slowly, rhythmically, her wicked hand swept up and down his shaft, pulling and stroking his dick. At times, her fist crept up over the tip and the water and last remnants of soap created a suction over the sensitive head. The pleasure was so intense, so erotic, his eyes rolled back in his head.

If that wasn't enough to short-circuit his brain, she grabbed a handful of his hair and gently pulled his head back so she could whisper in his ear how good he felt. She kissed his shoulder, licked the moisture from his skin, then gently bit the side of his neck, all the while her hips moved sinuously against his ass.

It was sensory overload. Desire coiled through him, his cock stretching and pulsing with a rush of blood. As if sensing how close he was to coming, she accelerated her pace, faster, tighter, each slick slide of her palm creating a heated friction that sent him over the razor-sharp edge of need and straight into oblivion. He groaned and shuddered violently as his climax roared through him, so powerful, so fierce, it drained him not only physically but emotionally, too.

It was the most amazing orgasm he'd ever had in his entire life, but it changed absolutely nothing between them.

Chapter Fifteen

Zoe was beginning to hate the conference room at the Reliance Group offices. Nothing good happened in this room, and she had a feeling that today's meeting would be no different.

At the moment, she was sitting alone, waiting for Caleb and Sean to arrive, which gave her too much time to think about what the two men wanted to discuss with her, and to also replay in her head this morning's sexy trysts with Sean.

Of course, the most prominent memory that was indelibly etched in her mind was the way he'd made her come undone with the deepest, most intimate kisses she'd ever had the pleasure of experiencing. His mouth had been ravenous, unrelenting, and earth-shattering. Even now, thinking about the scandalous things he'd done with his tongue had her shifting restlessly in her chair and her cheeks warming from the erotic recollection.

If that provocative encounter with Sean hadn't been enough to leave her aching for more, then walking in on him in the shower had been like adding fuel to her desire for him. Instead of being shocked by catching him in a blatantly sexual situation, she'd been turned on—and unable to turn away. He'd looked so masculine, so virile, so overwhelmingly male as his muscular body bunched and flexed as he stroked himself toward gratification.

She'd wanted to be the one to take him over the edge, just as he'd pleasured her. And while it had taken a bit of convincing on her part, when he'd finally relented she'd felt an undeniable streak of excitement bolt through her. She'd loved pressing her wet body up against his, enjoyed every moment of touching him and feeling him pulse and swell in her hand, and reveled in the heady sense of feminine power in being the one to make him lose control.

And that, in itself, had been magnificent to watch.

Even now, remembering every detail of his frantic, frenzied orgasm, along with the searing heat of his release against her palm, she bit back an inappropriate groan, even as an equally inappropriate rush of damp heat settled between her thighs.

Unfortunately, after their steamy encounter in the shower there was no mistaking the emotional walls Sean had erected, and she'd instinctively known it wasn't a good time to talk about what had happened between them or where it could possibly lead. Figuring he needed time to process everything, she'd let him have his space.

They'd each gotten dressed and ready for the day, then stopped for a quick breakfast quiche and a vanilla latte for her from a nearby French bakery before heading to her apartment so she could change from yesterday's clothes. She'd also packed an overnight bag to stay at Sean's place until they caught the guy stalking her.

Seeing her car in the parking garage right where she'd left it, the tires still brutally slashed, had caused her to shiver with a new dose of fear. Sean must have seen her reaction, because he'd quickly assured her that no one was going to hurt her, not while he was around. He'd promised to make the arrangements to get her car fixed, but for now he'd be her chauffeur and drive her wherever she needed to go.

And the first place on *his* agenda had been the Onyx, because according to Sean there were some things about her father he and Caleb needed to talk to her about. What those *things* entailed she didn't have a clue, but after what she'd learned from George at her father's office yesterday, she was preparing herself for the worst.

Growing increasingly anxious the longer she sat, she nearly jumped out of her seat when the door behind her abruptly opened and Sean and Caleb walked in.

"Sorry to leave you in here for so long," Sean said as he shut the door behind them for privacy, his demeanor as cool and professional as Caleb's. "We were talking to Lucas about your father's hard drive, and I gave him the one you recovered from Sheila's computer yesterday, which he'll start analyzing right away."

"Has he found anything on my father's hard drive yet?" Zoe asked hopefully.

"Nothing significant," Sean said with a shake of his head as he sat diagonally from her, and Caleb took the chair across the table, so they were all facing one another. "Your father's home computer is pretty clean."

Sean looked as disappointed as she felt.

Caleb set a file folder on the table in front of him but didn't open it. "Now that Lucas has Sheila's hard drive, he'll be sure to do a cross-check reference with any names he's already pulled from your father's computer, to see if there are any connections between the two."

She frowned, not quite following what he meant. "What do names have to do with anything?"

Caleb and Sean exchanged a glance, a silent look of understanding passing between the two men before Sean replied to her question.

"Because chances are your father has taken on a false identity."

"Oh." She didn't know what else to say, because *that* thought hadn't crossed her mind. The possibility that her father had gone so far as to assume a false identity made Zoe's mind reel, because it would mean that he was deliberately trying to hide something.

"Have you ever heard of the name Elliott Cooke?" Caleb asked.

She thought for a moment, but no recognition surfaced in her mind. "No. Why? Who is he?"

"Your father," Caleb stated in that blunt way of his. "Elliott Cooke is an alias he's used in the past."

Her stomach started a slow twist of dread. She looked at Sean, who, for now, was sitting quietly and letting Caleb carry the conversation—even though she was certain Sean had knowledge of all these details about her father, too.

"What would he use an alias for?" she asked, needing the answer, even though she instinctively knew she wasn't going to like what she heard.

Caleb paused for a moment, and a hint of compassion flashed in his gaze, as if he was well aware of how much his next words were going to hurt. "He used the name to help orchestrate a Ponzi scheme years ago."

Oh, God. She could hardly process the implications of Caleb's claim, but as much as she wanted to deny what he'd just told her, she'd come to learn that there was no reason for Caleb to lie.

Ignoring the pressure in her chest, she shored her fortitude for what she knew was going to be a very difficult conversation. "When did this Ponzi scheme take place?"

"Twelve years ago this summer," Caleb replied. "Do you remember your father being on trial during that time?"

Zoe mentally thought back and realized she'd been fifteen at the time and had just finished her sophomore year in high school. She also recalled how that particular summer had been a tumultuous one between her parents, filled with loud, hostile arguments that had ultimately led to their divorce. Then again, most of their marriage had been strained and antagonistic, but there had definitely been an added element of stress that summer that Zoe had been very aware of.

"I do remember that year," she said, and as those old memories emerged she tried to make sense of them now that Caleb had provided a solid reason why her parents' relationship had completely deteriorated. "I heard arguments between my parents, and I knew something was going on with my father, but not specifics."

She hesitated for a moment, then decided there was no reason for her to keep anything from Caleb, or Sean, either. "There was one time when I overheard them fighting about him being at the police station, and how humiliating it had been for my mother. When I asked her what was going on, she was vague with her answer and told me that my father's being at the police station was a big misunderstanding. A few days after that, my mother took me to Europe for the summer, and I only talked to my father a handful of times while we were gone. By the time we came back to the States, it seemed like nothing had ever happened."

"That's because your father cut a plea deal to cooperate with the prosecutor, which included testifying against the other man arrested in the same case," Caleb said as his fingers absently tapped the file folder still lying on the table in front of him. "The attorney who represented your father maintained that he had no role in the management of the investment deals and had just been a securities broker who marketed the investments to his clients."

She was feeling desperate enough to believe in her father's innocence that she latched onto the positive aspects of what Caleb had just told her. "He didn't go to jail, so that must be true."

Sean, who'd sat silently across from her while Caleb gave her the details of her father's past arrest, finally spoke up. "Your father knew *exactly* what was going on," he said, the terse tone of his voice catching Zoe off guard. "He was just very careful about his involvement so there was no direct evidence to trace him, or the name he was using at the time, to the crime."

She stiffened, a little wary of the sudden animosity radiating off Sean, and she couldn't help but wonder where his negative energy stemmed from. "How do you know that?"

A muscle in his jaw clenched. "Because Grant Russo's partner was *my* father, Casey O'Brien."

She stared at Sean in confusion and disbelief, certain she'd misheard him. And if what he'd said *was* true, why had he kept such a huge, shocking revelation from her when they'd already shared so much? Before she could find the words to respond, Caleb stood up, and she shifted her gaze to the other man, taking the much-needed moment to process the implications of Sean's statement.

"I think the two of you can handle the discussion from here and could use some privacy," Caleb said, obviously feeling the sudden strain in the room and knowing when to make a graceful exit.

But before he turned to go, he pushed the file folder across the table toward Zoe. "Here's an investigative report on your father, along with information on his past arrest for you to read. But I think Sean will be able to give you a more accurate account of your father's relationship with Casey O'Brien and what really happened between them."

Caleb left the conference room, and an uncomfortable

silence settled between her and Sean. Not sure what to say or do, she reached for the file folder, opened it, and scanned the reports and articles inside.

She felt Sean's gaze on her the entire time, watching her, no doubt waiting for some kind of reaction. But as she perused the contents of the file and evidence of her father's association to the case, she realized that most of the reports and newspaper articles provided only superficial information and lacked the depth and knowledge of what really had transpired between Grant Russo and Casey O'Brien.

Knowing that Sean was three years older than her, that put him at eighteen when his own father had been arrested. She suspected that Sean hadn't been as sheltered as she'd been before his father's arrest or during the actual trial. Which meant Sean most likely had a better understanding of the case, a deeper knowledge of the facts, and had been exposed to details and truths that the media wouldn't have known.

Zoe was torn between being pissed with Sean, wondering why he'd withheld such crucial information about both of their fathers from her, and wanting to know all the details about the dad she'd adored but hadn't known at all. Understanding what happened in the past had to come first, then she'd deal with Sean's second deception.

The realization that she was deeply hurt by this latest turn of events told her just how far she'd fallen for Sean, in such a short amount of time. But at least now she had a better idea of why he'd put up a wall between them and tried to reject her advances this morning. Apparently, he had some scruples about lying and sleeping with her. Just not enough to make him come clean earlier with the very fundamental fact that their fathers had shared a criminal past.

Exhaling a taut breath, she met Sean's gaze. He was

still watching her with eyes that were dark and shadowed, and his expression was more stoic than she'd ever seen it before. Every line in his body was tense, as if he was waiting for some kind of argument from her.

"I want you to tell me what you know about your father's relationship with mine, and what really happened between them," she said, closing the file Caleb had given her and pushing it aside. "Not the watered-down version I just read in the newspaper articles in that folder, but what *you* know. Then we'll talk about why you kept the truth from me."

A skeptical look passed over Sean's features. "Are you sure you're prepared to face the truth?"

She heard the doubt in his voice, along with the slight warning, and didn't let either sway her decision. "I already know I'm not going to like what I hear, but I need to find out what really happened. *All* of it this time."

Sean had known today's conversation with Zoe was going to be difficult, and he was amazed at how well and easily she'd accepted that her father had led the life of a con man so many years ago. Even before she'd seen the documents, she hadn't argued with Caleb's version of the past and had listened with a surprising calm.

But as soon as Caleb left the two of them alone, it became very clear just how upset she was with Sean for keeping their fathers' past association a secret from her. Honestly, Sean couldn't blame her for being angry, and while he questioned the wisdom in holding back this particular information until now, it was too late to change the decision he'd made. He'd only meant to spare her more heartache and protect her from the unpleasant reality of what and who her father really was.

Unfortunately, Sean's good intentions had backfired on him, and now the only thing he could do to try to repair the damage he'd done was divulge the truth about what had transpired between Grant Russo and Casey O'Brien all those years ago.

Needing a moment to gather his thoughts, he stood up and walked to the far side of the conference room and retrieved two bottles of water from the mini-refrigerator before returning to his seat next to Zoe. He gave her one of the chilled bottles, then twisted the cap open on his and chugged half of the liquid, wishing it were something much stronger than water. She took a sip of hers, and waited for him to speak.

Finally, he did. "Your father and mine were business partners and started a real estate investment company together, and over the course of three years they scammed hundreds of clients out of over five million dollars."

A flicker of pain flashed in her eyes as she listened to the extent of her father's deceit, and as much as Sean hated adding to her misery, he was relieved to finally get it all out in the open between the two of them.

"At the time, your father was using the name Elliott Cooke for all his business transactions, and he was very careful to make sure that my father was in control of all the investments so he wasn't linked to any of the fraud," Sean went on as he absently swiped the condensation on his bottle of water with the tips of his fingers. "All the paperwork pointed toward my father being the one who regulated all the securities and payouts to the investors, and even to himself and your dad. When things started falling apart and the company couldn't pay the promised returns to their clients, legal authorities figured out what was going on and arrested your father, and mine, for securities fraud."

Still, Zoe said nothing, though the anguish etching her features spoke volumes.

"After the arrest, your father insisted that he had no idea

that the money deposited into his bank account wasn't legitimate profits, since he hadn't been in charge of any of the accounting or payouts." Despite his attempts, Sean found it difficult to temper the bitterness he felt toward her father.

"Since prosecutors were unable to find any evidence to the contrary, your father struck a plea deal, which included his full cooperation in the investigation of the case and his testimony *against* his partner. Your father provided all the evidence to put my father away, using information he never would have known if he wasn't somehow involved in the Ponzi scheme from the very beginning."

"Oh, God." She looked both stunned and devastated, and Sean wasn't even finished yet.

"In return for your father's full cooperation, he pled no contest to a single misdemeanor securities violation, lost his broker's license for three years, and was sentenced to the twenty-seven days he'd already served in jail while waiting for the trail to begin. Then he was placed on probation for five years. My father, on the other hand, received a fifteen-year prison sentence, which he is still currently serving."

Sean exhaled a deep breath. "My father was guilty of fraud, but so was yours," he said, wanting to be sure she understood that Grant Russo had been equally responsible for what had happened.

"I believe you," she whispered in a strained voice, then pressed her fingers to her lips as tears filled her eyes. "And I'm so sorry."

He frowned, because he had no idea what she had to apologize for. "For what?"

She wiped away a single tear that fell down her cheek. "That my father betrayed yours and sent him to jail."

Sean felt his own chest tighten in response, and it took

effort to resist the urge to pull her into his arms and comfort her.

"You have nothing to be sorry for," he said, refusing to let her carry that burden.

"Why didn't you tell me all this sooner?" she asked. "Like the last time I was in this conference room learning that my father was being accused of investment fraud. Don't you think that would have been a good opportunity to let me in on the fact that your father and mine had once been partners in a Ponzi scheme?"

"In hindsight, yes," Sean said, and scrubbed a hand along his jaw, wishing now that he had done things differently. "But I wasn't sure you were ready to hear the whole truth about your father, or that you'd believe my story." He swallowed his pride and gave her the apology she deserved: "I made a mistake, Zoe, and I'm sorry."

She stared at him for long, tense seconds before exhaling a slow, even breath of air. "I just have one more question, and I'd appreciate an honest answer. Did you take on this case for revenge?"

He thought about his answer very carefully before replying. "I took the case because I work for The Reliance Group and that's my job. But I fully admit that I resent your father for what he did all those years ago. My father was guilty and he's paying the price for his actions, but your dad sold out mine and walked away without looking back. I'm not looking for revenge as much as I'm hoping for justice and retribution."

Unable to read her expression, Sean was left wondering where, exactly, things stood between them. She didn't strike him as a woman who held grudges, but he had a feeling that earning her complete forgiveness would take time.

A quick, brisk knock on the door echoed in the conference room, and a second later Nathan Fox stepped inside.

Grateful for the interruption, Sean introduced Zoe to his co-worker and the head of security at the Onyx; then Nathan got down to the reason why he was there.

"We've reviewed all the surveillance tapes from your apartment building around the time of your attack yesterday," he said, addressing Zoe. "And unfortunately, we weren't able to ID the guy on the bike. The license plate had been taped over, so there's no way to trace the bike's registration, or who the owner is."

"I can't say I'm surprised," Zoe said with a shake of her head. "The guy obviously knew what he was doing."

"Yes, he did," Nathan agreed as he slid his hands into the front pockets of his slacks. "Sean also told us about the things this man said to you, about being double-crossed by your father and someone named Bunny."

Zoe nodded, her expression pained. "I already told Sean that I don't know anyone named Bunny, so I'm afraid I'm not going to be able to help you much with that bit of information."

"That's okay." Nathan's gaze shone with compassion for Zoe's situation. "It's something new we didn't have a day ago and it might help us uncover some kind of lead on your father."

"I hope so," she said, her voice weary.

"Since we weren't able to nail the guy who attacked you, it's imperative that you're watched twenty-four/seven," Nathan told her. "If Sean can't be with you, then we'll make arrangements so someone else will be."

"Okay." Zoe's fingers absently played with the long crystal necklace draped along the front of her blouse as she talked to Nathan. "Construction inside the boutique is scheduled to start in a few days, and inventory will be arriving, too. Is that going to be a problem?"

"No. Anyone who steps foot into the boutique will have to submit to a thorough background check and you'll have an armed security guard posted inside the shop while you're there," Nathan assured her.

"Thank you," she said, and visibly relaxed. "I really do appreciate everything you're doing to keep me safe and protected."

It was hard not to notice how gracious Zoe was with Nathan, and Sean could only hope she extended the same reprieve to him for keeping the news about her father a secret for so long.

"You're welcome." Nathan clasped Sean's shoulder in his hand and graced Zoe with a friendly grin. "Trust me, we've got you covered, and I know for a fact that Sean isn't about to let anything bad happen to you, either."

"I know," she said.

Zoe met Sean's gaze, and in that instant, looking into her eyes, he experienced a small sense of satisfaction. While he might have caused her a wealth of disappointment today and shaken the foundation of what was between them, she ultimately trusted him to keep her safe. And right now, that's all that mattered to him.

As far as he was concerned, it was a good thing she no longer had that total faith in him, because his own past was marred with a criminal record that proved he was no better than her father.

And that, Sean reminded himself, was ultimately the reason why he and Zoe didn't stand a chance together beyond this case.

Chapter Sixteen

Sitting on the couch in Sean's living room later that evening, Zoe clutched her cell phone in her hand as the revealing conversation with Sean that morning played over in her mind like a bad horror movie—as it had on and off all day long.

After leaving the Onyx, she'd headed to the office with Sean in tow and done her best to concentrate on the work needing her attention. While Sean sat in the reception area and thumbed through magazines and took calls on his cell phone, she'd approved the jewelry and accessory samples she'd received for the new pieces in her fall collection for ZR Designs, then placed a large order to carry her through the holiday months. She finalized the drawings on the construction for the interior of the boutique, and after giving the okay to start the work on Thursday of that week she had the company e-mail her the names and identification for anyone who would be in her shop. She'd then forwarded the list to Nathan to run background security checks for those employees before they were allowed access inside her store.

She'd even managed to carve out a half hour of time for Jessica, who stopped by the office unannounced but came bearing their favorite treats—red velvet cupcakes with cream cheese frosting. Grateful for the sugar boost and her presence when Zoe needed it the most, she brought Jessica up to speed on the latest with Grant, as well as his connection to Sean's dad, then listened while Jessica told her all about her overnight date with Noah—which explained the glow on her cheeks, along with a bubbly, blissful disposition Zoe couldn't help but be happy for but also secretly envied.

A phone call from a local reporter interested in writing an article on the opening of her boutique brought her too-short time with Jessica to an end, and by five o'clock that afternoon Zoe felt drained and exhausted, as though she'd worked an eighteen-hour day when, in fact, only six hours had passed since she'd arrived at the office.

Sean had driven her back to his place, and while she'd taken a hot, relaxing shower and changed into a pair of comfortable Juicy sweats, he'd grilled chicken and vegetables for their dinner and served it over steamed brown rice. The man could cook, something she'd appreciate more if she wasn't so exhausted.

There was no outward animosity between them from that morning's discussion. As far as Zoe was concerned, it was a waste of energy to dwell on something that was already done and couldn't be changed.

But deep in her heart, in the part that had been steadily falling for Sean, she felt a normal amount of hurt and disappointment that he'd kept the truth from her. But she also understood that he'd been trying to protect her from the pain of knowing the extent of her father's deception. And to Sean's credit, he'd been man enough to apologize, to admit he'd been wrong.

For her, Sean's ability to express regret, and mean it, was huge. Because the only other man she'd ever fallen in love with had lacked any kind of decency when it came to lying to her and, worse, betraying her trust. For nearly a year Ian Croft had carried on a long-distance affair with another woman, and even after Zoe had confronted him with proof of his infidelity he'd expressed no remorse or contrition for his behavior. Nor had he ever apologized for breaking her heart.

Instead, when she'd asked him why he'd cheated on her, Ian had simply told her that she was sweet and classy and good for his image as an attorney, while the other woman he spent time with on his business trips was the kind of woman he could fuck.

As far as explanations went, it was a huge blow to Zoe's feminine pride, and his brutal comment had caused her to question her sexuality—until a pep talk with Jessica and a couple pints of Ben & Jerry's had helped Zoe come to the conclusion of just how much of a self-centered asshole Ian was and that she deserved so much better than being some man's arm candy.

She was smart enough to know that there were very few similarities between Ian and Sean, if any at all. Despite Sean's withholding the truth about his father's involvement with hers, Zoe instinctively knew that Sean would never deliberately hurt her. And that was what made all the difference in the world to her and made forgiveness possible.

Sean had insisted on doing the dinner dishes and was currently in the kitchen cleaning up, and while Zoe was tempted to call it an early night and crawl into bed and succumb to a deep sleep, there was one more thing she'd spent the entire day avoiding that she needed to take care of.

Before she changed her mind, she pressed the speed dial on her BlackBerry for her mother's cell phone. Even before the line began to ring, Zoe's stomach knotted in dread, because she knew the upcoming conversation wasn't going to be a pleasant one. But talking to her mother was necessary, because Zoe needed to hear from Collette exactly what she knew of Grant's arrest twelve years ago.

There was a three-hour time difference between Las Vegas and New York, where Collette was vacationing, which put it close to ten o'clock at night on the East Coast—as good a time as any to get the answers to the questions that had been on Zoe's mind since that morning.

"Zoe!" her mother exclaimed breathlessly as soon as she connected the call, just seconds before it would have gone to voice mail. "Tell me you've finally heard from your father."

Of course, the first thing on her mother's mind was that damn missing alimony check. "No, I haven't," Zoe said, unable to keep the annoyance from her voice. "I called because I need to talk to you *about* Dad."

"What about him?" Collette's voice was clipped with impatience.

Zoe clutched her cell phone against her ear, already feeling the tension between herself and her mother rising, and knew it was going to get a lot worse. "About his arrest twelve years ago."

A dead silence descended over the phone line. Zoe knew she'd caught her mother off guard, and it didn't take Collette long to recover.

"Zoe, is this really necessary?" her mother asked, her tone brusque. "It's late and I'm entertaining."

"Yes, it's *very* necessary." Zoe refused to let her mother dismiss her or brush off something that was so important to her. Not this time.

"Fine. Give me a second." Collette didn't even try to disguise the fact that she felt put out by Zoe's insistence on having this particular discussion with her.

Zoe glanced toward the kitchen, catching a glimpse of Sean as she listened to her mother tell someone that she needed to take this call and would be back in a few minutes. A male voice responded in the background, then a door shut, and Zoe's mother was back on the line, more annoyed than she'd been a few moments ago.

"Why is this so important now, Zoe?"

"Because Dad isn't on a business trip as he's led everyone to believe," she said, not mincing words but getting right to the point of the matter. "He's gone missing, and he's taken a lot of money with him. Money that doesn't belong to him, but to the clients who invested in the Meridian project."

"How do you know that?" her mother asked, her tone cautious.

"George at the office confirmed that checks are bouncing and money is missing from business accounts that only he and Dad have access to. There is also an investor claiming that Dad owes him millions of dollars."

"Unbelievable," Collette muttered in disgust. "I should have guessed something was up when I didn't receive my alimony payment."

Zoe shook her head at her mother's inconsiderate attitude. Of course, for Collette, it was all about the money *she* was out. Never mind the hundreds of other people who'd trusted Grant Russo with their investments and were now left wondering if they'd ever see another dime from him.

The one thing that really stood out for Zoe was the fact that Collette wasn't at all shocked by what her daughter had just told her—and Zoe called her on it. "You don't sound surprised to learn that Dad was most likely operating a Ponzi scheme under the guise of taking investments to develop the Meridian project. Is that because he's done it before and that's why he was arrested twelve years ago?"

When Collette didn't respond right away, Zoe went on, unloading the frustration that had been building within her. "I was only fifteen at the time, but I remember things, Mom. I remember loud, angry arguments between you and Dad about him being at the police station, and how he wanted you to take me to Europe for the summer to get me away from *everything*."

Other memories came rushing back, painful ones that had opened Zoe's eyes to just how manipulative and self-absorbed her mother truly was. Collette had agreed to take Zoe out of the country, for a price—Collette wanted a divorce, along with a hefty payout above and beyond monthly alimony. Zoe's father had obviously wanted to protect her from the scandal of the arrest and trial, while her mother had used her daughter as a bargaining chip for monetary gain.

"Your father's arrest was a misunderstanding," her mother said, refusing to admit the truth even now.

"Dad's arrest was legitimate," Zoe refuted in a straightforward manner her mother couldn't argue with. "But he cut a plea deal that sent his partner to jail for fifteen years, while Dad got off with a slap on the wrist in comparison."

Out of the corner of Zoe's eye she saw Sean in the kitchen again, and she knew he was done with the dishes but was giving her privacy to talk to her mother. Zoe wasn't modifying the level of her voice at all, so she was certain he could overhear her side of the conversation—not that she cared. She had nothing to hide from Sean and wanted him to know she was on his side when it came to what had happened between her father and his.

"Fine. It's true," her mother replied irritably. "What does it matter now? It's done and over with."

"It's not *over with*, Mom." This time, Zoe's voice did rise in pitch, and she didn't even try to temper it. "Did you not hear what I just told you? That Dad is being accused of scamming people *again*? God knows how many lost their investments!"

"They aren't my problem, Zoe. My missing alimony check is."

Zoe's jaw dropped open, and she promptly snapped it shut again, stunned by her mother's careless reply—though she shouldn't have been surprised. Collette didn't possess the capability to feel empathy for anyone but herself.

"I need to go," Zoe's mother said, making it clear she was done with the conversation.

"Fine." Zoe didn't push the issue. There was no reasoning with her narcissistic mother, so why even try? "Goodbye, Mother."

The line disconnected, and Zoe laid her head against the back of the sofa, closed her eyes, and released a heavy, defeated sigh. She'd called her mother hoping to get answers and closure, and instead Zoe had been forced to face the fact that Collette just didn't care about what Grant Russo had done in the past or even was doing in the present. As long as it didn't directly affect *her* in any way.

"I thought you could use some chocolate."

Zoe opened her eyes to find Sean standing next to the couch, a plate stacked with brown squares in one hand, a glass of cold milk in the other, and a charming smile on his lips that instantly lifted her spirits.

She sat up and took a closer look at what he was offering and laughed. "Brownies? What did you do, whip up a batch while I was on the phone with my mom?"

He set the milk and treats on the coffee table within Zoe's reach, then sat down on the sofa next to her. "I wish I could take the credit, but they're store-bought."

Regardless, she appreciated the sweet, thoughtful gesture

after dealing with her mother's cool and indifferent behavior. "Hey, it's chocolate. It'll do. Thank you."

She picked up one of the squares and took a bite of the moist, fudgy cake, the taste immediately making her feel better. Or maybe it was Sean's presence that calmed her. Either way, she was grateful for both, and that revealed far too much of her feelings toward Sean.

"Are you okay?" he asked.

She heard the concern reflected in his deep voice and shrugged. "I should be used to my mother's self-centered personality, but I just don't understand how she can be so cavalier about something so serious that has hurt so many people. Twice now."

Sean relaxed against the cushions and stretched an arm along the back of the couch, the tips of his fingers close enough to touch Zoe. "Maybe she's that way because she's been through all of this with your father before."

"It's just not normal." Zoe took a drink of milk, knowing that Sean was giving her mother the benefit of the doubt. But Zoe knew Collette so much better than he did, and she didn't deserve his consideration. "I know there's nothing she can do about the things my father has done and she's not responsible for his actions, but she can at least show a little compassion about the situation."

Zoe set the glass of milk back down on the table and waved a hand in the air between them, refusing to let any further thoughts of her mother bring her down. "There's no changing her, so I just need to let it go."

But the one thing Zoe couldn't stop thinking about was the fact that during her father's arrest twelve years ago, while she'd spent the summer in Europe having fun, oblivious to her father's trial and what he'd ultimately done to Casey O'Brien, she was pretty certain that for Sean there had been no escaping the painful trial process or listening as Grant Russo betrayed Sean's father.

There was so much she didn't know about Sean. Other than telling her that he was an only child and his mother had passed away when he'd been twelve, he never spoke of his past and childhood. But now Zoe was genuinely curious about how it had been for him, growing up without a mother and living with a father who'd ended up in jail by the time Sean had turned eighteen.

With the intention of getting the answers to her questions, she finished her brownie and felt a tug of awareness in her belly as Sean's dark blue gaze watched her lick a smudge of chocolate from the corner of her mouth. As she remembered everything that had happened between them just that morning, the slow burn of renewed lust prickled along her skin.

Pushing aside her sudden craving for more than just chocolate, she offered Sean a smile that would, she hoped, encourage him to open up to her. "What was your childhood like?"

Sean frowned at Zoe's unexpected question and the genuine interest glimmering in her eyes. Just a moment ago the air in the living room had been thick with the erotic memories of what had transpired between them this morning and everything that *hadn't*. While he was grateful for a change in topic, he wasn't thrilled about the subject she'd chosen. He wasn't comfortable talking about himself, especially his past and childhood.

"Why does it matter?" he asked, unable to mask the reluctance in his voice.

She shifted on the couch, tucking her legs beneath her and turning so that she was facing him straight on. "It couldn't have been easy, having your mother die when you were twelve. Were your parents married at the time?"

God, Sean so didn't want to have this too-personal discussion with Zoe. He didn't come from a conventional family, nor did he have a traditional kind of upbringing.

Far from it. He'd been raised by a con man and turned into one himself. He had a criminal record that would never be erased, mistakes he'd made that could never be forgiven, and his father was serving a fifteen-year term in prison for investment fraud. There was nothing pleasant about Sean's youth or the man he'd been shaped into because of his father's lifestyle.

She was waiting patiently for Sean to respond. Her expression was soft, caring, and kind. He didn't deserve any of it. Zoe Russo was much too good for him, and she didn't have the good sense to keep her distance from a man who was all wrong for her, in so many ways. This morning's tryst proved as much, that she was opening herself up to him and setting herself up for heartache in the end.

As much as he wanted to get up and walk away from the dreaded conversation, he saw it as the perfect opportunity to get the truth out in the open, all of it, and show her exactly what kind of man he was. And if Zoe was smart, which he knew she was, she'd shore up those walls to protect her own emotions and leave with her heart intact once they found her father and the case was over.

"My mother and father never married." Sean saw the immediate surprise widening Zoe's eyes and knew this was just the beginning of the shocking details he was about to share. "In fact, for the first twelve years of my life I only saw my father occasionally. My mother and I lived in Henderson, where she was a waitress at a coffee shop, and my father preferred the excitement and opportunities available for him in Las Vegas. When Casey came around, he always came bearing gifts for the both of us, as if that could make up for his absence."

And for Anna it had been enough. Sean, not so much. When he was a child, all he'd wanted was for the three of them to be a real family, which included a mother and father who were married, lived under the same roof, and spent time together like normal families.

"That must have been difficult," Zoe said quietly.

Sean's lips tightened as he remembered those old days and how much he'd resented his father. As a kid, Sean had been painfully aware of how much his mother loved Casey, and despite his wandering ways, Anna had always believed that one day he'd change and settle down. But what she never knew was that Casey loved the thrill and excitement of being a hustler, a man who always looked forward to the next con. And he'd never give that up for anything or anyone.

"When I was twelve, my mother was diagnosed with stage-three breast cancer. It was so invasive that within months she was gone," he said, feeling that familiar tightness in his chest whenever he thought of his mother's quick passing. "My father wasn't there when she died, and I was sent straight into foster care until he showed up a few weeks later to claim me."

Compassion softened Zoe's features. "I can't even imagine what that was like for you."

It had been hell for the twelve-year-old boy he'd been. He'd felt so lost and alone, and the time he'd spent in foster care believing he'd been completely abandoned had only cultivated his anger and bitterness toward his father. But at least Casey *had* shown up, instead of leaving Sean to the state's foster system. That was more than he'd expected his absentee father to do.

"I came to live here in Vegas with my father, who had absolutely no idea what to do with a defiant, rebellious kid with a huge chip on his shoulder," Sean went on. "So, he did the only thing a seasoned con man knew how to do. He taught his kid the tricks of the trade and recruited him to help whenever he needed it."

Zoe stared at Sean, her expression appalled. "He made you con people?"

She sounded so incredulous and looked so outraged on his behalf. While it would have been so easy to pin all the blame on his father for corrupting him, Sean had been genuinely intrigued by Casey's lifestyle and what he did for a living. At twelve, Sean had been drawn into his dad's world of cons and scams and eventually embraced it because it was the one thing that bonded him and his father. And even after Sean was old enough to realize that what Casey did was wrong, by then he'd been hooked, too—and was equally good as his father in using his charm and wit to his advantage.

"My father didn't force me to do anything, Zoe," he finally said, and looked her in the eye, knowing the next part of his story was going to change everything between them. As well as make her realize that he wasn't the kind of man she should pin her hopes on. "Even after I knew better, I didn't stop. A part of me liked the thrill and excitement of a good con. Just like my father did."

"Oh." The one word was spoken with shock.

Yeah, *oh*. And that wasn't even the worst of his offenses.

He leaned forward on the sofa cushion, clasped his hands between his spread legs, and tried to relax his clenched jaw. "I'd just turned eighteen when my father was arrested, along with yours, for investment fraud."

"Did you know about the Ponzi scheme?" she asked before Sean could continue.

"No." He shook his head. "When I asked my father what he was doing, he'd only tell me that he was working on something big and he didn't want me involved." At the time Sean had been annoyed that his father had excluded him, but in hindsight he'd wondered if his dad hadn't been trying to protect him somehow, just in case something went wrong—as it had.

"You already know what happened at the trial," he said, knowing it was unnecessary to rehash those details. "Right before my father was carted off to prison he looked at me in the courtroom and told me not to make the same mistakes that he had, to go and make something of my life and make him proud."

She drew her knees up to her chest and wrapped her arms around them, her gaze curious. "And did you do as he asked?"

"For a while. After realizing my father was going to spend fifteen years of his life in jail, I knew I didn't want to end up like him. I wanted to change, and I tried to. I went to college for a business degree while working nights and weekends as a bartender. But when I graduated and I was faced with a load of student loans, I felt overwhelmed financially. Even with a degree, it was difficult to find a decent-paying corporate job, and I kept falling further and further behind on my payments."

He dragged his fingers through his hair and released a deep breath that did nothing to ease the growing pressure in his chest. "One evening while I was working a double shift at the bar, I ran into one of my dad's old partners who was looking for someone to help him seal the deal on a con he'd already set up with a wealthy housewife looking to make a quick buck. Derrick offered me thirty percent of the take and all I had to do was back up the guy and convince the woman that the investment was a legitimate deal. It was quick, easy money, and the temptation was too great for me to resist."

When he was quiet for too long, Zoe finally prompted him. "What happened?" she asked.

He forced himself to finish the story, to relive the dark, unpleasant memories that still haunted him and probably always would. "The con went down as planned, except shortly after, the woman's husband found out about the missing money from their savings account and beat the shit out of his wife for losing it to a scam. The woman was so badly beaten that she ended up in the hospital, and when the police got involved they found out about the con and both Derrick and I were arrested for fraud."

Stomach churning with dread, he cast a glance at Zoe, certain he'd accomplished the feat of completely alienating her. Her fingers were pressed to her lips, but instead of the outrage he'd been expecting to see, her eyes were filled with a sadness and grief that wrenched at his heart.

He glanced away and swallowed hard. "At the trial, I found out that the woman had invested all of their savings in hopes of making some big money so she could finally leave her manipulative, abusive asshole of a husband and get a divorce. And knowing that I was partly responsible for those bruises on her face, her shattered jaw and broken arm . . . it had literally destroyed me to know that I put someone's life in danger like that."

Even now, so many years later, the thought leadened his conscience with guilt. And the only thing that made living with what he'd done the least bit bearable was the fact that he'd had Caleb check into the woman's whereabouts and he had discovered she was divorced from the abusive prick and was now living in South Carolina, where she'd grown up. She'd recently married her high school sweetheart and they'd just had a baby girl. Judging by the investigative reports, the woman appeared happy and healthy. Most important, she'd moved on and put her tumultuous past behind her.

Sean wished he could do the same. "I was sentenced to three years in county prison, rightly so, and was released after eight months for good behavior," he went on. "I was fortunate enough that the judge on the case was so lenient and saw something in me worth redeeming. He was also good friends with Caleb and set me up with a job interview with him as a bartender at the Onyx, and I was lucky enough that Caleb gave me a second chance when not many employers would have hired an ex-convict."

"Caleb believed in you, that you'd changed," Zoe said softly. "And he obviously trusted you enough that he eventually hired you on for The Reliance Group."

"Yes, and I don't *ever* want to let him down," Sean said adamantly.

She propped her chin on knee, her gaze much too perceptive. "Like you let your father down?"

Sean blinked at her, shocked that she'd managed to so accurately tap into one of his deepest regrets. All Casey O'Brien had wanted was for his son to turn his life around, to be a better person than his old man had been. Instead, Sean had done the exact opposite and now had a criminal record to show for his stupidity.

Yeah, he'd disappointed his father, in so many ways. Sean had been so ashamed by his own time in prison after promising his father he'd change that he'd never told Casey what had happened with that last con or about his own incarceration. Instead, over the years he kept his sporadic visits with his father in prison brief, the conversation light and superficial because Sean couldn't handle the guilt when his father praised him for being an honest, hardworking man.

He had a lot to make up for when it came to his father, and for Sean, catching Grant Russo and putting him away was a start to earning Casey O'Brien's pride and respect.

But in the meantime, Sean had Zoe staring at him, waiting for some kind of response to her comment. "I've let a lot of people down in my lifetime, Zoe," he said, his voice gruff. "And I've hurt a lot more with my selfish actions." And ultimately he was afraid of hurting and disappointing her, too.

Without thinking, Zoe reached out and touched Sean's

shoulder in a gentle, caring caress, and he stiffened against the bit of tenderness she'd tried to extend to him. She wasn't a psychic by any stretch of the imagination, but Zoe could practically read Sean's mind—as well as feel his physical withdrawal from her. She hated feeling like an outsider when all she wanted was to offer him the comfort and understanding he seemed to need so badly after spilling so much about his painful past, but it was obvious that he wasn't ready to accept any compassion, or concession, for the choices he'd made.

"Sean . . . we all make mistakes, some worse than others," she said, hoping her words would break through that burden of blame he still carried around and give him some kind of emotional relief. "But I do believe that everyone has the ability to change for the better, like you have. And despite what you think, you *are* a good, decent, honorable man, in every way that counts."

He shook his head in denial. "You're foolish to believe that."

Clearly, he still judged himself harshly, still saw himself as the con man he'd once been, instead of the trustworthy, respectable man he'd become. The man she saw when she looked at him, when she was with him.

"I'll admit that things between us haven't been ideal, far from it, but neither is this situation with my father," she pointed out. "But through it all, you've been there for me, whenever I needed you. And I know you'd never deliberately hurt me."

She trusted him with her life.

The thought came without hesitation or filters, and she knew it to be true. This man, despite what he'd done in the past, was someone who would never let her down. He was the kind of man she could rely on to keep her safe and protected, always.

She knew it and believed it.

Zoe's heart beat fast and hard in her chest as their gazes held, suspended by the silence in the room and the sudden awareness swirling between them. More than ever, she wanted to experience how good the two of them could be *together*. And not just foreplay this time. No, this time she wanted it all—to feel his strong, muscular body sliding over hers, his thick erection stroking hard and deep as he pushed them both toward the peak of a breathless climax.

Having sex with Sean wasn't a decision she made lightly or casually. Her desire for him was strong and undeniable, as it had been from the beginning, but it was the growing emotional connection to him that changed all the rules for her.

In that moment, all she wanted was to show him with her mouth, hands, and body how much she cared and what he'd come to mean to her. That despite all reasons not to, she was falling in love with him.

Placing her palm on his stubble-roughened cheek, she leaned in to kiss him and was gratified when he didn't pull away. At first touch, his mouth was firm, unyielding, but that didn't last long. A slow, sensual lick of her tongue, followed by a gentle tug of her teeth on his bottom lip, and he groaned deep in his throat and let her inside, right where she ached to be.

Feeling triumphant, she fisted her hands in his shirt, reclined against the corner of the sofa, and pulled Sean along with her. He followed, his strong body moving over hers, his hips settling between her thighs while his mouth ravished hers. Desperation radiated off him in waves as he tangled his fingers in her hair and angled her head for a harder, deeper, more possessive kiss.

And then, just as quickly, he stopped. He was off of her and standing by the couch before she realized what had happened, leaving her breathless and aroused but not entirely surprised that he'd put an end to things before the desire between them had spiraled out of control.

Disappointed, she slowly sat up, already knowing what he was going to say, even before he spoke.

"Zoe, we can't do this," he said, his voice a tortured rasp of sound while his eyes expressed a wealth of frustration . . . and a deeper, more personal agony, too. "You and I . . . it'll never work out, and I'm not going to take advantage of this, of *you,* because when this case is over and your father is in jail and we go our separate ways, I don't want you to walk away with regrets."

As if she could ever regret being with him.

For a man who thought so little of his own self-worth because of his past, he was very quick to protect her from himself. Clearly, he respected her and had a conscience and morals that proved he'd reformed over the years— even if he didn't believe he'd changed so drastically and for the better.

He scrubbed an agitated hand along his jaw, his entire body vibrating with sexual tension. "I'll be in my room if you need me for anything. Otherwise, I'll see you in the morning."

Even as Zoe watched Sean leave the living room, she knew that letting him shut her out tonight wasn't an option. If he thought he was doing her a favor by walking away, she was about to prove otherwise, because she was going to follow him into the master bedroom and demonstrate exactly what she *needed* from him, in a way he'd be hard-pressed to deny.

Without further hesitation, she stripped off all her clothes and tossed them onto the couch. Completely naked, with her pulse beating wildly in her veins, she headed in the direction he'd just disappeared.

For her, this wasn't a seduction tactic as much as it was an intimate, emotional message to Sean—that he meant something more to her than just a fling. She'd never felt so vulnerable in her entire life, so laid bare for a man, literally and figuratively. Her heart, body, and soul were his for the taking, unconditionally. All he had to do was trust in his own feelings for her.

With a final deep breath to bolster her courage, she opened his bedroom door without knocking and stepped inside. He was facing away from her, and he'd already taken off his shirt and his hands were in the middle of unzipping the fly of his jeans.

He jerked his head around, a dark, agitated glare in place. "I told you—"

Realizing she didn't have a stitch of clothing on, he snapped his mouth closed and stared in shock, his words forgotten as pure male instinct took over, just as she'd hoped. His expression darkened with lust as his gaze roamed hungrily over her firm, full breasts, down her flat stomach, to the apex of her thighs. Everywhere his eyes traveled she felt singed by the sweetest kind of sensual fire, and she shivered in response.

He forced his gaze back up to her face again and swallowed hard before attempting to speak. "Jesus, Zoe," he rasped. He sounded as though he were being strangled.

He didn't move, his entire body rigid. And aroused, judging by the outline of his erection straining the front of his jeans. His jaw clenched, and she could clearly see the desire and denial warring within him. Unwilling to give the latter the chance to take root, she slowly closed the distance between them.

"You said if I needed anything, you'd be in your room," she said, and smiled when she realized how hard he was trying to keep his gaze above her neck. "Right now, I need *you*. I also want you. And before you say another word about regrets, I can guarantee you that the only thing I'll regret in the morning is *not* making love with you."

He looked like a man so tormented and torn, but ultimately he didn't tell her to leave his room. Zoe took it as a positive sign, that Sean wanted this night together as much as she did, even if he didn't believe he deserved what she was offering.

Stopping in front of him, she placed both of her hands on his bare chest. The firm muscles beneath her palms bunched and rippled, and his skin was hot to the touch. "Give us tonight, Sean. *Please.*"

She lifted her lips to his, and with a harsh groan of surrender he crushed his mouth to hers in a wild, greedy, tongue-tangling kiss that stole the breath from her lungs and set the tone for what was about to come.

A fast, frenzied mating.

Liquid heat surged between her legs at the thought.

His fingers delved into her hair, tugging on the strands as she quickly dragged her hands down his abdomen, then lower. She finished unzipping his jeans and broke their frantic kiss so she could push the denim and his underwear down his legs. He stepped out of the restricting clothing and kicked it aside, and she gave herself only a second to admire his thick, jutting shaft before she made herself comfortable on his bed and waited for him to join her.

He opened the nightstand, retrieved a foil pack, and she watched in anticipation as he deftly rolled the condom in place. He climbed up onto the mattress and his hands pushed her legs wide apart to make room for him in between. He didn't waste any time with foreplay, and she was glad because she was already so hot for him, so wet, and beyond desperate to feel every inch of him inside her.

He moved over her, his hard body covering her soft curves, and she lifted her hips as the broad tip of his erection slid along the slick folds of her sex. Bracing his forearms on the mattress beside her head, he looked down at her, and the helpless need she saw in his eyes was her undoing.

She locked her ankles at the back of his thighs, urging him forward. "Take me, Sean," she whispered.

With a hard, powerful thrust, he filled her full, and she gasped as she adjusted to the sudden penetration. Her fingers clenched into the sinewy muscles along the slope of his back, and she instinctively arched into him, taking him deeper still.

They both moaned in unison at how perfectly they fit together, how amazingly good it finally felt to be as one, before Sean dropped his mouth over hers and began to move in earnest. He kissed her with a feverish heat and passion that matched the aggressive way he claimed her body. Primitive and raw, he pumped in and out of her in a steadily increasing rhythm, possessing her completely with a relentless, demanding urgency that pushed her closer and closer to climax.

She wanted to wait for him but couldn't. She cried out against his lips as her orgasm crashed over her like a wave and she was awash with the most exquisite, overwhelming pleasure. Her body rippled with the force of her release, and her inner muscles tightened around him as she came.

He wrenched his mouth from hers and stared into her eyes, all of the defenses he'd shored up against her stripped away in that moment. He seemed to know it, too, and didn't fight the emotions he was so obviously feeling.

"Oh, God, *Zoe*," he said in a reverent whisper, then let his head drop back as he thrust into her with a renewed sense of purpose and finally succumbed to his own soul-shattering orgasm.

Chapter Seventeen

Standing in the back of the Kids Zone playroom at the children's hospital, Noah watched while Jessica held a group of young kids enthralled as she read them a story. She sat on the floor with her young audience, her entire demeanor animated as she gave each character in the book a distinct voice and personality. Even Noah was captivated by her storytelling ability.

Or maybe he was just mesmerized by the woman herself, along with her generosity and selfless, giving heart, both of which he'd seen in spades the past couple of hours. After spending the last few days rekindling their romance, this morning Jessica had invited him to join her at the children's hospital, to see for himself how his charitable donation would benefit one particular recipient of her Wishes Are Forever organization. He hadn't been able to resist being a part of something she was so passionate about, and he was grateful for the invitation to this glimpse into her private life.

Jessica lowered her voice to imitate the sound of the gruff giant in the story, and Noah's own chuckle mingled along with the giggles and laughter erupting from the little people sitting around her. The children allowed in the

Kids Zone were the healthier ones who were on the road to recovery and would soon be released from the hospital to be with their families again. But there were other young patients who weren't as fortunate and were confined to their rooms and beds because they either were too weak or lacked the immunity to mingle with the other sick kids.

For those more unfortunate children, Jessica had already paid each one of them a special visit in their room, where they had her undivided attention and she did her best to bring a smile to their face. Upon request, she had sung one of her most popular songs to a young boy suffering from leukemia, then shown him how to play her guitar. In another private room, she had braided the hair of a little girl who was awaiting a kidney transplant, and somewhere from the bag of gifts that Jessica had brought with her she had withdrawn a sparkly princess crown, a small tea set, and a pretty new doll. The little girl's pale eyes had brightened with delight as the two of them enjoyed an impromptu tea party with graham crackers and apple juice. There were many more, and Jessica had treated them all as if they were friends. She had an easy, sweet way about her that drew out even the shyest of personalities—and it didn't hurt that Jessica came bearing presents for every single child. Toys, puzzles, books, videos, and even electronic games for them to pass the time.

As she turned the page on the book, she glanced up and met Noah's gaze from across the room. Then she sucker-punched him with a slow, intimate smile just for him before she continued her story. She looked so happy, vibrant, and beautiful—so reminiscent of the girl who'd been his high school sweetheart. The girl he'd fallen head over heels in love with.

The more time they spent together, the more comfortable they became. And as long as he didn't bring up the past and her reasons for leaving him, everything remained fun and flirty, and very, very sexy.

It was becoming increasingly clear to Noah that for Jessica this was a temporary fling with an old flame until her concert tour began in a few weeks and she was back on the road. But for him, every moment they shared was heartfelt and real and made him crave more of her. He didn't want a casual sexual relationship with Jessica and refused to settle for anything less than her whole heart and the truth of what had torn them apart.

Only then, with the past resolved, could they work on building a future together.

"She's amazing with the kids, isn't she?"

A female voice pulled him from his deep thoughts, and he glanced at the smiling nurse standing beside him, who obviously appreciated Jessica as much as the patients did.

"Yes, she is," he agreed, not at all surprised that Jessica was so at ease with the younger ones. Way back when, he and Jessica had talked about having children when they married, and he'd always known she'd be a wonderful mother someday. Her doting nature and affectionate interaction with the sick children today proved she possessed those maternal instincts.

The nurse smiled as the kids laughed at something Jessica said to them. "Whenever she drops by the hospital, she's like a bright ray of sunshine for those kids in an otherwise quiet and lonely day filled with shots and chemo and surgery and other unpleasant procedures. The kids absolutely adore her."

"It's hard not to," Noah said, and grinned.

"True," the woman agreed, then tipped her head curiously at him. "Jessica has been coming here for years, and she's *never* brought a guy before. Are the two of you dating?"

Noah didn't know if Jessica would classify what they were doing as *dating,* but he definitely did and he didn't mind saying so. "Yes, we are."

The nurse appeared pleased to hear that bit of news. "Well, good for her. That certainly explains the extra sparkle in her eyes and the flush on her cheeks every time she glances your way. She looks very smitten with you."

He liked the way that sounded. And hearing it from an impartial bystander gave him hope that Jessica was letting down her guard, and her emotions, with him.

A soft beep pierced the air, and the nurse checked the pager on the waistband of her uniform, then sighed. "Duty calls. Enjoy your time with the kids today."

"Thanks. I already am."

The woman left the area just as Jessica finished the storybook—much to the kids' disappointment. She spent a few more minutes giving them hugs and ruffling their hair before grabbing her guitar case and a colorful gift bag, then making her way to the back of the room, where Noah was waiting for her. He smiled as she neared, because her green eyes *were* bright and joyful and her complexion seemed to glow with a happiness that radiated from the inside out—just as the nurse had observed.

Today Jessica was wearing a yellow summer dress and flat white sandals. Her auburn curls fell softly down her back, and she'd applied minimal makeup to her features. Without all the flash and fanfare of being Jessica Morgan the pop star, she actually looked very young and a lot like the girl he'd known in high school.

Before everything had changed between them.

As soon as Jessica reached him, she hooked her free arm through his and guided him down a hallway and away from the Kids Zone. "Before we leave, there's someone special I want you to meet. His name is Timmy, he's eight years old, and he has Batten disease."

Noah had never heard of the condition before. "What's that?"

"It's a disorder that affects the nervous system of a child, usually between the ages of five and ten," she explained, her voice more somber than it had been all day. "Timmy has been in and out of the hospital over the past few months because of increasing seizures, and now he's starting to show signs of mental impairment, too, so they've been putting him through a battery of tests to see how far the disease has progressed."

"Is there a cure for this Batten disease?"

"Unfortunately, no. Statistically, the disease is often fatal by the late teens or early twenties. So, since Timmy's condition is worsening, I decided that it's time to grant him a wish." She came to a stop in front of a closed door and looked up at Noah. "I know it sounds bad, but despite what Timmy is going through, he's a cheerful, happy kid. And he's so excited about having his wish granted."

"What did he ask for?" Noah asked curiously.

Jessica gave him a secretive smile. "I'll let Timmy tell you himself, since it's the donation *you* made to Wishes Are Forever that's going to fund his wish. Are you ready to meet him?"

Noah grinned back at her. "Absolutely."

She pushed open the closed door, and he followed her into a hospital room that was situated farther away from the children's ward. Inside, a young boy was sitting up in his bed, watching the Disney movie *Toy Story* on the TV mounted on the wall in front of him. At first glance, he appeared to be a perfectly normal eight-year-old, wearing blue pajamas and wire-rimmed glasses and giggling at something Woody had just said to Buzz Lightyear.

"Hey, Timmy," Jessica said.

As soon as the little boy saw her, his eyes lit up with excitement and a big lopsided grin split across his face. "Jessica! You c-c-came to s-s-see me!" he stuttered.

"Of course I came to see you, silly boy," she chastised in a fun-loving tone. "Today, I saved the very best visit for last. And that's *you*." After setting her guitar case and gift bag down on a nearby table, she went to Timmy's side and gave him a warm, affectionate hug that he returned with equal adoration, though a bit clumsily.

Once the embrace ended, Jessica motioned for Noah to move closer to where she was standing by the side of the bed. "There's someone I want you to meet," she said, speaking slower than normal. "This is my friend Noah, and he's the one who helped to grant you your wish."

Up close, there were subtle things about Timmy Noah noticed that were most likely part of Batten disease. While the boy seemed physically healthy, behind the thick lenses of his glasses his eyes tended to roll back, and he twitched occasionally, as if he couldn't control the neurological disorder.

"Hey, buddy," Noah greeted Timmy, with a smile. "So, what did you wish for?"

Timmy's eyes widened behind his glasses, his face expressing his enthusiasm. "I g-g-get to g-g-go to Disney World," he said, struggling to get the words out around his stuttering. "I g-g-get to have b-b-breakfast with B-b-buzz and Woody!"

Noah chuckled at Timmy's growing excitement. The best part for Noah was feeling a sense of pride and satisfaction that his donation had helped to give this sick boy something that meant so much to him. "Wow, that's quite an adventure. You are so lucky!"

"Isn't he, though?" Jessica agreed. "He gets to go with his mom and dad and his other brothers and sisters for a weeklong vacation to the happiest place on earth."

"With B-b-buzz and W-w-woody!"

Jessica laughed and picked up the colorful gift bag she'd brought into the room with her and placed it by Timmy's side on the bed. "So, guess what I brought for you to take to Disney World with you?"

"Toys?" Timmy asked guilelessly.

Pulling a wrapped present from the bag, Jessica placed it on Timmy's lap for him to open. "No, something much better," she promised.

When the boy struggled with the task of tearing off the paper, Jessica helped him unwrap the gift. Once it was uncovered, Timmy stared at the box with a confused frown, and Jessica immediately explained what it was.

"It's a video camera," she said, pointing to the image on the box. "That way, your mom and dad can record a video of you meeting Buzz and Woody and having fun at Disney World, and when you come back home, you can show it to me so I can see what a blast you had."

Understanding now, Timmy grinned. "C-c-cool!"

"And this other gift is all for you." Jessica retrieved another item from the bag, and this time she placed her hands around Timmy's and helped him through the motions of tearing the wrapping paper away, then opening the box until the present inside was finally revealed.

Timmy released a squeal of glee as he pulled out a replica of Woody's hat, along with the rest of the entire cowboy costume—a vest, a bandana, boots with spurs, and a shiny sheriff's badge. Jessica settled the cowboy hat on Timmy's head and pinned the badge on his pajama top.

Beyond happy, Timmy gave Jessica a hopeful look. "Will you guys st-t-tay and watch the r-r-rest of *Toy Story* with m-m-me?"

"We'd love to." Jessica helped Timmy move over so she could sit on the bed beside him while Noah sat in a nearby chair.

They finished watching the Disney movie together, and while Noah had never seen the animated flick before, he was truly amused by the story line and laughed right along with Jessica and Timmy. But during the quieter moments Noah found himself casting surreptitious looks at Jessica, drawn to her warm and caring spirit and the ease with which she interacted with Timmy and the rest of the children in the hospital.

When the movie ended, Jessica brought out her guitar and sang a few of her songs to Timmy, until he began to yawn and his eyelids started to droop. She fluffed his pillow and tucked the bedcovers around the little boy and told him to have the best time ever in Disney World before she and Noah left Timmy's room and headed to the parking structure where Noah had parked his car.

What amazed him the most was while many people would have walked away from a similar experience feeling sad, or despondent even, she was smiling and appeared cheerful and content. Obviously, she chose to make her visits a joyful thing and creating a fun, playful atmosphere for the children, even for a few hours, made her extremely happy.

Once she and Noah were both in the car, she reached across the console separating them and placed her hand on his arm to get his attention before he backed out of their parking spot. He met her gaze and lifted a curious brow.

"Thank you," she said softly.

"For what?"

"For coming with me today." She trailed her fingers along his forearm, her sensual touch raising the level of awareness between them. "There's not many people I'd share this part of my life with because it's very personal and it means so much to me, but I knew you'd appreciate seeing up close everything Wishes Are Forever does for those children."

Her strolling fingers reached the back of his hand, and he turned it over so her palm slid over his, skin to skin. "Actually, what *you* do for them," he corrected her, and entwined his fingers through hers.

She gave a modest shrug. "I'm just the spokesperson for the organization."

Jessica was so much more than that, especially when it came to the kids. He loved that she'd trusted him enough to allow him to be a part of something that meant so much to her. It was a step in the right direction, a definite sign that she was gradually letting him become a part of her life again.

He glanced at the clock on the dashboard and realized that they'd been at the hospital for nearly four hours and it was past lunchtime. "I have about three more hours before I have to be at work for tonight's shift. Would you like to grab something to eat somewhere?"

A slow, sexy smile curved her lips. "I can eat anytime." Her voice dropped to a husky note, and she leaned across the console and nuzzled his neck. "I'd rather spend the time alone with you, at your place."

Noah wasn't about to turn down such a provocative invitation. He couldn't drive home fast enough, and every excruciating mile of the way Jessica continued to seduce him with her hand stroking his thigh, her fingers grazing along the solid bulge in his pants, and her breathing hot and heavy in his ear.

By the time they arrived at his place, he was beyond aroused. Once he had her inside the house, they pulled eagerly at each other's clothes, leaving a trail of haphazardly tossed garments all the way to his bedroom. Light laughter mingled with sultry groans as their mouths and hands touched and teased, and as soon as they were completely naked she pushed him back onto the bed and climbed on top of him, taking control.

Straddling his hips, she grasped his erection in her hand and guided it between her legs. She slid the sensitive head through her wet folds so he could feel how turned on she was before slowly, leisurely, taking every hard inch of him deep inside her body. When he was in her to the hilt, her lashes fell half-mast and a moan of utter bliss escaped her parted lips as she savored the sensation of fullness.

Splaying her hands on his stomach, she started to move, circling her hips as she slid up and down his shaft. The position afforded him the luxury of watching her and touching her . . . everywhere. He took her full, firm breasts in his palms and plucked at her nipples, rolling them between his fingers, lightly pinching them until they were rock hard. He skimmed his hands down her slim torso, tracing the curve of her waist with his fingers, caressing her belly, then slid his thumbs into the soft, wet flesh at the apex of her thighs.

She stared down at him, her face flushed and her eyes dark with desire as she rode him hard while he stroked her intimately, escalating her pleasure. She took him without inhibition, holding nothing back. Not her need for him and not the strong, powerful emotions he saw reflected in her gaze.

"Come for me, sweetheart," he urged, his voice low and deep, his own body tightening and drawing closer to release with every slick slide of her sex against his. "Come for me, Jessie."

He increased the pressure and friction of his thumbs on her clit, increased the timing of his deep, upward thrusts, and felt her start to unravel and let go. Her head fell back, and her wild spiral curls spilled over her shoulders like a cloud of silk, making her look like a stunning goddess. The hot core of her gripped him tight, then pulsed around his cock as she gave herself over to an unbridled climax.

"Noah . . . ," she said on a long drawn-out moan.

His name on her lips as she came was the sweetest thing he'd ever heard and sent him over the edge right along with her. Grasping her hips in his hands, he held her in place and drove into her one last time, high and hard, and growled deep in his throat as his own release ripped through him.

She collapsed on top of him in a boneless heap, soft and warm and sated. Welcoming her slight weight, he wrapped his arm around her and held her close, feeling the wild beat of her heart against his chest and the gradual slowing of her breath along his neck.

The moment was sublime, absolutely perfect, and he didn't want to let her go.

After a while, she moved off of him and stretched like a lazy, content cat. He rolled to his side and grinned down at her, enjoying the flush of satisfaction on her skin and her lack of modesty with him.

When she was done, she blinked up at him and caught him watching her. "What are you smiling about?"

Unable to help himself, he skimmed a finger over one of her nipples, which immediately puckered at his touch. "I'm just thinking about what a lucky guy I am to get to sleep with *the* Jessica Morgan." He waggled his brows at her.

She laughed, the husky sound soft and intimate between them. "Yeah, well, don't let it go to your head, mister."

He'd been teasing her, and he suddenly grew serious, because he wanted her to know that what she did for a living made no difference to him. "The thing is, you're not *the* Jessica Morgan to me. You're still just Jessie, the girl I met in high school. That won't ever change."

"I don't ever want it to." Her eyes shone with an unmistakable honesty. "It's hard to know who your real friends are in this business, and you're one of the few that knew me before I became this international pop star."

He didn't miss her reference to them being *friends* and decided to pick his battles carefully. "But there's a lot I don't know about you *now*." He knew he was traveling into dangerous territory, *the past,* but it had to be done.

Deliberately, he traced the thin white line of a five-inch scar where it marred her otherwise-perfect skin across the top of her pubic bone, and felt her stiffen in response. He'd seen the mark before, but there had never been a good time to ask about it . . . until now.

"Like this scar right here. That's new to me," he said gently as he stared down at her, thrown off by the rise of panic he saw in her eyes. But it wasn't enough to dissuade him. "What happened, Jessie?"

"It's nothing." Visibly upset, she pushed his hand away and rushed off the bed.

Judging by her reaction, the reasons behind the scar were anything but insignificant. Calmly he said, "If it's nothing, then tell me what happened."

When she realized that her clothes were scattered somewhere in the other room, she went straight for his dresser and rummaged through his drawers until she found one of his gray T-shirts. She pulled it over her head, and once she had all her curves covered up she turned to face him again, her chin lifted defiantly. "Don't you need to get ready for work?"

Clearly, she wanted to avoid the discussion. He didn't. "Not for another hour," he said, and slid from the bed.

Warily, she watched as he crossed the room, her entire demeanor now guarded. "How about lunch, then? Are you hungry?"

"I can eat anytime," he said, using the same words she had just a while ago.

Besides, since he knew they were on the precipice of

something huge, something that would possibly explain her past behavior, the last thing on his mind was food. And if there was any chance of them having a real, lasting relationship, he wanted everything out in the open so they could deal with it and move forward.

Finding a pair of cotton sweatpants, he pulled them on and faced her again, prepared to pursue this issue until he got the answers he needed. "This is more important, Jessie."

"It's really none of your business."

"Yeah, well, I'm making it my business," he said with just as much determination.

Arms crossed over her chest, she glared at him. For a moment he fully expected her to storm out of the bedroom in her refusal to talk, but instead a combination of resolve and purpose flashed in her gaze.

"You're right," she stated, her tone still tinged with anger. "This *is* important."

Despite their being only feet apart physically, emotionally Noah felt as though a mile separated them. Something in her eyes went cold, and even before she spoke his gut tightened with a sense of unease.

"The scar is from an ectopic pregnancy," she said, her tone flat and perfunctory, as if she were discussing something as mundane as the weather. "The fetus ruptured the fallopian tube, and I had an emergency hysterectomy to remove my left ovary and uterus, and that's what left a scar."

The only word his mind latched onto was *pregnancy*. She'd been *pregnant*. His mind reeled at the revelation, even as his heart squeezed at the loss she'd suffered.

"When?" he asked, already tormenting himself with thoughts of Jessica being with another man, getting *pregnant* by another man. But he'd started this conversation, and he knew he wouldn't be satisfied until he had all the excruciating details. "When did this happen?"

She swallowed hard. "A few months after you left for college," she said, her voice barely above a whisper.

The timeline hit him like a freight train, knocking the breath from his lungs. "Jesus, Jessie." Still stunned by her confession, he scrubbed a hand along his jaw, trying to process everything. "Why didn't you tell me you were pregnant? I should have been there for you, especially if there were problems!"

She closed her eyes, and when she opened them again the depths brimmed with such pain and regret. "Because it wasn't your baby."

Another blow, but this time it destroyed him on a personal level. He stared at her, his mind warring between disbelief and outrage as he battled the sense of betrayal crushing his chest. "You slept with someone else right after I left for college?" His voice sounded like he'd swallowed crushed gravel.

Tears filled her eyes, and she pressed trembling fingers to her lips.

"Dammit, Jessica, answer me!" he demanded furiously. "I deserve to know the truth. *All* of it."

Turning pale, Jessica backed up until her legs hit the bed, and she sat down on the mattress. Unable to meet his gaze, she blinked, and tears rolled down her cheeks. "I . . . I was raped."

Her voice was so soft and low, Noah thought he'd misheard her. But there was no mistaking the pain etching her features or the agony that radiated off her.

"My mother's much younger boyfriend at the time, Boyd, was the one who assaulted me," she continued without any more prompting from Noah, though she still wouldn't look at him. "I'd been laying out by the pool that day, and afterward, when I came walking through the house to head up to my bedroom, he was in the living room just sitting on the couch. My mother wasn't home, but she'd given Boyd a key, and he started coming on to me. The things he said to me were so crude . . ." Her voice trailed off, and she visibly shuddered.

Noah swore beneath his breath. He could only imagine how difficult it was for her to relive that terrifying day, and he attempted to stop her. "Jessie, you don't have to finish."

"Yes, I do." Now that her secret was out, she seemingly wanted to purge herself of the terrifying incident. "When he cornered me and started getting physically aggressive, I fought as hard as I could to get away from him, but he was much bigger and stronger than me, and it was so easy for him to pin me down on the couch and tear my bathing suit off."

She didn't give him the details of what happened next, but Noah's own mind easily filled in the blanks. He clenched his hands into fists at his sides, feeling so damn helpless hearing all this years after the fact.

She swiped away the moisture on her face and drew a deep breath. "Just as he was done, my mother walked in, saw me half-naked on the couch and Boyd pulling his pants back on, and freaked out. Boyd told her that I'd instigated the whole thing and came on to *him,* and, of course, my mother believed him. After calling me some horrible names and blaming me for everything wrong in her life, she slapped me hard, then kicked me out of the house." Absently Jessica pressed her palm to her cheek, as if remembering the sting of her mother's hand.

Noah always knew that Jessica's mother was pure evil and that the two had never had a loving mother–daughter relationship, but it was unfathomable to him that any parent would treat a child so viciously. He sat down next to Jessica on the bed and took her hand in his to offer his silent support.

Finally, she looked at him. Her eyes were dry but

puffy, and she looked so young and vulnerable, just as she'd undoubtedly been that day. "At the time, the only place I could think of to go to was Zoe's in Los Angeles, and that's where I went. I was so devastated by what had happened, and a part of me wondered if maybe I *had* done something to provoke him. Emotionally, I withdrew from everything and everyone. The guilt and shame were overwhelming, and I just couldn't bring myself to tell you that another man . . . that I was raped."

Noah wasn't a psychologist, but it made sense to him that she'd suffered from some kind of post-traumatic stress disorder after the assault, which would account for her embarrassment, emotional retreat, and inability to reach out to him.

"I didn't even know I was pregnant until the night I started hemorrhaging and had these sharp, excruciating pains in my belly." She paused for a moment, her free hand traveling to her stomach. "Zoe rushed me to the hospital, where I was diagnosed with an ectopic pregnancy. By the time the doctors got me into surgery, the fetus had already ruptured the fallopian tube, damaging my uterus and leaving the surgeon with no option than to give me an emergency hysterectomy. I can never have children."

"God, Jessie. I'm so sorry." Paltry words for everything she'd lost. The ache in Noah's chest expanded, a part of him grieving for what *they'd* lost as a couple, all their hopes and dreams for an idyllic future stolen from them both in a cruel twist of fate. No wonder she never wanted him to know.

She stood up, disconnecting their clasped hands as she stepped away, clearly putting distance between them—emotionally and physically. "So, now you know everything, and it's about time for you to go to work."

Heading off to the nightclub for the evening was the last thing Noah wanted to do right now, because he instinctively knew that once he took Jessica home and gave her time alone he was going to lose her for good. He could already feel her pushing him away, evading him, and her reaction frustrated the hell out of him.

Moving to his feet, he slowly crossed to where she stood and gently tucked an errant curl behind her ear. "What happened in the past, as horrible as it was, wasn't your fault, Jessie. And it certainly doesn't mean the end of us now."

She crossed her arms over her chest in a protective, guarded gesture. "Did you *not* hear the part about me not being able to have children? That's something that will *never* change."

"I know," he said, wishing he had the power to undo the damage that was already done, for both of their sakes. He didn't, of course, but he wasn't willing to let her go so easily, either. "We can work through this together, if you just give us the chance."

She shook her head, those soft curls of hers framing her somber expression. "You might feel that way now, but in time my inability to give you the life you want, the life we both talked about having together, *will* matter, and you'll come to resent me and the situation." She sounded certain.

"You don't know that." He was equally sure.

"It's my biggest fear, Noah, which is why I'm making the decision to end things now, so you'll never be in the position where you'll have to make that choice yourself, or possibly stay with me out of some kind of misplaced obligation." She shifted on her bare feet, a sad smile on her lips. "I gave you what you wanted . . . answers about the past and why I left you the way I did, so now you need to move on with your life. One day you'll be grateful that I let you go so you can find a woman who can give you everything you want in life. And everything you deserve."

He clenched his jaw and exhaled a deep, calming

breath. She thought she was doing him some kind of a favor, and the conviction in her voice told him just how serious she was, how deeply she believed that she wasn't good enough for him because of everything that had happened to her.

With effort, he tamped down his anger and reminded himself that Jessica had spent *years* with these skewed thoughts and her distorted perception of herself as a woman. She honestly believed what she was saying, and Noah was at a loss as to what he could do to prove her wrong about him, about them, when she wouldn't even give the two of them a chance.

She released a weary sigh and dragged her fingers through her hair, pulling the soft strands away from her face. "I've really enjoyed this time with you, Noah, but I have my career to think about, and an upcoming tour, and the truth is, I just don't have the time for any kind of relationship right now, anyway."

Her emotionless brush-off after everything they'd shared chafed his hide, and he responded without couching his words. "That's a load of bullshit, and you know it."

She flinched at his straightforward assessment but didn't argue his point.

Noah saw her excuses for what they were, and while he wanted to force her to acknowledge that the relationship between the two of them was more than just a passing fling, he knew her issues went so much deeper than one quick discussion could fix.

She turned away, effectively putting an end to the heated conversation. "I need to get dressed, and so do you. I'll wait for you out in the living room," she said; then she was gone.

Knowing it would do absolutely no good to follow her when she was so unwilling to compromise in any way, Noah admitted defeat for now.

He took a quick shower and changed for work, and in

silence he drove Jessica to her complex. He brought the car to a stop in front of the main doors to the building, and she leaned across the console and gave him a too-chaste kiss on his cheek. As if every intimate moment they'd shared the past few weeks had never happened.

"Good-bye, Noah," she said, the look in her eyes bittersweet.

"No, this isn't good-bye, Jessie," he refuted, his voice vibrating with determination. "I'm not letting you go this time."

She shook her head. "It's not your choice."

Before he could say anything more, she stepped out of the car, shut the door, and walked away. It took every bit of willpower he possessed to let her go with so many issues unresolved between them.

She was wrong, and he wasn't about to give up on them without a fight. Despite everything he'd learned today, from the awful rape to her being unable to have the children they'd both wanted so badly together, he loved Jessica enough to work through any obstacles thrown in their path.

Now he just had to figure out a way to convince her that what the two of them shared was rare, precious, and lasting. Because living without her for the rest of his life wasn't an option for him.

Chapter Eighteen

Finally, a possible break in the case.

Sean strode purposefully across the casino toward the gallery of shops where Zoe's boutique was located at the Onyx. He was a man on a mission to bring Zoe back to Caleb at the Reliance Group offices. This morning, they'd apprehended a man who had attempted to breach Zoe's security detail at work. Now they needed her to ID the suspect so they could turn him over to Metro P.D. With a little luck, Sean thought, they'd found Zoe's stalker.

Sean turned the corner, and even from a distance his gaze was automatically drawn to the beautiful, vibrant woman inside the store who occupied way too many of his thoughts. In deference to all the work involved in putting together the boutique, she'd opted out of wearing her normal sophisticated attire. Today, her hair was up in a sleek ponytail and she was dressed casually in jeans and a pink T-shirt that outlined those perfect breasts that he'd stroked with his hands, the hard nipples he'd tasted with his tongue before sucking the sensitive tips deep into his mouth.

The erotic recollection sent a shaft of heat straight to his groin—no big surprise there. Two days had passed since he'd given into temptation and selfishly taken what Zoe had offered—solace in her soft and willing body. While every moment of that incredibly hot and sexy night was indelibly etched in his mind, he'd somehow managed to revert to a businesslike relationship with her. Not an easy feat when he now had detailed knowledge of what it was like to be a part of Zoe in ways that went beyond just physical pleasure.

Making love with Zoe had been so different, the level of intimacy between them more intense than anything he'd ever experienced with any other woman. And because Sean had known that being with her was a one-night deal, he'd been a greedy son of a bitch and taken her three separate times, until they were both too exhausted to do anything else but sleep in each other's arms.

But in the light of day, he was forced to remind himself of what had brought them together in the first place . . . and what would eventually tear them apart. Her father's guilt and Sean's own tumultuous past. And he couldn't change either of those things.

As much as Sean cared for Zoe, as much as he loved being with her and wished he could embrace the feelings stirring to life inside of him when it came to her, he knew that in time she'd find it more difficult to accept the man he was—his mistakes, flaws, and everything else that went along with the stigma of being a con man. And he'd never expect her to.

Arriving at the boutique, he rapped his knuckles on the glass door, and the armed guard standing at his post instantly recognized Sean and unlocked the door to let him inside. Along with the construction crew that had been screened by security for Zoe's protection, her assistant, Brittany, was also present, as well as another young woman Zoe had hired as a store manager.

Boxes of product were stacked wherever there was extra room, and large, blown-up snapshots of Jessica wear-

ıg different accessories from the ZR Design collections
vere stacked on the counter behind the register. Eventu-
lly, those glammed-up pictures of the pop star would
race the walls of the boutique to lure shoppers into the
ıpscale store.

"Hey, stranger," Zoe said, greeting him with a bright
ımile.

Just as she'd promised, she'd given him no indication
hat she regretted anything about their one night together.
f anything, he was the one providing all the tension in his
ıttempt to keep things professional between them when it
vas clear she wanted so much more.

"Everything is coming together quite well," he said,
ındicating the work inside the boutique.

"It's getting there." She glanced at her watch, saw that
t was early afternoon, then tipped her head curiously.
'What brings you by? I still have another few hours with
he contractors before I can leave."

Obviously, she recognized his sudden appearance in
he middle of the day as an unexpected change in the rou-
ine he'd established with her—which included dropping
ıer off in the morning and not seeing her again until he
ɔicked her up in the evening and making sure she was un-
ler security watch every minute in between. So, yeah, him
ıtopping by unannounced was out of the norm.

"Caleb would like to see you up at his office." Noah
ıaw the questions in her eyes but didn't offer specifics in
ront of everyone. "Do you think Brittany can take care
ɔf things while you're gone?"

Zoe looked back at her assistant, who assured her with
ı confident wave of her hand. "Don't worry. Go do what
you have to do," Brittany said as she set a crystal-encrusted
ɔelt on the counter. "We've already discussed how you
vant things laid out, and Sarah and I can work on getting
he accessories in the boxes unpacked and inventoried."

"Okay." Zoe grabbed her purse and slung it over he shoulder. "If you need me for anything, or have any ques tions, don't hesitate to call me."

Brittany rolled her eyes good-naturedly at her boss. " know this place is your baby, but we'll be fine, Zoe Promise."

"I can't help but be a little neurotic," Zoe admitte with a grin. "I'll be back in a while."

Zoe fell into step beside Sean as he escorted her bac through the gaming area, his gaze automatically scannin the area to make sure there wasn't anything, or anyone that struck him as out of place. Just because the Relianc Group had diffused one threat against Zoe this morning he wasn't about to assume she was now in the clear.

Once they were by themselves and away from listenin ears, her curiosity obviously got the best of her. "So, what' up?" she asked, her voice tinged with hope. "Is there fi nally some news on my father?"

"Nothing specific yet."

Between the information Lucas had retrieved from Sheila's hard drive and the man TRG now had in custody there had been a lot of revelations that morning, but Sear wasn't about to discuss any of it with Zoe out in public But as soon as they were enclosed in the private elevators leading to the security area, he told her the main reason why Caleb wanted to talk to her.

Sean pushed his hands into the front pockets of his khaki pants and met her gaze. "We think we apprehended your stalker."

"What?!" The news caused a startled look to pass over her features. "Where? When?"

"You know all those packages that were delivered about an hour ago through the back corridor by UPS?"

"Yes," she said with a nod. "It took the guy four sepa rate trips to deliver them all."

"One of the security guards we posted at the entrance to the corridor made sure the UPS guy was legitimate, but there was another man in a blue uniform who tried to pass through right behind UPS, but the guard stopped him. The guy was carrying a package and claimed he had a delivery for ZR Designs, but when security insisted he show a company ID and he couldn't provide one they got suspicious and called Caleb for backup. The guy bolted, but luckily they were able to catch him before he could get away."

"Thank God." Her eyes were wide with relief. "How do you know he's the guy who was stalking me?"

"We don't, not for sure. That's where you come in," Sean said just as the elevator came to a smooth stop and a soft ping announced their arrival. "The guy was concealing a very lethal-looking hunting knife on him, and that does seem to be your stalker's weapon of choice."

She visibly shuddered, obviously remembering the guy's last vicious attack as she followed Sean from the elevator and into the security offices. "Where is he now?"

"We're holding him for questioning to see if he's involved with your father or Sheila in any way, and we need you to give us a positive identification that he's the guy who's been threatening you before we call Metro and press charges against him." Knowing how difficult this had to be for her, Sean stopped and gently cupped her shoulders in his hands. "Are you going to be okay with that?"

His touch seemed to calm her, and she relaxed against his hands. "As long as he's restrained."

"He's in handcuffs and they have him in a secured holding room." Unable to help himself, Sean let his palm slide down her arms until he held her hands in his in a show of silent support. "You only have to see the guy through a one-way mirror."

"Okay." She exhaled a deep breath and put on a brave face. "Let's get it over with."

Sean led her into a private room where Caleb was waiting for them. After a quick hello, Zoe stepped up to the one-way mirror to take a closer look at the man in a connecting room, who was sitting at a table with his hands cuffed behind his back. It only took her a few seconds to turn back to Caleb with her response.

"That's him," she said, her tone ringing with certainty. "I've been up close and personal with that face twice now, and I'm one hundred percent positive that's the man who attacked me."

"All right, then," Caleb said with a nod. "Here's what we know so far. According to his driver's license, his name is Ray Omie. We're running a background check on him right now, so hopefully that will give us better insight as to who the guy is and if he has a criminal record."

Zoe crossed her arms over her chest. "And find out what his connection is to my father?"

"If there's anything to know, we'll have to find that information from him firsthand." Caleb glanced at the man named Ray, who wore a hostile expression, and back to Zoe again. "Now that you're here and ID'd the guy, I can start the questioning process. You two can stay in here and watch and listen, and I'll see what I can get out of Ray."

Once Caleb was gone, Sean pulled up two chairs for them to sit in front of the mirror. He took a seat next to Zoe just as Caleb entered the adjoining room and sat down at the table across from Ray.

Caleb didn't waste time with pleasantries. "You've been positively ID'd as the man who has threatened Zoe Russo in two separate incidents. And today you tried to breach security to get to her with a concealed deadly weapon. Why?"

Ray thrust his chin out belligerently. "Go to hell."

The man's reply didn't deter Caleb in the least. "Whatever your reasons for stalking Zoe, all we're looking for are some answers. You cooperate and provide them, and I'll see what I can do about lessening the charges against you."

In response, Ray's jaw clenched tight and an angry snarl turned up the corner of his mouth.

"This doesn't seem to be going well," Zoe said, her brow furrowed with concern.

Sean knew that his boss was just getting started and was far from finished with his interrogation. "Don't worry. I've seen Caleb break stronger men than this guy. By the time Caleb is done, we'll have answers."

"I hope so," she murmured.

"Let me tell you what I *do* know," Caleb went on, his tone direct. "The last time you attacked Zoe, you said something to her about how you'd put your ass on the line to get all that money, only for Bunny and that bastard to screw you over. I'm assuming 'that bastard' you referred to is Grant Russo, which leads me to believe you're somehow involved in the embezzlement scheme."

Ray just glared insolently at Caleb, neither confirming nor denying anything.

Caleb's cell phone rang, and he took one look at the caller ID before answering the call with a brisk, "What've you got for me?"

The room was quiet as Caleb listened to whoever was on the other end of the line. Caleb said a few brief words to the caller and after a minute snapped his phone shut and looked back at Ray.

"Now we're getting somewhere," Caleb said, a confident smile making an appearance. "That was Lucas, my computer analysis technician, who excels in computer hacking. And he discovered some very interesting information on Grant Russo's secretary's hard drive, despite the fact that someone tried to erase the data."

A spark of panic flashed in Ray's eyes, and Sean had no doubt that Caleb had caught the fleeting emotion as well, and would use it to his advantage.

"He retrieved deleted e-mails between Sheila and yourself that were filled with all sorts of incriminating evidence," Caleb continued, calm and confident in the report Lucas had given him. "You're a computer programmer who works for Quest Software, the same company that Grant Russo uses for his accounting program. A few months ago, you were hired to work on a glitch Russo's company was having with their system, but Lucas also found correspondences between you and a woman named 'Bunny,' who appears to be Sheila, about creating a dummy account to divert company investment funds and payments to a nonexistent supplier. How am I doing so far?"

Ray's face flushed a deep red, a combination of guilt and fury playing across his features. Clearly, Caleb had hit a couple of bull's-eyes with his knowledge of facts.

Sean glanced at Zoe, who sat quietly beside him watching the whole scene play out with fascination and interest. "The man doesn't have much of a poker face, does he?"

"No," she said with a shake of her head. "He looks guilty as charged."

Caleb clasped his hands casually on the table. "All the evidence points to you and Sheila engaging in an embezzlement scheme," he said, provoking Ray further. "The charges keep piling up against you, man. And I can't help you if you don't let me know what's going on."

Finally, Ray's anger boiled to the surface and he exploded. "That bitch double-crossed me!" he said furiously, his shoulders jerking in an attempt to release his confined hands. "Bunny . . . *Sheila* came to me about her plan to siphon the money from the main accounts and offered me fifty percent to help her. I did all the work and programming for the dummy account, and she stole millions of dollars, and just when we were going to leave the country with the money, she tells me that Grant caught on to what we were doing and took the cash for himself and disappeared with it."

"And that's when you first confronted Zoe about her father's whereabouts?" Caleb guessed, since he was now familiar with the timeline of Zoe's attacks.

Ray nodded, his jaw working angrily. "I was still hoping I could find Russo and demand my portion of the money. I'm the one who created the account and did all the programming, and half of that was *mine*."

Caleb didn't bother to correct the guy that the money had been stolen, therefore he had no legitimate claim to it. Sean figured Ray was too caught up in his own greed to see reason, anyway.

"Then, when Sheila went missing, that's when I realized that both Russo and Sheila had duped me," Ray went on, his outrage fueling his need to tell his side of the story. "They fucking used me to funnel all that money into the dummy account so it couldn't be easily traced, and all along they'd planned on cutting me out of the deal!"

"So, you upped your attack on Zoe, slashed her tires, and threatened to slit her throat if Russo didn't pay up," Caleb said, summarizing the events. "Were you going to follow through on that threat today?"

"I just wanted to scare her, so my message would get back to her old man," Ray admitted. "So he'd know how serious I was about getting my share of the money."

"Except Zoe doesn't know where her father is," Caleb told Ray.

Ray's lip curled up in a sneer. "Russo and Sheila are probably out of the country by now with all that goddamn money."

Zoe shifted in her chair at the accusation and glanced at Sean, her gaze conflicted. "Do you think that's true?" she asked him.

"I honestly don't know." Sean refused to give her any kind of false hopes. "But I can tell you that Lucas can't find anything on either hard drive that indicates they've left the country, or even the state of Nevada for that matter. Caleb used his connections at Las Vegas Metro to see if Grant's or Sheila's name came up on a database search of flight records, and there isn't any documentation of either of them boarding a plane recently. That is, if they used their real names."

"God, I just want all this to end." Zoe rubbed her fingers across her forehead and released a weary sigh. "But at least Ray provided some answers about the missing money, though I have to admit a small part of me held out hope that my father was somehow innocent in all this."

"That's completely understandable," Sean replied, his tone gentle. Clearly, Zoe was no longer devastated by the notion that her father was guilty of fraud, but considering how much Zoe adored her father, Sean knew it would take time for her pain to ease.

Caleb wrapped up his conversation with Ray, then left a guard with the man until the authorities arrived. A minute later, Caleb walked into the office Sean and Zoe were still in.

"So now we know how and why millions of dollars are missing from Russo's company accounts," Caleb said without preamble, though he didn't point out Grant Russo's obvious involvement in the embezzlement. "And, most important, we diffused the threat against Zoe."

"Thank you," she said, her tone sincere. "At least I don't have to fear for my life any longer."

Caleb's diligent gaze didn't waver. "Regardless, we'll keep the guards posted as they are now, and Sean will remain on security detail until the case is resolved."

Smiling, Zoe shook her head. "I appreciate your concern, but that really isn't necessary."

"Yes, it is," Sean replied in a tone that was firm and adamant. He knew things were uncomfortable between them since their night together, but he'd never forgive himself if something happened to Zoe because he hadn't been there to protect her.

Before she could argue further, Nathan Fox stepped into the room and approached Caleb and Sean, his intense and direct demeanor a reflection of his days as a vice cop for Metro P.D. "Sorry to interrupt, but the background check on Sheila came through, and there's something on the report that caught my attention."

"And what's that?" Caleb asked, his interest piqued, as was Sean's.

"She owns a place in Pahrump," Nathan said, telling them what he knew. "According to county records, it belonged to her parents, and when they died she inherited the piece of property. Her main residence is listed as an apartment here in Vegas, and the house in Pahrump doesn't appear to be occupied by renters or any other tenants. Lucas checked out the property on Google Earth, and the house itself actually looks run-down and dilapidated."

Caleb lifted a dark brow. "Well, it looks like you and Sean will be taking a drive to Pahrump to check the place out and see if you can find anything that might give us more answers."

Since Sean was unable to carry any kind of weapon because of his criminal record, he knew Caleb was sending Nathan with him because the other man never left home without his gun, and there was no telling what they'd encounter in Pahrump.

"I'm going with you," Zoe announced.

Caleb's and Nathan's gazes shifted to Zoe, as if they'd forgotten she was standing there, listening to their verbal exchange. "No," they both said in unison.

Zoe looked taken aback by their joint refusal, and Sean attempted to soften the stern rejection: "It's really not a big deal."

Her shoulders straightened in a show of determination, matching the fortitude brightening her eyes. "If it's not a big deal, then you won't mind if I go, too," she said reasonably. "This pertains to my father, and I have just as much at stake in finding him as you all do."

Caleb looked far from happy about Zoe accompanying the two men, but as tough as Caleb could be, Sean knew his boss was also a compassionate man who knew when to bend the rules. Like now.

"Fine," Caleb relented, but not without a strict, nonnegotiable request of his own. "But they're in charge and you'll do exactly as they say, understood?"

Zoe barely concealed a triumphant smile. "Understood."

Chapter Nineteen

Less than half an hour later, they were on the road heading to Pahrump, about an hour's drive outside of Las Vegas. Zoe sat in the backseat of the car, quiet on the drive there while Nathan and Sean talked about mundane things to pass the time. Sean supposed Zoe was lost in thoughts of her father and the new amount of evidence Ray had provided during Caleb's interrogation. None of it good, either.

The farther away from Vegas they drove, the more the glitz and glamour of the city segued into flat, dry desert, which eventually gave way to the small town of Pahrump. A mix of old and new businesses, along with a few modest casinos, lined Highway 160, which were quickly left behind as they followed the GPS directions to a more rural, sparsely populated area, where huge expanses of land separated each house they passed. As the GPS indicated, Nathan turned the vehicle onto an unpaved road, and a couple of minutes later they finally saw a lone house appear a half mile up the isolated road.

"That must be the place," Sean said, his tone wry. Obviously, since there was nothing else around for miles.

Another turn led them directly to the house, a bumpy dirt road that forced Nathan to slow the car to keep the jostling and a trail of dust to a minimum. Dried brown weeds and more dirt landscaped the acreage surrounding the property, and two old trees flanked a run-down manufactured home in dire need of repair. The siding was peeling away from the structure, the metal roof was rusted out, and the screens covering the windows were torn and shredded from years of weathering.

Except for the dusty blue Toyota Camry parked in front of the trailer, the place looked abandoned.

"That's Sheila's car," Zoe said from the backseat.

Nathan parked directly behind the Camry, deliberately blocking in the vehicle. "That's a positive sign."

But it also made for a potentially dangerous situation, Sean knew, depending on who was inside the house. Then again, this could have been just a dropping-off point for the car before Sheila and Russo used another form of transportation to leave the area.

As soon as Nathan and Sean stepped from the car, the back door opened and Zoe started to get out to join them. Sean caught Nathan's quick shake of his head and knew exactly what the other man was thinking.

Sean put a hand up to stop her exit. "Zoe, you need to stay in the car until we check the place out and make sure everything's safe."

She frowned, and for a moment Sean thought she was going to insist on accompanying them. But then she either thought better of it or remembered her promise to Caleb to do as they asked and sat back down on the leather seat.

"Just sit tight, and we'll be right back." Sean locked and shut the car door, then met up with Nathan. Since he had the experience of being a cop on his side and had dealt with more complicated situations than this, Sean followed Nathan's lead.

They walked up to the trailer's entrance and knocked on the aged and deteriorating door. The panel of fabricated wood rattled on its loose hinges and provided no real protection against an intruder intent on breaking into the house. When no one answered, Nathan rapped on the door again, louder and harder this time.

Again, no reply.

Nathan nodded his head to the side to indicate he was going to inspect the trailer from the outside, and Sean fell into step behind the other man as he strolled around the perimeter of the small home. He tried to look into the windows, but curtains blocked their view. Just as they started to walk away from the trailer, Sean heard a distinct creak of sound from inside and out of the corner of his eye saw the fabric covering the window closest to the door flutter, as if someone had been peering outside.

A quick exchanged look with Nathan told Sean that his friend had heard and seen the same thing.

Nathan stepped back up to the window and thumped the glass pane with his knuckles. "We know someone is in there," he announced in a deep voice. "We need to talk to you."

Complete silence.

Nathan exhaled an impatient sigh and crossed the few steps to the door. "You can do this the easy way by opening the door and talking to us, or I can call in local law enforcement to handle things a bit more forcefully. What's it going to be, Sheila?"

Sean wasn't sure if Nathan's threat was legitimate, but he sounded convincing and that's all they needed right now to gain some ground with the woman.

The door unlatched from inside, then slowly opened about six inches. The part of the woman's face that appeared in the crack matched the photo Caleb had acquired of Grant's secretary, Sheila. She was an older woman, in her mid-fifties, with chin-length brunette hair and brown eyes and a medium frame. Even with a light application of makeup, her features were plain and ordinary, and she looked her age, if not older.

Her wary gaze flickered from Sean to Nathan. "Who are you and what do you want?"

"We just want to ask you some questions about your boss, Grant Russo," Nathan said easily. "He's gone missing and we're investigating his case. We're hoping you can help us out and give us some insight as to where he might be."

Nathan played the part of good cop extremely well. Instead of making direct accusations, to gain Sheila's trust he made it seem like Russo was his only focus. Except she wasn't easily swayed.

"I don't know anything, and you're trespassing on private property."

As soon as she tried to shut the door, Sean automatically used his shoe to keep the door wedged open. He and Nathan didn't force their way in, but the move implied that they could.

Sheila glared at them.

"Do you really want to go the route of bringing the cops into this?" Nathan asked calmly. "Just a few minutes of your time is all we're asking, and then we'll be on our way."

Nathan's request was nonthreatening, asked in a way that would lead her to believe she could be rid of them quickly if she cooperated, rather than hindered, their investigation. And that's exactly what she did.

Reluctantly, she opened the door and let them inside. Sean glanced back at Zoe, who was still waiting in the car, where he knew she'd be the safest. But even from a distance he could see her wondering what was going on and what he and Nathan were up to.

As soon as they stepped across the threshold, they were standing in a small living room that looked as though it had been decorated back in the seventies. Dark wood paneling lined the walls, and worn and matted shag carpeting in a gawd-awful burnt orange shade covered the floor. The couch was covered in a puke green slipcover with tassels along the edges, and judging by the stale smell in the air and the thick amount of dust covering everything, it appeared that it had been a while since anyone had truly occupied the trailer.

To Sean, it seemed like a sad place for anyone to live, much less for a young girl to grow up in, as Sheila probably had, since she had inherited the property from her deceased parents.

Sheila kept the door open and didn't invite them farther into the trailer. "I doubt I can help you in any way."

"You might be surprised," Nathan said with a charming smile meant to put her at ease. "There's some speculation that Grant Russo embezzled millions of dollars from his company and has taken off with the money."

"So I've heard." She crossed her arms over her chest, her posture slightly defensive. "All I know is that things started falling apart at the company. Contractors weren't getting paid, payroll checks started bouncing, and the Meridian project came to a halt. Everyone was walking away, and since my payroll check bounced as well, I wasn't about to stay and work for free."

Her explanation sounded logical, except that Ray, her partner in crime, had already implicated her in the embezzlement. But Nathan and Sean didn't have the power or authority to arrest her, so that was a moot point.

"What brought you out here to this place?" Sean asked, purposely keeping his tone neutral so she didn't feel like she was being interrogated.

Her lips pursed in agitation. "Since I had time on my hands, I thought I'd clean this place up so I could put it on the market and sell it. How did you know where to find me?"

"You inherited the place," Nathan interjected smoothly. "It's a matter of public record."

She shifted nervously, even as her annoyance increased. "And it was that important for you to come out all this way just to talk to me?"

Nathan shrugged. "We figured you knew Grant's habits better than anyone, so it was worth a shot to see if you were here and find out if you might know anything."

She gave a bitter laugh that was at odds with the situation. "Considering what Grant is being accused of, it seems I don't know my boss at all."

"Do you know where he might have gone?" Nathan continued questioning her, using the tactic to see if he could get anything in her demeanor to crack.

"No." Her brown eyes flashed with impatience. "A few weeks ago he didn't come into work, and he's been gone ever since. That's all I know."

As Nathan kept asking questions, Sean looked everywhere he could see, searching for something, anything, that would indicate that Grant Russo had been there or still was—but found nothing to either confirm or deny his presence.

"We'd like to take a look around the place," Nathan finally said.

"No." Not only was Sheila's tone brutally sharp, but Sean didn't miss the panic that had flashed in her gaze before she regained her composure. "You don't have a warrant, and you have no right to search the trailer. In fact, I think we're done with this conversation and I'd like you to leave."

Unfortunately, she was right. Legally, they were pushing their limits and they had no real jurisdiction to search the place without her permission. Just as they started to leave, a loud, distinct *thump* from the far end of the trailer reverberated all the way to the living room.

Every muscle in Sean's body tensed, and a quick glance at Nathan told him his friend was just as alert. "Is somebody here with you?" he asked.

"No." Unmistakable fear etched Sheila's expression, and she shook her head, a bit more frantically than necessary. "That was . . . probably my cat, who's always knocking down things."

Sean didn't believe Sheila's story. Not for a second. And when the sound came again—*thump, thump, thump*—Nathan didn't hesitate, or wait for permission, to find out the source of the heavy, pounding noise.

With a cop's instinct, Nathan withdrew the gun he carried beneath his lightweight jacket and headed down the hallway toward the bedrooms. Not wanting Nathan to face the threat alone, Sean grabbed Sheila's arm, giving her no choice but to come along—and felt her resistance every step of the way.

Thump, thump, thump.

"It's coming from in here," Nathan said, his voice low as he tried to turn the knob, only to realize that the door was locked—and bolted from the *outside*. Whoever or whatever was in this room had been deliberately secured inside.

Thump, thump, thump. The sound came quicker, harder, more urgent than before.

Nathan flipped the bolt, then pushed open the door. Gun at the ready, he rushed inside and came to an abrupt stop in the middle of the room. Behind him, Sean did the same, shocked, even a little horrified, at what they'd discovered.

"What the hell?" Sean said, trying to make sense of the disturbing scene they'd stumbled upon.

"Jesus Christ," Nathan muttered, and lowered his gun to his side.

They'd found Grant Russo, but not as Sean had expected.

The man had been tied up with twine, his hands secured to the metal railing of a bed frame while his ankles had been cinched together with the thin rope, and silver duct tape sealed his mouth shut. Obviously, having heard other strange voices in the trailer, he'd used his feet to kick the wall, which had worked to get their attention.

The white dress shirt he wore was dirty and wrinkled, as if he'd worn it for days, weeks even, and had been un-buttoned down the front so it lay open on either side of him. His bare chest and abdomen had brown burn marks seared onto the flesh, which looked to Sean like the probe marks of a high-voltage stun gun. Russo's whiskered face was pale and gaunt, his dark hair a greasy, matted mess around his head, and dried, caked blood was encrusted on an open wound on his lower lip. As he was unable to speak, his gaze pleaded with them to help him.

Good God, he looked as though he'd been treated like a wild animal, or worse, and even Sean felt a twinge of pity for what the man had endured.

Taking advantage of Sean's distraction, Sheila wrenched her arm from his grasp and ran back down the hallway. Sean swore and, knowing that Nathan would take care of Russo, bolted after Sheila before she could get away. In the living room, she shoved an old rocking chair at the end of the hallway, blocking his path and giving her just enough time to grab her purse and head out the door, slamming it shut behind her.

Letting loose a ripe curse, Sean tossed the chair out of his way and reached the door seconds after her. He turned the handle, only to realize that she'd somehow jimmied the lock, and it took him precious moments he didn't have to spare to get the lock to finally release.

He wrenched open the door, his gaze searching the yard for Sheila. Instead, his worst fears were realized.

His heart slammed hard in his chest and he struggled

to breathe. Zoe was out of the car and Sheila was standing behind her, holding her hostage and pointing a pistol at her head. And judging by the barbaric way Sheila had treated Grant, Sean suspected the crazy psycho woman wasn't afraid to use the gun if provoked.

"What is taking them so long?" Zoe muttered to herself as she glanced at her watch for the tenth time in as many minutes.

As much as she was tempted to get out of the car to find out what was going on, she stayed put, which wasn't an easy feat. She'd seen Sheila answer the door, then begrudgingly allow the guys to enter, and even though she'd left the trailer door open, Zoe couldn't see a thing. Which left her to speculate on what might be happening inside.

Not knowing was driving her nuts. Making her anxious and antsy. But she wouldn't break her word to Caleb, even if it was killing her to just sit there and do nothing.

A few minutes later Sheila came running out of the trailer. Slamming the door shut behind her, she dug into her purse and retrieved her keys and what appeared to be a gun. Her eyes were wild and wide and distraught as she headed toward her Camry.

Zoe gripped the backseat, attempting to watch Sheila while remaining out of the other woman's sight.

As soon as Sheila realized that Nathan's vehicle parked so close behind hers prevented any kind of easy escape, her expression grew furious . . . and then she started toward his car.

Before Zoe could think or formulate a plan, Sheila came up to the passenger window and pointed her gun at Zoe.

A malicious smile lifted the corners of Sheila's mouth. "Get out of the car," she ordered.

Since Sheila was holding a deadly weapon, Zoe knew

it would be stupid to refuse. Slowly, she unlocked the door, opened it, and stepped out.

"Move over there," Sheila demanded, indicating the open area in front of the house with a jerk of her gun.

Not wanting to agitate the other woman further, Zoe did as she was told, which left her facing the trailer with her father's secretary right behind her. "What's going on, Sheila?" Even though she was quaking inside, Zoe's voice was surprisingly steady. "Why are you doing this?"

"You wouldn't be in this position if your goddamn father would just give me what I want, and what is *mine*!" Sheila said angrily.

Zoe had no idea what the woman was talking about. The information that Ray had given Caleb indicated that Zoe's father and Sheila had double-crossed Ray, that they'd taken the money and left him high and dry. So why was Sheila so enraged with Zoe's father? And where *was* her dad?

The door to the trailer flung open and hit the outside of the fabricated house with a loud bang. Sean filled the doorway, and as soon as he saw the scene outside and realized the danger she was in his entire body went rigid. Despite the initial flicker of worry she saw in his eyes, his features hardened into a grim mask of determination.

"Whatever's going on here, leave Zoe out of it," Sean said in a level tone.

"Are you kidding me?" Sheila laughed, the crazy, maniacal sound making Zoe shiver deep inside. "Grant's precious daughter is the only leverage I've got left. Her life for the pass code he refuses to give to me sounds like a fair exchange, don't you think? Now tell that other guy you're with that I want Grant out here *now,* or else Zoe is going to take a bullet straight to her heart for her father."

Zoe felt the barrel of Sheila's gun nudge the middle of

her back, and said heart leapt in response. Sean must have seen her terror, because he didn't waste another second in following through on Sheila's request.

"Nathan, we've got a situation out in the yard," Sean said, loud enough that the other man would hear him. "And I need you and Grant out here right now."

"Nicely done," Sheila said, a sarcastic edge to her voice. "Now why don't you come out here and join us and stand right there. Don't make any sudden moves or try to be a hero, because you won't like the consequences."

Right there was a good ten feet away from where Zoe stood, too far away for Sean to do anything to diffuse the situation. She saw the helpless look in his eyes and could feel his frustration that Sheila had managed to get the upper hand.

A moment later Nathan and another man Zoe barely recognized as her father came out of the trailer. She gasped in shock at her father's appearance. Along with red, raw marks on his chest and stomach, he had a swollen and bloodied lip, and his clothes looked wrinkled, unwashed, and torn. Her father stumbled beside Nathan, so weak and unstable that Nathan had to hold on to his arm to keep Grant upright and on his feet.

"Oh my God, Dad!" Zoe wanted to go to him in the worst way, but the muzzle of the gun grazing her back kept her from making any sudden moves.

Grant squinted against the bright sun. "Zoe?" he rasped. "What are you doing here?"

Before she could answer, Sheila spoke. "Gun on the ground," she said to Nathan. "And move over there, closer to your buddy."

Nathan hesitated, but obviously realizing that Zoe's life was ultimately in jeopardy, he reluctantly relinquished his weapon. Setting the gun on the dirt, he then guided Grant over to Sean, so that the three of them were standing together and too far away from Zoe to help her in any way.

Zoe couldn't stop staring at her father, stunned by the realization that Sheila had been holding him *captive* in her isolated trailer all this time. The man Zoe knew and loved looked like a shell of himself, and she couldn't even begin to imagine the horrors he'd been through—all because Sheila wanted some kind of code from him.

"What have you done to my father?" Zoe spat at the woman.

"What have *I* done to *him*?" Sheila responded incredulously. "Your father is making *my* life hell. I should have been out of the country by now with millions of dollars, living the kind of life I've always dreamed about and deserve, but he refuses to give me a simple little code that I need."

"So you can finally get your hands on the millions of dollars you and Ray embezzled from Russo's company accounts?" Nathan said, playing the same game with Sheila as Caleb had with Ray. "He's a little pissed off that you double-crossed him, you know."

"He was nothing more than a means to an end, and he got too damn clingy for my liking. That money belongs to *me*," Sheila said, her temper flaring. "I've planned this for years, ever since I realized that my boss had an interesting past as *Elliott Cooke*, a man who knew his way around Ponzi schemes and investment fraud. I realized what a perfect patsy he'd provide for my plan. And once the authorities discovered the missing money, he'd be the main suspect."

Sheila's idea *had* worked, because everyone had believed that Grant was the guilty party. Zoe couldn't help but feel relief that her father was completely innocent, but she never would have imagined that Sheila was so sick and twisted as to use Zoe's father to cover her own crimes.

"But the money is still sitting in an account," Sheila ranted, her voice rising along with her anger. "And I can't retrieve it because your father discovered what I was doing before I could transfer the funds into an offshore account, and changed the password."

Grant narrowed his gaze at Sheila. "I'm not about to let you get away with this."

"Are you willing to bet your daughter's life on that?" Sheila asked, her tone far too smug. "No, I didn't think so. In fact, you'd do anything for your darling daughter, wouldn't you?" Sheila's voice dripped with disgust as she glanced back at Zoe. "That's all he talked about while he was here, how much you meant to him and how he didn't want you to be disappointed to find out the kind of man he really *is*. That's why he wouldn't give me the code, because he refused to take the blame for something he didn't do. Wasn't that fucking noble of him?"

"I'm not that man anymore," Grant said gruffly, seemingly still having a bit of fight left in him, despite his lack of physical strength.

Much to Zoe's dismay, she felt her throat tighten with emotion. "I know, Dad," she said, wanting to be sure he realized that his past didn't matter to her. That she loved him, regardless.

Regret filled her father's gaze. "I'm so sorry, Zoe. I never wanted you to find out about everything, or have it taint you in any way."

She bit her bottom lip to keep herself from giving in to the tears burning the backs of her eyes. "You're a good man, Dad. You made mistakes, but you changed, and that's all I care about."

She shifted her gaze to Sean, because her words were meant for him, too. But while his body was tense because of the standoff, his expression was unreadable.

"This is all so sweet and touching," Sheila snapped

impatiently, "but there's only one thing I'm interested in. Give. Me. The code. The *real* one this time."

"It's over, Sheila," Nathan said, a calm voice of reason. "We have a confession from Ray, along with evidence on your hard drive. I'm sure the Feds are already involved and it's just a matter of time before you're arrested for fraud. Don't make things any worse than they already are."

"It's not over until I say it's over!" she screamed hysterically.

Still holding her gun on Zoe, Sheila dug into her purse with her free hand and withdrew a long, black rectangular device. Only when she pressed the metal prongs against Zoe's torso did she realize, too late, that the implement was a stun gun.

Zoe barely registered a loud crackling, popping sound before her entire body seized up and the air was sucked from her lungs. Shafts of white-hot electrical currents zapped her nerve endings, causing her muscles to convulse and intense pain to radiate through her. She felt as though she were being electrocuted by a live wire, and when Sheila finally pulled the device away Zoe could only moan and drop to the ground on her hands and knees, barely able to hold herself up even that much.

"Zoe, no!" her father shouted, his voice hoarse with anguish and worry.

Zoe couldn't even lift her heavy head to acknowledge her dad, to let him know that despite the excruciating pain, she was okay. Her muscles continued to twitch, her heart raced, and she struggled to breathe through the burning sensation licking along her skin.

"Jesus Christ!" Zoe heard Sean yell, his voice sounding as though it were far, far away. "You're a fucking lunatic!"

"Stay back!" Sheila screamed, letting Zoe know with that command that the men had tried to come to her aid.

"That was to let you know how serious I am. I have no qualms about killing her, so give me the fucking code. *Now!*"

"*Cupcake,*" Zoe's father said without hesitation. "The password is *cupcake!*"

Cupcake. The nickname Zoe's father had given her when she'd been a little girl. If the situation weren't so dire, she would have smiled at the sweet sentiment.

"*Finally,*" Sheila muttered irritably.

Fighting the nausea rolling through her, Zoe forced her head up and pried her eyes open. After a few blinks, her gaze focused in on the three men still standing too far away. Nathan's expression was grim, her father was watching her, unable to conceal his fear, and Sean's gaze blazed with fury. Sheila, her attention on the men, stood to the right of where Zoe was still crouched.

Sheila waved her gun at Nathan. "Now hand over the keys to the car that's blocking mine so I can get the hell out of here."

Nathan reached into his front pocket and in her general direction tossed the ring of keys, which landed in the dirt a few feet from Zoe. Sheila stepped in front of Zoe to pick them up.

"Do you really think you're going to get away with this?" Nathan asked.

"Of course I am." Sheila laughed, the demented sound making Zoe's skin crawl. "Especially since I don't plan on leaving any witnesses behind," she said, and fired off a shot at Grant before anyone could stop her.

Zoe watched in horror as her father fell to the ground in a heap, then Sheila trained her gun on Sean. Refusing to let Sheila get away with murder along with her other crimes, Zoe gathered every last bit of strength she possessed and lunged at Sheila's legs. With her muscles still spasming, agility wasn't on Zoe's side, and she clipped the back of

Sheila's knees with her shoulder, but it was enough to knock the other woman off balance.

Another shot rang out somewhere in the air as she flailed and tried to steady herself, and Sean seized the opportunity to take down Sheila in a full body tackle while Nathan went for his gun. Knowing that the men had Sheila under control, Zoe crawled across the dirt to her father, who lay unmoving on the ground.

Oh, God. She knelt beside him. There was so much blood on his chest she didn't know where he'd been wounded. Cupping his face in her hands, she gently caressed the pads of her thumbs across his pale cheeks. "Dad," she croaked, unable to stop the tears that spilled over her lashes.

He looked up at her and smiled. "Cupcake," he whispered, and then he closed his eyes and his body went lax.

"We need to get him to a hospital right away," she said in a panic, the thought of losing her father unbearable to her. "Hang on, Dad," she told him, even though he was passed out cold. "You're going to be okay."

Even as she said the words, she prayed they were true.

Chapter Twenty

Zoe sat next to her father's hospital bed, holding his hand and watching him as he slept, so grateful that he was going to be okay.

Nearly twenty-four hours had passed since he'd been shot, and luckily, Sheila had horrible aim. The bullet had gone clean through his left shoulder, missing his heart and any other vital organs. And other than being severely dehydrated because of lack of fluids while he'd been held hostage, he was in fairly decent condition. A week or two of rest and TLC and he'd be as good as new and back at work.

Yesterday, after Zoe's father had been shot, Sean had driven her to the nearest hospital while Nathan had taken care of Sheila. As soon as Sean pulled up to the emergency circular drive, the doctors had taken one look at Grant and wheeled him immediately into surgery. Sean had stayed with Zoe until Jessica arrived and the surgeon came out to tell them that Zoe's father would be fine and was in recovery. Then Sean left to return to Vegas to deal with the police and federal agents who wanted to question him and Nathan about what had transpired with Sheila.

Zoe hadn't heard from Sean since.

She'd called her mother in New York to let her know what had happened to Grant. Collette, who'd been in the middle of a spa treatment, had told Zoe that she was glad he was okay, but if he wasn't dying, then she saw no need to fly all the way to Vegas when she still had a few days left of her vacation to enjoy. Never mind that Zoe herself might have needed the emotional support. But thinking only of herself was par for the course for Collette, and Zoe would have been more shocked if her mother had insisted on being there for her daughter.

Zoe sighed and rubbed her fingers along her forehead, her own exhaustion catching up to her. She'd been by her father's side since he'd gotten out of surgery the day before. She'd slept in the chair by his bed and only left to walk the halls to stretch her legs or to get a cup of coffee. She'd been in the room earlier that morning when two detectives arrived to take her and her father's statements, and after they'd left she and her father had had an open and honest discussion about Grant's past.

The most important thing she'd taken away from that conversation was her father's genuine remorse. There was no doubt in Zoe's mind that her father harbored a ton of regret for testifying against Casey O'Brien and for his part in sending Casey to prison. Knowing that he was paying for a crime they'd both committed had been the catalyst for Grant to start his life over, to be a better man and earn a legitimate living, while the guilt he carried with him was his personal penance. Her father was proof that people could, and did, change for the better.

Just as Zoe knew that Sean had changed for the better. But there wasn't anything left she could say or do that could convince him of his own self-worth. That he deserved to be happy and loved—by her.

Emotionally and physically drained, she laid her head on the mattress by her father's hand and closed her eyes.

She desperately needed a shower and a few good hours of sleep in her own bed. As soon as her father woke up again she'd let him know she was heading home for a while but would be back early tomorrow morning.

A soft knock on the open door brought her head back up, and she glanced over, expecting to see a nurse. Instead, Sean stood there, looking as gorgeous—and as distant—as ever. But despite the fact that he clearly held himself aloof and remote, Zoe couldn't stop the racing of her pulse or the warm curl of awareness settling deep in the pit of her belly.

"Hey," he said softly, keeping his voice low because of her sleeping father. "I wanted to come by and give you an update on the case. Would you like to go get a cup of coffee in the cafeteria?"

Of course it was all about business for him. "Sure."

She stood, quietly crossed the room, and once they were in the corridor he spoke again. "How is your father doing?"

"Fairly well, actually. His doctor said it was a clean shot and he'll be as good as new in a few weeks."

"I'm glad to hear that." Though this was Grant they were talking about, Sean seemed sincere.

As he and Zoe walked side by side, he shoved his hands into the front pockets of his jeans and glanced at her, his sexy blue eyes filled with concern. "And how about you? Are you okay? Getting hit with a hundred thousand volts of electricity is enough to knock the strongest of men on their asses."

"Good to know I wasn't just being a wuss," she said, and laughed. "My muscles are definitely sore, but the doctor assured me there won't be any lasting effects. It's definitely not something I want to repeat anytime soon, that's for sure. I don't know how my father endured so many shock treatments without giving Sheila what she wanted."

They reached the cafeteria, and Sean poured each of them a generous amount of coffee into two disposable paper cups.

"Your father was determined not to give in to Sheila's demands," Sean said as he and Zoe each added cream and sugar to their coffee. "He didn't want to take the fall for something he didn't do, and he probably knew that she'd kill him once he gave her the password."

Believing that was true, Zoe was so glad she, Nathan, and Sean had found her father when they had. "What happened to Sheila?"

After Sean paid for his and Zoe's drinks, they found a vacant table away from everyone else and he sat across from her. "Both Sheila and Ray were taken into custody. Between all the incriminating evidence on her hard drive and their own personal confessions, they'll both be spending a considerable amount of time in prison."

"Good." It was nothing less than they both deserved, Zoe thought.

Sean took a drink of his coffee and continued. "Your father will also be absolved of any involvement in the embezzlement." Sean held her gaze, his expression contrite. "I'm sorry I was so adamant about his guilt."

The last thing Zoe wanted was for Sean to carry that burden around with him, along with all the other anguish he carried on those broad shoulders of his.

Reaching across the table, she placed her hand over his and saw that reciprocating attraction between them darken his eyes. "Considering my father's past, it's understandable that he'd be suspect. And for what it's worth, my father genuinely regrets everything that happened with your father. He told me that if he had the chance to do it all over again, he would share the blame and accept whatever punishment was handed to him."

Very gently, Sean pulled his hand from under hers, as

if her touching him was too difficult for him to endure. "Thanks for telling me that. It's worth a lot," he said, his tone husky.

She knew he meant it and she was glad that she could give him that bit of closure and hoped maybe someday he could forgive her father for what he'd done to Casey O'Brien.

"Two detectives from Las Vegas Metro came this morning to talk to both of us," she said, changing the subject to something less personal. "My father told them he started to realize there was something seriously wrong with the company accounts a few weeks ago. He'd been getting calls from contractors that checks were bouncing and investors like Davenport were contacting him to let them know that they were concerned about the fact that the Meridian project was shut down for lack of funds." Her father had specifically mentioned the man who'd started the ball rolling in The Reliance Group's attempt to find her father.

"How did he end up with Sheila?" Sean asked.

"He went into the office one morning before anyone else was scheduled to arrive and searched through Sheila's computer. He came across an unfamiliar file, followed the links, and eventually came across a dummy account under Sheila's name with *millions* of dollars in it."

"How did he get the original password?" Sean asked curiously, and took another long drink of his coffee.

"First he tried all the logical things, like her birth date, her middle name, her license number, and other personal information. But it wasn't until he came across the e-mails between her and Ray with the nickname Bunny that he gave the word a try and he was able to get into the account."

"And that's when he changed it to *Cupcake*," Sean said wryly.

She laughed and absently swirled her coffee in her

cup. "Yeah. He wanted to lock Sheila out of the account until he figured out what was going on. But she came in early, saw him at her computer, and realized that he'd probably discovered what she'd done."

"Then what?" Sean asked.

"He confronted her and threatened to call the police, and she panicked and pulled a gun from her purse. She took him to her trailer in Pahrump and figured she'd hold him there until he gave her the new code to access the account again."

"That makes sense, and now I see why Ray believed they'd run off together and double-crossed him."

Zoe nodded. "Sheila wanted the money for herself, and as soon as she could get the new password and transfer all that money into an offshore account she planned on leaving the country. And, well, you know how it all ends."

A ghost of a smile touched Sean's lips. "That we do."

A beeping sound pierced the air, and Sean checked his cell phone for the text that had come through. Then he glanced back up at Zoe. "Looks like Caleb needs me back at the office."

Sean stood, and so did she. They tossed their cups into the trash, and she accompanied him to the entrance of the hospital, since it was on her way to her father's room anyway. When she and Sean reached the automatic doors, he stopped and turned to face her.

"I guess I'll see you around at the Onyx," he said, his tone casual. "I'll be back to bartending soon, and you'll be working at your new boutique, so I'm sure our paths will cross."

God, he made it sound like they were virtual strangers, and she hated it. But despite how hard he tried to remain impassive and composed, the caring in his eyes told her that he wasn't immune to the emotions between them. He just refused to believe in what the two of them could have together.

In that moment, she decided that she wasn't going to make it easy on him, wasn't going to let him walk out of her life with the most important thing between them left unsaid, even if he might not like what he heard.

She drew a deep breath and held his gaze. "Before you go, there's something I need to tell you."

His expression turned cautious, as if he feared what she was about to divulge. "What's that?"

"I love you," she said. Like she'd never, ever, loved another man. "I. Love. *You,* Sean O'Brien."

He stiffened, looking more agonized than elated. "Love isn't enough." His voice sounded as rough as sandpaper, telling her in not so many words he loved her, too.

"It's enough for me." And that's all he needed to know. The rest was up to him.

When he didn't reply, she turned and headed back down the hall to her father's hospital room, hoping to God the heartbreak of losing Sean would ease in time.

If Sean believed that the emptiness consuming him without Zoe in his life would fade as the days went by, he was dead wrong. Over two weeks later, the gnawing ache in his gut was as strong as ever, overwhelmingly so. Letting Zoe walk away had affected every aspect of his life, dominating his thoughts and making him too much of a loner. Even spending time with the people he considered a second family couldn't snap him out of the funk he was in.

He was usually the life of the party, laughing and joking with everyone, flirting with the girls, even. But today at Caleb's, with the rest of The Reliance Group gathered for one of the weekend BBQs their boss liked to have on occasion, Sean just didn't feel like joining in on the fun.

Hell, he probably shouldn't have even come today. He wasn't in the mood to be around anyone, and watching Nathan with his wife, Nicole, and seeing just how happy in love the two of them were was a painful reminder of Zoe and what Sean had walked away from.

He was so damned convinced she deserved better than the life of a con man's wife. The same kind of lifestyle Zoe's father had once embraced, yet she still loved and adored him unconditionally, Sean was now coming to realize.

He exhaled a deep, frustrated stream of breath and dragged his fingers through his already-mussed hair. His head and his heart were tugging him in two different directions, making it impossible for him to think straight. And everyone else's good mood was seriously getting on his nerves.

Just when Sean decided to cut his visit short and head home early, Caleb strode determinedly across the yard, a bottle of beer in his hand, and sat across from Sean at the bench-style picnic table.

Without hesitation, Caleb spoke. "I think it's about time you and I had a talk."

Sean eyed his boss warily. In this casual setting, Caleb was far more relaxed than at work, his demeanor more that of a friend than a supervisor, but he was still as direct as ever. "About what?"

"This damn attitude of yours," he said, not mincing words. "I've given you over two weeks to snap out of this pity party you've been having for yourself. Now, I'm going to flat-out tell you to get your shit together. If you care about Zoe, then find a way to make it work."

Sean bristled in annoyance. "What makes you think I have feelings for Zoe?"

"You're kidding me, right?" Caleb took a drink of his beer, and when Sean didn't respond he continued. "I saw it whenever the two of you were together. So did Nathan. And Valerie . . . well, we all know that she sees things a lot more clearly than any of us ever do."

Sean glanced across the yard and found Valerie standing by the patio, watching him in that unnerving way of hers. He switched his gaze back to Caleb. "It doesn't matter how I feel about Zoe. She's way too good for me, and I never should have let myself fall for her."

"But you did fall for her, and she obviously saw something in you that made her do the same," Caleb said, matter-of-fact. "But you're only as worthy as you believe you are, and that's a big part of your problem."

Sean couldn't disagree, and that wasn't a good sign.

"I like to give people second chances to prove to themselves that they can be a better person," Caleb continued. "You, especially, have always been extremely tough on yourself for the things you've done in the past. Right now you're at a crossroad and you have a choice to make. Either you can let the past follow you around like a dark cloud hanging over your head or you can start fresh and new. But ultimately, *you* have to be the one to want to change. No one can do it for you."

"I *have* changed," Sean stated a bit defensively.

Caleb lifted a dark brow. "Not if the past still has the ability to affect your future. Stop carrying around all that excess guilt and go and do what you've been putting off for years."

"And what's that?" Sean asked, not sure he wanted to hear what Caleb had to say.

"Go and see your father and set things right," Caleb said, his tone filled with compassion and understanding of the situation. "Put it all out there, then forgive yourself for the mistakes you've made and move on."

Sean knew exactly what his boss meant and Caleb was right. It was time.

Leave it to Caleb to put things into perspective, Sean thought. He was so convinced that Zoe wouldn't be able to love him completely, but in reality it was *he* who was having a difficult time coming to terms with his past and accepting that he was a changed man. One who would never, ever, do anything to deliberately hurt the people he cared about and loved.

Including Zoe.

Especially her.

Caleb stood, clearly done with his lecture. "Just keep in mind that life doesn't have to be complicated unless you make it that way."

Sean laughed. He *had* made his life complicated for way too long, and it was damned time he stopped and made everything right.

After a long seven-hour drive to the Nevada State Prison, Sean sat at a table in the minimum-security visitation area, waiting anxiously for a guard to escort his father into the room. Sean had a lot to discuss with his father today, things that should have been aired long ago, and was so ready to get everything out in the open between them.

As soon as Casey arrived and saw Sean, a huge grin transformed his features as he made his way to Sean's table, and for a brief moment Sean experienced a stab of guilt that it had been far too long since he'd seen or talked to his father. Just as quickly, Sean released those regrets. Today was the beginning of a new relationship with his father, one built on honesty and mutual respect.

Sean greeted Casey with a firm handshake and a smile. "Hi, Dad."

"It's been a while, hasn't it?" Casey said as he slid into the seat opposite Sean. Casey wore standard inmate issue—a blue shirt and pants—and though his dark hair had some gray at the temples, he still looked the same to Sean. "That job of yours must be keeping you real busy."

As always, his father's tone was laced with understanding. Despite the long lengths of time in between Sean's visits, Casey never made him feel bad for his absence, as if he knew how difficult it was for his son to see him in a prison setting. But for Sean, his reasons for keeping his distance were a lot deeper and more emotional than that.

"Work has been interesting," Sean said, describing the past few weeks the only way he could, leaving out the mention of Zoe and Grant Russo—for now. Sean would get there, but he and Casey only had an hour of time and he didn't want to waste it with surface talk. "I was hoping that you and I could talk. There's some things I need to tell you."

Worry darkened Casey's blue eyes. "Sure. What's on your mind, son?"

Sean exhaled a deep breath and jumped right in. "I never told you, but six years ago I served eight months at High Desert State Prison," he said in a rush. "I should have told you when it happened, but I didn't want you to know how stupid I'd been."

Sean didn't notice any shock from Casey when he learned his son had been incarcerated.

"What happened?" his father asked calmly.

Sean clasped his hands on the table in front of him and told his father about that last con and what had happened to the woman involved and how overwhelmed with shame Sean had been that he'd inadvertently hurt an innocent person for his own selfish reasons.

Once he was done, he waited for his father to express his disappointment, but it never came. Instead, oddly enough, Casey's gaze turned compassionate. "You're my son," he said, his deep voice conveying how much he cared for Sean. "You learned what you knew from me.

And after everything I've done, the last thing I'm going to do is judge you. Now it's my turn to be honest. I knew about your time in High Desert."

"You did?" Sean asked, shocked. "How?"

"An inmate from High Desert transferred here to Nevada State. He knew who you were, and when he found out my last name he asked if you were my son."

Sean searched his father's gaze. "Why didn't you say something to me?"

"I figured when you were ready, you'd tell me yourself," Casey said with a shrug, making it very clear that Sean's time in prison wasn't an issue for him. "Now tell me what changed that made you feel the need to tell me about your past. Did you meet someone special?"

Geez, were his feelings for Zoe stamped on his forehead for the entire world to see? "What makes you ask that?" Sean asked, curious to hear what his father had to say.

Casey smiled, the slight wrinkles around his eyes making an appearance. "Because there's something different about you today. You used to come here with your guard up, and now it's gone. I'm guessing it's due to some woman's influence. They have a way of softening a man's hard edges."

Sean laughed and shook his head. "Yes, I met a woman. Her name is Zoe Russo. And you know her father, Grant Russo."

Casey's dark brows rose high, his expression concerned. "Well, now, I'm sure there's an interesting story to go along with *that*."

"There is," Sean said, and summarized the events of the past few weeks and the case Caleb had assigned to him that had brought Zoe into his life.

"The thing is, when I took the case, I wanted revenge for you," Sean said once he was finished with his story. "I wanted to bring Grant down and make him pay for sending you to prison while he got off scot-free."

"You don't need to fight my battles, son," Casey said, even as a ghost of a smile touched the corner of his mouth. "Grant was out to save himself, and given the chance, I would have done the same thing to save my own ass. That said, I'm glad to hear that Russo *has* changed for the better."

Sean was so thrown by his father's easy acceptance that he didn't know what to say.

Casey flattened his hands on the table, his gaze softening as he stared at Sean. "Now that we're getting things off our chests, I think it's a good time to tell you how sorry I am."

"Why are *you* sorry?"

"Because I should have been a better father to you," Casey said, a wealth of emotion ringing in his voice. "When you were just a kid, I should have been there for you on a regular basis, and not just sporadically. And when your mother died and you came to live with me, I should have set a better example than teaching you the life of a con man. It was all I knew, but it wasn't fair that I exposed you to that kind of lifestyle."

It was clear to Sean that his father had lived with his own regrets and, just as Sean had done, spent a lot of his time in prison ruminating over those things he wished he'd done differently.

"It's okay," Sean said, wanting to ease his dad's conscience.

"No, it wasn't okay," he replied, cutting himself no slack as a parent. "But I do believe it's going to be okay from here on out. For both of us. I still have a few more years to serve before I'm out of this joint and then I'll have the chance to start over. But right now, you need to live your life to the fullest. And don't ever take the love of a good woman for granted like I did. I loved your mother, and I should have been a better man for her, too."

Sean nodded, accepting his father's apology.

"So, this Zoe, she doesn't hold what happened with me and her father against you?" Casey asked curiously.

Sean shook his head. "No, she doesn't. She's an amazing woman, Dad."

Just then, one of the guards announced that the visiting hour was over, and for the first time ever Sean wished he had more time to spend talking with his father. But Sean had only minutes to say good-bye, and instead of the handshake he usually shared with his dad, Sean pulled Casey into a hug. The gesture was so unexpected that it took him a moment to realize what Sean had done and return the embrace.

When Casey pulled back, a hint of moisture glinted in his eyes. "Don't wait so long in between visits the next time, okay?"

Sean smiled. "I won't," he promised.

"And bring Zoe with you sometime, so I can meet her myself."

Sean knew his father would adore Zoe as much as he did. "I will, if she'll have me." Because even though he'd resolved things with his father, there was a whole lot more between himself and Zoe he'd left unsaid, and he had no idea where he stood with her.

But the one thing he did know for certain: He was prepared to fight for the woman he loved.

Chapter Twenty-one

Zoe strolled into her living room, two plates of chocolate cake in hand, and sat down next to Jessica. She handed one of the desserts to her friend, which Zoe had made especially for Jessica earlier that day, since this would be their last evening together for a while. Tomorrow night at Mandalay Bay was the opening of her new tour, and after that her life would be busy and chaotic for the next few months as she traveled across the country performing for her fans.

Jessica took a bite of the rich, decadent cake and sighed blissfully. "You're so good to me, Zoe. I'm not sure I deserve you."

"You do," Zoe assured her friend with a smile, and ate a bite of the dessert, too. This same chocolate cake reminded Zoe of her first date with Sean, which had led to the hottest, most arousing make-out session she'd ever had the pleasure of indulging in.

Everything she did these days reminded her of Sean, and she didn't see that ending anytime soon. Once her boutique was open, she had a feeling she'd be seeing a lot more of him at the Onyx, which would be painful, but she was determined to make it work.

"I'm going to miss you, Jess," Zoe said, suddenly feeling

a bit melancholy at the thought of not seeing her best friend on a regular basis. "You know that, right?"

"Yeah, I know, and I feel the same way." Jessica picked up a morsel of cake and popped it into her mouth. "But I'll be back next week for the opening of your boutique. It might only be for a few hours, but you know I wouldn't miss your big day for anything."

"Thanks." She was grateful that Jessica, as the face of ZR Designs, was able to squeeze in an appearance at the boutique to celebrate the opening. "So, how excited are you about kicking off your tour at Mandalay Bay tomorrow night?"

Jessica slanted her an anxious look. "I'm more nervous than anything else."

"Why?" Zoe frowned in concern. "You're not usually prone to pre-show jitters."

"Yeah, well, I don't usually have Noah Young sitting in the VIP section watching me," Jessica said wryly. "He won those VIP and backstage-pass tickets at the auction." She paused in thought. "Then again, maybe he won't show at all."

Realizing that the conversation had taken a serious turn, Zoe set her half-eaten cake on the coffee table in front of the couch and gave her friend her full attention. "Is that what you want? Noah to be a no-show?"

"Yes . . . no . . ." Jessica groaned in frustration. "I honestly don't know anymore. A part of me is hoping he'll be there, and the other part is so afraid that he won't come at all. And if that happens, it's a good indication that he's done with me, for good."

"You're the one who walked away, Jessica," Zoe reminded her, and she knew how badly such a rejection could sting, considering Sean had done the same to her. "If you want him in your life, you need to tell him how you feel before you go on tour."

Jessica worried on her bottom lip. "What if he's changed his mind? What if he's had too much time to think about not being able to have a family of his own if we're together and he's moved on?"

Zoe seriously doubted that was a possibility, but she understood Jessica's fears. Recalling the two slips of paper she'd come across just that morning, Zoe decided to share them with her best friend. "There's something I want to show you," she said, and headed back into the kitchen.

She opened what she fondly referred to as her junk drawer, which was filled with small miscellaneous household items she didn't have a specific place for, and grabbed the two notes, then returned to the living room. Once she was sitting on the couch again, she presented Jessica with one of the small rectangular pieces of paper.

"Do you remember a couple of weeks ago when we had Chinese and read our fortunes from the cookies?" Zoe asked. "I must have put them in my junk drawer and found them this morning. Read yours again."

Jessica glanced down at the writing on the paper. " 'Something you lost will soon turn up.' "

"At the time you thought you might find your favorite Cartier pen that you'd lost," Zoe reminded her. "But I think it meant something far more personal. Like you losing Noah, then finding him again."

Jessica rolled her eyes. "Come on, do you really think a Chinese fortune cookie can predict the future?"

"No, I don't," Zoe said with a laugh. "But I'd like to believe that you did find something you'd lost. Something precious and rare and irreplaceable. Like love, and Noah."

Jessica hesitated as she considered what Zoe had said, then she exhaled a shaky breath. "You know what? I think you're right."

Zoe grinned. "Of course I am."

"Remind me what your piece of paper says," Jessica said, suddenly interested in dissecting Zoe's fortune, too.

She'd fully expected her friend to turn the tables on her, which was only fair, she knew. " 'Sometimes the object of the journey is not the end, but the journey itself.' " Zoe glanced back up at Jessica. "At the time, you thought maybe it had something to do with ZR Designs and the boutique, but I think it has more to do with the journey of meeting Sean, discovering everything about my father's past, and learning that people can and do change."

"I like that," Jessica said with a smile.

Zoe did, too, but she didn't want the conversation to focus on her. "You asked me a few minutes ago what if Noah has changed his mind about you and he's moved on. And to that I want to tell you that life is full of what-ifs, Jess. But you'll never know the true answer to your question if you don't give a relationship with Noah a chance. Wouldn't you rather risk your heart one more time with Noah than spend years wondering what could have been?"

"My heart is already involved," Jessica said, her voice emotion-filled. "Always has been. There's been no one else for me since Noah; you know that."

Zoe reached out and grabbed Jessica's hand. "I *do* know that, but I think it's time that you told Noah exactly how you feel about him and let him know that you're willing to see what the future holds for the two of you."

Jessica nodded, then tipped her head curiously at Zoe. "What about you and Sean?"

Zoe shrugged past the ache in her chest she'd been living with since Sean had walked away. "I risked my heart, and I have no regrets. You need to do the same with Noah."

"I will," Jessica promised, her voice infused with a newfound confidence.

Zoe smiled. "Good." At least one of them would get the happy ending they deserved.

The moment Jessica stepped out onstage the following evening to kick off the opening night of her new tour, the sold-out crowd packing the Mandalay Bay arena let out a deafening roar that reverberated through the entire stadium and sent a rush of adrenaline through her veins. Wearing a black beaded, skintight minidress and a pair of thigh-high stiletto boots—the first of a dozen costume changes she had planned for the show—she strutted along the perimeter of the stage and welcomed everyone with a wave.

"Hello, Las Vegas!" she said into her microphone. "Is everybody ready to have a great time tonight?"

Her question was met with thunderous applause and cheers of approval. As she passed the VIP section, her gaze scanned the seats, searching for the specific set of chairs that had been given to Noah as part of the VIP package he'd won.

He wasn't there. Instead, Jessica recognized the seven-year-old girl beaming up at her as Emily, one of the patients she'd visited at the children's hospital, with her mother sitting beside her. The only way the duo could have gotten the seats was if Noah had given his tickets to them. While it was a generous and sweet gesture on Noah's part, the fact that he'd opted *not* to be at the concert on Jessica's opening night spoke volumes.

But she had no time to dwell on the pain and disappointment of Noah's absence, not when she had twelve thousand people to entertain. Emily waved at her, and Jessica blew the little girl a kiss just as her band played the intro to her opening number, "It's All for You." With a feisty toss of her wild mane of curls, she rocked the house with the upbeat tune that had everyone jumping to their feet and dancing in the aisles.

Over the next two hours there was no room in her mind for anything but the lineup of songs she performed, the numerous costume changes that were required throughout the show, and the complex choreographed routines that required her complete focus and concentration. Even after the concert ended, she spent another hour at a special meet and greet with VIP fans backstage where she signed autographs, answered questions, and had her picture taken with them.

It wasn't until she was finally alone in her dressing room where it was quiet that she began to relax and unwind and thoughts of Noah returned. While the night hadn't turned out the way she'd planned as far as he was concerned, she refused to give up hope that he still loved and wanted her. She needed to take a shower and change, and as soon as she did she intended to find Noah and lay her heart on the line.

The upscale changing room came with a large bathroom, complete with a shower and other necessities, which Jessica took full advantage of. Once the night's sweat and makeup were washed away, she stepped out of the stall, dried off, and slipped into the casual cotton dress she'd brought in with her. Deciding to let her curls air-dry to save time, she exited the bathroom and came to an abrupt halt when she saw Noah standing in the middle of the room.

Shock rendered her speechless, while her heart beat double time in her chest. The slow, sexy smile curving his lips made her weak in the knees, and she knew that no matter how many years passed, he'd always have that effect on her. He was her first love, and she knew without a doubt he would also be her last and only love. There would be no other man for her except Noah. Ever.

"You were amazing tonight," he said, his deep, husky voice adding to the slow heat of awareness building inside her. "So hot and sexy and exciting to watch."

He'd been there tonight, and the realization made her incredibly happy, even as a half-dozen questions swirled in her head, the first of which was how in the world he had breached her tight security. "How did you get in here?"

"Simon," he said with a sheepish shrug. "What can I say? The guy likes me."

She shook her head, her mind still reeling with confusion. "I was hoping you'd come tonight, but I didn't see you in the VIP section."

"I had a regular seat." Still standing too far away, he pushed his hands into the front pockets of his jeans. "Granted, the section I was in wasn't nearly as good as VIP, but I didn't want you to see me and be distracted on your opening night, so I offered those seats to Emily and her mother."

"That was very sweet of you," Jessica said, recalling how excited Emily had been during the concert. Then Jessica asked the biggest question of all. "So, what are you doing here *now*?"

He tipped his head, his body language exuding pure male confidence. "Did you really think I was going to let you leave on tour with so much left unsettled between us?"

She swallowed hard, not sure what to make of that, considering the last time they'd been together she'd been adamant that things between them were over. "What do you mean, unsettled?"

"You being stubborn and so certain things between us just couldn't work," he said, still keeping his distance. "I wanted to give you time and space to come to your senses, but I have to admit that being apart was a good thing. It gave me the chance to think about what a life with you unable to have children would be like."

Oh, God. She found it difficult to breathe, for fear that he'd come to the conclusion that her inability to give them a family was a deal-breaker for him. "And?" The one word escaped her on a croak of sound.

"I realized that there is one thing I'm absolutely certain of." He paused for a moment, his gaze so tender and caring as it held hers. "My life isn't complete without you in it."

Tears filled her eyes, because she felt the exact same way about him.

He walked toward her, finally closing the distance between them until he was standing only inches away. Grabbing her hand, he placed her palm right over his rapidly beating heart, making her wonder how she could have ever doubted his love, his acceptance. This was a man who would care for her, protect her, and always be there for her.

With his free hand, he stroked his thumb gently along her jawline. "As for having kids with you . . . there are so many ways for us to have a family together. We can foster kids. We can adopt children who need loving parents. And then there are all those kids at the hospital who are a part of Wishes Are Forever that you absolutely adore, and who adore you. There will be no shortage of children in our lives."

So overwhelmed with joy, she started to cry in earnest. He looked panicked, as if he feared he'd said something wrong. Or that she might turn him away again.

He framed her face in both of his hands and used his thumbs to wipe away the moisture on her cheeks. "I love you, Jessie," he said roughly. "That's all that matters, and if you—"

She pressed her fingers over his lips, stopping his flow of words. "Stop."

He frowned and gently pulled her hand away. "But I'm not done."

"Yes, you are," she said, and managed a smile. He'd already said enough. *More* than enough. "You don't need to say another word. It's my turn to talk. I want you to know that I wasn't going to leave on tour until I talked to you."

"Okay," he said hesitantly.

"I'm so sorry about the way I handled things in the past," she said. "The only excuse I have is that I was young and scared and I thought I was doing the right thing. But there wasn't a day that went by that I didn't think about you, and I never stopped loving you. Whatever the future holds for us, however we're able to have a family, I want it with you. That's all I ever wanted."

"It's yours, Jessie," he said earnestly. "*I'm* yours."

And then he kissed her, slow and deep and passionate. Until she was boneless and breathless and so deliriously happy.

Once he let her up for air, she expressed one of her concerns. "My career and touring might make things difficult for us to be together on a regular basis," she said, unsure how he felt about that.

"We'll find a way to make it all work, *guaranteed,*" he promised, making it clear he was supportive of her career. "You being gone isn't going to be for forever. I'll fly out to see you on tour on my days off, and I have a lot of vacation time I still need to take. All that matters is that you'll always come home to *me.*"

Smiling, she wrapped her arms around his neck and hugged him tight. "I will, *guaranteed.*"

Zoe finished rinsing the dinner dishes and loaded them into her father's dishwasher. Since the incident with Sheila, Zoe had made a point of stopping by his house at least a few times a week to check up on Grant, and this evening she'd baked him a casserole, which they'd both enjoyed for dinner.

She figured in another hour she'd head home. With the opening of her boutique happening that weekend, there was so much she needed to get done. But spending time with her father had become equally important to her, especially after how close she'd come to losing him.

With the kitchen cleaned, she headed to the wet bar in the living room and poured a snifter of the cognac her father liked to drink after dinner, then took the glass to him where he was sitting in his favorite leather recliner.

"Thank you, honey," he said with a smile. "Though I could have gotten the drink myself. I'm perfectly fine, you know."

"Yeah, I do know," she replied good-naturedly. Her father had received a clean bill of health from his doctor and had returned to work. The Meridian project was back in progress, and things were looking up for her father's company, despite the embezzlement issue.

She sat down on the couch and curled her legs beneath her. "While I'm here, just let me spoil you a little bit, okay?"

Amusement danced in his eyes as he swirled the amber liquid in his glass. "Problem is, I might get used to being waited on."

She quirked a brow at him. "In that case, you need to find yourself a wife," she teased.

He swallowed a drink of cognac and chuckled. "And you need to find yourself a husband to dote on, instead of me."

Her father meant it as a joke, of course, but his comment made her heart squeeze tight and caused images of Sean to fill her head. "You're the only man I have time for right now, Dad," she lied. Truth was, while her days were full and busy, her nights were excruciatingly empty and lonely without Sean around. She missed not having someone to share the day's events with, to bounce ideas off of, to be physically and emotionally intimate with.

The doorbell rang, startling Zoe from her thoughts. She glanced curiously at her father. "Were you expecting company?" A silly question, considering the only way someone could get to her father's house was if he had given the guard at the main gate the name of the visitor.

"Yes, I am expecting someone." Her father didn't move from his comfortable position on the recliner. Instead, he focused on his drink and said, "Would you mind getting the door?"

She narrowed her gaze. "I thought you said you were perfectly fine and didn't want me waiting on you."

"I know what I said, but the person at the door is more for you than me."

Curious now, she got to her feet and headed to the foyer just as the person rang the doorbell again. She opened the door and wondered if she was dreaming. A wonderful, sexy dream starring the man who'd become a part of her heart and soul.

Pulse racing, she blinked again, but the apparition didn't disappear, which told her the man standing in front of her was flesh-and-blood real. "Sean?"

He smiled past the nervousness she saw in his eyes. "Hi, Zoe."

Still, she stared at him, trying to make sense of what he was doing at her father's house.

"Invite him in, honey," Zoe heard her father say from the living room. "He's welcome here."

She snapped herself out of her shock and opened the door wider for him to enter. "Yes, come in."

Sean followed her into the adjoining room. Her father stood from his chair, and Sean walked up to Grant and shook his hand. "Hello, sir."

Grant nodded in a friendly greeting. "Good to see you, Sean."

What was going on? Head spinning with confusion, she looked at her father. "What is he doing here?"

"He called me at work today and we had a nice chat about things that had happened in the past and, most important, you," her father said, though he didn't get into specifics. "When I told Sean you were coming over for dinner tonight, he asked if he could stop by to talk to you."

She switched her gaze back to Sean, realizing there was something different about him but unable to put her finger on what it was that had changed. "Why didn't you just call and tell me you wanted to talk to me?"

He shifted on his feet, looking more uncertain than she'd ever seen him. "Considering how we parted ways at the hospital, I wasn't sure you'd *want* to talk to me."

"On that note, I'm going to retire upstairs and let the two of you work things out." Grant walked over to Zoe, pressed a light kiss on her cheek, and said in a low voice, "He's a good man, Zoe, and he deserves a second chance."

She had no idea what her father and Sean had discussed on the telephone, but she didn't need her dad to tell her what kind of man Sean was. She already knew. But it was nice to know that her father thought highly of Sean, respected him even.

Once her dad was gone, she folded her arms over her chest and faced Sean again, waiting patiently for him to speak.

After a moment, he did. "When I took on this case through The Reliance Group, my main goal was to find your father and deal out a bit of justice for what he did to my dad," Sean began, his intense blue eyes bright and clear. "But instead I met the sweetest, most amazing woman. A woman with the ability to believe the best in the people she cared about. Including me. That's never happened before."

With each word he spoke she felt herself relax, felt the tension drain from her body, and she couldn't resist stating the obvious. "That's because you hadn't met the right woman before me," she said, injecting a bit of humor into the conversation.

"So true," he admitted, and grinned. "You saw the good in me, even when I didn't think there was anything decent left because of the things I'd done in the past."

"What changed?" she asked, needing to know.

"I paid a visit to my father in prison and we had a long-overdue heart-to-heart about a lot of things. It made me realize I was hanging on to a lot of shit that just doesn't matter anymore and it was past time to let it go and move on with my life."

For Sean, the revelation was huge. "Did you figure out what does matter?"

"You," he replied without hesitation, his voice stronger and more certain than she'd ever heard it before. He approached her and clasped both of her hands in his bigger, stronger ones, holding on tight. "*You* matter. And what I feel for you matters."

Hope swelled in her heart, filling it to overflowing. "I like the way that sounds."

It was then that she realized what was different about Sean. He was calmer now, more at peace with the man he was. The blame and recriminations he'd carried with him for so long were gone, and she knew he'd finally forgiven himself for the past.

"I want you in my life, Zoe," he said, entwining their fingers so they were intimately connected. "I *need* you in my life. You make me want to be a better man. A great husband, and the best father possible."

Before she could respond to that, he dropped to one knee

in front of her and pushed his hand into his front pocket, trying awkwardly to retrieve something from inside.

Unable to make sense of his sudden move, she frowned. "What are you doing?"

"I'm only going to do this once in my lifetime, so I want to do it right," he said seriously, and finally withdrew a small black velvet box.

Picking up her left hand, he flipped open the top of the jeweler's box and presented her with a generous-sized diamond solitaire engagement ring. "Will you marry me, Zoe Russo?" he asked, his voice wavering ever so slightly with nerves. "Will you be my wife, the mother of our children, and the woman I spend the rest of my life with?"

She was so shocked by his unexpected proposal, so elated, she couldn't speak.

"I've already talked to your father, and he gave us his blessing," Sean rushed on to assure her. "All you need to do is say yes."

Not that she needed her father's permission to accept Sean's proposal, but it was nice to know her dad approved of the man she planned to marry.

"With you by my side, I know I can have all the things I never believed I deserved," he said when she took too long to give him an answer. "A real home. A complete family. Love and total acceptance."

Seeing just how anxious he was, she knelt in front of him on the carpeted floor, so that they were face-to-face and on equal ground, which was how she intended for their life together to be. Equal, in all ways.

She reached out, laid her palm against his cheek, and smiled. "Yes, Sean O'Brien. Yes, I'll marry you."

"Thank God," she heard him mutter, right before he slipped the ring on her finger. Then he slid his hand around to the back of her neck and brought her mouth to his for a hungry, possessive, forever kind of kiss.

Losing herself in the wonderful, splendid moment, she fisted her fingers in his shirt and tipped backward, so that she was flat on her back and he was on top of her, right where she wanted him to be. She moaned as he settled his hips between her thighs and gasped as his hand squeezed her breast.

Even as the heat of desire spiked inside of her, she realized that there was one very important thing missing from his proposal. She tangled her fingers in his hair and slowly, reluctantly, pulled his head back until he was staring down at her.

"I think there's still something left for you to say," she said huskily.

He thought long and hard, then understanding dawned in his eyes. " 'I love you'?"

She laughed in amusement. "Is that a question?"

"Hell, no. It's the truth." He grinned, looking like a man who had everything he wanted in life and more. "I love you, Zoe Russo. And damn, but it feels good!"

She sighed, the sound blissful even to her own ears. "Yeah, it does feel good, doesn't it?"

"Don't you have something to say to me, too?" He gave her a mock-stern look.

She bit her bottom lip to keep from laughing again when he was trying to be so serious. "I love you, too," she said, staring up at his gorgeous face. "But you already knew that."

"Yeah, I did," he said as he lowered his head and touched his lips to hers. "I just like hearing you say it."

He kissed her again, the intoxicating blend of passion and emotion heightening the pleasure escalating within her. His hands moved over her body, seeking, caressing, and she instinctively wrapped her legs around his waist, groaning as the hard length of him caused a scintillating heat and friction between her thighs that made her restless and wild.

She wanted him naked, and she wanted him inside her.

With a low, deep growl, he tore his mouth from hers. He was breathing hard, and the hot need blazing in his eyes told her he wanted the same thing.

"We need to get out of here, because there are so many inappropriate things I want to do to you right now," he said, his voice vibrating with the sexy threat. "And for that we need a whole lot of privacy."

She shivered, knowing they had a lot of great sex to make up for. Knowing, too, that her father would understand when he found them gone.

"Then what are you waiting for?" she asked as she gave Sean a sassy, sexy smile. "Take me home."